This book is dedicated to everyone currently stuck in a meeting that could have been an email, wishing your boss looked like Medard Carter instead of… well, your actual boss.

Since the universe failed to provide, here's your fictional compensation.

You're welcome.

May your real bosses be respectful and appropriate, and your fictional ones be morally grey with exceptional bone structure.

A full list of trigger warnings can be found in the back matter.

One Man's Control

Men Of London - Book One

R.K. Everleigh

Copyright © 2025 R.K. Everleigh

All rights reserved.

Chapters

Stone-faced, Career-driven Bastard	1
Viking God	4
Chauvinistic Pig	12
Cut-throat Lawyer	18
Arrogant Prick	22
Most Feared Man	29
One-Night-Fuck	34
Fool	42
Ignorant Asshole	46
Savvy Bastard	53
Ordinary Guy	65
Decent Guy	75
Professional	79
Billy Big Bollocks	87
Control Freak	93
Loser	101
Sadistic Bastard	111
Flawless Gentleman	123
Psychopath	133
Boss	144
Antichrist	148
Tyrant	155
Boyfriend	164

Satan	174
The Accused	183
Devil	200
Saviour	208
Batman	213
Lunatic	230
Husband	238
Stalker	248
Tosser	260
Git	267
Smug Man	276
Groom	286
Conniving Dick	291
Arrogant Bastard	299
Protector	310
Benefactor	316
Idiot	319
Madman	328
Executioner	342
Moron	348
Liar	351
Oxygen	356
Hypocrite	371
Leech	385
Backstabber	388

Bad Catch	395
Man Of Steel	404
Beggar	414
Roadblock	420
Gentle Heart	424
Partner	430
Lion	438
Epilogue	459
Teaser	472
About The Author	474
Trigger Warning	475

Stone-faced, Career-driven Bastard

Medard

"You can't hide behind your work forever." Dad's sigh crackles down the line, heavy with worry and cigar smoke.

If only he knew what, or who, I'm really hiding from.

I wedge the phone between my shoulder and ear, hands busy rifling through the chaos my predecessor, Charles Harman, left behind. Paperwork everywhere, as if my desk threw up bureaucracy. Filing? Foreign concept. Scanning? Mythical beast. Honestly, the man must've viewed administrative order as some quaint hobby for lesser mortals. When you hit sixty, maybe it's time to retire and stop inflicting paper avalanches on the rest of us.

Of course, Dad is the exception. He's sixty-four and still sharper than the blade he metaphorically loves to twist in the backs of his opponents.

"I know, Dad. But it's just the rehearsal," I murmur, my voice a mere whisper amid the clutter of papers.

The telltale drag of his cigar filters through the line, followed by a sigh of smoke. "Fair enough," he says, the hint of amusement colouring his tone. "Suppose it's your funeral."

Typical. A veiled warning wrapped in sarcasm.

My father's mornings are ritualistic. He parks himself beneath my mother's rose pavilion, has one cigar, and one lecture to himself about yesterday's successes or failures. Mum once swore the smoke would kill her beloved roses. Joke's on her as the ashes turned out to be fertiliser on steroids. She hasn't lost the 'Rose of the Year' trophy since.

"Yes, I know," I mutter, irritated at myself for sounding like a schoolboy begging to be excused from PE. "It's not like I'm missing the actual wedding."

And then, like a banshee through the receiver, my mother screeches. "I will not allow you to skip your little brother's wedding rehearsal!"

I yank the phone from my ear, grimacing.

God save me.

"Mum, my work takes prior—"

"No, it doesn't!" Her tone is razor-sharp, laced with that maternal venom that reduces grown men to toddlers. "Your family should come first."

I pinch the bridge of my nose, mirroring her, because yes, I inherited the same tell when frustration claws too deep.

I'm mostly my father, though. A stone-faced, career-driven bastard in a suit. We keep our emotions under lock and key, because that's what survival demands. The only person who's ever cracked my father's armour is my mother. She's the only one who knows where his soft underbelly lies.

I'll never forget the day we laid my nan to rest. He didn't shed a tear at the funeral. Didn't waver through the wake. Rock solid. But later that night, I saw through a sliver in their bedroom door. Mum sat on the edge of their bed, hand outstretched, and when he reached her, he fell apart, knees to the floor, sobbing into her lap like a broken boy while she stroked his hair. That's the kind of bond they have. Terrifying. Beautiful. Rare.

"I understand your career is important," Mum continues, her voice softer but no less insistent. "But you live thirty minutes away, and we haven't seen you in four months."

"I know, Mum. I'll be up soon." I'm lying. We both know it.

"You said that the last time we spoke!"

I sigh, frustration tingling at the edges of my being. "I know. It was three days ago."

The exasperation in her voice cuts deeper than it should. "And you still haven't been home! I really need you to come to the reh—" She starts in again with that bloody rehearsal, and my patience disintegrates.

"I've gotta go. Love you." I hang up before she can wind herself into another guilt-soaked crescendo.

The truth? I can't stomach going. Not now. Not when Theo's engagement has them circling me like vultures, waiting for me to pick out a nice woman, settle down, sprout kids, and smile behind some white picket fence. My aunt has even taken to texting me numbers of 'eligible young ladies'. I block them faster than spam calls about extended car warranties.

They don't understand. I don't crave that life. Not anymore, or maybe I never have. I don't want clingy women clawing at me for my money, nagging about late nights, or smashing dinnerware because I've prioritised my clients over candlelight.

What I want is simple: power, reputation, influence. Corporate law feeds me in a way no domestic fairytale ever could.

The office door swings open, and Joseph Buckman's voice slices through my thoughts.

"Carter, are you ready to address the staff?"

I straighten, masking the residue of family drama beneath steel composure. "Always."

Viking God

Sophie

"This is your last chance to abandon that sinking ship, Sophie."

My father's warning crackles through the phone. I roll my eyes—thankfully, he can't witness the disrespect.

The mere thought of working at his prestigious firm makes my stomach churn. If I were foolish enough to join Rosen & Smith, even temporarily, he would hover over my every move like a helicopter parent with a law degree, nitpicking every microscopic detail that doesn't meet his impossibly high standards.

Absolutely bloody not!

No matter how dire my current professional situation appears, I would rather perform legal services for free in a cardboard box under London Bridge than submit to his suffocating micromanagement.

"I'm fine," I reply with the kind of dismissive tone I perfected during my teenage years.

I push the plastic lid firmly onto my takeaway cup before stepping out of the coffee shop and into London's morning rush hour.

The autumn wind picks up with vindictive enthusiasm, and I clutch my precious caffeine against my chest, using it as both hand warmer and shield.

Despite the weather's best efforts, I genuinely love this city. There's something intoxicating about the financial district in Canary Wharf, where ambition radiates from the very pavement. The towering skyscrapers stretch towards the grey sky like monuments to power and success.

Harman & Buckman used to fit seamlessly into this landscape, standing proudly as one of the most influential law firms in the United Kingdom. We were second only to my father's firm—a fact he never lets me forget—commanding respect and fear throughout the legal community.

That glorious reputation lasted right up until everything crumbled under the weight of a single allegation against our managing director.

"The papers are making it sound worse than it actually is," I explain, partly to reassure my father but mostly to convince myself. "Harman simply played golf with the judge because they've been close friends for decades. The opposing counsel took a few photos and suddenly transformed a perfectly innocent friendship into some kind of corruption scandal."

"They are not merely allegations anymore, Sophie." His voice drops. "The Law Society has opened a formal investigation. The preliminary findings are not encouraging."

A quick glance at my watch reveals I'm running dangerously late for the town hall meeting. I quicken my pace, weaving through the crowd of commuters.

Just as I'm mentally congratulating myself on my superior pedestrian skills, a solid shoulder slams into me. I lose my footing completely, spinning in an ungraceful half-circle, but somehow manage to maintain my death grip on my coffee cup.

My lungs release a sigh of epic proportions. The absolute last thing I need today—especially when new management is being announced and first impressions could literally determine my professional future—is to arrive looking like I've been in a fight with a coffee shop and lost.

"Sophie! Are you listening to me?" The sharp sound of my father's voice jolts me. "They have disbarred him."

The words hit like a physical blow.

"I'll be fine," I mutter, though it feels more like a mantra than a promise. "I have to go. I'll talk to you later."

Before he can protest, I end the call.

I can't quite believe Harman is guilty. He was my mentor for three years, someone who showed me the ropes after I graduated, who believed in me when others saw only my father's daughter.

A specific memory surfaces—my first week, fumbling through a contract review, convinced I was about to be fired. Harman pulled me aside, made me a cup of truly terrible tea, and told me that doubt was just ambition in disguise.

I can't wrap my head around him manipulating a case. It doesn't fit the man I know.

But then again, I've been wrong about people before.

I bolt down the street, making it to work in the nick of time. Pushing through the towering glass double doors, I find the entire firm gathered like a flock of gossiping birds. Joseph Buckman stands on the landing above, deep in conversation with a group of unfamiliar, impeccably dressed men.

"Who do you think they've chosen to be the new MD?"

I turn to find my colleague, Ben, standing beside me, eyes bright with curiosity.

"What do you mean?" I ask, distracted, scrolling through my flooded inbox of texts and emails from concerned clients, some threatening to bolt since Harman's disbarment two weeks ago.

"They're not just rearranging management. Buckman is staying second in command, and they've brought in someone new to replace Harman," Ben says, lowering his voice. "Haven't you heard?"

"No," I reply, still fixated on the chaos of my emails. "I've been busy trying to convince my clients we're still a force to be reckoned with."

"Tell me about it," Ben mutters. "Have you heard from Harman?"

I shake my head, cautious of prying ears. "No. I've tried calling him a few times, but he never answers."

Since the scandal broke, everyone has been distancing themselves, fearful they might be drawn into the mess. It's smart, albeit cowardly. But not me. I refuse to turn my back on Harman.

Though I wouldn't dare voice this opinion to anyone but Ben. He's been my closest confidant at the firm, someone I can count on for honesty. In return, I assure him that his latest fling didn't end things due to a few extra pounds or his love for Danish pastries.

He leans in, whispering conspiratorially. "Why would you do that? Do you want to get in trouble?"

"I don't care what people think. It's not right to ostracise him after everything he's done for this firm," I retort, perhaps louder than intended.

A few heads turn our way, then quickly pivot back.

"This isn't about fairness. Trust me, if the tables were turned, Harman would be the first to cut you lose," he says, eyes sharp.

I snort. He's dead right, but it leaves a bitter taste.

My hand moves unconsciously to my thigh, rubbing through the fabric of my skirt. The motion is automatic, soothing. I catch myself and stop, shoving my hand into my coat pocket instead.

Find something to let go, Mrs Saunders had said five years ago in her office with that hideous goose lamp watching me fall apart.

I'd quit therapy the next week, convinced I could just power through. That Rosens don't need help managing stress.

I joined Krav Maga instead. Turns out punching things is excellent therapy, and far less likely to disappoint my father.

Suddenly, Ben yanks my arm, nearly knocking the coffee out of my hand. "Oh my god! Sophie, look! Medard Carter. Medard fucking Carter!"

My head snaps up, and I follow his stare. And then I see him, standing on the landing beside Buckman with his back turned to the crowd below.

He's tall. Broad-shouldered. His suit fits so well it has to be custom. Dark blond hair, cut short but not severe, falling into easy, natural waves. His hands rest in his pockets, shoulders drawn back in a way that says he's fully aware of his own presence.

Calm. Controlled. Dangerous in that quiet, self-assured way.

"Who's Medard Carter?" I ask.

Ben spins towards me like I've just confessed I've never heard of electricity. "Jesus, Soph! Have you been working under a rock? He's like fucking royalty. He's undefeated in court, closes every deal he touches, and if he's our new MD, he'll be the youngest managing director in the history of corporate law!"

"Right," I drawl, sipping my coffee with deliberate boredom that I definitely don't feel. My eyes flick back to the landing where the mystery man holds court with a few other suits who look like they'd lick his shoes for approval. "How old is he then?"

"Thirty-five," Ben declares with relish, then leans in, voice dropping theatrically. "And let me tell you this: he's hot as sin. I'm telling you, he's a turner."

"A what?" My eyebrow lifts.

Ben gives me the most dramatic eye-roll known to humankind and takes a savage bite of his Danish. "A turner. As in, he could bend my heterosexually straight arrow into a perfect rainbow."

I blink. "You're joking."

"I'm not." He gestures with his pastry for emphasis, scattering flaky evidence all over the floor. "One look and you'd beg to be his personal assistant."

"Don't be silly—" I begin to tease him when my gaze drifts back up, and my breath stumbles right out of my lungs.

He's turned.

Oh, hell.

I want to fetch this man his coffee.

He's perfection incarnate. Strong nose, clean-shaven jaw, symmetrical features that were clearly carved by angels with very dirty minds.

His eyes sweep across the room, sharp and assessing, and I swear the air changes. That stern mouth—God help me—looks like it could order nations to war or whisper filth against a lover's skin.

This man doesn't just sit at the boardroom table. He owns it like some Viking God, whose probably built it from the bones of his vanquished legal opponents.

Take me to Valhalla! I'll pack light.

"Good morning, everyone!" Buckman's voice carries across the marble lobby, and the spell shatters.

I blink, drag in a breath, and try to remember I'm a professional woman, not a hormonal fan girl.

Buckman was supposed to take over, but I suppose at sixty-one, he's clearly counting the minutes until he can retreat to his countryside estate, drink wine by the fire, and pretend none of us ever happened.

Honestly?

I don't blame him.

Three decades of blood, sweat, and lawsuits, only to watch it all unravel. And now, here comes Medard Carter. The myth, the legend, the legal world's golden boy, according to Ben. The last shining lifeboat on this sinking ship.

I wonder how they convinced him to climb aboard. Probably offered him the wheel and a challenge big enough to feed that ego of his for years.

Buckman continues with his introduction, praising Carter's unprecedented track record, his vision, his dedication to excellence. The usual corporate worship.

And then Carter steps forward.

"Thank you all." A deep, rasping voice fills the space, vibrating through the air and straight into my bloodstream. I swear the sound of him alone could seduce a nun.

His presence commands the entire lobby without even trying. His tone is rich, controlled, like a man who's used to people listening when he speaks and obeying when he finishes.

"Not only for gracing us with your presence this morning," he continues, "but for your unwavering loyalty to this firm during these challenging times."

I try to focus on what he's actually saying, but my brain has officially checked out, and my hormones have taken charge.

That voice. That face. That everything.

Good lord, when was the last time I had some fun in the bedroom?

"I know many of you are uncertain about the future," he continues, his voice dropping lower, more intimate somehow despite addressing a crowd. "And I won't insult your intelligence by pretending everything will stay the same. It won't. This firm has been operating with inefficiencies and tolerating mediocrity for too long. That ends now."

The shift in the room is palpable. Bodies stiffen. The comfortable murmur of conversation dies completely.

He pauses, letting the words land like stones into still water.

"I expect dedication. I expect excellence. And I will not hesitate to remove anyone who cannot meet that standard."

My stomach drops. The coffee in my hand suddenly feels too hot.

Around me, I can feel the collective anxiety rising. People shifting weight from foot to foot. A few nervous coughs. Ben's gone absolutely still beside me, his Danish forgotten halfway to his mouth.

Carter's expression doesn't change. If anything, he looks more resolved, more certain.

"But for those of you who prove you belong here—who fight for this firm's reputation as hard as I intend to—I will move mountains to ensure you succeed."

The silence that follows is deafening.

It's not a motivational speech. It's a declaration of war.

And we've all just been put on notice.

I swallow hard, my mind already racing. Client acquisition. Billable hours. Case wins. Whatever metric he's going to use to separate the wheat from the chaff, I need to be on the right side of it.

My father's firm is not an option. Which means I need to prove I belong here.

No matter what it takes.

Carter's eyes begin to scan the crowd.

Methodically. Deliberately. Like he's cataloguing each face, each person, filing them away in that sharp mind of his.

My heart kicks up a notch.

There's something predatory about the way he assesses us. Not cruel, just... exacting. Like he's already separating the wheat from the chaff, deciding who's worth his time.

His gaze moves across the front row. Past the senior partners standing at attention. Past the cluster of associates trying to look impressive.

And then his eyes land on me.

The world narrows.

Impossibly sharp eyes are holding mine with an intensity that makes my breath catch.

Everyone else gets a sweep, a passing glance.

I get a beat. Two. Three.

Long enough that I feel it. Long enough that my pulse hammers in my throat. Long enough that I can't look away even though every professional instinct screams at me to break eye contact, to not challenge the new managing director on his first bloody day.

But I don't look away.

And neither does he.

Something passes between us in that suspended moment. Recognition, maybe. Or a challenge. Or the universe clicking two puzzle pieces together and whispering *Oh, you're fucked.*

Then, as smoothly as it began, his gaze moves on. Continues its systematic sweep of the room like nothing happened.

But my heart is still racing.

My palms are damp.

And I have the strangest, most unnerving sensation that my entire life just shifted on its axis, and I didn't even feel it happen until it was already done.

"Well," Ben whispers beside me, voice strangled. "Did you see that?"

"See what?" I manage, my voice barely steady.

"The way he looked at you." Ben's eyes are wide. "Sophie, he looked at you like he was trying to solve a particularly interesting equation."

I swallow hard. "You're imagining things."

"I'm really not."

But deep down, beneath the professional denial and the rational voice telling me I'm being ridiculous, I know he's right.

Medard Carter looked at me.

And something tells me that's going to be a problem.

Chauvinistic Pig

Sophie

Since the firm was introduced to the new management this morning, the atmosphere in the pit has been charged with tension.

No one dares to speak louder than a whisper. Colleagues who usually chat in the kitchen while their soup heats up in the microwave now suspiciously glance at each other in passing. Although we were assured earlier that the new management would do everything in its power to turn things around, they didn't explicitly confirm that there wouldn't be any layoffs.

Hence, everyone is on edge today.

To top it all off, Medard Carter has started calling people to his office. So, one by one, they scuttle off like frightened little mice.

"Julia, how did it go?" I lean over my desk and whisper to her as she returns from her conversation with him.

Julia Michaels has been here for twelve years and has become part of the foundation. She's often the first to know the latest gossip and even topics that have been discussed behind closed doors. So much so that I sometimes wonder if she has listening devices installed across the entire building. If there's anyone who can shed light on these mysterious talks, it's her.

She scans the room briefly before answering with a furrowed brow, "It was fine. Mr Carter seems nice enough. He just asked me a bunch of questions."

"What kind of questions?" I press eagerly.

"Just about my clients. You know, how they're performing, which ones could use improvement for increased revenue. It was strange, really. I mean, everything he asked me, he could have easily found in the client files."

"Hmm," I lean back in my chair and steal a glance at Ben, who sits at the desk next to mine. "Do you think he's trying to figure out who should be getting the boot?"

He briefly glances at Julia before shrugging his shoulders and letting out a sigh.

"At this point, anything is possible. I don't trust a word they said this morning. When the numbers are down, cuts have to be made, and salaries are one of the biggest expenses."

Before Julia or I can respond to his statement, his laptop chimes with a notification from the company messenger, indicating that he's the next one to speak with Mr Carter.

"Wish me luck!" he says as he adjusts his tie and downs the last of his water, then heads out of the pit.

I try to focus on my work, responding to emails and scheduling meetings with almost every client I have on the books. Next week I'll be absolutely swamped with back-to-back meetings that will likely keep me locked in the conference room. That is, if I still have a job.

Ben's words about potential layoffs keep echoing in my mind. He's right in saying salaries are usually the first expense to cut. So, the question is: how deep will the cut be?

I look around at the other twelve people in the office, all of whom have put in years of hard work to become corporate lawyers. Joining Harman & Buckman was a dream come true for all of us, but now it feels like that dream is slipping away. And all it took was one little cog in this whole machinery to break for everything to crumble to pieces. I rub my thighs anxiously, feeling the synthetic fabric of my pencil skirt heating up beneath my palms.

A message suddenly pops up on my Messenger, informing me that Mr Carter is ready to see me. I take a deep breath and stand up from my desk.

"Good luck!" Julia gives me a weak smile, to which I only nod in response. The lump in my throat has already stolen my voice.

As I walk down the corridor towards his office, I run into Ben, who looks surprisingly calm.

"You'll be fine, Soph. Mr Carter is actually a decent guy," he reassures me, giving a thumbs-up.

Before I can respond to him, I'm met by a tall middle-aged woman with a black pixie cut and an unfriendly face who instructs me to go right in. She must be Mr Carter's assistant.

I take one final deep breath, trying to steady my nerves, before pushing open the door to Harman's old office. Except, it's not quite what I remember.

My eyes widen in surprise as I step inside. It's been remodelled. Gone are the dark mahogany shelves and heavy desk that belonged in a gentleman's club. Instead, the space is sleek and minimalist—light beechwood furniture, upholstery in calming greens, glass shelves that somehow support law books, and a coffee table that looks like a concrete block. It reminds me of Mrs Saunders' therapy office, except with sharper edges. Fitting.

Medard Carter sits behind the desk and scribbles notes into a file, then casually tosses it onto a stack of paperwork like it's nothing.

"Mrs Rosen, please have a seat," he says without looking up. He reaches for another folder and gestures vaguely with his hand towards the armchair opposite him.

"It's Miss Rosen. I'm not married," I clarify, forcing a polite smile to get his attention, but he just nods absentmindedly, still engrossed in his papers.

I settle into the plush armchair, which should be comfortable but feels like a cheap plastic chair outside a headmaster's office. I shift in my seat, and he finally looks up. A moment goes by, then two. He studies my face as if he's weighing whether I'm worth his time. Then he begins rummaging through the sea of folders on the desk.

"Hard to believe," he deadpans.

"Pardon?"

"So, tell me about yourself. Got a boyfriend? Kids, maybe?"

He continues flipping through a file—scanning from page to page—before his gaze lifts to mine in anticipation of an answer.

Alarm bells go off in my head. He wants to know something personal about me. I can't go down that road again. Harman knew me on a personal level, and where did that get me? My colleagues still tiptoe around me, wondering if I knew about the scheme, if I was complicit just because he mentored me.

No, this is my chance to draw a line. To keep it strictly professional.

"My biggest client—" I start, but he cuts me off.

"Not a big fan of small talk?" he says, the corner of his mouth lifting in what might be amusement.

"If you don't mind, Mr Carter, I'd prefer to focus on my client files," I say, keeping my tone even but firm.

His eyebrows lift in surprise. He leans back, props his ankle on the opposite knee and rests his chin on his hand, like he's the king of the world and I'm just here to entertain him.

"We'll get to that in a minute," he says, casually sliding the file onto his lap and flipping through it as if he's bored out of his mind.

"So, you've graduated from Oxford. Top of your class."

If he's impressed by my academic achievements, he's hiding it well. So far, I'm seeing less of the decent guy Ben described and more of the cocky, self-assured alpha type. Handsome? Sure. Like he stepped right out of a magazine. But charming? Not so much.

"Internship at Rosen & Smith's. Are you related to Andrew Rosen?" he asks, raising a brow.

I shouldn't be surprised that he knows of my father. Everyone in Corporate does. And if I've learnt anything, it's that most of them see me as just the Rosen girl, nothing more. Except Harman, and look where that got me. Maybe Carter's just looking for a reason to dismiss me, too.

"Yes, he's my father," I admit.

"So, how come you've been here since graduation? Surely, it's easier to make your way at his firm."

"I'm not interested in easy. I want to earn my place."

It's the standard line I've rehearsed a hundred times. But I wish, just once, that these middle-aged men would entertain the idea that a woman might want to carve out her own path instead of relying on her father's influence.

He pauses, studying me. His index finger brushes over his bottom lip, a slow, deliberate motion that radiates arrogance. It's like he's savouring every second of this power play. He's lucky he's attractive, because his personality is testing the limits of my tolerance.

"Good answer," he finally says. "Albeit, it will take you longer, and with the clock ticking—" He gestures vaguely, implying something. Nothing good.

"Excuse me?"

"Tick tock, tick tock," he says, his gaze flickering briefly to my midsection before returning to my face with that infuriating smirk.

Chauvinistic pig.

Heat floods my cheeks.

He wants me to react. Wants me to storm out or threaten HR. Wants an excuse to dismiss me as emotional, unprofessional, exactly what he expects from "the Rosen girl."

I won't give him the satisfaction.

Our gazes lock, and despite my fury, I notice his eyes are grey—

not quite silver, with flecks of amber that catch the light. Sharp eyes. Assessing eyes. The kind that catalogues your weaknesses before you even know you have them.

I shift in my seat again, suddenly feeling the familiar urge to rub my thighs. I resist, keeping my hands still on the armrests.

"Mr Carter, with all due respect—" I start, but he cuts me off again.

"Or perhaps you're simply not interested in establishing a family of your own," he says, his tone mocking.

He meets my gaze with that same infuriating expression.

Decent guy, my arse!

Beneath his composed facade, he may seem amiable when talking to other men, but towards women like me, he appears to be nothing more than an egotistical dick. And if he thinks I will play into his hands by confirming his stereotypical view of an emotional and sensitive woman, he can choke on his own dick!

"I'm not so easily flustered," I say, voice steady. "And I'd appreciate it if we stayed focused on my achievements at this firm."

I haven't worked this hard, only to be subjected to this interrogation, and even worse, judged for the choices I make in my personal life.

The nerve.

He lets out a soft laugh, dismissively waving my protest away. "Unnecessary. Your file tells me everything I need to know," he says, nodding towards the file on his desk.

"Then why did you want to talk to me?"

What's the point of this charade? If he doesn't care about my clients then what is this? Some twisted test?

I don't have time for this nonsense. He obviously hasn't realised yet that we're losing clients on all sides. I should be out there talking to them, not enduring his scrutiny and judgement regarding my lack of offspring.

"Like I said, I wanted to gain insight into the employees here. Now I've done that," he declares, closing my file with a decisive snap. "You may leave. Thank you for your time."

That's it? No questions about my responsibilities, no indication that he even cares about my work. Just a dismissive wave.

"Mr Carter, I—" I begin, but he raises a hand to silence me, his expression unreadable.

Panic rises in my chest, tightening my throat and making my palms sweat. I'm sure I just lost my job. After four years of blood, sweat, and countless late nights, it's all crumbling. My hands move unconsciously to my thighs, rubbing through the fabric of my skirt in quick, anxious strokes before I force myself to stop and stand slowly. Every movement is watched by his sharp gaze. When I reach the door I turn back, hoping for some sign, any sign, of what's to come. His body remains still, one leg casually crossed over the other, his sharp jaw resting in his palm. His index finger continues to leisurely stroke his bottom lip.

Even as my mind races with worst-case scenarios, I can't help but wonder if he's planning to fire me because of my father or because of me.

"And there you have it," he says smoothly, his voice hanging in the air like a final note.

"Pardon?"

That infuriating smirk returns, his gaze locking onto mine. "You're flustered. Good day, MISS Rosen."

Cut-throat Lawyer

Medard

I talked to thirty-four employees today. Each one of them, a mere cog in the intricate machinery of this firm, a machinery that is about to implode if I don't wrench it back on course. And today, I've had to sit across from every single one of them, pry into their values, peel apart their dynamics, assess whether they're worth keeping. I loathe it. Every second feels like grit under my tongue.

Until her. Sophie Rosen.

Just another file on my desk—tucked between the hopeless and the mediocre—a folder labelled number twenty-two to be precise. I'd scanned the crowd during this morning's town hall, cataloguing faces with detached efficiency. And then my gaze snagged on her. Blonde hair, striking features, the kind of woman who turns heads without trying. I held her gaze a beat longer than the others, though I couldn't explain why. Something about the way she held herself—chin lifted, shoulders back, refusing to look away even when I clearly unsettled her. Intriguing. But just another pretty face in a sea of anxious employees.

Or so I thought.

Then she walked into my office, and I realised pretty didn't begin to cover it. The oxygen in the room shifted. Her scent—something maddeningly sweet—wrapped itself around me, and for a heartbeat, I forgot who the hell I am. I forgot the clients. Forgot the firm. Forgot that she is my subordinate. My pulse spiked, palms damp, stomach twisting like I was green again and facing my first jury. The words I usually wield with ease became a jumbled mess, spilling from my lips before I could halt their escape.

I lost control. Me.

So much so, I actually asked if she was involved with someone. Audacious. Unprofessional. Ridiculous.

And not one ounce of me regrets it. Because I want her. Want her enough to burn everything in my path.

How could I not? She's stunning. Those blue eyes—sharp and defiant. That blonde hair I want wrapped around my fist. A body that makes every professional boundary feel like a personal insult. She possesses an unwavering confidence and a touch of defiance that begged me to test her, to push until she broke. And when she didn't? Christ, it was the most satisfying thing I've felt in years.

Fuck.

I want to unravel her layer by layer, strip her down to her most vulnerable self, and claim every inch. Her on her knees, blue eyes glazed, lips swollen, giving me everything while I take even more. The image alone makes my cock ache, straining against tailored wool.

And yet, I can't.

She's forbidden. A subordinate. Worse, Rosen's daughter. The daughter of my biggest competitor.

I pinch the bridge of my nose, exhale hard, and remind myself I can fuck any woman in London tonight. Anyone but her. I'll bleed out this ache, drain it until Sophie Rosen is nothing but a fleeting distraction.

"Carter, how was your first day? Have you settled in alright?" Buckman's voice yanks me back, gravelly and annoyingly chipper.

I turn from the window, surprised to find him still here at eight o'clock. The place is a ghost town by now, save for the interns killing themselves to prove a point. Buckman though, lingers like a relic. He reminds me of my grand-father—once formidable, now outdated, and still sur-viving on decades of loyalty and nostalgia.

I cross to the bar cart and pour two scotches. "I have. You've got some interesting people working here."

"Only the finest," he declares, swelling with pride.

I drop a stack of files onto the coffee table, the thud cutting him down a peg. I hand him his drink and take a seat opposite. "These eight will be gone by tomorrow."

He sputters into his scotch, choking with wide eyes. "Tomorrow?"

"Yes."

He fumbles through the files, scanning names with shaky hands. Concern etches into the lines of his face as I lean back, relaxed, sipping my drink.

"Carter, firing people this soon. This morning, we told them we'd fight to save the firm. How do you think that will look?"

"It'll look like what it is," I counter, swirling the scotch in my glass. "A company hemorrhaging money. We're down twenty-seven percent in revenue. You cut costs, or you bury the corpse."

He tries again, the seasoned negotiator in him refusing to die quietly. "We should carefully consider alternatives before swinging the axe."

I smile, cold and amused. "Buckman, you misunder-stand. I'm not asking your permission. This is a courtesy. You hired me because this shit-show is out of your depth. So, make no mistake, this will be done my way. Understood?"

The old man gapes. He sees no deference in me, no bow to his age or tenure. I don't give a damn. He's climbed the ladder here by staying put. I've built empires by moving, merging, cutting, and conquering. He clings. I dismantle and rebuild. That's the difference.

"They warned me about your cut-throat approach," he mutters finally, taking another gulp.

I raise my tumbler, toast him with a smirk. "Then you were well informed."

Impulse strikes, reckless and deliberate, as I pluck Rosen's file from my desk and toss it onto the table between us.

"Sophie Rosen, what do you know?"

He flips it open and skims the pages. "Smart woman. She got us Fern Institute, Horizon Pharmaceuticals, Farm Valleys, and—" He snaps his fingers.

"Laren Automotives." I finish for him, sharper than his fading memory.

"Yes, she's an asset," he concedes, clutching his glass. His Adam's apple bobs. He thinks I'll cut her. He doesn't know that I could never. Not her.

My mind betrays me again—blue eyes, pouty lips, the subtle way she rubbed her thighs when flustered. I imagine those hands, long and delicate, wrapped around my cock. Heat coils low, urgent. I cross my legs to force composure.

"I'm concerned about her ties to Rosen & Smith," I say flatly, daring him to contradict me.

"Her father?" he frowns. "He's been trying to lure her over for years. She refuses. Their relationship is... rocky, from what I gather."

"In what way?"

He hesitates, his gaze sliding to the window. "He's always been 'firm' with her. That's the word Harman used. But he wouldn't share details."

My jaw tightens. Andrew Rosen is no joke—cut-throat, cunning, vicious in court. If he's firm with his daughter, it means Sophie has survived a battlefield.

"So, Harman knew her personally," I press.

"To a degree," Buckman allows. "He was her mentor, so naturally, they spent a lot of time together in a pro-fessional setting."

It's not enough. A red flag screams in the silence. Proximity to Harman. Blood ties to Rosen. She's a risk. A delicious, intoxicating, unbearable risk. As much as she's piqued my interest, this situation needs to be handled immediately.

Buckman shifts in his seat, pulling me from thoughts I have no business entertaining while discussing employee files.

"She's a liability," I conclude, masking desire with cold steel.

Buckman exhales resigned, bowing to my decision. "Whatever you think is best."

Arrogant Prick

Sophie

I make it back to my desk on autopilot, my professional mask barely holding together. My hands are still shaking when I drop into my chair, and I have to grip the edge of my desk to steady myself.

I want to scream. Want to storm back into Carter's office and demand he treat me with the basic respect I've earned. But beneath the anger, there's something worse—cold, creeping dread. The kind that whispers I've just failed some test I didn't even know I was taking, and now I'm going to pay for it with my job.

"Soph! How did it go?" Ben appears at my desk, practically vibrating with curiosity.

I force a smile that feels like it might crack my face. "Fine. He just asked about my clients, you know. Performance, areas for improvement. Same as Julia."

Ben's eyes light up, and I know what's coming before he even opens his mouth.

"Oh man, mine was brilliant! He's actually really sound, you know? We talked about client acquisition strategies, and he had some absolutely genius ideas about how I could restructure the Franco account to maximise billable hours. And then—get this—we got onto football. Can you believe it? I'm telling you, Soph, he's not just a legal genius, he actually gets it, you know? The whole work-life balance thing. He asked about my hobbies, my interests outside work—"

I nod along, making appropriate sounds of interest while my mind spirals.

Why didn't he ask me anything about my clients? He could have asked whether I enjoyed knitting, baking, underwater hobby horsing. Literally anything would have been better than forcing me to confront the uncomfortable truth that my life revolves entirely around my career.

"—and then he mentioned...Soph? You listening?"

I blink, refocusing on Ben's expectant face. "Sorry, yes. That's great."

"You alright?" His brow furrows with genuine concern. "You seem a bit off."

"Just tired," I lie, turning back to my computer screen. "Long day."

He lingers for a moment, clearly wanting to press, but eventually returns to his own desk, still buzzing with enthusiasm about our new managing director.

If I'm being honest, I feel embarrassed. It's evident I failed to capture his attention, so I'm sure he'll let me go soon. But I can't bring myself to share these thoughts with Ben. Some humiliations are best kept private.

The afternoon drags on with excruciating slowness. I throw myself into work, responding to emails, reviewing contracts, anything to stop replaying that final moment—You're flustered. Good day, MISS Rosen—on an endless loop in my head.

He's an arrogant prick. Unprofessional when it comes to handling his staff. And annoyingly attractive, which somehow makes it worse.

At five-fifty-five p.m., my phone buzzes with a reminder: Dinner with Father - six-thirty p.m.

My stomach sinks.

As if this day couldn't get any worse, I have my weekly obligation with Andrew Rosen to look forward to. Two hours of being interrogated, corrected, and found wanting in every possible way.

I watch the clock tick towards six o' clock with a sense of impending doom usually reserved for root canals and insurance renewals.

When it finally strikes, I gather my things with mechanical efficiency and head for the exit, trying not to think about how I'm trading one condescending man for another.

I'm staring at the white tablecloth, tracing the pattern of the damask weave with my eyes, when my father's voice cuts through my spiralling thoughts like a knife.

"It is disrespectful not to give me your undivided attention. I have rearranged my entire schedule to share this dinner with you."

I blink, pulling myself back to the present, to my father's disapproving face across the table.

"My apologies, Father."

As always, his lips tighten disapprovingly, aimed not just at this particular instance but perhaps at my general existence. The fact that he pulled me away from my busy schedule—insisting we have dinner—seems to have conveniently eluded him. I straighten my posture and take a sip of my Chardonnay, attempting to look composed rather than like someone contemplating whether it's possible to drown yourself in a wine glass.

"Let us have the sea bass. They say it is worth its sixty pounds," he concludes, folding his menu with the finality of a judge's gavel and snatching mine from my grasp before placing both on the edge of the table.

"I'd prefer the steak." The words hang in the air for approximately half a second before he ignores them completely.

I glance around the restaurant where I've spent most of my evenings when dining with my father—which is to say—far too many evenings for a healthy father-daughter relationship. When I left for Oxford, he sold our family home and moved into a penthouse in the city. I suppose he saw no point in keeping relics from my childhood now that I was off being educated at his alma mater. Since then, he's never invited me to his new abode, and I've never felt inclined to pry. Some doors are better left closed.

"So, I hear that Medard Carter is your new boss. What is your impression of him?"

I snatch my wine glass, taking a long sip, hoping the alcohol will somehow formulate a plan to evade any discussion about that cocky bastard. Revealing the truth about my encounter with my new boss is absolutely out of the question. My father would surely interpret it as a failure on my part. And perhaps he's not entirely wrong. After all, none of my colleagues seemed to have endured as uncomfortable and confrontational a meeting as I did.

"We will have the sea bass," he informs the waiter with the authority of someone whose never been told no in his life, before returning his attention to me. "So, have you had the pleasure of speaking to him yet?"

"I have," I respond, perhaps too quickly.

"Yes, I have had the pleasure." He corrects me as though I'm a particularly slow student. "Speak in full sentences. I have not spent a fortune on your education to listen to you speak like a commoner."

He tightens his grip on the whiskey tumbler, which accentuates the disappearing lips within his greying goatee. It's a look I've seen countless times—the expression of a man perpetually disappointed by the world's failure to meet his exacting standards.

We're only twenty minutes into this dinner, and I've already managed to disappoint him twice. A new record, perhaps. At this rate, I might actually achieve something impressive tonight.

"My apologies. You're right," I clear my throat, tasting bile and Chardonnay.

He nods, acknowledging my apology with all the warmth of a tax audit, then motions for me to elaborate on my meeting with Carter.

"He briefly spoke to each employee today. I assume it was to gain an understanding of the dynamics within the firm."

"Did he enquire about your clients' performances? Your contributions to the firm? What did you tell him?" He fires questions at me like a prosecutor cross-examining a hostile witness.

"You know I can't tell you any details." I idly rotate the stem of my wine glass, stealing a glance at him to gauge his reaction.

This is our customary dance whenever we dine together, like a choreographed performance we've perfected over the years. He poses questions that I'm legally unable to answer without breaching my confidentiality agreements. I remind him of the oath I took as a lawyer. He insists I abandon the firm and join his instead.

Same shit, different day.

"Fair enough," he huffs before shaking out his napkin and laying it across his lap with unnecessary precision. "But let me explain this to you. He is currently evaluating the entire situation.

Assessing everything from the firm's assets, profits, and risks to all manner of expenses. He will scrutinise it all. The cost of high-earning lawyers, the profits they bring in, the company cars, and even the price of a single paper clip. Do you understand, Sophie?"

"I understand," I huff, downing the remnants of my wine before signalling the waiter for a refill with perhaps more desperation than is dignified.

Of course, I know what's involved in running a law firm. I've been working at one for four bloody years. There's no need for him to explain it to me as if I were an ignorant child just learning about life's birds and bees.

"In that case, you should know that he will have to make cuts. People will lose their jobs. If you are not deemed valuable enough, you will be axed," he exhales while running a hand over his goatee in that contemplative way that always precedes something particularly cutting. "Before that happens, you should consider jumping ship and working for me."

Here we go again.

I thought my father couldn't belittle me any further after implying I'd be a better lawyer under his tutelage. Now he's suggesting that Harman & Buckman— scratch that, Carter & Buckman— won't keep me around. That I'm disposable. Expendable. Not quite good enough to survive the cull.

I try to hide the anger brewing inside me by layering my voice with false sweetness. "What makes you think they would fire me?"

I want to scream at him, to make him see that I'm a successful lawyer in my own right, deserving of his respect. What will it take for him to view me as his equal? A signed affidavit? A billboard in Piccadilly Circus? An act of bloody Parliament?

"Do not fool yourself, Sophie. You have not been there for very long," he finishes his whiskey, then beckons for the waiter to refill his glass. "And let us not forget, you were Harman's little pet."

"I was not," I gasp, shaking my head in disbelief at his insinuation, heat flooding my cheeks. "He was my mentor, teaching me like any other senior associate."

To my surprise, he chuckles at my defiance. It's a sound completely devoid of warmth or humour.

The waiter approaches our table, serving our meals with the

quiet efficiency of someone who's learnt not to make eye contact during family disputes. The limp fish on my plate serves as a perfect metaphor—at the age of twenty-eight, Andrew Rosen still believes he holds the reins to my decisions, my choices, my entire bloody life.

Working at this law firm is one of the few things I've managed to defy him on. I won't allow him to take it away from me. So, I'll remain at Carter & Buckman until they physically show me the door and change the locks.

"I do not believe that," he takes a bite, then points his fork at my plate like a weapon. "Eat! The fish was the right choice."

Against every inner voice shouting "Anarchy!", I act like the good, obedient daughter and pick up my fork. The fish tastes mediocre at best, and I yearn desperately for the steak I actually wanted. But that would require having autonomy, and we can't have that, can we?

"You had a special station with him. Wherever he went, you followed like a devoted puppy. People talk, Sophie. They wonder if you knew about his scheme, if you were complicit, or if perhaps—" he pauses meaningfully, "your relationship was more than professional."

His insinuation slams directly into my chest like a physical blow, causing a piece of fish to lodge in my windpipe. I cough violently into my napkin as he points his fork towards my glass of water. I grab the wine glass instead.

Anarchy!

"Are you insinuating that I had romantic relations with my boss?" I hiss across the table, mindful of the other diners nearby who are definitely pretending not to listen.

"You tell me." He counters with a shrug so dismissive it borders on obscene. "He promoted you from junior to senior associate rather swiftly."

Unbelievable. Bravo. He's just earned himself the award for shittiest father of the century.

I'm finished with this putrid fish.

"Have you ever considered the possibility that I may actually be good at my job?" My voice rises slightly despite my best efforts. "That there are people out there who believe in me and my abilities?"

Adding insult to considerable injury, he huffs at my response like I'm a naive child. "Petulance is not a becoming look on a young woman."

I open my mouth to argue, to tell him exactly where he can shove his opinions about becoming looks, but he raises one hand, instantly silencing me.

It works. It always works. And I hate myself for it.

"If you have slept with him, I will not judge you." The lie sits between us like a third guest at the table. "But I need to know so that I can handle the situation. After all, as your father, my reputation is just as much on the line as yours."

Of course.

That's all it comes down to. Daddy dearest doesn't want his pristine image tarnished. It would be a scandal— his only daughter caught in a romantic entanglement with a married, disbarred lawyer, a managing director no less.

It shouldn't surprise me that, once again, he doesn't care about me or my feelings. Only about how my failures might reflect on him.

I toss the napkin onto my plate and grab my purse, my hands shaking with suppressed rage. "As always, it's been a pleasure. Enjoy the rest of your evening."

He seizes my wrist as I pass by him, his grip tight enough to bruise. "Answer me!" He grinds the words through clenched teeth.

"Contrary to your beliefs, I do know how to be professional." I yank my wrist out of his grasp and hurry towards the exit before my last ounce of resolve crumbles, or worse—before I confess that the truth is far more complicated than his accusations.

Most Feared Man

Sophie

Twenty-four hours after my humiliating meeting with Carter, I sit at my desk in catatonic shock. Five straight minutes, and I'm still mentally screaming at my finger to just. Bloody. Click. But my index finger has declared independence, frozen while the cursor hovers over the 'send' button.

It's just a meeting request. Farm Valleys. Despite Richard being equal parts sleazy uncle and greasy used-car salesman, they're still a solid client. So why can't I send the damn invite?

Because if I hit 'send,' I'm promising Farm Valleys I'll be here next week. And what if, by then, I've already been handed a cardboard box and have to send a humiliating cancellation?

Chaos is rippling through the office like aftershocks from an earthquake. Security's been called. People are pacing like caffeinated lunatics or crouched behind their screens, whispering panicked theories into phones.

Ben and I fall into the second camp—desk-huggers, pretending that if we huddle close enough to our computers, we might become invisible.

Ben is convinced this is it. The layoffs. The purge. And if my name is on that list, it won't just be losing my job. It'll be the humiliation of cancelling on Farm Valleys, explaining to Richard why I'm no longer employed.

As a senior associate, I should be safe. I have good clients, solid numbers. Maybe I should wait until tonight to send the invite.

"I can't fit all my outfits into my nan's spare room," Ben's voice infiltrates my spiralling panic. He's got a Danish in his hand. Seventh? Eighth? When I'm stressed, I rub my thighs raw. Ben eats his body weight in sugar and butter.

I blink at him, confused.

"If they let me go, I'll have to move into my nan's spare room," he says around a mouthful of pastry. "With my student debt? No way I can afford Shoreditch rent without this job."

I narrow my eyes. "What outfits? You mean your garish tie collection?" I lift my coffee cup in mock toast, but he just mutters a half-hearted "sure" and swivels back to his screen.

Fine.

I've never had to stare down overdue rent or choose between electricity and food. I could crawl back to Andrew Rosen's platinum safety net if I had to. Though I'd rather chew glass.

It's not a lack of money that terrifies me. It's failure. Proof that my father's right, and I'll never be as exceptional as him. That I'll always be the disappointment.

That thought alone snaps me out of my paralysis.

Screw it.

I slam my finger down and send the bloody invite. As long as I've still got a desk, I'll fight tooth and nail to keep it.

And then Julia explodes through the doors like a Shakespearean tragedy in vintage Prada. Tears pour down her face in black rivers; an empty cardboard box clutched in her hand. She slams it onto her desk with a bang that reverberates around the pit.

"Twelve years!" she wails.

Without missing a beat, Ben and I survey the carnage. Mark Thomas is shouting at security as they escort him back to his desk. Kabir is packing his life into a box while screaming in Hindi down the phone. Through the glass panels, I spot management parading past with arms full of boxes. Three senior partners. Gone.

I glance at Ben, and the look we share says everything. The guillotine has dropped.

"What happened?" I whisper, shoving tissues in Julia's direction.

"He fired us! Can you believe it? Twelve years, and I'm tossed aside like a used napkin."

Ben lets out a sharp sigh, tossing the remnants of his Danish in the bin.

"On what grounds?" I ask.

"Some nonsense about cost-cutting and unsatisfactory performance," she scoffs. "Oh, what does it matter?"

As she tosses her hole punch into the box, something shatters. The picture frame of her beloved sausage dog, Ludo. Julia squares her shoulders, tosses the frame back in, and fixes us with one last watery glare.

"Good luck, you two. You're going to need it."

And she's gone.

Shit.

"Relax!" Ben chirps, noticing the frantic way I'm rubbing my thighs. He's suddenly whistling.

"How are you calm right now?" I hiss.

He shrugs. "Better her than us." Then he winks.

I roll my eyes, about to tell him exactly where he can shove his optimism, when I freeze.

The most feared man in this firm walks in.

Carter.

Silence falls. He strides to the front of the pit, sleeves rolled to his elbows, forearms dusted with dark blond hair.

His gaze begins to sweep across the room. My breath catches in anticipation. But as soon as he spots Ben, his attention diverts from me entirely, moving along like I'm part of the furniture.

Why won't he look at me? After yesterday's interrogation, after humiliating me, now I'm not even worth acknowledging?

I rise, intent on fleeing to the bathroom before I do something monumentally stupid. But as I reach the doorway, his voice anchors me in place.

"At present, eight people have been made redundant."

Gasps. Whispers. He doesn't flinch.

"Further cuts have not yet been determined. Retain your accounts. Bring in business. That is how you survive."

I glance at Ben. He's practically glowing with relief.

"Muhammad, Reynolds, and Rosen—" Carter continues, his gaze zeroing in on Amina and Ben as their names escape his lips. I, however, remain completely unacknowledged, like I'm invisible.

There's no denying it now—he's deliberately ignoring me. Anger courses through my veins.

What the hell have I done to deserve this?

"Congratulations. You've been promoted to junior partner."

My gasp is audible. Ben's jaw drops. Even Amina looks floored.

Promoted. He promoted me.

You don't promote people you hate. Did I misread him this entire time? Or is this some elaborate setup—give me more responsibility so my failure is more spectacular?

Excitement rockets through me, chasing away the suspicion. Carter moves through the room with purpose, shaking hands, offering congratulations. He stops at Ben's desk. A solid handshake. Words exchanged. My pulse quickens as he approaches me.

He's going to stop. He has to.

But he doesn't.

He pauses just long enough for me to drown in the amber flecks of his eyes, close enough that I can smell his cologne, and then he turns and walks away.

The humiliation is sharp enough to flay me alive.

Ben is suddenly at my side, his hand clamping around my elbow. His eyes are wide, frantic.

"What the hell was that?" he hisses.

Shit. He saw it.

I nod quickly towards the corridor, motioning for Ben to follow.

Out of sight, he leans in again. "Did you see that coming? My meeting with Carter went well enough, but a promotion?"

"Neither did I," I admit, the words tasting oddly flat.

Ben scrubs a hand through his hair. "Why even hand out promotions when they've just axed people?"

"Stability. Clients want consistency. Cut too deep and no one's left to handle the accounts. It's brutal math, really."

He nods slowly. "Huh. Didn't think of it like that."

Carter's assistant is striding towards us.

"Mr Reynolds." Her voice is brisk, clipped. "I'm Janet, Mr Carter's assistant. I'll show you to your new office." She jabs at her tablet, then her eyes flick to me. "Miss Rosen, there's been a clerical error with your assistant assignment. I'll fetch you once it's sorted."

She pivots on her heel and stalks away.

Ben follows, grinning. Halfway down the corridor, he spins around and starts walking backwards. Hands curled like paws against his chest, tongue lolling out, he pants at me like an eager puppy.

I fight the laugh clawing up my throat. With a subtle swipe at my shoulder, I flip him off. He barks a laugh before trotting after Janet.

An hour later, Janet's back, pushing open a heavy oak door. "And this will be your office."

My office.

I step in, and the air leaves me in a rush. A corner office. Floor-to-ceiling glass spilling light across rich furnishings. Canary

Wharf stretched out like a promise.

"This... can't be right," I murmur.

Corner offices aren't handed out like sweets. They're reserved. Power seats. Carter has one. Buckman another. The boardroom takes the third. The fourth? Linda Marks. Head of Litigation. Third in command. Until this morning, when she was walked out with a cardboard box.

And now, they—no, he—gave it to me.

"Are you sure?" I ask.

She raises a brow, then nods. "Quite certain. Now, if you'll excuse me, Mr Carter's lunch won't fetch itself."

"What's he having?" I blurt out before I can stop myself.

Her eyes roll heavenward. "Unagi Donburi. From Nobu. And no, I won't get you anything. You have your own assistant for that now." Then she's gone.

I lean back against the desk. This office should feel like victory, but instead I think of Betty—Harman's assistant who believed in me, who nudged him to take me under his wing when I was fresh out of Oxford. She's gone too, walked out because she was too close to Harman, too loyal to the wrong person.

Janet will never bake cookies like Betty did. And if I'm not careful, I'll end up just like Betty—discarded for backing the wrong horse.

A tentative knock pulls me from my thoughts, and a girl who barely looks old enough to drink legally steps in.

"Miss Rosen? I'm Melissa, your new assistant."

Relief loosens the tension in my shoulders. "Come in, please."

She bounces forward with an eager smile. "Sorry, I'm late. HR had me down for Amina Muhammad, then switched me last minute. Guess they thought we'd be a better fit personality-wise."

I catch the implication. Amina's intense, no-nonsense. Melissa is... bubbly. Apparently, Carter thinks I need handling with enthusiasm and encouragement. I'm not sure if that's insulting or oddly thoughtful.

"Oh, and everyone calls me Millie," she adds.

"Millie." I return her smile. "Nice to meet you. Let's start by syncing our calendars, shall we?"

Because apparently—whether I like it or not, whether I understand it or not—I've just been catapulted into the big leagues. And I have absolutely no idea what Carter's game is.

One-Night-Fuck

Medard

Leaning forward, elbows braced on my knees, I clench my fists until my knuckles scream white. The tension ripples through my arms, biceps straining. If I'd looked into those eyes—those impossible, piercing, bright-blue orbs—for one more second, I would've been done for. Finished.

Every muscle in me is strung tight, pulling me towards her like I'm on some invisible leash. My fingers twitch with the urge to touch her, but not to shake her hand. Not professional, polite, sterile contact.

No, my mind betrays me with the image of my hand sliding over hers, then higher to find her pulse, feeling it thrum beneath my touch. And that's when my carefully constructed restraint would shatter.

Because I wouldn't stop there.

I'd pull her against me. Fill my lungs with her intoxicating scent. Find the delicate curve where her shoulder meets her neck, and taste her. Devour her. Claim her.

I want her. No, crave her.

But I can't. I won't.

This firm is supposed to be my endgame. The final act that takes Andrew Rosen's empire to its knees—his firm crumbling while I rise as the undisputed head of the most powerful law firm in the country.

And Sophie Rosen? She's the one temptation that could wreck the entire plan. An employee. Worse, his daughter.

Unfuckingtouchable.

But Jesus Christ, I need to get laid.

I yank my phone from my pocket, thumb flying across the screen.

Me: Free now? Graphix Bar.

Alex: Let's paint the town red

Alex never fails me. Twenty years of friendship means we don't need to say more than three words.

Shoving my phone into my pocket, I snap my laptop shut, grab my coat, and stalk out. The place hums with uneasy silence, eyes following me. Can't blame them. I've only been here two days and already turned their world upside down.

People despise change. And me? I thrive on it. Their hatred feeds me. They'll adapt. Or they won't, and I'll replace them.

I round the corner towards the lift and—

Fuck.

Her.

She's there. Folders clutched to her chest, watching the indicator lights. My heart gives a traitorous lurch. It was an idiotic move keeping her on this floor. Sharing lifts with Sophie Rosen is like locking myself in a cage with a lioness—too close, too dangerous, too bloody tempting.

I spin on my heel, aiming for the stairs, but she catches the movement.

"Mr Carter!" Her voice slices through the air.

I don't stop. The metal door clangs shut behind me, cutting off whatever she was going to say.

Christ.

I'm running. From a subordinate. From a woman. What the hell is wrong with me?

I force myself to slow before I hit the lobby, straightening my coat. I'm a grown man. Her boss. Fully in control.

"Carter!" Buckman's voice barrels towards me as he steps out of the lift.

Miss Rosen is right behind him, head bowed, slipping past like a shadow.

"If you have a moment," Buckman begins, "there's something I wanted to discuss."

I track her with my gaze as she walks away, that tight pencil skirt cupping her arse like a gift from heaven. My throat dries.

"Carter?" Buckman presses.

"Yes. What is it?" I snap.

"I was surprised to see you promoting three staff members after you'd just axed eight. I know you don't like being questioned—"

"You had three under-performing, overpaid dinosaurs," I cut him off. "Cutting them saved us 2.4%. Promoting three younger employees costs us 0.6%. Net gain, Buckman. And with half-term coming up, students will be scouting internships. Promoting from within tells them this place has upward mobility."

He blinks, clearly still processing. "I see. And what about Miss Rosen?"

"What about her?" I reply coolly.

"Well, I just assumed—"

Pathetic.

"If that's all, I'll see you tomorrow." I cut him off and stride for the exit.

Keep your friends close, your enemies closer.

And Sophie Rosen? She's both.

If she'd settled for working for her father, none of this would be a question. But she didn't. She clawed her way here on her own merit. That gives me just enough doubt that she's clean.

And if I'm wrong?

Then there's no better way to uncover the truth than keeping her under my roof, under my eye... Under me.

"Long day?" Alex greets me as I drop into our usual booth at Graphix, the neon glow casting half his face in electric orange. He's already nursing a beer, sleeves rolled up.

I tug at my own tie, loosen it, and pop two buttons.

"You have no idea. The new project I've taken on is a complete disaster."

He slides a bottle across the table. "You want to talk about it?"

I shake my head and take a long pull. "Not tonight. I need some fun."

Alex's brows lift. "How much fun are we talking about? Your definition tends to range from 'harmlessly reckless' to 'I'm questioning my choice in friends.'"

"Fun-fun," I say vaguely.

"Define. Because remember the last time you said that? Karaoke night? You tried to hit that high note and your voice cracked so bad the bartender ducked like someone had fired a gun."

I groan. "You're one to talk. You forgot the second verse entirely and started serenading grandmas with made-up lyrics about hookers and tequila."

Alex throws his head back laughing. "They loved it!"

I shake my head, grinning. "Alright, I'll give you that one. Although the night was rather low-key."

"Low-key," he snorts, nearly choking on his beer. "Sure. Exhibit B then. Cian's summer party two years ago."

Ah, Christ.

Cian's parties are legendary—equal parts debauchery and blackout survival test.

"We decided shots weren't strong enough and started drinking the punch straight from the paddling pool."

I groan at the memory. "Until you fell into that damn thing and dragged me with you."

Alex is practically choking on laughter. "And then... the twins. The Eiffel Tower incident."

I groan. "We swore never to speak of that."

"Still," Alex says with a shrug, "not bad for two drowned rats sticky with sangria."

"At Cian's party? That was hardly a challenge. That man-whore has more pussy in his house than a cat sanctuary."

We both burst out laughing.

"So, what's it gonna be tonight?" Alex asks once we've calmed down.

I shake my head. "Tonight, I'm aiming for quick, clean relief."

He raises his bottle in mock salute. "Mild blowout it is."

I take another swallow, already scoping out potential candidates, when Alex clears his throat.

"Well, your fun might have to wait a second. There's something I need to talk to you about."

My gaze slides to the bar. Two women have been watching us. Pretty. One blond, one brunette. The blond catches me looking and flashes a shy smile.

"Go on," I nudge Alex. "Let's get this over with."

"Your mum called me."

That drags my attention back. "About?"

"Your brother's wedding rehearsal."

I groan. "She shouldn't have done that."

Alex smirks. "I told her I'd pass it on."

At the bar, Blondie's fishing olives out of her martini glass, lips closing around the pick.

Alex snaps his fingers in front of my face. "Mírame, look at me. Whatever is between you and Theo, it's not worth blowing off his wedding. Just suck it up and go."

I bark out a laugh. "That's your advice? Stick to numbers, mate."

He shrugs. "Numbers don't lie. Neither does family."

He follows my gaze back to the bar and grins. "Vale, I'll take the blond, you take the brunette?"

The blond flicks her hair over her shoulder, locking eyes with me.

I let a slow smile spread across my face.

"Not this time, mate."

Game on.

5:58 a.m. Like every morning, I dismiss my alarm before it has the chance to go off.

Glancing over my shoulder, I take in the aftermath of last night. She's still wrapped in my sheets; her long blond hair sprawled across the pillow. I make a mental note to tell Mrs Ruthers to change the sheets. Immediately.

I head for the bathroom, but not before clocking Alex sprawled on my sofa like a fallen gladiator. He's half-crushed under the brunette—Jessy? Jenny? Something with a J.

I nudge him with my foot. He groans, disentangles himself, and stumbles after me.

Our routine is so well-oiled it's almost domestic.

The bathroom fills with the hiss of water. Alex grabs two toothbrushes from the drawer, loads them both up with paste, and passes me mine.

"You feeling better?" he asks, voice rough with sleep.

I shrug, slipping under the stream. "The itch is gone."

Alex doesn't buy it. "You don't look at ease. Something's different."

Twenty years of friendship, and the man reads me like a profit-and-loss sheet.

But I refuse to admit it, because admitting it means it's real.

Nothing has changed. Sophie Rosen is nothing more than a temporary glitch—a dazzling, sharp-tongued, blue-eyed glitch. But I scratched the itch, and now I'm back in the game.

"I'm just stressed about the new firm," I throw over my shoulder as I swap places with him.

My reflection greets me in the mirror as I scrape the razor across my jaw.

From the shower, Alex calls out, "Is it more of a shambles than you bargained for?"

"You could say that. Despite the former MD being an unethical and useless prick, I was hoping his partner could be helpful."

I wash my face, and when I look back, he's standing next to me with a towel around his waist.

He slaps aftershave onto his jaw and smirks. "Well, if it isn't gross profit—"

"It's growth."

"Exactly, my friend." He hands me the bottle, claps me on the shoulder, and saunters out.

In the walk-in wardrobe, I pass him a crisp white shirt. In return, he passes me my espresso.

"How's your promotion going?" I ask.

He exhales sharply. "I thought bringing in that last account guaranteed me a seat at the big boy's table. Instead of promoting me, the bastard asked me to tutor his daughter in Spanish."

I raise a brow. "I hope you told him to shove it."

Before he can answer, the woman stirs in my bed—all honeyed smiles and bare breasts. She stretches, then clutches the sheets when she notices Alex.

"Morning," Alex nods politely, turning back to me. "And no. I didn't refuse. If I'd said no, I'd be at the bottom of the ladder again."

"Or," I counter, "you could've gained respect by standing up for your worth."

I stride past Blondie without a glance, but she blocks my path with a hopeful smile.

"Last night was great. Maybe we could continue—" She flicks a lock of hair over her shoulder.

I became incredibly turned on last night when she exposed her delicate neck. I imagined wrapping my hands around it while I stretched her wide. Now, I just wish she'd get herself a bloody hair tie and quit the performance. Her attempt at innocent coyness is laughable. She took every filthy thing I gave her—hard thrusts and rough hands pulling her hair. And the whole time, I never once let her see my face.

Because she wasn't the fantasy I was chasing.

"You thought wrong," I cut her off. "I'm a one-night fuck, nothing more."

She retreats into the pillows, her confidence deflating.

Alex's conquest drifts into the bedroom, wearing a broad smile and very little else. "What about me, handsome?"

Alex freezes, eyes going wide, then stammers, "What he said," pointing at me before bolting for the door.

Pussy.

I join him at the entrance while he looks like he's just escaped a firing squad.

"Do you think they'll be all right?" he asks.

"They'll be fine. Mrs Ruthers will whip up breakfast, then send them on their way."

As if summoned, the lift pings and out steps Mrs Ruthers herself. She barely glances at us before sighing.

"Good morning," I say smoothly. "If you don't mind. And change the sheets, please."

Another sigh. "Again, Mr Carter?" Her tone is bone-dry.

"Again."

She marches past us without another word.

In the lift, Alex hunches slightly. "You know that's not what I meant. I feel bad discarding them like that."

Only Alex—a hopeless romantic trapped in a sinner's body—would carry guilt over a mutually agreed one-night stand.

"Don't," I say flatly. "They knew what they were signing up for."

Silence fills the small metal box, and for the first time in longer than I care to admit, I feel something that shouldn't be there.

A flicker. The faintest trace of guilt.

Not for the women still in my penthouse, but for the fierce, blue-eyed beauty.

I shake it off. Guilt is a luxury I can't afford. Not when I'm this close to everything I've worked for.

Fool

Medard

22 years ago, Medard, 13 years old

The school bell shrills through the old loudspeakers. My classmates flood the classroom in a chaotic chorus of chatter and laughter. My mates are talking about last night's Premier League Final, but I pay no attention. Instead, I unzip my pencil case and flick my gaze to the note Susie slipped me yesterday.

I carefully unfold it, trying to ignore the nervous flutter in my stomach.

"Medard, do you want to be my boyfriend?" her handwriting reads in neat, curly letters.

Butterflies. Big, stupid butterflies. I stare at the words, my cheeks burning hot.

"Come on, Med! Parker was ace last night, right?" Rob nudges me.

I glance down at my open backpack. Nestled amid my books is the pink rose I plucked from Mum's garden this morning. Its petals are soft, delicate, and perfect.

My heart beats faster at the thought of giving it to Susie after class. Mum always says flowers brighten her day. So maybe, just maybe, it's worth the risk.

My thoughts are interrupted when the teacher, Mr Burns, calls out, "Alexander Weatherford."

I glance over my shoulder. Sitting alone behind me is a boy I've never seen before. He's tall, tanned, with black hair down to his chin. He looks completely out of place.

"Weatherford," Mr Burns repeats, voice sharper. "Where's your history book?"

The boy blushes. "Sorry, sir. I arrived yesterday from Spain. I've had no time to get my books."

From Spain? That makes sense. His skin is darker than ours, and that accent—thick and warm—makes my curiosity spike.

"Well, then," Mr Burns sighs, "can someone please give him their book?"

Everyone stares at him, causing him to retreat into his seat. I feel a twinge of sympathy and turn around, handing him my History book. He looks surprised but takes it gratefully.

"Thanks," he whispers. "Really."

The class resumes, but my mind keeps drifting back to Susie, the note, and the rose.

The bell rings again, and everyone shuffles out. I stay behind a moment, gathering my courage. Then I head outside, where Susie and her friends sit on a bench, chatting.

My stomach twists. I take a deep breath and walk over.

"Hey," I manage, voice cracking slightly.

Susie notices me first. She smiles warmly. "Hi, Medard."

My palms sweat as I reach for my backpack.

"Um... I brought you something," I say, fumbling with the zipper. I pull out the pink rose, holding it out to her.

She stares at it, giggling softly. "That's sweet," she finally says, taking the flower.

Her friends giggle and whisper, until one suddenly squeals, "Aww, that's so cheesy!"

Susie glances at her friends. Something flickers across her face—uncertainty maybe, or embarrassment. But then her expression hardens into pity.

Without warning, she drops the rose. It hits the hard bricks with a soft thud, petals scattering. Her white trainer crushes the delicate flower beneath her foot, grinding it into the pavement.

I stare, stunned.

"I...I don't under—" I start, but she's already giggling with her friends.

"You silly fool! That note was just a joke. I wasn't serious about... all that."

My heart sinks. Heat rises in my cheeks, and a sting prickles at the corners of my eyes. I turn and run, my footsteps pounding away.

I don't stop until I reach the park. I find a bench and sink onto it, feeling tears prickling behind my eyelids. Why did I think she would like me?

As I sit there, head bowed, a book appears in front of me. I look up to find Alex, the new boy from Spain, holding my History book out with a small smile.

"Here," he says softly, "thank you."

I quickly wipe my eyes. "No sweat," I whisper.

To my surprise, he sits down next to me.

"You okay?"

I nod, trying to settle my racing heart.

"The girl doesn't deserve your kindness. She's mean."

"Maybe it was just a cheesy, stupid idea of mine," I shrug.

He stares at me in disbelief. "No way! You're brave for trying. She's just a stupid girl."

"Brave?" I echo, feeling a flicker of warmth despite the ache. "I looked like a complete fool."

He chuckles. "No, you looked like someone that cares. Someone not afraid to show it. Mi abuela, my grandmother, always says a real man shows his feelings and only a coward hides behind his moustache."

I laugh—a genuine, relieved laugh that bubbles up unexpectedly.

Alex joins in, shrugging.

"So, you're from Spain?" I ask.

"Sí. Mi papá got a job here, so we had to move quick. Like one day I'm in school with my friends, the next I'm on a plane to England."

"Wow," I breathe, "that sucks."

That awkward, crushing feeling begins to fade. I've got my friends, Mum and Dad, and Theo. I can't imagine being ripped out of my life like that.

"It's just you and your dad then?"

"No, I have three little brothers and my abuela has come too, to help with them."

"Alright, and your mum?"

"She's gone," he says quietly, then looks up to the sky and pulls out a golden necklace with a cross from under his shirt, kissing it.

"Descansa en paz, mamá," he whispers.

"I'm sorry for your loss," I whisper.

He nods, lips pressed thin.

I can't imagine losing my mum. The thought alone makes my chest tight. How is he even sitting here, smiling, being kind to me when he's dealing with that?

But then something shifts. He smiles again, a little brighter.

"But I like it here. I'm just looking forward to summer," he says, pulling his denim jacket tighter.

I laugh. "Oh, mate! You should know, this is summer."

His face falters. "De verdad? Really?"

"Yeah. It's actually been boiling lately."

"¡Ay, qué putada!" he throws his arms up in dramatic exasperation, pulling a laugh from me.

"Welcome to Britain!" I say gleefully, giving his shoulder a friendly squeeze before I stand up and stretch my legs.

"I'm heading to football practice. You want to come?"

His eyes light up. "Sí! I love football!"

"Brilliant. Come on then."

We walk together, the cold sun shining down on us, and it's in that moment that I decide I will give it my best to become Alex's friend.

Ignorant Asshole

Sophie

I flick my empty coffee cup into the bin, the hollow clatter echoing my mood. Four hours of broken sleep, and somehow, I'm supposed to function. The promotion should feel like champagne bubbles in my veins, but instead it's a rock in my chest, heavy and suffocating. And the name carved into the damn thing?

Medard Carter.

Two days since the promotion, and I still haven't heard from him about my accounts.

The lift doors close, and I stare at my reflection. Maybe I'm overthinking. Maybe Carter is drowning in work, too consumed with salvaging the firm to notice me. Except Ben's words replay in my head. Carter scheduled a meeting with him and Amina about rearranging the clients. Ben and Amina. Not Sophie.

By the time the doors open, my thighs tingle from nervous rubs.

"Morning. Any meetings today?" I ask Millie when I reach her desk.

Millie glances at her notepad. "Nope. Just Horizon Pharmaceuticals at two."

So that's it. No meeting with Carter.

My nails dig into my thighs. How did I get here? First, the whispers—Harman's little protege, tainted by association. Then the near job loss, flipped last-second into a promotion that should have screamed trust. Now, a new MD who acts like I'm invisible.

"Anything else?" Millie asks.

"Coffee. Milk, no sugar. Keep them coming. Thanks," I mutter, already walking to my desk.

I slam open my laptop to find my calendar glaring back at me mockingly.

Fine.

If Carter won't invite me, I'll drag him to the table myself. I hammer in a new meeting request, title it 'Discussion regarding new clients', and give him generous notice—three days from now. I hit send and lean back. I'm not waiting for a man's permission.

Horizon's file takes over my screen next. Rupert—lecherous,

oily Rupert—who thinks women can't see his eyes wander.

Millie reappears with coffee. I'm halfway through my first gulp when my screen pings. Carter.

Meeting request—declined.

No explanation. No alternate date. Just cold refusal.

My hands move to my thighs instinctively, nails digging in through my skirt. I jab the intercom to summon Millie, and she appears instantly.

"Have you met Carter's assistant? Can you find out when he's free?"

She nods. "Friday at eleven?"

"How do you know?"

Her shrug is casual. "I saw your request and his decline."

Great. Now she knows he's dodging me.

"Please go confirm with his assistant," I order, dismissing her.

Work becomes my weapon. I drown in contracts, depositions, and potential client briefs. Four hours pass until my stomach growls.

As I rise, my phone buzzes. Father's name lights the screen. I hit decline without hesitation. I haven't spoken to him since our dinner two nights ago, and I'm fine with that. My anger hasn't cooled enough for guilt to creep in yet, but it will. It always does.

The pit is a storm as I make my way to the kitchen—phones ringing, papers shuffling, voices colliding.

Ben's laugh carries before I even see him. Then Carter's deep, smooth voice. I round the corner and freeze. He's there. His suit is impeccable, the crisp white shirt blinding under the fluorescents.

Perfect chance to confront him.

His gaze lifts and snags on mine. Electricity bolts through me in a sharp, traitorous jolt. His eyes hold mine for a beat too long, searing and unreadable. His aftershave ghosts over my senses—fresh, oceanic, expensive sin. Without a word, he lifts his phone, presses it to his ear, and strolls past.

The phone didn't ring. I know it didn't ring because I was watching him. He just... picked it up. Pretended.

Ignorant arsehole.

"Hello, stranger," Ben sings as I walk into the kitchen.

I pull out my salad, grateful for his sunshine.

"Oh, honey, you miss me." He squeezes my shoulder. "I miss

you too. The new office is gorgeous, all this space to myself, but without my favourite blond bombshell?" He sighs dramatically. "Tragic."

A giggle slips out, my anger dissolving. Ben's been calling me that since my first week here. That's Ben—flirty, fun, and never creepy. My ally.

"You're right," I grin. "I miss you dearly, my little tattletale."

"I knew it." He winks. "So? Meeting with Carter yet? Which clients did you snag?"

And just like that, my anger re-ignites. Luckily, before I can come up with an excuse, he rambles on.

"He gave me Visage d'or," Ben cuts in, practically glowing. "Cosmetics. One of the biggest names in the game, and they're mine."

"That's great." I mean it. "I've got to run, but coffee later this week?"

"Send me an invite, or better—have your assistant send my assistant an invite!" he calls after me.

I stride down the hall, too fast, too wound up. Reception looms, and I realise I've gone the wrong way. But before I can turn, Amina spots me.

"Sophie!" She waves, surrounded by colleagues, and one particular set of broad shoulders. Carter. He turns, his gaze crawling up my body before locking on mine. Then, just as quickly, he turns away, mutters something to the group, and walks off.

Of course.

"Congrats on your promotion!" Amina beams.

"Likewise." I force a smile.

She falls into step beside me. "How are the kids?"

"Good, thanks to my parents." She slows her steps as we walk past Carter's office.

He's there, leaning forward with elbows on his knees, his voice sharp into the phone. Watching him feels somehow indecent.

"What clients did you get?" she asks.

"Oh, I don't know yet. I've got a meeting with Carter later this week." The lie escapes without thought.

"That's odd. He split the accounts between me and Ben." Her frown deepens.

My stomach drops. He split them between Amina and Ben. Not me. He's not just ignoring me—he's actively excluding me from the work.

"Miss Rosen," Millie appears in the doorway, "can we go through tomorrow's schedule before you're heading out for your meeting?"

"Of course." I nod, grateful.

Amina studies me for a moment, but then she finally walks away.

Inside, I exhale as Millie hands me paperwork.

"Thanks for rescuing me."

She smiles. "No worries. That's my job."

"Any luck with Carter?"

Millie hesitates. "Yes and no. His assistant confirmed Friday at eleven, but when I asked to schedule, she put me on hold. Then she came back saying he had no availability. Like, none."

I blink. "What?"

"She said he's very busy, but she'll 'let me know' if something opens up."

Translation—he's dodging me.

Confirmation—I'm officially screwed.

"Harder! I said, Harder!" Baron barks, his voice ricocheting off the gym walls.

It's two hours after work, and my body's screaming mutiny. Muscles burn, lungs claw for air, but I feed the fire with every strike. Anger at Carter surges through my veins, and I swing like it's his smug jaw under my glove.

Baron braces. I snarl, coil, and unleash. My fist collides with leather, the crack ringing in my ears. Pain shoots through my knuckles—I'm hitting too hard, but I don't care. Before he can recover, I grab his bicep—the thick muscle hot and solid—and lock my other arm around the back of his neck. My knee rockets up, slamming the pad.

"Break!" His command slices through my frenzy.

I stagger back, chest heaving, sweat pouring down my temples. This is the only place I can breathe.

My old counsellor's voice whispers through my head—'Find a healthy outlet.' It took me two years to listen, but she was right. Krav Maga saved me. I need this, at least every other day, like my mother needed her fix.

Baron lowers the pad, handing me a water bottle. "Feeling better?"

I gulp greedily. "Better."

Baron's been my anchor for three years, carved from granite on the outside but with the kind of heart that makes saints look stingy. Somewhere between bruises and banter, he became family.

"Now," he says, crouching in front of me, "tell me what's going on."

"Nothing," I mutter, sinking onto the bench.

Baron tilts his head towards the pad. "If it weren't for this, Lucy would have no chance at having another kid with me."

A smirk tugs my lips. "How's that going? The little one finally sleeping through the night?"

"No chance, woman." His voice is steel. "Now talk."

"I got promoted," I blurt out.

Baron leans back, then barks a laugh. "Fuck! What are you going to do with all that extra cash?"

I laugh and throw my grappling glove at him, but he dodges with a grin.

"It's not the money," I sigh. "It's my new boss."

Baron settles beside me. "I still don't get it."

"As you know, they hired a new managing director. What I didn't tell you is that we got off on the wrong foot. I thought he'd fire me. Instead, he promoted me."

Baron studies me. His gaze is steady, blue like the sea, and relentless. They're nothing like Carter's stormy greys, but both have the power to cut right through me.

Baron is an angel, all guidance and loyalty. But Carter? He's a dark demon, dangerous and magnetic. He won't even tell me the time of day.

"Well," Baron says slowly, "if he promoted you, things can't be that bad."

"They are," I snap. "We haven't spoken since. He avoids me. He declined two meeting requests and pretended to take a phone call in the corridor just to dodge me."

Baron winces. "Yeah, he's avoiding you."

"Exactly! What the hell am I supposed to do?" My face drops into my hands.

Baron rubs my back with soothing circles. "It'll work itself out. Be patient."

"I can't." My voice cracks. "Layoffs are still looming. If I don't prove myself, I'm out."

He considers my words. "Catch him off guard. Kitchen, maybe."

I bark a bitter laugh. "Where anyone could overhear? Absolutely not."

"Then knock on his office door."

"No!" Too sharp, too fast.

Baron leans in. "There's more to this."

I resist the urge to defend myself, remaining motionless.

"Well, well, well," he chuckles, "you're intimidated."

A grunt escapes me.

"I knew it! First time in three years, there's actually a man who intimidates Sophie Rosen."

"You're wrong," I retort. "My father intimidates me. Not Carter."

He shakes his head. "Your father manipulates you. Different beast entirely."

Over the years, Baron's heard enough about the dynamic between my father and I to know—despite never having met him—what kind of a man he is.

"Is he attractive?" he asks suddenly.

"Sure. If you fancy steely-eyed wankers."

Baron stares, then explodes into laughter.

"You're an arse," I glare.

He wipes his eyes. "Intimidation and attraction. Lethal combo."

"Perhaps for you. I can acknowledge his looks without compromising my integrity."

"I hope you're right," he exhales. "Let's switch, payback time."

Before I can protest, he hauls me up and slams the pad against my chest.

"What should I do about Carter?"

"Nothing. It'll work itself out." His tone is flat. "In the meantime, you just need a distraction."

"And what do you suggest?"

"I can't believe I'm saying this, but—" he says, wrinkling his nose. "You need to get laid."

I nearly drop the pad. "Don't be ridiculous."

"I'm serious. It's either that, or you'll combust." He squares up. "Up."

I brace as he pummels the pad. Baron's strikes are forceful and rapid, steadily pushing me back. I muster all my strength, tensing my muscles and widening my stance.

Finally, he relents, pacing the mat. "I have a mate at the Met."

"A police officer?"

"Yes. A copper. Good guy. Nice-looking. Has a dick. The essentials."

I roll my eyes. "Seriously?"

He grins. "His name's Gareth. Met him through him catching me speeding three times in the span of a month, believe it or not. He's single, emotionally available, and—most importantly—nothing like your father or your boss."

I want to argue. Want to tell him I don't need a man to fix this. But maybe he's right. Maybe a distraction is exactly what I need.

Because sitting around waiting for Carter to acknowledge my existence is driving me insane.

Baron grins wolfishly. "Trust me, Soph. He's exactly what you need."

Savvy Bastard

Medard

I'm in desperate need of a major client. A lawsuit, a deal, a miracle, anything. What I don't need is Sophie Rosen stalking my every waking thought, or my mother blowing up my phone for the eighth time today.

I decline her call again, jaw tight. If she keeps this up, I'll change my number, fake my death, or both.

Three weeks. Three weeks since I promoted Sophie Rosen, and I've managed to avoid direct contact. Until now.

By the time I park my Lexus in front of the Argentinian restaurant, my head is already pounding. Thank God, it's Wednesday. My weekly lunch with Alex—the one island of reprieve in an ocean of bullshit.

I should be walking in here triumphant. I had the perfect client lined up. A golden goose of a lawsuit. A wealthy couple—CEOs of their respective empires—were at each other's throats over corporate shares while navigating a messy divorce. The kind of case that would have dragged my firm back from the brink.

Then he called this morning. Apparently, they've reconciled. My hands still twitch at the memory.

Bullshit.

She gave him a blowjob. That's all it took. A sloppy, desperate reconciliation ritual, because she knew she didn't stand a chance in hell of beating him in court. And judging by how smug he sounded, that blowjob was one hell of a suck-fest.

I even tried to save the situation by proposing a contingency contract. But no, apparently love conquers all.

Idiot.

And if that wasn't enough, Sophie Rosen has managed to materialise at every damn turn, like some celestial punishment tailored just for me.

The autumn wind whips at my collar as I step onto the pavement. Inside, warmth greets me. So does Aletha.

"Good afternoon, Mr Carter." Her smile is sweet enough to rot teeth.

I give her a polite nod, hand her my coat, and spot Alex waving from the window table. Sliding onto the bench opposite him, I mutter, "Apologies for my tardiness. The board's been breathing down my neck again."

Aletha trails after me with a pot of tea, her perfume curling into my lungs.

"Do you gentlemen know what you'd like to order?" she asks sweetly.

But her eyes? Locked on me like Alex doesn't exist.

"I'll have the rib-eye with patatas bravas," Alex orders, handing her the menu.

"Medium rare?" she purrs, still watching me.

Alex exhales like a man wronged. He doesn't even bother answering, just fishes out his phone.

"Yes, darling. Medium rare. And I'll take the sea bass." I return her smile.

"You sure about that?" Alex cuts in, his tone sharp. "Word on the street is the sea bass at that French place on Park Lane is miles better."

Aletha stiffens, then stomps away.

I smirk into my teacup. "That place is pretentious and overpriced, but you know that."

Alex slams his phone onto the table with a sigh. "Are you ever going to release her from your clutches? You've been toying with her emotions for over a year now."

Normally, this would amuse him. Normally, Aletha's infatuation with me is our running joke. But not today. Today, he's prickly.

I laugh anyway. "No cagues donde comes, my friend."

"I'd rather have a well-done steak served by a scorned woman at this point," he mutters darkly.

"You're in a foul mood. What's up with you?"

He runs a hand through his hair, hesitating, before blurting, "I've met someone." His face softens, almost glowing. "She's kind, funny, beautiful. Puto carajo, she's the most stunning woman I've ever seen!"

Ah, there it is.

Alex, the eternal romantic. I've lost count of how many "perfect women" he's discovered. But I don't say that.

"That's great, man. I'm happy for you."

"And we can talk for hours," he swoons, completely ignoring

me.

"So why the storm cloud?" I frown. "Is she not interested?"

He groans into his hands. "It happened too fast. We were talking, then she bolted onto a tube because of some emergency. Before I could get her number, she was gone."

"No full name to stalk her socials?"

He shakes his head, then smirks faintly. "Doesn't matter. I've seen her again."

"Well, that's good. What are the odds in this city?"

He looks up at me, face grim. "Even more so, what are the odds that she's my boss's daughter?"

My jaw drops.

"The one he asked you to tutor?"

"The very same. Sí." His whole frame deflates, the hopelessness palpable.

He knows he's screwed. One wrong move and Daddy Boss will have him fired faster than he can say Te quiero.

"Looks like you need another woman. Or another job if you're dumb enough," I say.

"You really think I shouldn't pursue this?"

I arch a brow. "Mixing business with pleasure never ends well. You know that." I keep Sophie Rosen firmly out of my thoughts as I say it.

My phone chimes. Another meeting request from her. My pulse jumps. I unlock the screen, ready to decline... again. But Janet has already accepted it.

For fuck's sake.

I told her to ignore those requests.

Aletha reappears with another pot of tea. I ignore her smile, glaring at my phone instead as I cancel Sophie's meeting with a forceful jab.

"What's got you all hot and bothered?" Alex asks, watching me drop my phone like it's radioactive.

"Nothing," I bite out.

He isn't buying it. "The other night, I let it slide. But you're still in your head. So, spill."

I trace a finger around the edge of my phone, debating. If I mention Sophie, he'll start spouting destiny bullshit. Sparks, fate, cosmic connections. But this isn't romance. Not even close.

It's biology. She's beautiful. I'm a man in his prime. Her

pheromones just happen to scramble my brain chemistry. Nothing more.

"An employee. She's irritating. Keeps insisting on meetings."

"You find half the world irritating. So how is she different?"

He knows me too well. But I'm not giving him more. I glare at him over the rim of my teacup. He studies me, brows lifting as the realisation dawns. And then, laughter—loud, grating, merciless.

"What was that saying again? No cagues donde comes?"

"I have no intention of sleeping with her," I snap.

"Maybe not. But you clearly don't trust yourself around her. Otherwise, why decline her requests?"

Because I have a firm to salvage. Because she's one of many partners. Because I don't trust myself around her.

Thankfully, Aletha returns with our food before I have to answer. Her eyes plead with me. Begging.

Before I can think better of it, I push back from the table and stalk after her. She barely has time to squeak before I catch her elbow and steer her to the restrooms.

"One good hard fuck is all you get from me. Understood?" I grit out, every word sharp, every muscle in my body straining with the desire to take and obliterate.

"Yes," she breathes, eyes dark with want. "I want it."

I study her face, searching for hesitation. There's none. Just hunger.

"This won't be sweet," I warn, voice low.

"I don't want sweet." Her fingers curl into my jacket. "I want you."

Permission granted. Game on.

I steer her into the restroom, the lock clicking behind us. Her mouth finds mine, eager and willing. I spin her around, my palm flat between her shoulder blades.

"Not like that," I snarl against her ear, dragging her skirt up and yanking her panties down. My trousers are open, and a condom is rolled on before she can process the shift.

"Mr Carter—" she moans, anticipation thick in her voice.

I slam into her in one punishing thrust. The sound she makes is guttural, raw. I grip her hips so hard I know I'll leave bruises. She braces against the door, gasping, pushing back against me.

Aletha. Dark curls, brown eyes. She's beautiful, objectively. But my head betrays me, conjuring Sophie Rosen. Bright blue eyes, that defiant mouth, the sharp curve of her smile that haunts me.

Fuck. Focus.

I dig deeper, harder, ramming into Aletha with the single-minded promise I made—one brutal fuck. No tenderness. No fantasy. She yelps when her forehead knocks the door.

My hand snakes up and closes around her throat, tight enough to send her arching. She gasps, the sound strangled and desperate, her body clenching around me.

And still, it's Sophie. Sophie's hair spilling like gold over my hand. Sophie's lips parting with gasps that aren't hers to give me. Sophie's throat beneath my palm.

I snap, driving in one final, merciless thrust that tears my release out of me. For one glorious second, there's nothing but the blind haze of orgasm.

Then reality hits me like ice water.

Aletha. Not Sophie.

The thought of being inside Aletha suddenly sickens me. I pull out, strip off the condom and flush it down the toilet before she's even adjusted her skirt. She's trembling, fumbling with her clothes, wide eyes glassy with disappointment.

I should feel bad, but I don't.

"I'm sorry if I just ruined the fantasy you've been nursing," I say with a caress of her cheek.

Her throat bobs. No words. No eye contact. Just silence.

Fine. Silence, I can handle.

I unlock the door and stride out, the sudden need for a drink clawing at me. Alex's head snaps up as I pass, his eyes widening when Aletha scurries past me, one hand clutching her throat, the other her pride. She bolts through the staff-only door without a glance back.

Yeah, that fantasy is well and truly dead.

I plant myself at the bar, knock my knuckles against the counter. "Highland Park eighteen," I mutter.

"Glenfiddich," a voice cuts in from my right.

I turn, ready to tell the bastard to fuck off. But then recognition strikes. Square jaw, sharp eyes, late fifties but exuding power—Gerald Ravens. The golden boy I read about in the Technology Digest. The man who ditched a thirty-year cushy post to gamble on his own tech company.

Maybe the universe is throwing me a bone after all.

"Apologies," he says. "I didn't see you there. My mind's elsewhere."

"No problem." I slide a hand out. "Medard Carter. Pleasure to meet you."

He grips it firmly. "Gerald Ravens."

"Not a fan?" I gesture at the scotch he sips, his face twisting with distaste.

"Truth? I'm tea-total. But apparently, whisky is what a man drinks when he wants to project power."

I smirk. "Only if it's the right whisky. Let me fix that for you." I nod to the bartender. "Two Glenmorangie Signets."

His brows rise. "Signet, hm? That's a bold call."

"So am I." I tap my phone to his, dropping my digital card into his contact list.

"Corporate law. Carter & Buckman," he chuckles. "I've already got legal covered."

"Of course you do." I lift my glass. "But tell me—when Skiron Anemos comes knocking with a lawsuit, will your legal team be prepared?"

That stops him.

I press. "You left them. Eighteen months later, you're selling lidar with obstruction detection—the very feature they announced before you bailed. You think they won't come after you?"

His lips twitch into a smirk, impressed. "You've done your homework."

Of course, I have.

"And I always play three moves ahead." I tilt my glass towards him. "If you like this whisky, you let me compete for your business."

A pause. Then, with a slow grin, he clinks his glass to mine. "Deal."

The sip seals it. His eyes widen at the Signet's complexity. Jackpot.

"Mr Carter, you have impeccable taste," Ravens says, clapping a hand on my shoulder. "I'll be in touch."

I watch him leave, satisfaction humming in my veins. I return to the table, and Alex's glare could light a campfire.

"I can't believe you just did that," he says, stabbing his steak like it owes him money.

"You know I don't stop working, even when I'm on a date with you, my honey bear," I wink.

"Fuck off. I'm way out of your league," he snorts, laughing despite himself. "But jokes aside, I'm talking about Aletha. What happened to 'Don't shit where you eat'?"

I shrug, unapologetic. "You said it yourself. Now she's cured. No more swooning."

"Puto," he sighs, raking a hand through his jet-black hair. "When did you become so heartless?"

"The day I realised women only stick around if you're useful to them," I say flatly.

Alex's face falls. "That's... sad, man."

"It's realistic," I counter, before letting the scotch slide over my tongue like victory—the cold fish and hotter mistake forgotten. "Now, how's tutoring Miss Soul Mate?"

His fork clatters. "Don't ask." He shoves his plate away. "Unlike you, I still have a heart, and it's currently not doing me any favours."

His insinuation should sting, but it doesn't. Not even close. Maybe that's the evidence right there that he's right. That my chest houses nothing but a piece of muscle pumping blood.

"You want to talk about it?" I offer.

Alex exhales sharply. "Do you? About Theo's wedding?"

My jaw tightens. "There's nothing to talk about."

"Medard, your ex is marrying your brother. That's—"

"Ancient history," I cut him off, the words sharper than intended.

"It's been seven years, and you still won't even—"

"Drop it, Alex."

He studies me for a long moment, then shakes his head. Already pushing back from the table, he pulls a couple of notes from his wallet and tosses them down.

"I've got to get back to work." His voice is clipped. "I'll see you around."

Before I can say anything else, he strides off.

Poor bastard.

He still believes in love, still thinks it's something worth bleeding for.

My phone buzzes. Mum. Again.

I silence it without looking.

She wants me at Theo's wedding rehearsal. Wants me to play the dutiful brother while my ex becomes my sister-in-law. Wants me

to pretend my heart wasn't shredded seven years ago.

Not happening.

I'm just glad my heart is nothing but a muscle. It's easier that way. Cleaner. Safer.

And infinitely less pathetic.

"Mr Carter, a moment, please."

She doesn't knock. Of course, she doesn't. Sophie Rosen bursts into my office like she owns the air in it, her confidence slamming into me before I can blink.

Not now. Christ, not now.

"Not now, Miss Rosen." My eyes snap back to the screen, clinging to spreadsheets like they're a lifeline. If I look at her too long, I'll forget how to breathe, let alone how to lead a firm on the brink of collapse.

I'd just managed to salvage my mood with Ravens. Finally, a lead worth celebrating. And now? One glimpse of her and it's in tatters again. Because three weeks ago, a pretty blond should have cleared Sophie from my system. And the messy fuck with Aletha earlier today definitely should have. They didn't. Not even close.

She's still here—under my skin, haunting every thought. I still want her. Still want to know how her breasts would feel in my palms. How her body would arch when I drove into her.

"I understand you're very busy, but I would appreciate it if we could address the situation," she says, ignoring my brush-off and sliding into the chair opposite me.

The 'situation' in my slacks is begging for her attention, but that's not what she means.

Shame.

She crosses her legs, and my peripheral vision betrays me. White dress, rising hemline and a sliver of creamy thigh exposed. I want to shove that dress higher, see what delicate fabric waits beneath.

"And what situation might that be, Miss Rosen?" My voice is steady, but my exhale betrays my intrigue.

She squirms, nails digging into her thighs, eyes darting. Is she nervous? Intimidated?

"I mean, we didn't exactly get off to a great start—" she admits, her voice barely above a whisper.

"We didn't?" I ask, like it's news.

"Well, I don't think so. I mean, I just thought—"

Pathetic.

My stomach sinks. This isn't the fiery woman from our first meeting. This is a mouse who's cornered, stammering. Disappointment douses my desire. Maybe this is what I needed, the reminder that she's just like the rest. Not special. Not dangerous.

"Miss Rosen, I'm an extremely busy man. So next time you request an impromptu meeting, come prepared. Don't waste my time."

I lean back, savouring the way her composure frays. Call it sadistic, but watching her doubt herself feeds something dark in me. The flutter she stirred in my chest starts to die. She's nothing. She can't touch me.

Or so I think.

Because then she breathes deep, folds her hands, and meets my gaze dead-on. Her spine straightens. Her eyes sharpen. And when she speaks, it's like a punch to the gut.

"Thank you for the promotion. I will do my best to prove you made the right decision. But in order to do so, an active dialogue is necessary so that I understand your expectations." She smiles—calm, confident, radiant.

The brave little lioness just found her claws. My cock reacts instantly, swelling hard enough to make sitting uncomfortable.

Fuck.

She's back. She's not a mouse, but a predator in sheep's clothing, and I've just underestimated her.

"My expectations," I say carefully, "are that you know what is expected of you."

I signal her dismissal, but she leans forward, elbows nearly kissing the edge of my desk, and smirks like she knows exactly what she's doing to me.

"So, your expectations of me differ from those of my colleagues. May I ask why?"

Of course, she's clocked my avoiding her.

"Weren't you the one who barged in here?" I shoot back, my voice clipped. "Looks to me like you're the one expecting special treatment."

"You left me no choice. You declined all my meeting requests," she counters, her arms folded now, lips pressed into a pout that would look better wrapped around my cock.

Fuck.

I picture her over my knees, arse bared, me teaching her not to pout at her boss. Since when do I think about spanking?

"As I said," I force out, "I am a busy man, Mrs Rosen."

"Miss Rosen," she corrects, sharp as a whip.

I know it's Miss. I've known since our first meeting. But watching her correct me again gives me a perverse satisfaction.

"Sophie," I breathe, savouring her name, "what do you need from me to excel in your role?"

Her eyes spark as she leans closer, and then she drops it. "You."

The word hangs between us, loaded with meaning neither of us can acknowledge. Her eyes widen slightly—she hears it too, the double meaning.

Two seconds. That's all it would take for me to launch over this desk, shred her dress, and fuck her until she couldn't walk. My blood pounds in my ears, cock straining, restraint splintering. But then, mercifully, she clarifies. "I mean, I would like a meeting with you to discuss my new clients."

Christ. Get a grip, Medard.

"You haven't been assigned any new clients," I mutter, walking to the bar cart, pouring a scotch just to get space between us.

Her lips purse, but she schools her face quickly. She's annoyed.

Good. Bad. Fuck, I don't know anymore.

"What about the clients handled by the former partners?"

"Muhammad and Reynolds have them." I sip casually, masking the fact that I'm seconds away from tearing into her.

She squints, barely, but I see it. A flicker of rage.

Oh, she hates me. Delicious.

"Thank you for clarifying," she says sweetly, venom coating every syllable.

And then she storms out. Right into Buckman.

"What was that about?" he asks, ambling in, taking Sophie's still-warm seat.

"Nothing. Minor difference of opinion." I wave him off, eyes already darting to the email that just pinged. Gerald Ravens. He's confirmed an impending lawsuit. We're in.

"Good news?" Buckman prods.

"The best. We've been invited to tender for a major case."

"Tender?" he repeats like a schoolboy.

"That's how it works," I snap. "Multi-million-pound case, Buckman. No one hands it to us. We prove ourselves."

He scratches his beard, leans back like the concept of work is beneath him. "Sounds like a lot."

"It is. But if we win, the firm's back on track."

"Good. Sophie Rosen will support you, yes?"

My blood stills. Absolutely not. Locking myself in strategy sessions with Sophie Rosen is like handing a pyromaniac a can of gasoline.

"No. Muhammad's a better fit."

"Impossible. Muhammad's overloaded. Sophie's clear. She'll dedicate herself fully to you and this case."

That's what I'm afraid of.

"Of course," I grit, swallowing the inevitable.

"Good. For a moment, I thought you were avoiding her." He leaves before I can respond. Avoiding her? If only.

Now I'm fucked. Completely fucked.

Ordinary Guy

Sophie

It's a good day. No, scratch that. It's an excellent day.

I wake before my alarm. Not because of insomnia, not because of a nightmare about missed deadlines or, my new personal favourite—Carter ignoring my pleas while I burn at the stake like it's 1692, Salem. No, it's simply because my body, for once, decides it doesn't need the blaring alarm.

Usually, I'm timed to precision—wake, shower, dress, out the door, coffee shop. But this morning, I've been gifted extra time. And what does a woman like me do with bonus minutes?

She plans her private and work schedule for the remainder of the year. I sit cross-legged on my bed with my laptop, syncing calendars, blocking out Krav Maga sessions, noting Baron's birthday in March, scheduling quarterly reviews, and colour-coding everything by priority. By the time I'm done, my life is mapped out in neat, predictable blocks. Exactly how I like it.

By the time I step out of the shower and slip into the dress that's finally been returned from the dry cleaners, I'm positively humming.

It's my favourite. Baby blue, off-shoulder neckline, fitted skirt. It's the kind of dress that lengthens my spine and sharpens my stride.

The universe, apparently, agrees. At the coffee shop, Lewis the barista has my latte waiting before I've even reached the counter.

And then, just when I think things cannot possibly get better, it happens.

A meeting request from him. Medard Carter.

I stop dead in the middle of the pavement, coffee halfway to my lips. It's been almost a week since I stood in his office, demanding he see me. Six days of radio silence, and then this morning—a meeting request. Not a response to any of mine—which he's ignored all week—but a new request entirely. He's asking me to support him in acquiring a client.

I left that day convinced I'd failed. But maybe I was wrong, because he's not requesting Ben. Not Amina. Me.

He wants me.

My heart does a ridiculous flip. Which is absurd, because Carter is not my crush. He is my boss. My infuriatingly unreadable, frustratingly handsome boss who has ignored me at every turn.

Until now.

Maybe it's the dress. Maybe it's the latte. But I don't want to stay mad at Carter anymore. All I want now is a fresh start. And the chance to prove myself worthy of that promotion.

I sip my latte like it's champagne and glide towards my office.

"Hey, Soph!" Ben calls out. "Coffee at noon?"

"Definitely," I grin, shooting him a thumbs-up before spotting Millie. "Morning, can you cancel my ten a.m. with Farm Valleys? Something came up."

"I know," she says around a bite of her bagel. "Who do you think this mysterious new client is?"

I throw her a cautious look. "It doesn't matter. What matters is that they remain confidential. If anyone asks where I am, just say I'm with a client, or in a meeting with Carter. Nothing more."

I leave my bag and coat in my office and walk down the corridor towards Carter's.

Each step feels heavier than the last. My palms sweat and I try to discreetly wipe them against the dress. I'm rigid in my ways. I like order. Predictability. Yet, with every stride, chaos creeps in.

This is ridiculous. It's just a meeting. With my boss. About a client. A chance to show him exactly what I'm capable of.

Except...what if it's not? What if we clash again?

I push the thoughts down, breathe deep, and approach Janet's desk.

"Morning, is he ready to see me?"

"It's 9:01a.m. He's ready, you're late." She glances up, her lips pinched.

The sting of her tone is sharp, but I don't flinch. I spent six years at an all-girls boarding school where women like Janet reigned supreme. If I survived them, I can survive her.

I knock, inhale once more, and step inside when I hear his voice.

"Have a seat," he says without lifting his eyes from the papers, his voice clipped.

I slide onto the opposite sofa, deliberately choosing distance.

If there's space between us, maybe my pulse will behave itself. But the illusion of control doesn't last. He rises almost instantly and thrusts a folder into my hands before prowling back to his seat.

I quickly flip through the pages. A run-of-the-mill intellectual property case. Skiron Anemos vs. Windpower, two companies locked in a battle over patent rights. This should be a straightforward win.

"Give me a few days," I say smoothly, snapping the folder closed. "I'll finalise a strategy."

"You can't leave." The steel in his tone roots me to the sofa. "This is a high-profile case. Windpower's legal team failed to anticipate the lawsuit, so they'll likely be ousted. No one in the market knows about this yet. If we can keep this under wraps, we'll have no competition. It'll all be down to us proving that we have more to offer than winning a simple IP-case."

"What's to stop Windpower from seeking representation elsewhere?" I ask.

"They won't. Ravens is giving us the first shot. If he doesn't like our offer, it's a feeding frenzy. And we both know this firm currently can't go toe-to-toe with the likes of Rosen & Smiths."

He grinds out the name like it's poison. My father's firm. Clearly Carter despises him just as much as Harman did.

"So," I ask evenly, "how do you propose we tackle this?"

"I take the technical reports and drawings. You handle the contracts, NDAs, all the legal scaffolding."

He gestures at the mountain of folders on the coffee table and we immediately fall into work.

It doesn't take long for me to realise that the contracts are airtight. Skiron has left no loophole uncovered. Even the exit protocol was executed flawlessly. If Carter cannot find any technical evidence differentiating Ravens' device from theirs, I will have to search for a loophole within the NDAs. I sneak glances at Carter, hoping his face might betray something—an idea, a lead, the tiniest sign of breakthrough. But he doesn't move. In fact, he hasn't moved an inch for the past two hours.

Even when Janet brings us coffee, his focus remains steadfast on the papers. I, on the other hand, sip, scan, and steal more glances, and every damn one leaves me with the same thought— replace the papers with a whiskey tumbler and he could be a cologne ad. One ankle propped, finger grazing his bottom lip, jaw set in masculine perfection.

Gorgeous man. Arrogant man. Unfair combination.

The shrill ring of his phone startles me, guilt flashing through me like a schoolgirl caught staring. He answers without looking at the screen.

"Carter speaking," his deep baritone resonates, causing a warm, fuzzy tingle to flare in my lower abdomen.

That's new.

A pause, then his voice shifts to a warm tone. "No, it's fine. Don't worry about cooking dinner. I'll grab something on the way home."

Dinner? I freeze. Cooking? His gaze flickers up, pinning me even as I hunch deeper into my fortress of contracts. My ears burn as I pretend not to listen. Who is he talking to? His wife? No. Google assured me he isn't married. Girlfriend, then? Hidden away, safe from gossip columns and LinkedIn stalkers like me?

"I'll see you tomorrow."

The call ends. His focus returns to the papers, as if nothing had happened. As if my pulse hasn't just tripled.

It's hard to picture anyone caring for him. His cold detachment is a mirror of my father—men carved from stone, incapable of investing in anything that doesn't advance their own ambitions. To them, relationships are transactions, only useful as long as they gain something from it. Sometimes I wonder if my father ever loved my mother at all, or if she was simply a vessel, an efficient way to produce the heir who would carry his legacy. If that was his grand plan, then I must be his greatest disappointment.

"Your wife?" I blurt out, before I can rein myself in.

The question hangs in the air. He raises a slow and deliberate eyebrow.

"Miss Rosen, you continue to surprise me," he retorts with bemusement. "After our first meeting, I assumed you didn't care for small talk."

A surge of adrenaline propels me forward, determined to smooth over any rough edges between us. Despite the fact that he rubs me in all the wrong ways, he's still my boss.

"On the contrary, there's nothing wrong with a bit of chit chat when the timing's right," I counter with a smile.

He studies me for a long moment. "It was my housekeeper."

To my surprise and shock, relief punches out of me in a ridiculous laugh. "Of course."

"Elaborate," he requests, his composure unwavering.

"You don't strike me as the type to fold laundry." I shrug casually. "Hiring help suits."

"And you do?" His gaze sharpens, pinning me to the sofa.

"I do. It keeps me grounded. Humble." And because paying someone to do it would gut my savings, but he doesn't need to know that.

He doesn't respond, just returns to his papers.

The silence between us quickly becomes deafening. Why can't we break the ice? Every interaction seems forced, every word cautiously considered by him. If this continues, working with him will feel nothing short of a walk to the gallows.

"Your turn."

My head snaps up. "Pardon?"

"Small talk shouldn't be one-sided," he says.

That smirk—it's infuriating.

If I hadn't probed about his phone call, he wouldn't have put me in the position now where I have to share something personal.

"I just told you that I don't have a housekeeper," I say with a shrug.

"That doesn't count."

"Says who?"

"I'm the boss," he replies with a shrug of his own, mimicking my nonchalance. "I make the rules."

I'll wait for eternity before surrendering anything personal to him. I can't let myself become vulnerable again. Not while Harman still won't pick up my calls.

"The relationship between me and my father is one of tolerance. The less I have to engage with him, the better."

He can chew on that bit of information. My loyalty to this firm is unwavering, regardless of what he may think about me. As he processes my words, his gaze softens unexpectedly. "I'm sorry to hear that."

The pity in his tone cuts like a blade. I don't want his sympathy. I want his respect.

With a sharp bite to my tongue, I force my focus back to the work. Engaging with him in any argument feels like a losing battle.

Must he be so devastatingly handsome?

A managing director should be seasoned, grey-haired, cutting a dad-bod figure. But Medard Carter defies every expectation. His physique is a vision of strength, his jawline carved with precision, and his eyes? They're captivating and hold depths that dazzle yet intimidate. Even his cologne exudes God-like powers. I could easily believe he's the kind of man who knows how to wield his charm and skill between the sheets just as effortlessly as he navigates this office.

He leans forward to grab another file, and his shirt pulls tight across his shoulders. The fabric strains over muscle, and my traitorous brain supplies an image before I can stop it—those same shoulders flexing as he pins me against a wall.

The heated, unwelcome rush between my legs jolts me from my thoughts. I clamp my thighs together, desperate to stifle the treacherous sensation. My imagination betrays me—flashes of his body claiming mine with brutal precision. Heat floods my skin, pooling low in my belly, shameful and undeniable. I squeeze my thighs, fight to regulate my breathing, bite my lip hard enough to draw blood.

The stack of papers slips from his hands. His eyes meet mine.

And I just know—he knows.

He can see it written all over my face. The flush. The rapid pulse at my throat. The way I can't quite meet his gaze without my breath hitching. I might as well be holding a neon sign that reads: "Currently Having Extremely Unprofessional Thoughts About My Boss."

Before the air between us can combust, Janet barges in with salvation wrapped in a plastic carrier bag.

Thank God.

She unloads containers of Chinese food onto the table. Sweet and sour chicken. Fried rice. Spring rolls.

For once, I'm absolutely delighted to see her unfriendly expression.

She nods at Carter, then leaves. The door clicks shut.

And it's just him again.

The reprieve lasted all of fifteen seconds. Brilliant.

I brace myself, forcing my eyes up from the floor. They travel slowly, cautiously, up the line of buttons on his impeccably pressed shirt until they finally lock onto his silver stare.

He's watching me with the scrutiny of a lawyer who knows the witness is about to slip.

"I hope you're hungry." His voice is casual, but there's something underneath it. Something dark and knowing. He studies my face with a subtle smirk that's barely hidden behind the finger resting against his bottom lip. "I had Janet order us Chinese."

He definitely knows.

He knows exactly what I was just thinking. Probably knows what I'm still thinking. Can probably read my entire back catalogue of inappropriate fantasies like they're subtitled across my forehead.

This is fine. Everything is fine.

I am a professional woman having a professional meeting with her professional boss, and I am absolutely not imagining what that finger on his lip might feel like elsewhere.

Stop it. Stop it right now.

The mortification has me leaping to my feet like the sofa's on fire. I hastily gather up my papers, hands trembling slightly, pulse hammering in places it has no business hammering.

"No thank you. I'm meeting Ben for coffee."

"Reynolds?" His frown is genuine, something flickering across his face that I can't quite read. "We have a tight schedule. I have a few meetings this afternoon, but I expect you back here at five p.m." His tone leaves no room for negotiation.

I bite my lip hard, summon my most professional smile, and nod. "Of course."

"There you are! I was beginning to think you'd bailed on me," Ben calls out from the lifts as I power-walk towards him.

"Sorry!" I quicken my pace, heels snapping against the marble as if to punctuate my apology. "Carter ran over."

"No sweat," he says breezily, flicking open his tobacco pouch as I step into the lift with him. I press for the ground floor, determined to leave my earlier embarrassment behind—if only for the next hour.

"So, tell me—" he says breezily, already halfway through rolling a cigarette, "what accounts has Carter given you? I skimmed the client list yesterday, and unless I'm losing my touch, Amina and I seem to be babysitting most of the roster."

You mean all of it. It was only a matter of time, before Ben would notice what Amina realised within seconds. But at least now I've got something to tell him. Something, that makes me look a little less forgotten.

"It's a new account, a big one. We're still at the acquisition stage so there's a lot of leg-work at the moment."

We step out onto the street and walk the short distance to our usual cafe. The wind has picked up again, lashing unforgivably against my cheeks. I wrap my coat tighter around myself, trying not to look as though I'm sprinting to keep pace with Ben's easy six-foot strides.

"One more account?" he gasps incredulously. "Seriously? Just the one?"

He pushes open the café door with a flourish, holding it for me like I should curtsy on my way through.

"It's a big one though. Hence, he asked me to support him."

Ben whistles low, dropping a ten-pound note on the counter. "Lucky bitch! With my client list now being longer than Santa's bloody naughty-list, I can barely catch a break. Meanwhile, you get to work closely with Carter. I'd give my right arm to spend hours with him confined in his office."

Be my guest. I'd happily offer up my whole body if it meant escaping his office, especially after this morning, when my imagination staged an indecent spectacle starring Carter and me against his office wall. I shake the thought away, pay for my coffee, and keep my expression neutral.

"I don't know. He's pretty ordinary."

Ben barks out a laugh so loud the barista shoots him a glare. "Ordinary? The man's a bloody legend. He sweats wisdom. If he bottled it, I'd drink it for breakfast."

"Please don't." I accept my latte and trail him to an available table by the window.

He shrugs out of his coat and collapses into the chair opposite me. "Trouble in paradise already?" His grin is pure mischief.

I wish I could confide in him about my confusing interactions with Carter, and the unwelcoming effects he has on me. But if I've learnt anything in the past few weeks, it's that drawing attention to the way my boss treats me—positively or negatively—is not a wise course of action.

"There's no paradise. Everything's fine," I dismiss him, hoping he drops the subject.

I busy myself with stirring my coffee.

Ben lifts a brow, but I steamroll ahead, needing safer territory. "Actually, I could use your advice. Baron has given me a friend's phone number. He thinks it'll do me good—"

"Do it!" Ben cuts in while pouring an unhealthy amount of sugar into his latte.

How his doctor hasn't declared him diabetic yet is beyond me.

"I haven't even told you anything about this guy," I protest in amusement.

He waves me off. "Fair enough. Has he got a criminal record? A wife? A dick?"

"No, no and yes," I fire back, wondering where he's going with this.

"Then I stand by what I said—do it. You work too much. You need fun, Soph. Real fun. The kind that doesn't involve NDAs or highlighters."

"I do go out. I work out every week," I object.

"Yeah, with that very handsome and very married model." He waves me off again, wiping the latte foam from his upper lip.

"Baron and I are just friends," I clarify, horrified at the thought of ever crossing that line. "He's like a brother."

Ben snorts. "I don't believe in friendships between men and women."

"But we're friends!"

"We're ... different. Now, text him," he insists, sliding my phone towards me.

"Who? Baron?"

Ben releases a loud huff, picks up my phone and places it into the palm of my hand.

"Dick-man, text him. Now!"

I hesitate, but his stare is relentless. Before I can talk myself out of it, I fire off a quick message to Gareth, the policeman.

He leans back, triumphant. "I'm proud of you. Finally asking for some cock."

"Charming," I mutter, rolling my eyes.

He winks, then mercifully shifts the conversation to his latest client debacle. I half-listen, half-stare at my phone, wondering if Gareth will reply. Not that I want him to. Relationships take time and effort, both of which I have no intention of wasting. Daniel, my last boyfriend, proved as much. He tolerated my schedule until, one day, he didn't. End of story.

No, I'm at my best alone. Or I was until Carter's presence stirred something in me, I wish had stayed dormant. I'm not built for messy desires. Especially not when they're directed at my boss.

A sharp chime cuts through my thoughts. My gaze snaps to my phone, pulse skipping, only to find nothing.

"Shit!" Ben blurts.

"What's wrong?"

His face turns as white as the foam on his oat milk vanilla latte.

"I've lost the Bradford account!"

My eyes widen. "Shit!"

He rakes a hand through his chocolate brown curls before jumping up and yanking his coat off the chair.

"Carter wants to see me asap."

"Double shit," I breathe, scrambling for reassurance. "I'm sure it'll be fine."

But Ben's already shrugging into his coat, downing the last of his latte in one painful gulp.

"I doubt it. Later, Soph."

He storms out, leaving me staring after him with my own dread simmering at the thought of Carter's silver stare.

Decent Guy

Medard

Yet another account lost in my first month here, not due to the firm's reputation, but an oversight from Reynolds. I had high hopes for him, seeing growth in his client base, but now I question my judgement. The setback stains my plan, irritatingly.

Tossing the Bradford file into the bin, I focus on the screen, analysing KPIs and profitability checks. Though a smaller client, their acquisition plans showed potential for expansion. Thankfully, the revenue won't take a significant hit. Windpower could easily balance it out. I'm still pissed off with Reynolds, though. After his recent promotion, I expected him to work his arse off, not cause me to lose business.

Cutting his coffee break short with Sophie seems insignificant in comparison.

A spontaneous decision prompts me to reach for the intercom. "Janet, reschedule my appointments for the next two weeks. I need daily meetings with Sophie Rosen during the lunch hour. Noon to two."

"Noted," Janet confirms.

"And make it clear that Miss Rosen can have her lunch after two, once everyone else has already eaten."

There's a pause. "Of course, Mr Carter."

I end the call, satisfaction curling through me. No more coffee dates with Reynolds. No more convenient twelve o'clock breaks where she can slip away to giggle over lattes. If she's working on my case, she works on my schedule. And my schedule doesn't include Ben fucking Reynolds.

I'm being rewarded for my strategic thinking with yet another voice mail from my mother.

> Mum: Darling, please call me back. We need to discuss your brother's wedding rehearsal.

I rather not.

> Mum: I understand you're busy with work but we haven't heard from you in weeks.

It's been days but who's counting? Clearly not you.

> Mum: Medard Alfred Carter! Call me!

I hate when she calls me by my full name.

> Mum: Frankly, I'm not even angry anymore. I'm just disappointed.

No, you're still very much angry with me.

> Mum: I just spoke with your father. We're heading to the city now.

Good luck, you don't even know where I work.

> Mum: I just wanted to say how proud I am of you, darling. Having your name on the door is such a great accomplishment, and it really helps when looking up the address online. We'll be there in an hour.

Shit.

Without wasting a moment, I dial my mother's number and she answers immediately.

"Darling, how wonderful to hear from you at last! How have you been?" she purrs, triumph evident in her voice.

"Mum, what do you want?" I ask wearily, trying to shake off the exhaustion of the day, my job, and now Mum.

"About the wedding rehearsal, darling. Will you be staying overnight? Should I book you a room at St. James?" she enquires eagerly.

I'd rather spend a night at His Majesty's pleasure than with my entire family in that outdated hotel at the arse-end-of-nowhere. And the thought of celebrating their union is even less appealing.

"Why can't Theo have the rehearsal at your place? It's big enough."

She lets out an annoyed sigh. "Because that's what he wants so that's what he'll get."

As always.

"Listen, darling," she switches to a caring tone, trying to act as the mediator between her two estranged sons. "Maybe one day you'll meet a woman and get married, and then you'll understand how important it is to have your special day just the way you want it. Until then, it would be nice to see you happy for your brother and Lisa."

"I am happy for them," I assure her, forcing the words out.

"Good, I'll book you a single room then," she says with relief. "Or are you planning to bring a plus one?"

"No!" I reply automatically but the word suddenly leaves a bitter taste in my mouth.

"Actually—" Sophie's face flashes through my mind. Her in that blue dress. Standing beside me at the wedding. "Never mind. I have a meeting now. I'll talk to you soon."

I end the call just as Reynolds hovers in the doorway like a schoolboy about to be hauled in for detention.

"Mr Carter, you wanted to see me?" His voice wobbles even though he tries to square his shoulders. The effect is laughable. His Adam's apple bobs so violently I half-expect it to dislodge and roll across the polished marble floor.

"Yes. Sit." I don't bother softening the order, just gesture to the chair opposite me.

He lowers himself into it with the kind of hesitation usually reserved for people about to face a death sentence.

"The Bradford account," I start, my tone clipped. "Care to explain?"

"Of course." He clears his throat again. "I apologise. I thought I'd covered everything regarding the land. I even triple-checked the trees weren't protected, confirmed they could be cleared—"

"But you didn't check the soil," I cut in, slicing straight through his excuses.

He flinches. "No, I didn't. I didn't think it was necessary."

I glare at the incompetence before me. My fingers pinch the bridge of my nose because if I don't physically restrain my frustration, it's going to explode all over him. What does Sophie see in him? All I see is a man who mistakes confidence for competence. A man who forgets the most basic due diligence because he's too busy grinning his way through meetings.

"Tell me something, Reynolds—" I lean forward, voice dropping to a low, deadly tone. "What does Bradford specialise in?"

He blinks, sensing the trap but too slow to avoid it. "Frozen food."

"What specifically?"

"Potato products. Chips, curly fries, smileys—" he continues, rambling off the entire content of a fucking freezer as if it will make up for his oversight.

I sit back, silent, letting him hang himself with every word. My eyes drift across the desk, landing on the Baccarat crystal pencil holder Mum gave me for my first job as a lawyer. For a fleeting, delicious second, I imagine hurling it at his head. Or maybe at my own, just to put myself out of the misery of listening to him. Either option feels more productive than enduring another second of his incompetence. A monkey in a suit, that's what I've promoted.

"Reynolds, you fucked up," I sigh. "If the client hadn't caught your oversight, they'd have sunk nearly six million into land crawling with late blight—a fungus that wipes out potato crops. The land would have been worthless for their purposes."

His complexion pales. "I know, and I apologise. I'll... I'll double-check everything next time."

At least he admits it. Still, this isn't a slap-on-the-wrist situation. This is scorched earth, or in this case—late-blight-infested earth.

"You won't be handling new or ongoing acquisitions," I state flatly. "Muhammad will take over. Effective immediately."

He hangs his head. His shoulders sag. The finality of it sinking in.

Part of me knows I'm being harsh. One mistake, however costly, doesn't erase his wins. But imagining him sitting across from Sophie in a café, making her laugh, their easy friendship—

No. He fucked up. He deserves this.

In a last pathetic effort to dampen the blow, he blurts, "What about... could I assist on the new case? Work with Sophie perhaps?"

The sheer audacity nearly makes me laugh. Sophie is many things—intelligent, relentless, far too tempting for my own sanity—but she's not his saving grace. No, she's mine. And as such, she belongs under my close supervision. And I'll be damned if I hand her over to Reynolds, of all people, to squander her potential.

"Absolutely not," I snap before he can even exhale. "I'm handling this case, and Miss Rosen's support is more than enough. You'll support Muhammad."

He opens his mouth, maybe to beg, maybe to dig the hole deeper, but I lift a hand towards the door as a silent dismissal. His sluggish entrance is nothing like his exit as he scurries out. His fate sealed.

I turn back to my screen, but Sophie's schedule glows on the calendar. Two weeks. Two hours daily during lunch. Twenty hours of her undivided attention.

Suddenly, losing the Bradford account doesn't seem quite so irritating after all.

Professional

Medard

Her face is an open book, and I read every line. Confusion has her play with her earrings, interest flares in her eyes, and nerves make her rub her thighs.

We've been here for hours, side by side in my office, heads bent over paperwork for the Windpower account. It's been mostly silence, bar her phone ringing from time to time.

"I'm sorry," she murmurs when it chimes yet again.

She finally mutes it and lays it on the coffee table. I caught the name on the caller ID. Her father. The man who happens to be my biggest competitor. Part of me is smug that she's ignoring him for work. Another darker part wants to hear exactly how she speaks to him.

"Can I offer you a glass of wine?" My voice sounds more like gravel than charm.

"Yes, please," she nods, swiping her palms on her skirt again, a nervous tick she probably doesn't even know she's doing.

I wonder if she's on edge because of her father's persistent calls, or because of this morning, when I caught her squirming in her seat. If I wasn't convinced that she disliked me, I'd swear she had me starring in one of her dirtiest daydreams.

I stand and stroll to the bar cart, my hand closing around a bottle of Chardonnay. Something about her says she's a white-wine girl.

"Is he always this persistent?" I ask as I pour.

I hand her the glass and, against my better judgement, choose the seat right beside her.

"Are you asking as my colleague," she tilts her head, "or his biggest rival?"

"Just trying small talk," I shrug.

She exhales, clearly exhausted by the topic. "He can be, when things don't go his way."

"Like you not joining his firm?"

Her jaw tightens as she sets her glass down. "What does it take? What do I have to do to make you trust me?"

The boldness catches me off guard, but it also stirs something low in my gut. My cock twitches. If she dropped to her knees right now, if she sucked me without sinking her teeth in... well, that would certainly be a fast track on my trust scale.

She's waiting, eyes locked on mine, her expression a cocktail of challenge and hope.

"I only trust people I know," I say casually, "and I don't know you."

"Fair enough. I didn't want to do this, but here we are." She leans back, but there's a spark in her eyes. "Let's engage in some small talk."

I chuckle, because she's got guts. Most employees shrink under my stare. Not her.

"Isn't this something that should happen naturally?"

"It should," she says, "yet here we are. We'll take turns asking one question. A question answered can't be thrown back."

A game. Clever girl. Perfect way to test her.

"Any topics off-limits?" I ask.

"Politics, religion, and work."

I nod, intrigued. "Ladies first."

"Do you have any siblings?"

"I have a younger brother. His name is Theo. What does your mother think about the relationship between you and your father?"

She blinks, surprised at how quickly I've gone for the jugular.

"Nothing. She's dead. What is your highest priority in life?"

So, she's not playing at surface-level fluff either. "Success in my career. How long has it been just you and your father?"

"As long as I can remember." Her voice flicks sharp now. "What do you detest most in people?"

"Disobedience."

"In private or at work?"

I shake my head slowly, smirking at her for trying to break her own rules. "My turn. What's your greatest fear?"

She picks at a phantom imperfection on her skirt, her gaze darting across the floor.

"Sophie?"

Our eyes meet, and for a heartbeat she feels familiar. Like someone from my past, someone who'd stand with me when things turn ugly.

"I'm scared to become mentally...unwell," she almost whispers before her hand flies to her mouth as though she's shocked by the admission.

"What makes you think that?" Concern tugs at me, uninvited, before she snuffs it out with a soft tut.

"My turn. What is your greatest weakness?"

I exhale, dragging a hand over my mouth to buy time. "I used to believe I had none," I admit.

"And now?" Her curiosity is unflinching. "You haven't answered my question."

Now, I think you might become my greatest weakness.

"And I won't. It's work related." I drain my glass.

I need to get my shit together. I'm a professional. She's just my subordinate—my beautiful, fiery, captivating subordinate.

I silently challenge her to look away. She smooths down her skirt again but holds my gaze.

"Are you seeing someone?" The question escapes before I can stop it.

"You mean a shrink?" she asks, clearing her throat.

I shake my head slowly. She digs her nails into her thighs, and the sight feels like a starting pistol. Her lips part, and I'm gradually leaning towards her when her damn phone buzzes again.

She stands, answers, walks to the window. "You were?" she murmurs, glancing over her shoulder.

I make no attempt to hide my presence. This is my office.

"No, not at all. What have you got in mind?" she says, pacing softly.

Who is she talking to? Not her father. She's too relaxed. Too soft. The little giggle she lets out twists my gut. This one is reserved for lovers.

Tension surges through my arms as I fist my hands.

"Alright, you've caught me with that. I'll see you soon." She ends the call, drops the phone into her handbag, and grabs her coat.

"Where do you think you're off to?" My voice is steady, though my fingers are white-knuckled. "I didn't say we were finished."

"I'm sorry, I've got to go."

"It's only half-past seven," I reason.

"Are you going to dock my pay?" she fires back, sparking an urge in me to drag her across my knee. I swallow it down.

"I'll see you tomorrow," I bite out.

As the door clicks shut, silence swallows the room. It feels suffocating without her. Loneliness rarely gets a hold of me, but tonight it seeps through the cracks.

Maybe Alex is up for a few beers. No, he's busy tutoring his latest soul mate.

I scroll through my contacts. There's only one name that makes my pulse tick faster. Sophie Rosen.

I agreed to her little game out of curiosity. But somehow this curiosity has turned into obsession. She hides herself well. But that just makes the hunt more interesting.

I will uncover her secrets. Every last one of them, before they blow up in my face. And tonight feels like the night to start.

I grab my coat and phone, locking the office behind me. The moment I step onto the pavement, London greets me with its usual chaos. A group of women strut past, their laughter bubbling, their cheap perfume clinging to the air. Their eyes drag over me like they're checking stock. Normally, I'd smirk, indulge in the ego boost. Tonight, though, their attention irritates more than flatters.

I need focus, not flirtation. And I need dinner. The Tesco Express near the office will do.

I pull out my phone and call the one person who can provide me with answers.

"Harris," I say as soon as the line connects. "Long time no hear. I've got another job for you."

A hoarse laugh greets me. "I was wondering when you'd call again. Who's the target this time?"

"The daughter of my biggest rival. Sophie Rosen. She's under my employ."

"Ah, a delicate matter," he says between drags from a cigarette. "Any particular angle you want me to dig into?"

"Find out everything. Who she's meeting. What she's doing when she's not at the office. Her father. Her old boss Harman. Down to who she went to school with."

The words taste wrong even as I say them. This is too far. I know it's too far. But I need to know if she's a threat.

Harris doesn't miss a beat. "Consider it done."

I end the call and step into the shop. The calming folk song oozing through the tinny speakers does nothing for my pulse, which still hammers with residual anger at whoever just stole my evening with Sophie.

I force my attention to the list on my phone. Garlic, pasta, passata, chili flakes. Normal, mundane, manageable. Mrs Ruthers usually handles this, but tonight I needed the distraction.

I'm still on edge, my thoughts circling the image of Sophie's soft laugh during that phone call. The way she lit up for someone who wasn't me. It shouldn't bother me. She's an employee, nothing more. Yet every muscle in my body feels strung too tight.

I round the corner into the sauce aisle and reach for my usual jar of passata. Then, from nowhere, a slender hand slides into view, fingers pointing towards a higher shelf.

"If I may suggest," says a voice I could identify blindfolded, "this sauce tastes far better."

Every nerve in me sharpens.

"Do you always hand out free advice to fellow patrons?" I manage.

Sophie's eyes widen as recognition hits. She steps back. And she's not alone. Standing beside her is a man—tall, dark-haired, wearing a police jacket.

"Carter. I didn't realise it was you. I didn't think you actually do your own food shop." She says it like a joke.

"And why's that?" I ask, plucking the jar she pointed to and dropping it into my basket.

She tilts her head, teasing. "I don't know... isn't that one of the many tasks reserved for your housekeeper?"

I give a short laugh. "I've heard dabbling in first-world consumerism can be quite the thrill." The second the words are out, I want to strangle myself.

Who says that?

But she laughs. "Next you'll tell me you actually cook."

This is where a professional man would stop, smile and walk away. But apparently, I left professionalism back in the office.

"As a matter of fact, I do so occasionally. Tonight, I thought I'd try my hand at a Penne Arrabbiata," I announce, like I expect her to give me a pad on the back for being a grown man able to feed himself.

Her brows rise, impressed. "Really? That sounds... delicious. The best one I ever had was in Rome, at this tiny restaurant with an olive tree right in the middle of the terrace, and—"

"Mirrors on the walls," I cut in before my brain can veto it.

She blinks, startled. "You've been there too?"

I nod, caught off guard by the rush of memory. "Years ago. I dragged my brother there after graduation."

Of all the restaurants in Rome, what are the odds we both ended up at the same tiny trattoria?

Her smile softens. "Then you must have tried the olives from the tree. Please tell me you did."

She leans in, her hand grazing my arm in a feather-light touch that ignites a spark. I silently curse the sleeve of my coat for existing.

"The best olives I've ever had," I say, my voice rougher than intended. "And I usually prefer black over green."

"Exactly!" she exclaims, laughing at the unexpected connection.

Then she reaches for a small tube on the shelf and hands it to me. "If you want your Penne to taste even half as good, you'll need to make your sauce from scratch with charred San Marzano tomatoes and a dash of this paprika paste."

I stare at the tube like it's a live grenade. "Right, of course."

My mind scrambles for coherence and fails spectacularly. "Maybe I could… give it a try. With your guidance."

Her brows lift slightly.

Brilliant, Medard. Well done. Maybe next ask her to hold your hand while you boil water.

"I mean," I backpedal, heat climbing my neck, "perhaps you have a recipe I could follow."

Her expression shifts—something flickers across her face. Wariness? She takes a small step back, the easy warmth between us cooling.

"I don't have one, I'm sorry," she says, her voice quieter now. "I just remember those tips from a cooking show I watched once."

The wall goes up so quickly I almost hear it slam into place. This is the same retreat I saw in my office after she admitted her fear. The same pulling away.

Like she's realised we've strayed too close to something personal. Something dangerous.

Before I can dig myself deeper, she glances past me towards the copper. "I should go."

And she does. Straight back towards him, standing at the far end of the aisle. He greets her with too-familiar ease, his hand finding the small of her back. I expect her to lean in but she doesn't. Instead, she stiffens slightly, offering him a polite smile that doesn't quite reach her eyes.

I stand there, still clutching the damn paprika paste, pulse hammering. Driven by equal parts curiosity and something that tastes suspiciously like possessiveness, I stride after them.

They're about to turn into the next aisle when I speak. "Sophie, one more thing."

She stops. Shoulders tense. When she turns to face me, there's weariness in her eyes.

"Let's review our notes before my meeting with the board," I say, deliberately neutral. It's nonsense, we've already reviewed them twice. But I need her attention.

"Sure," she says slowly. "But isn't that meeting at eight a.m.?"

"Yes." The single word leaves my mouth in a sharp tone, because my gaze has already drifted towards the copper.

He looks me over, then steps closer, his hand still at the small of her back. She doesn't lean into him, doesn't melt against his side. The rigidity in her posture speaks volumes.

My jaw tightens. "Medard Carter," I say, extending a hand. My smile is perfectly civil. My grip, not so much.

He eyes me for a moment, then takes my hand. His palm is warm and his shake firm, but not firm enough.

"Gareth Hayes," he replies, offering no context.

I can play too.

"An early start shouldn't be an issue, right?" I ask, turning back to Sophie, my tone all business, my eyes anything but.

She blinks, caught off guard. "Of course not."

"Good." I let the word linger, low and certain. "I'll see you in my office at six thirty sharp."

She simply nods, though her body leans subtly towards me, breaking the contact with his chest.

One-nil for me.

But as I watch her disappear into the London night with him, the victory feels hollow. Because she's still leaving with him, and I'm going home alone.

Billy Big Bollocks

Sophie

"I can't believe you've never been on the London Eye!" Gareth calls from the kitchen, his voice rising above the extractor fan.

The air is thick with the scent of something savoury and buttery. Despite the clutter, his home feels lived in and warm. Two bookcases dominate the living room, groaning under the weight of books and souvenirs. Tiny motorbikes and peculiar rocks perch between travel guides and cookbooks.

"To be honest," I call back, "I've never been to any of the typical attractions. Aren't they for tourists?"

"Absolutely not." He emerges, wiping his hands on a tea towel and offering me a glass of red wine. "You ever asked yourself why you don't feel the same sense of wonder about your own city as you do when you visit somewhere new?"

I take the glass, ignoring the fact that I'd kill for a chilled Chardonnay instead. The kind Carter poured for me in his office. "Probably because you're too used to it."

He chuckles. "Spoken like someone who needs a change of scenery."

He's not wrong. I can count the countries I've visited on one hand. Father and my job made sure of that. Duty over desire. But Gareth lives like the world's an open buffet. He wears adventure like a second skin.

"Please, make yourself comfortable," he says, gesturing towards the sofa. "If you don't mind, I'm going to change a minute."

"Of course," I reply as he disappears down the hall.

He's so different from Carter. Easy, approachable and kind. If I'd met him a couple of months ago, I might have fallen for him without hesitation. But now there's Carter—complicated, unreadable Carter—wedged like a splinter under my skin. Not that I would ever entertain the idea of getting involved with him. I've learnt my lesson when it comes to blurring the lines between personal and professional.

Still, that moment in his office earlier lingers—the almost-kiss that probably wasn't one. And then the encounter at the shop. The way he looked at Gareth as if assessing a threat. I should have been annoyed. Instead, I was... flustered.

"Food's ready!" Gareth's voice pulls me back.

He returns balancing two plates piled high with shepherd's pie. It's hearty, golden, and unapologetically British. I should have insisted Gareth tells me his dinner plans, rather than letting him "surprise" me. Because neither the thick layer of carbs nor the minced lamb hiding underneath looks appealing.

"Thank you for cooking and your hospitality," I say, smiling.

"It's nothing," he replies, settling beside me.

Gareth digs right in, while I push the food around on my plate, mentally preparing myself for the first bite.

"You don't like it, do you?"

I hesitate. "It's... very thoughtful. I'm just not used to heavy food."

He chuckles, sliding my plate aside. "That's alright. I may not win you over with my cooking, but I'm hoping for better luck with my company."

He places his hand over mine. His touch is warm and comforting, reminding me it's been almost two years since anyone has touched me with tenderness. Since Daniel. Since I decided work was safer than relationships.

The moment stretches. Then my work phone pings. For a heartbeat, instinct takes over. I almost reach for it. But then Gareth's thumb strokes my hand, grounding me.

What has all this constant vigilance ever given me? A shaky career, a father who measures affection in disapproval, and a boss whose every word manages to both infuriate and fascinate me.

Maybe Ben was right. It's time to take that dick.

I set my phone into Do-not-disturb mode and look at Gareth. "Let's find—"

Before I can finish, Gareth leans in and cups my jaw, and then his lips find mine. It's confident, assured. Everything Carter isn't—except Carter is. And damn it, why am I thinking about Carter?

His tongue teases at the seam of my lips until they part. I focus on this—on Gareth, on the present moment.

My hands find the hem of his T-shirt, brushing against his solid chest before tugging the fabric upward. He breaks the kiss just long enough to pull it over his head.

Good grief. The man is carved.

His fingers slide up, brushing the straps of my dress off my shoulders. The fabric slides down, pooling near my hips before he helps it the rest of the way.

Insecurity claws at me. It's been too long. But then Gareth's gaze finds mine. There's no judgement, no arrogance, just quiet appreciation.

"You're beautiful," he murmurs.

I thread my fingers through his hair, pulling him closer. I answer with my mouth instead of words, trying to lose myself in sensation rather than thought.

Between moans and hurried sighs, there's the rustle of a condom wrapper. He pulls down his sweatpants and sheaths himself. He gently nudges my shoulders to lie back, before sliding down my knickers.

Every thought, every worry that's been clawing at my mind for weeks—I want them to burn away under the heat of his touch. I'm trying to lose myself in this moment, in him. Our lips reconnect. My hand wanders down the firm planes of his chest.

But my treacherous mind won't cooperate. When I close my eyes, I see grey instead of brown. Sharp suits instead of bare skin. A corner office instead of this warm, cluttered flat.

"Jeez, Sophie!" he groans as he tilts his hips forward. The tip of his length nudges at my entrance; and then I push my hips off the sofa, meeting him as he finally slides into me.

After almost two years of abstinence, my inner walls stretch around his deep thrusts. He pulls down the cups of my bra and flicks his tongue over my nipples. He murmurs my name like it's a secret while he thrusts into me in a slow and measured pace.

I focus on the physical sensations—his hands, his mouth, the pleasant pressure. But my mind begins to blur, another face flashing behind my closed eyes. Grey eyes, sharp and unrelenting, cut through the haze.

No. Not now.

I try to banish the image, but it lingers. The phantom of Carter's deep, authoritative voice slides into the quiet between Gareth's whispers, and my body reacts before my brain can fight it.

My orgasm builds with each slow thrust, but it's no longer Gareth's voice I hear. It's his, Carter's. It's his hand I imagine gripping my waist, his mouth I feel ghosting over my neck. His quiet, dangerous restraint that drives me to the brink.

And it's his name I barely stop myself from crying out when I come.

"Oh god, please!" I gasp instead, as the orgasm crashes through me.

"I'm coming," Gareth's voice yanks me into the here and now as he stills inside me.

My eyes snap open to find him pulling out with concern flickering behind his eyes. Red-hot guilt blooms in my chest. My stomach churns.

I just had sex with one man while fantasising about another. What kind of person does that?

I'm the worst!

Before I can speak, he pushes himself off me and leaves to discard the condom. My hands fall to my face, too ashamed to watch him walk out. He didn't deserve this. He gave me a mind-blowing orgasm and I didn't even have the decency to keep my mind off another man.

"You okay?" he asks, his voice soft.

I peek through my fingers and—thank God—he's back in his boxers. He's watching me with a faint grin, then holds out my underwear. I snatch them back, mustering a smile that doesn't quite reach my eyes.

I scramble to fix my dress. "I'm fine," I say, too quickly, too brightly.

Gareth tugs on his T-shirt, pours himself another glass of wine, and studies me with a steady, detective's gaze.

"So," he says, voice light but curious, "who was it you were thinking about?"

My heart stutters. "Pardon?"

"You know," he drawls. "My job is to observe people. And you were clearly thinking of somebody else as I was shagging you." He pauses, his expression gentle. "Your body was here, but your mind wasn't. I could tell. It's alright, I'm not offended. I'm just curious."

God, kill me now.

I bury my face in my hands, groaning. He's not even angry, but amused. That somehow makes it worse.

"I can't. I don't even want to admit—"

There's a pause. Then a low whistle. "It's Billy Big Bollocks, innit? The guy from the shop earlier?"

I nod without looking up.

He lets out a slow exhale. "I thought he makes you uncomfortable. So, what, you didn't want him seeing us together?"

I glance up. "Maybe. Or maybe I didn't want to admit that he gets under my skin. He drives me insane, but—" I let the words trail off, because what follows is the problem—I. Can't. Stop. Thinking. About. Him.

My hands move to my thighs automatically. I drag my nails down until I feel that familiar sharp sting. The same thing I do in Carter's office when he looks at me like that.

"But you're still drawn to him," Gareth says.

His eyes flick down to my hands. "You do that a lot. The thigh thing."

I freeze, then force my hands still. "Anxiety tell."

"I noticed. You were doing it in the shop too, when Billy Big Bollocks showed up."

Heat crawls up my neck. Of course he noticed. He's a bloody police officer.

"Exactly," I mutter. "He makes me anxious. It's infuriating. I should hate it, hate him, but—" My hands twitch towards my thighs again. I clench them into fists instead. "Apparently, my libido didn't get that memo."

He chuckles warmly. "Either that, or she simply acknowledges what your brain refuses to believe."

"No chance," I say, dragging my nails down my thighs until I feel that sharp sting again. "She's just a treacherous little weasel."

Gareth lets out a loud, genuine laugh. "At least she doesn't bite!"

I roll my eyes, but can't stop the smile creeping onto my face, glad that Gareth's more about compassion than ego.

He reaches for the bottle again; brow raised in silent offer. I nod, then hurriedly cover the glass. "Actually, do you have any white wine?"

His brows lift in mock surprise.

"I got that wrong too, huh? Jeez, I really need to work on my form." He winks. "At least I got you to gush around my cock," he adds with a grin, and I laugh.

The tension breaks. This won't be a romance. But maybe, just maybe, it'll be something better: a real friendship.

My phone buzzes on the table. I ignore it. Carter can wait until morning.

Control Freak

Sophie

When I stride into Carter's office at precisely six-thirty a.m., his gaze hits me like a wrecking ball. His scowl could curdle milk, and judging by the thunderclouds brewing behind his eyes, my morning will most certainly turn for the worst now.

"What were you doing last night?" His voice is sharp enough to slice through marble, and my composure.

What was I doing? Thinking of you, you arrogant prick, while I was with an actually decent man.

"Why do you ask?" I manage, forcing my tone to sound neutral, professional. Calm, even. Because I have no idea where this ambush is coming from. When we parted ways in the shop last night, everything seemed... fine. Tense, sure, but that's our normal.

Carter takes two measured steps towards me before snapping, "I want to know what possessed you to prioritise your bloody boyfriend over your career."

The words detonate between us.

My jaw drops. "My... what?"

He closes the distance entirely now, his presence an onslaught on my senses— heat, authority, and that infuriating ocean scent that scrambles my brain chemistry. I stumble back a fraction, which, of course, he notices. His gaze flicks to my mouth before locking back on my eyes.

"My boyfriend?" I repeat, finally finding my voice. And then it hits me—Gareth. He thinks I'm with Gareth. "I don't think that's any of your concern," I retort, my voice trembling with a blend of nerves and defiance.

He steps closer still, and I swear he's choking me with his furious glare alone.

"Everything you do is my concern," he growls, "especially when you decide to ignore your clients."

There it is, the reason for his wrath. He produces his phone with the theatrical flair of a prosecutor, taps the screen and shoves it my way.

The subject line blares like an alarm: Termination of Contract

– Farm Valleys.

My stomach drops.

"I can explain," I start but he cuts me off with a sharp flick of his hand, the look in his eyes saying I'd better not.

My fingers fly to my bag, fumbling for my phone. One click on the 'Do-not-disturb'-toggle, and my heart sinks further. Fifteen missed calls and five emails from Richard, six missed calls from Carter.

Shit!

My hands shake as I lower the phone. This is exactly what Father always said would happen—I'd fail, lose everything, prove him right. The familiar spiral of anxiety starts, but then I look up and see Carter watching me with that hard, assessing stare.

And suddenly, instead of crumbling, I feel anger. White-hot and clarifying.

I had silenced my phone last night, so I could have one tiny, blissfully undisturbed evening. And of course, it's come back to bite me squarely on the arse.

"What's there to explain, Sophie?" he presses, voice low and lethal. "That you'd rather play house with your boyfriend while your client's trying to reach you? Repeatedly?"

"I'm entitled to a private life," I bite out, clutching what little dignity I can still salvage.

This man is insufferable! How could I have ever wasted a single romantic thought on him?

He tilts his head, his expression unreadable. "And I'm entitled, as your boss, to reprimand you for your failure."

Failure.

The word cuts deeper than it should. Deeper than he could possibly know. My mind takes me back to Father's office where I had to face the sharp reprimands, the disappointment marring his face, the cane swooshing down on my tiny fingers.

I was six. He'd told me to memorise a poem for his colleagues. I'd stuttered on one line. One line. And he'd made sure I never forgot it.

I swallow hard, forcing down the sting, and dig my nails into my palms. It's not enough though. Nowhere near enough. I want to pull up my skirt and claw at my thighs until the hurt bleeds out of them.

"I apologise," I murmur, hating the wobble in my voice.

Why did I silence my phone? Carter is right—I shouldn't have allowed myself a moment's respite when so much is at stake.

Carter's jaw flexes, the muscle ticking in quiet restraint. For a moment, his anger seems to falter, replaced by something that almost looks like concern. But then it's gone again, buried under ice and authority.

"Sophie," he says, quieter now. The sound of my name from his mouth does terrible, traitorous things to me. "Go stand in the corner."

I blink. "Excuse me?"

He gestures towards the empty space beside his sleek bar cart. "Go. Think about whether sacrificing a client was worth it."

My jaw drops. "You want me to stand in the naughty corner? I'm not a child."

His lips twitch. Not quite a smile, but more like the ghost of one that knows how ridiculous this is.

"Anyone can take a moment to re-evaluate their actions," he says smoothly.

Before I can summon a proper comeback, his hand finds the small of my back. His touch feels warm, guiding and utterly inappropriate. I hate the heat that coils low in my stomach as he gently manoeuvres me towards the corner, like he's taming something feral.

Is Gareth right? Carter's touch is affecting me more than it should.

When we reach the corner, my reflection catches in the glass top of the bar cart. And what I see, knocks the breath right out of my lungs. Heat pools between my legs as I watch Carter lean into me. His lips ghost my neck, his eyes closed while he inhales my perfume.

"If self-reflection is the goal," I say, keeping my voice light and watch him straightening up quickly, "wouldn't the sofa be more comfortable?"

I glance over my shoulder, expecting him to retreat, but he doesn't. He's still close enough that the lapels of his suit jacket brush my back. My pulse stutters, and I have to fight the absurd impulse to lean back into him. To see what would happen if I did. Instead, I allow the walls to close in as I lean forward.

"No, because a well-delivered reprimand induces a sense of embarrassment," he murmurs, his tone calm and controlled.

His footsteps echo sharp against the marble, swallowed moments later by the quiet, methodical tapping of his keyboard.

Minutes tick by agonisingly slow as I debate whether to challenge his authority. Ultimately, though, I resign myself to the rather harmless punishment for losing the firm so much money. Papers rustle behind me, followed by him clearing his throat.

I should feel humiliated. Mortified, even. But instead, a bubble of laughter swells in my chest, fighting to escape. The absurdity of this entire situation is just too much.

How the hell did I end up here, standing in the corner of my boss's office like a misbehaving child? Either the desperate need to keep my job has officially stripped me of all self-respect, or I've got some deep-rooted daddy issues I should probably unpack with a therapist.

A ridiculous image pops into my head—me draped over Carter's knee in a short plaid skirt and knee-high socks, his large hand coming down in slow, authoritative smacks. *You've been a very naughty girl, Miss Rosen* he'd say. And thanks to Father's schooling in etiquette, I'd probably thank him for it.

I clasp a hand over my mouth, trying to smother the laugh that escapes anyway.

"Sophie!" Carter's voice cuts through the air like a whip, jolting me back to reality and ironically, feeding straight into my wayward fantasy.

I lose it. Laughter bursts from me in uncontrollable waves.

"Is this a joke to you?" he snaps, tone brimming with disbelief. But the more severe he sounds, the harder it hits me. I double over slightly, clutching my stomach, tears threatening to spill.

"I'm so sorry," I gasp between giggles, brushing at my cheeks. "It's just, standing here doesn't embarrass me. It just feels like I'm a naughty little schoolgirl waiting for detention."

The sound of my own laughter feels foreign, startlingly light. When was the last time I laughed this hard? This genuine? It floods through me, sweeping away the shame, the tension, even the exhaustion. For a moment, I feel free.

Carter, of course, does not share my amusement. His expression is stoic, not a hint of a smile, just that infuriating self-control.

"Compose yourself," he warns, voice dropping an octave, "or I might have to give that naughty little schoolgirl a firm hand."

The words hit like a punch to the gut. My laughter dies instantly.

Did he just—?

I stare at him, mouth slightly open, trying to determine if he actually said what I think he did. Surely not. It goes against every paragraph in the book of ethics.

He leans forward slightly, unflinching.

"What do you mean?" I manage, the air suddenly feeling thick between us.

"The firm is built on sand," he replies, his tone clipped, all business now. He starts towards me, each step deliberate and commanding. "We cannot afford any mishaps, let alone losing another client. So, if I ever find myself in a similar situation with you again—" His gaze locks on mine, hard and unyielding. "I will ensure that you learn your lesson."

His words are professional, but the delivery is anything but. The way his eyes darken, the rough edge to his voice—he knows exactly what images he's putting in my head. And damn him, it's working.

My lips part. "Is that a threat?"

"You take it in whichever way it pleases you the most," he says, voice low and utterly infuriating in its calmness.

How dare he threatening me like this? I might be willing to entertain his unconventional method of standing in a corner, but I won't be threatened with physical abuse.

My temper spikes, hot and sharp. "You will never see me standing in a corner again," I bite out, each word laced with defiance.

His mouth curves into a smirk. "Time will tell."

My lips part to retort but his words spark a sudden realisation. I push past him and stumble to my knees, frantically rummaging through the paperwork laid out on the coffee table. Somewhere in here, there's proof, the missing piece we need.

"The applications for the patent, where are they?" I call over my shoulder as more papers sail to the ground.

He launches at his desk in pursuit of the paperwork, only finding it by the time I've already cleared the table.

He hands me the applications and takes a seat on the sofa. I hastily flip through the pages, knowing exactly what I'm looking for. Comparing both applications, I check the issuing dates and signatures, followed by the statement of case.

"This is it!" I shout triumphantly, my pulse thrumming with adrenaline.

Still kneeling, I turn towards him with the evidence clutched in my hand, and find myself perfectly framed between his open legs. He leans forward slightly, bringing himself too close, his cologne hitting me like a drug.

"Check the dates," I say quickly, ignoring the heat crawling up my neck. "Windpower filed their patent on the fifteenth of August."

"We know that," he counters, impatient. "And we know Skiron filed four months earlier, tenth of April."

"Have they though?" I press, flipping to the last page and leaning closer, my elbow leaning on his solid thigh. "The signature states fourth of October. Look at the address of the patent office where it was issued."

He leans in, eyes narrowing as he reads. "New York City." A pause, then his brow lifts. "They've written the date in American format."

I can't help it. I beam. The victory tastes sweeter than champagne.

"Windpower filed first," I declare, the words spilling out in a breathless laugh. "We win!"

"We win," he echoes, and for the first time this morning, his voice softens.

A slow smile blooms across his face, showcasing utterly captivating dimples I didn't know he had. My poor, overworked heart forgets how to function.

The sun breaks over the buildings, catching his face in golden light. The amber flecks in his eyes shimmer against the silver-grey, and for a moment, I forget how to breathe. For a moment, the chaos fades. It's just him, me, and the heady hum of victory between us.

My elbow slides off his thigh as he stands up, bringing my face level with his crotch. I try to swallow the abundance of saliva coating my tongue as my gaze traverses the significant bulge of his pants. Heat floods my core. Is he hard? For me? Or is he just... blessed? Either way, I can't look away.

"Sophie," his deep voice calls out in the distance, its tone like a warning.

The papers scrunch in my fist as the urge to touch his bulge floods my foggy braincells. Just one touch to feel his length resting against my palm. Just to know if he's hard because of me. Because of this moment. Because he wants me the way I—

My hand lifts off my thigh, fingers trembling.

His hands are suddenly under my arms, lifting me with deliberate speed. Did he see? Does he know what I was about to do?

His grip lingers—too long, too deliberate. The warmth of his palms seeps through the thin fabric of my blouse, igniting tiny fires across my skin. Like he's steadying himself as much as me.

I look up, ready to share another triumphant smile, but the softness in his eyes has vanished, replaced by something harder, colder.

"I'm running late for the board meeting," he murmurs, his voice low and throaty, "I will arrange a meeting with Ravens for tomorrow morning."

He sidesteps me, but when he reaches the door, he glances back with a perfectly neutral expression. "And do consider dressing a little more… conservatively."

My jaw drops, but he's gone before I can summon a single word.

I just stand there, rooted to the spot, the echo of his last words ricocheting around my head.

Dress more conservatively.

I look down at myself. Is he serious? What's wrong with my clothes? A pencil skirt that reaches my knees and a dress shirt buttoned to the collar—how much more conservative can I get?

The audacity.

My fists clench at my sides, and the anger starts to bloom. Of all the things he could have said. Of all the ways he could've thanked me for winning the account, for helping him, he chose that? Not Well done, Sophie, or even a professional nod of respect. No, apparently the problem is my damn wardrobe.

"Conservatively," I mutter under my breath, the word dripping from my tongue like poison. "I'll show you conservative."

I glance around the office. The early light pours through the tall windows, glinting off the whiskey bottles on his bar cart, the sleek glass of his bookshelves, the leather of his perfectly aligned chair. Everything in here is meant to look like a cosy retreat, but in truth, it all screams control. He's a control freak. It's like he's built an entire fortress to protect himself from human emotion, just like Father has.

And yet, every time I think of Carter's smug expression, his commanding tone, I imagine him taking control...of me.

I start gathering the scattered papers from the floor, forcing myself to breathe through the inappropriate thoughts. I can do better. I can prove to him that I'm the best employee he'll ever have.

By the time I straighten up and smooth my skirt, my plan is already forming. A slow and wicked grin spreads across my face.

Tomorrow, I'll walk into this meeting looking so professional he won't be able to breathe without choking on his own hypocrisy. I'll give him conservative. But it'll be the kind of conservative that commands attention. The kind that says power, not penance.

A tailored dress that fits like a glove, hugging every curve with ruthless precision. Hair pulled back, sleek and defiant. No pink, no flower-print. Just authority, wrapped in elegance and sharpened to a blade.

He won't know where to look, and I'll meet his eyes without a flicker of hesitation. Because the truth is, Medard Carter can command, scowl, and criticise all he wants, but he can't control what he doesn't understand.

Me.

And when he tells me I look professional, I'll smile and say "Thank you, Mr Carter." And he'll know—he'll absolutely know—that I won.

Loser

Medard

"Good morning, are you alright?" Buckman's voice cuts through my thoughts as he steps into the conference room. His gaze settles on the dark shadows under my eyes like I'm a case study in burnout.

I can practically hear what he's thinking—another sleepless night, another round of over-thinking and scotch-fuelled self-destruction. He's not wrong. When I wasn't torturing myself over this morning's meeting with Windpower, my mind kept circling back to Sophie.

The way her eyes lit up when she cracked the case. That look—a cocktail of pride and delight—did something to me. When I helped her to her feet, something small and fragile fluttered in my chest. Like the first tentative flap of a butterfly's wings. And then fear came crashing down, grinding that delicate thing into dust before it could take flight.

I can't allow myself those feelings. Not for her. Not for anyone. The firm takes priority, and Sophie made it clear where her priorities lie.

She let her personal life interfere with business. Chose a man—a bloody policeman, no less— over a client.

A tiny voice in the back of my mind whispers that I'm overreacting. That one evening off after weeks of dedicated work shouldn't warrant this level of fury. That she more than made up for it by cracking the patent case.

I tell that voice to shut the fuck up.

I thought we were finally on the same wavelength, but one call from her boyfriend and she vanished, leaving me to handle the fallout. Richard's voice still echoes in my skull, venomous with frustration as he recounted Sophie's endless rescheduling and lack of communication. He was right to be furious. Hell, even I couldn't talk him down.

The entire debacle left me pacing my home half the night, stewing in equal parts fury and unwelcome mental images of her with her bloody lover.

By the time she walked into my office the next morning, all cool poise and zero remorse, I was ready to lose it. Part of me wanted to haul her over my knee and give her a proper lesson in discipline. Not that I'm into that sort of thing. Though lately, I can't seem to stop imagining it. It's ridiculous, I'm being ridiculous, and yet that image has somehow set up permanent residence in my mind.

It took every ounce of my self-control to confine myself to a verbal reprimand and a stint in the naughty corner. God knows, what shit show I would have evoked, if I'd acted on the fantasy instead.

"Anything I can help you with? If not, I'd like to get prepared for the meeting," I cut off Buckman's polite probing with a flick of my hand. I'm in no mood for small talk.

Normally, I'm composed. Controlled. But with Sophie? She has a way of heightening my emotions. She doesn't just irritate me, she infuriates me. I don't find her interesting, I fixate on her. It's maddening. But I can't let her throw me off-balance again, not today. Not with Ravens walking through that door any minute.

"It's best if I sit in on the meeting with Ravens," Buckman presses, his persistence grinding against my frayed nerves. "After all, there's much at stake."

"You're not needed," I bite out. "Miss Rosen and I have it covered."

He doesn't take the hint.

"I'm sure you do," he says with a smile, "but there's no harm in having a bit of extra expertise in the room."

If his name weren't on the letterhead, I'd have escorted him to the door myself. But with the firm's reputation already hanging by a thread after Harman's dismissal, I can't afford to make any more waves.

"There will be plenty of expertise present to ensure this project is completed success—," I say, but the words die on my tongue the moment Sophie walks in.

She's dressed like sin wrapped in silk. A dark red dress clings to every curve of her body like it was sewn on her skin. The neckline dips too low, the hem rides too high. It's not so much a dress as a provocation, and—fuck me sideways—it's working.

"Dismissed," I snap at Buckman, my voice harsh. I can't stand having witnesses while I'm trying to maintain the barest thread of professionalism with her in the room.

She stiffens, causing her full breasts to jut out and strain as much against the fabric of her dress as my dick is now straining against my boxer briefs.

"I'm sorry, I thought I was supposed to participate," she stammers, her fingers brushing against her thighs, as if she knows exactly where my mind's gone.

God, this woman is going to ruin me.

"Not you," I manage through gritted teeth, my eyes flicking to Buckman. "I said out."

He shoots me a glare but wisely takes his leave. The moment the door shuts, my attention returns helplessly to Sophie. She leans forward to arrange the proposals on the table, and I swear she's doing it on purpose. The fabric shifts, her legs elongate, and my pulse hammers so violently I almost forget to pick my jaw off the floor.

"You look—" I start, then stop, because the word 'perfect' is hovering too close to the tip of my tongue.

"Professional? Pretty?" she teases with that cock-teasing sweet smile.

"I was going to say—" I start again, but the universe spares me from finishing as the door opens.

"Mr Ravens, it's a pleasure to meet you," Sophie chimes, instantly slipping into her professional persona. Her voice, soft and melodic, carries across the room.

I swallow the unspoken words and step beside her. Ravens eats it up. Of course, he does. His gaze lingers on her curves far longer than appropriate, and when I glance at his wife, the tightness around her mouth tells me she's noticed too.

Brilliant.

This meeting is already circling the drain.

"Gerald, please, have a seat," I gesture towards the chair I'd arranged earlier, complete with carefully prepared documents.

As I move to take my seat opposite, Sophie swoops in, claiming it like it's her throne. I hesitate, but not one to cause a scene, I resign myself to the chair beside her.

We dive into the discussion, presenting our strategy. Or rather, I try to present it. Sophie, in her infinite enthusiasm, keeps cutting in. She's quick, clever, charming in a way that makes my chest swell with pride, but somehow also infuriates me. Every time Ravens raises a question, she's there with an answer, her smile bright, her voice honeyed. And Ravens? He's captivated and practically drooling.

"Mr Ravens, rest assured our firm has a longstanding record of success in the technology sector," she says, flashing that killer smile.

I grind my teeth so hard my jaw aches.

"I must say, you're quite persuasive," Ravens chuckles, and Sophie laughs in return in that soft, lilting sound that's far too intimate for a professional setting.

"It's all part of the job," she says sweetly, "making sure our clients are well taken care of. But it certainly helps when I have such a powerhouse of a man to impress."

Did she actually say that? Or am I hearing it through the filter of my jealousy? Either way, Ravens is eating it up.

I want to scoff. Instead, I ball my hands into fists beneath the table.

"Oh, you flatter me, Miss Rosen. Your confidence is truly captivating," Ravens replies, oblivious to the ice radiating from my side of the table, let alone his own wife.

Mrs Ravens hasn't said a word since we started. She just sits there, perfectly still, her wedding ring catching the light as she taps one finger against the armrest. I've seen that expression before—on my own mother's face when my father's eyes lingered too long on the hostess.

I need to get this meeting back on track. Winning over Ravens is crucial for our firm.

"Sophie," I interject sharply, desperate to salvage what's left of our dignity. "Perhaps you could retrieve another copy of the statement of case while I go over the specifics with Mr Ravens."

Her hand moves to one of her little dangling earrings, and she twists it while looking confused at three copies in front of her.

Ravens rises, smiling, with his associates quick to follow suit. "No need. I believe we've covered everything. I'll be in touch."

He shakes my hand, his grip smugly firm, then turns back to Sophie. "Miss Rosen, it's been a delight."

"Likewise," she beams. "Allow me to escort you to the lifts."

As Ravens' entourage filters out of the conference room, I turn to the window, needing the distraction. Sunlight dances off the towering skyscrapers outside, but my mind is clouded with unease. A knot tightens in my gut, hard and unrelenting.

The meeting didn't go as I'd hoped. Not even close. And it's all because Sophie—my beautiful, impossible subordinate—refused to follow my bloody lead.

I thought the events of the other morning would've straightened her out, reminded her that disobedience has consequences. But no. Sophie doesn't learn her lessons, she rewrites them. She fights her own battles without considering the bigger picture.

"Medard," Buckman's voice slices through the air, sharp with accusation. "Did you manage to win the client over?"

I pinch the bridge of my nose, the weight of defeat pressing on my shoulders. "It's not looking promising," I admit, my voice flat with exhaustion.

"This could've been avoided if you'd allowed me to join the meeting," he fires back.

The anger that's been simmering in my chest flares dangerously close to the surface. I spin to face him, jaw tight. I don't have the time or energy for his fragile ego. The firm is hanging by a thread, and I have one employee who seems hellbent on cutting it entirely.

"One failed meeting hardly compares to the damage you caused with your former partner," I snap, my tone low and cutting. "Don't lecture me on damage control, Buckman."

His face reddens, the veins in his temple twitching. "How dare you speak to me like that!" he bellows, fists trembling at his sides. "My name is still on that door! You will treat me with the respect I've earned, not cast me aside like some incompetent fool. And certainly not in front of another employee!"

His voice booms through the glass walls, echoing into the corridor.

Fucking perfect.

Just what I need—another public spectacle.

From the corner of my eye, I catch movement. Sophie's unmistakable silhouette passes by. Her brows pinch together, no doubt catching enough of Buckman's outburst to draw her own conclusions. She probably assumes the meeting went swimmingly and I'm now venting about some minor inconvenience. The idea almost makes me laugh.

When she's out of sight, I turn back to the old man.

"I acknowledge your years of service," I begin evenly, though the effort it takes to keep my voice steady is monumental. "But I won't put you on a pedestal just because you've outlasted everyone else. You, like every other employee of this firm, share responsibility for where we are now. Act like a subordinate, and I'll treat you like one."

His mouth opens and closes. Then finally, he exhales. The fight bleeds out of him.

"I apologise, Carter," he mutters, voice softening. "I only want us to succeed... together."

I narrow my eyes, studying him. His sudden humility smells suspiciously like self-preservation.

"If you truly want us to succeed," I tell him coolly, "then start by trusting my leadership, and follow my direction."

I don't wait for a reply. I've spent enough time dancing around egos for one morning. The moment I step into the corridor, the air-conditioning hits me, cool and sharp against my heated skin. It helps. A little. But my mind still spins. The failed meeting, the firm's fragile future, and Sophie's infuriating defiance collide like storm fronts in my head.

Buckman may have been out of line, but he's not entirely wrong. Maybe I should have let him sit in. Maybe I wouldn't have let my conflicted feelings for Sophie cloud my judgement.

If I'd been the one steering that meeting, Ravens wouldn't have had the chance to ogle her like she was dessert while his wife sat stewing across the table. I would've controlled the flow, led the conversation, not sat there like an idiot trying to ignore the fact that my subordinate was batting her lashes at a married man, wearing a red dress that belonged in a bar, not a boardroom.

I round the corner, my resolve hardening with every step, only to freeze when I spot Sophie's assistant perched behind her desk.

A reminder.

Another decision influenced by my personal feelings. Maybe now isn't the time to confront her. Not yet. Not when we don't even know if we've lost the business. Holding onto a glimmer of hope that our proposal will shine brighter than Sophie's charms, I take a breath, straighten my spine, and pivot on my heel to retreat down the hall.

"Carter, wait!" Sophie's voice calls out from behind me.

I don't turn. I can't. If I look at her now, at those wide eyes, that soft mouth, I'll lose what little composure I have left.

So, I keep walking. Ignoring the pull. Ignoring her. Even though every instinct in me screams to turn around.

An hour later, I'm trying to exorcise my temper at the gym. The treadmill whirs beneath me, each heavy footfall pounding in time with the chaos in my head. I crank the speed up another notch, my calves screaming their protest. I don't care. I need the punishment.

My original plan was to head straight back to my office and bury myself in the mountain of work I neglected while Windpower consumed every waking thought. But instead, my feet brought me here. Maybe instinct knows what the mind can't admit—the walls of my office would've driven me mad. Because if Sophie had shown up, all red dress and defiant eyes, I'd have done something reckless.

I push harder, jaw locked, lungs burning. Still, her voice trails me like a ghost. Carter, please wait.

Damn her.

The ache in my legs finally matches the one she left in my chest. I slam my hand on the stop button and grab the towel to wipe the sweat from my face. The woman on the treadmill next to me gives me a coy smile. She's pretty in an unassuming way, with sleek brown hair pulled back in a ponytail. Mid-twenties at most. There's an invitation in her look. It's subtle, deliberate, like she's testing the waters to see if I'll bite.

She'd be a good distraction. Not because I want her, but because I want the noise in my head to stop.

I step off the treadmill and grab my water bottle, pretending not to notice her gaze dip lower. I take a slow breath, run a hand through my damp hair, and look her squarely in the eyes.

"You should be careful where you aim that smile," I tell her, my tone cool, a little amused. "Some men might take it as a challenge."

She blinks, momentarily thrown off, then smirks. "Maybe that's the point."

Her gaze drifts down to my crotch again, and I laugh quietly. Not out of amusement, but disbelief.

Christ, I'm becoming predictable.

"Well, it's working," I say, throwing the towel over my shoulder and head towards the changing room.

It merely takes a few steps, before I hear her hit the stop button on the tread mill and follow me. We walk to the ladies' changing room in silence. No more words are required. She and I both know what we just signed up for. She peaks into the room to confirm no one's there, then pulls me in for a hungry kiss. She quickly works on untying the string of my joggers while I guide her further into the room. But then a sudden concern creeps into my mind.

"Are you legal? Show me your licence," I nod towards the lockers.

I may be self-destructive, but I'm not stupid. The last thing I need is an underage girl and a court case.

"For real?" she teases, the youth evident in her tone as she tries to pull me closer.

I'm up for a quick fuck to get Sophie and the shit show at the firm out of my head. I won't risk going to prison for it though.

"For real," I assert.

With an eye roll, she retrieves her license and a condom from her locker. Rebecca Hartford, twenty-two years old. That's all I need to see before tossing the card aside and focusing on the moment at hand. Her smile grows wider as she leaps into my arms. I guide us to a nearby bench, trailing kisses down her neck and over her breasts. She lets out a soft moan, eagerly pressing herself against me. I peel off her leggings to reveal her wetness ready for me. My fingers dance over her clit, prompting her to beg for more. I capture her lips, my hand sliding down my waistband to free my cock. He's not fully hard yet, but grinding her wet pussy over it, should get him there in no time. I focus on our kiss, dragging her bottom lip between my teeth as she shamelessly coats my shaft in her slickness. I tear open the condom wrapper with my teeth, and try to roll it on, but it bunches around the tip. Frustration bubbles to the surface as I grip the stubborn fucker to will him to stiffen, but he refuses to cooperate.

"What's going on?" she asks, glancing down between us.

"Nothing," I mutter, trying to focus, to will him to stand at attention, "just give me a sec."

But then Sophie's bewildered expression flashes through my mind and all I feel is guilt chasing through my veins. My dick deflates completely.

"Great," she snorts, slipping off my lap and readjusting her leggings, "should have known a guy your age wouldn't get it up."

A guy my age? I'm thirty-five, for fucks sake! Not seventy!

She shoots me a disgusted look before striding out, leaving me on the bench with my pants around my ankles and my flaccid dick drooping between my thighs.

Fuck, fuck fuck!

I can't fuck other women anymore. Because of her. Because of Sophie fucking Rosen. She's ruined me for anyone else.

My phone buzzes, pulling me away from my self-pity. I yank up my joggers and retrieve it. It's an email from Ravens confirming they won't be working with us.

"You loser!" I curse myself, hurling the phone against the wall, the screen shattering on impact. "You fucking loser!"

Sadistic Bastard

Sophie

"Did the meeting not go well?" Millie asks, her gaze tracking mine as Carter storms down the corridor like a bull stuffed into a three-thousand-pound suit.

Despite the meeting having gone perfectly well, I feel queasy at the thought that Carter's mood might indicate otherwise.

"I'm sure it went fine," I say, brushing her off while my eyes follow those broad shoulders until they disappear around the corner.

Millie hums nervously beside me, wringing her wrists.

"I mean, he looked angry," she ventures. "Do you think something else is bothering him?"

"Maybe." I shrug, forcing a breezy tone I absolutely don't feel. "Who the hell knows with him?"

Because truly, who does?

I flop into my chair and wake my laptop, refreshing my inbox like it's deliberately withholding good news. Nothing. No email.

Come on, Ravens. Be a decisive man.

Millie hovers, gnawing her lip, clearly unsure whether to stay or make a run for it.

"Whatever it is," I sigh, flicking my eyes to my phone where a message from Gareth waits, "I'm sure we'll find out soon enough."

She takes the hint and scurries off. I try to focus on mentally recapping the meeting, but Carter's expression keeps flashing behind my eyelids—all hard lines and barely leashed frustration.

I shake it off and open Gareth's text instead.

> Gareth: Sauvignon blanc or Pinot Grigio?
>
> Me: Are you asking me for advice? I thought you drank red.
>
> Gareth: Like I said, I need to work on my form. So, Sauvignon or Pinot?
>
> Me: Chardonnay

> Gareth: Jeez, really? I took you for a Sauvignon-kinda-girl.

> Me: Better luck next time! :)

A smile sneaks onto my face. Gareth might not be the distraction Baron suggested, but he's turned out to be a decent friend. Someone easy. Uncomplicated.

Unlike bloody Carter.

I set my phone aside with a determined huff and bury myself in clauses and strategy notes, losing track of time until a new notification blinks onto my screen—Ravens.

Finally.

My pulse spikes as I click open the email, eyes darting past the polite formalities and corporate waffle and straight to the line that guts me: Thank you for your proposal, but we have decided to decline your offer.

I stare at the screen, blinking stupidly. But the sharp sting in my thighs where my nails have dug in confirms my brain has already processed what my pride is still refusing to believe.

We lost. I lost.

The one account Carter wanted. The second failure in three days.

Ravens was enthusiastic. Engaged. So, where the hell did it all go wrong?

I shoot out of my chair and march down the corridor. Janet's typing furiously at her desk when I reach Carter's office.

"Is he here?" I demand, scanning the glass walls of his conspicuously empty office.

She doesn't even glance up. "He left this morning after the meeting. Your assistant can schedule an appointment when he's available."

Right. The assistant line. Corporate speak for piss off.

I cross my arms. "No, thank you. I'll wait here."

That gets her attention. Her eyes flick up, thoroughly unimpressed. "Miss Rosen."

But I'm already pacing, my heels snapping against the floor in a relentless rhythm that mirrors the chaos ricocheting through my chest.

Something's not right. Carter doesn't just lose clients. Windpower was his golden ticket, his obsession. If he's angry, it's not about the pitch.

It's about something else.

God help me if it's me.

"Miss Rosen, please return to your office," Janet tries again.

I ignore her. My mind's too busy spinning through every possible scenario.

"Miss Rosen," Janet snaps, "leave."

"No," I bite out. "I'm staying."

I need answers. If I'm at fault, I need to face whatever punishment Carter decides to dish out.

But if he thinks he can order me into a corner again, he's bloody delusional.

The thought makes me bristle and, annoyingly, flush.

Finally, the lift dings.

Carter strides out, all sharp lines and quiet dominance, his presence hitting me like a punch to the chest.

Oh, he's angry.

God help me, I can't decide if I want to run or find out exactly how angry he is.

I step in beside him, matching his stride until we reach his office, where I make sure to shut the door behind me.

"Carter, I'm so sorry. I don't know why Windpower pulled out at the last minute, but I will find out and fix it."

He says nothing as he settles into his chair, but the frustration radiating off him is practically visible.

"I'll review the papers today and arrange another meeting," I add, sliding into the chair opposite him. "Maybe I can get him to reconsider."

His gaze pins me in place as he drags a finger pensively along his lower lip.

"Them," he says finally.

"Pardon?"

"Gerald Ravens and his wife, Eloise," he clarifies. "She attended the meeting this morning."

The name clicks into place. Mrs Ravens—the woman in the peach suit.

"What does that have to do with anything?" I ask, genuinely confused.

He stands and paces to the bar cart, pouring himself a scotch.

He turns back slowly, swirling the amber liquid. "Mrs Ravens is quite conservative. Very involved in church and community commitments. I told you to dress accordingly today. You chose not to."

My jaw tightens. Is he seriously blaming my outfit for losing a client?

"My competence isn't decided by what I wear," I say, too sharp. "The meeting was solid. Ravens appeared invested. There was no reason for them to decline."

He raises a single brow and takes a long swallow. "Your skills aren't defined by your clothes, Sophie. But the way you presented yourself—charming Ravens while his wife sat there watching—sent a message."

"I was being professional," I protest.

"Were you?" He sets the glass down with a sharp click. "Or were you trying to prove something to me?"

The accusation hangs between us.

Was I? The red dress, the way I dominated the conversation, taking his seat—was I trying to win the client or punish Carter?

"You're a good lawyer," he says, voice low and precise. "But you let your personal feelings cloud your judgment. You made that meeting about us instead of the client."

My hands grip the armrests. "That's not fair."

"Fair?" His voice rises. "You want to talk about fair? Two accounts gone in three days because you can't separate your emotions from your work."

"Farm Valleys was one evening—"

"One evening that cost us a client!" He moves closer, his control fracturing. "And now Ravens. You're letting your personal agenda sabotage this firm."

"My personal agenda?" I stand, fury coursing through me. "You're the one who's been—"

"What?" he challenges, closing the distance. "Say it."

My throat works. "You've been—"

"I'm what, Sophie?"

His jaw flexes. "You've messed up again. I'm starting to question my decision to promote you. You've cost the firm six figures so far."

His words cut through me like knives, but I refuse to take all the blame.

"That's not fair. Ravens—I wasn't the only one in that meeting,"

I snap. "You can't pin all of this on me."

"Not fair?" he shouts, charging at me until there's barely an inch between us. His hands grip the armrests on either side of my chair as he barks in my face. "I don't give a fuck about fairness! You chose to defy me. You made a conscious decision to wear that dress, to take control of that meeting, and it backfired!" He pushes off the chair with abrupt force.

If I wasn't seething with rage, I'd be downright terrified. I square my shoulders and meet him head-on.

"I'm a damn good lawyer, and if you don't start appreciating it, I'll leave this bloody firm," I declare, my voice fierce.

But he's quick to cut me down, his words dripping with superiority, his smile suggesting he's been waiting for exactly that threat. "And then what? Who will hire you? You'll come from a tarnished place. Harman's little protégée." He steps closer, his eyes roaming over my face as he whispers, "But then, there's always Daddy Rosen to fall back on."

My throat works overtime trying to swallow the lump forming there. The urge to dig my nails into my thighs is overwhelming, but I refuse to let him see just how much his words affect me. If only he understood how hard I've been fighting to step out from under Father's shadow.

But he's right.

Painfully, infuriatingly right.

Everyone who's left Carter & Buckman in recent weeks has struggled to find new employment. Leaving now would be difficult. I could go to Father's firm, but that would feel like admitting defeat. Like proving Carter right about everything.

"So, what now?" I snap, desperate to conceal how trapped I feel. "Are you going to put me in the naughty corner again?"

He gives a single, dry laugh as he strolls back to his desk.

"No. That didn't work." He taps his lower lip, thinking, the motion annoyingly casual. "Manitore Industries. Get it sorted."

My eyes widen.

"No. Absolutely not. I'm not humiliating myself like that in front of the entire firm," I protest, crossing my arms.

Manitore Industries was recently converted to a public company, which means we have to change their title on thousands of pages. It's mind-numbing work.

He leans back, clearly amused by my revolt. "Look at you, little lioness."

There's a mocking tenderness to the pet name that makes my skin crawl.

"I accept I made mistakes, and I apologise," I say, attempting to sound reasonable for once. "But I will not waste the firm's time or money doing work that can literally be done by a trained monkey."

I didn't work my arse off for years to now be degraded by a chauvinistic dick.

"I am this firm, Sophie." The words are both vow and threat. "So, you can throw as many tantrums as you like, but if you want to keep your job, you will not leave my office without bearing the consequences."

I meet his eyes, fury and calculation locked together. "I will not take the Manitore account. Nor will I stand in a corner."

He eyes me with zero surprise, as if he's been waiting for my stubbornness.

We're at an impasse.

His phone cuts through the charged silence. He doesn't even glance at the screen, but lets it ring out and places it face-down on the desk. His focus slides to a long wooden ruler resting beside his files.

He picks it up, testing its weight. Studies me for a long, loaded moment.

Oh boy.

Something tells me he's lethal when he looks at me like that.

"There's a third option," he says finally, his voice low.

My stomach flips. "Which is?"

"You already know." His eyes never leave mine. "Don't pretend you haven't thought about it."

Heat floods my face because he's absolutely right. The corner punishment, the "firm hand" threat, that damned fantasy that won't leave me alone—

"This is insane," I breathe.

"Probably." He sets the ruler down on the desk between us like a gauntlet. "But it's your choice, Sophie."

My pulse hammers in my throat. "Are you seriously suggesting—"

"Eight strikes," he says calmly. "For the eight million Windpower would have brought in. Or you take Manitore. Your call."

I should walk out. Tell him exactly where he can shove his ruler and his twisted power games.

But that fantasy—the one I've been trying to ignore since he put me in that corner—roars back to life.

"Yes or no, Sophie," he presses. "I have a meeting in ten minutes."

The clock on the wall ticks loudly in the silence.

I hold his gaze, searching for any hint that this is a joke. But his expression is deadly serious.

"Fine," I bite out, moving towards his desk. "Just get it over with."

"Hands on the desk."

I place my palms flat against the polished wood, my heart thundering.

The first strike lands, and my entire body jolts. It's sharp, stinging—nothing like the fantasy.

"Fuck!" I gasp.

"Language," he warns, but there's something almost amused in his tone.

The second strike follows quickly. Then the third. Each one builds on the last, the sting intensifying until my knuckles are white against the desk.

By the fifth, I'm biting my lip hard enough to taste blood.

"Breathe," his voice cuts through the haze.

I don't feel like I'm breathing. I feel like I'm coming apart.

The sixth strike lands, and I can't hold back the small cry that escapes.

"Do you want to stop?" His voice is suddenly closer, quieter.

I should. I should stop this madness right now.

But that would mean admitting defeat, and I won't allow him the satisfaction while he's standing there all smug.

"No," I grit out. "Finish it."

"You're sure?" he chuckles darkly.

"Why? You're feeling guilty?" I can't help but mock him with a smirk of my own. "Just do—"

The strike hits harder than the others. As though he wants to make a point. I cry out, loud and unrestrained. Before I can recover, his hand covers my mouth—firm enough to muffle the sound.

"Quiet," he murmurs. "One more."

The final strike lands, and I'm shaking, tears pricking at the corners of my eyes.

The moment he releases me, I straighten, sucking in air. My face burns. My backside burns. Everything burns.

He steps back, sets the ruler down with deliberate care, and straightens his cuffs like nothing happened.

"There," he says, his tone casual, almost dismissive. "Consider it a lesson learnt, lioness. You'll think twice before challenging me again."

The words hit like ice water.

A lesson learnt. Like I'm a child who needed correcting. Like he's the one who held all the power, all the control, and I was just—what? A disobedient employee who needed to be put in her place?

The rage comes roaring back, white-hot and clarifying.

"I'll have bruises tomorrow, you sadistic bastard," I hiss.

He actually smirks. "You agreed to this."

"Screw you," I bite out, glaring at him with every ounce of defiance I can muster.

He closes the distance between us in a blink. "Watch your tone," he grates through his teeth, leaning in close, "or the next time, I won't be holding back."

"There won't be a next time," I fire back, lifting my chin.

His eyebrows rise, and that infuriating smirk returns. "So, you're going to be a good little lioness from now on?"

"Screw you, arsehole! And I'm not your little anything."

Something flashes in his eyes. Something dangerous. But before I can step back, his hand grips my throat with such force that I stumble backwards, my backside hitting the desk.

"Never speak to me like that again," he murmurs, leaning in close. "And don't you dare contact Ravens. You've done enough damage. I'll try to salvage the deal."

I can barely breathe as I wait for the panic to set in, for my self-defence training to kick in. Yet, for some reason, I make no effort to escape him.

What's wrong with me? Where's the fear?

He shouldn't touch me like this. I shouldn't feel so…exhilarated.

Like magnets drawing together, I lean into his hold. All the fight, the anger, the defiance drain out of me until there's nothing left but sweet, bewildering surrender. It feels freeing. Peaceful, even. Our breathing syncs. I'm powerless. He has all the control. But strangely, I trust him fully.

My breath hitches, my body swaying closer still.

But then he releases his grip, and the cold air hits my throat. I gulp down one deep breath after another. He takes a large step back, as though the idea of being in my vicinity sickens him. And then, without another word, he strides to his desk to retrieve his jacket.

His abrupt dismissal stings more than the burn in my throat or my backside.

"If you don't like me," I manage between pants, my voice raw and broken, "why don't you just kick me out?"

He stops—hand on the door handle, jacket slung over his arm—and without even turning around, he answers. "That's where you're wrong, Sophie. It's not a matter of liking you."

"Then what is it?" The plea escapes before I can stop it, desperate and small.

He shakes his head, still refusing to face me, and just walks out. The windows rattle as the door slams shut.

I perch against the backrest of the sofa, hand clutching my chest as if I can physically hold myself together. My heart hammers wildly, my throat and backside burn, and my mind is spinning.

The humiliation. The heat. The way his hand felt around my throat. The way I let it happen.

I don't hate Medard Carter.

I loathe him.

I loathe his arrogant, patronising tone. I loathe the smug control he wields. And I especially loathe the calculated humiliation he just put me through.

But mostly, I loathe myself for letting it happen.

For letting him speak to me like that. For letting him spank me. For standing there and taking it like some pathetic, broken thing instead of telling him exactly where he could shove his threats and his condescension and his bloody choke-hold.

I should have walked out. But I didn't.

I stayed. I submitted.

I let my boss cross every professional line in existence, and I did it willingly.

And that burns more than anything else.

My hands find their way to my thighs almost of their own accord. I yank up my skirt with shaking fingers and dig my nails into the flesh above my kneecaps. Then I drag them upwards, hard, letting the sharp bite of pain cut through the fog.

The skin instantly burns, leaving thin red scratch lines in their wake—visible evidence of something I can actually control.

I take a deep breath, let the sting settle over me, grounding me. Anchoring me back to white-hot anger instead of the pathetic, broken girl threatening to surface and fall apart completely.

Another breath. Deeper this time.

I can work with anger. Anger is useful.

I stand upright, adjust my skirt with sharp movements, and storm out of his office. Rage propels me forward with each step.

I have no destination in mind, just a mountain of humiliation and fury I desperately need to outrun.

Maybe if I walk fast enough, far enough, I can leave this entire disaster behind me. If I don't stop moving, I won't have to acknowledge the traitorous part of my brain that's already replaying his hand around my throat, the heat in his eyes, the way my body responded despite everything.

I barrel past Millie without a word, grab my coat and bag, and make a beeline for the lifts.

If I just keep going, I won't have to admit that the worst part of all this isn't what he did.

It's that some twisted, fucked-up part of me wanted him to.

"Hey, Soph!" Ben's voice calls out as he steps out of the restroom. "Coffee later?"

I shoot him a look. The kind of look that makes his hands go up in immediate surrender.

"You know what, never mind. I'll just... re-label Amina's stationery again." He does a one-eighty so fast I almost feel bad for him.

The lift dings, and I dive in before anyone can stop me. My heart pounds so hard I can feel it in my throat.

How can I ever face Carter again? How can I look him in the eye after allowing him to treat me like that?

Losing Windpower would've been bad enough. But this? This is worse.

This is personal.

The mirrored wall catches my reflection, and I almost laugh at the tragic sight. My hair's wild, strands sticking out everywhere. My mascara's smudged. And my nose? Red enough to audition for Rudolph the bloody reindeer.

I look exactly how I feel—wrecked.

And that's when the dam breaks.

Hot, angry tears spill down my cheeks before I can stop them. I furiously wipe at them, but they keep coming, fast and unrelenting.

Because this isn't just about what happened. It's the fact that he treated the whole thing like a transaction. A punishment delivered and lesson learnt.

Like none of it mattered.

Like I didn't matter.

The lift pings open, spilling me into the lobby. I keep my head down and move fast.

Three streets later, I find myself in the small park tucked behind the main road. I drop onto a bench, exhaling a shaky breath, and instantly regret it when a flare of pain shoots through my backside.

Perfect. Just perfect. Even sitting hurts now.

"Sophie?"

I glance up to see Lucy walking towards me, pushing a pram.

"Hey," I say, quickly swiping at my cheeks and forcing a brittle smile. "Fancy seeing you here."

For crying out loud. Can this day get any worse?

She tilts her head, concern written all over her face. "Are you okay?"

"Yes, I'm fine," I lie automatically. "Just a difficult day at work."

She sits beside me, rocking the pram absently. "Do you want to talk about it?"

"No." The word comes out sharper than I want it to. "Honestly, I just need to... not think for five minutes."

She nods slowly, studying me with those perceptive eyes. Then, gently: "Can I ask you something personal?"

I tense. "I suppose."

"Are you struggling to sit comfortably?"

My head whips towards her, heat flooding my face. "What?"

"It's okay," she says quickly, softly. "I'm not judging. I just...Baron and I... I know the signs."

I stare at her, speechless.

"You don't have to tell me anything," she continues. "But if something happened that you weren't ready for, or if someone crossed a line—"

"It was consensual," I blurt out.

Her expression shifts to something like relief. "Okay. Good. That's good." She pauses. "But you're upset."

"He left," I whisper, the words tumbling out before I can stop them. "Right after. He just...walked away. Like it was nothing. Like I was just another employee he'd disciplined and dismissed."

Understanding floods her face. "Oh, Sophie."

"We agreed to it," I say quickly, defensively. "It was my choice. But then he acted like...like he'd just taught me a lesson. Like he was always the one in control and I was just—" My voice cracks. "He didn't even stay to make sure I was okay."

Lucy reaches over and squeezes my hand. "That's not okay."

The tears start again, and this time I don't try to stop them.

"I could really do with a friend right now," I manage.

Lucy pulls me into a hug, careful and warm. "You've got one."

Flawless Gentleman

Medard

"Mr Carter, you're early," Mrs Ruthers remarks as I close the front door behind me.

"My last meeting didn't last long," I respond dismissively, ignoring her curiosity and the fact that I'm never home before eight.

I hang up my coat and loosen my tie, desperate to wash away the remnants of the day, but she follows me like a persistent shadow.

"Is everything all right?"

"I had a long day. Thank you for your service today. I'll see you tomorrow." The words come out sharper than intended, but I need to be alone. Now.

"Very well then, have a nice evening," she concludes before retreating.

I head into the bathroom and strip off my clothes with efficiency born of desperation. I spent two agonising hours in that board meeting, my mind reeling with images of Sophie bent over my desk. It was nothing but a one-dimensional thought when I offered the spanking, free from any ethical considerations. All I cared about was shifting the dynamic between us back into place. I had to show her that I'm in charge, that she belongs under my tutelage.

I never thought she'd agree to it.

Stepping into the shower, I let the warm spray work at the tension coiled in my muscles. I shouldn't have crossed that line with her, but Christ, it was mesmerising watching her whimper and arch her back with each strike. She's intoxicating. Dangerously so.

My hand moves down to my thick shaft before I can stop it, images of that beautiful, fierce lioness consuming my thoughts. I pump with a firm grip; my forehead pressed against the tiles as water lashes down on me.

I want her. Crave her.

Even more now than I did after our first meeting.

She's like a wildcat—elegant and gracious enough to beckon

any man under her spell—with a tongue and claws so sharp she could shred a man's biggest ego to ribbons. How I'd love to take on that challenge, to overpower her and bend her to my will until she's nothing but a purring kitten in my palm.

But I can't have her. And I cannot lose my shit around her again. She could be my downfall.

I punch the tile above my head, release my cock before the release can hit, and step out of the shower. Grabbing my phone, I dial. It rings several times before the mailbox picks up.

I speak into the receiver with a lightness I don't feel. "Gerald, I have a bottle of that scotch you like. How about I come by your office tomorrow, we crack that baby open and discuss how we can make this contract work for you?"

I hang up, exhaustion burning behind my eyes.

I have to find a way back in with Windpower before the firm closes its doors for good. If we can't secure a reputable client after the scandal with Harman, the market will lose its last shred of trust in our capabilities.

"Medard, darling, are you home?" Mum's voice travels down the length of my hallway as I step out of the bathroom, dressed in nothing but a towel.

I'm certain I gave her that key for emergencies only, not for unannounced visits.

"Mum, did I forget we had something arranged?" I ask, walking towards her when Lisa appears by her side.

She quickly averts her gaze, wringing her wrists in discomfort over my lack of attire. It's a sight to behold, and one I have no intention of rectifying quickly.

Closing the distance, I give Mum a peck on the cheek before greeting Lisa with a hug that leaves her blouse speckled with water from my chest.

"Lisa, I never thought I'd see you standing in my living room."

Her cheeks blush, her gaze aimlessly searching for somewhere to land that isn't my half-naked form.

"You get dressed, darling," Mum instructs, heading to the kitchen, "and I'll make us a nice cup of tea."

My mother, ever the hospitable woman, regardless of whose house she's at. I still don't know why she's here or why she's brought my soon-to-be sister-in-law. I don't expect to get an answer from her, though. And I'm certainly in no rush to get dressed.

"You've got it nice here," Lisa says, drawing my attention as she takes in the open-plan concept. "It looks very masculine with the neutral tones and concrete features."

"Well, I am a man. So, I'd say the interior is fitting." I brush off her compliment. Why the hell is she here?

She studies me for a moment, her eyes perusing the planes of my chest and travelling down to the towel before they snap back up as I clear my throat.

"I heard you got your name on the door. Congrat-ulations!"

"Thank you," I respond out of mere courtesy. "How's Theo doing? Any promising projects on the horizon?"

Hitting the raw spot, she exhales sharply. She hates discussing my brother's non-existent achievements. She'd always hoped he'd become a reputable politician, granting her the wealth and prestige she thinks she deserves.

"He was able to secure funds for another food bank," she forces out with a smile that never reaches her eyes.

"That's good. I'm sure if you keep him encouraged, something promising will come up soon."

"What about you? Is there anyone to cheer you on?"

"I don't need a cheerleader for my success," I shrug her off, though my response instantly evokes that glimmer of hope on her soft features.

"I suppose it's difficult for a woman to catch the attention of a flawless gentleman like yourself," she says with a meek smile.

I've always enjoyed making her believe there's still an opening for her. Now I just want to slam that book shut.

"But yes, I'm seeing someone."

"You are?" Mum squeals with delight as she hands Lisa a cup of tea. "Well, who is it? Tell me all about her."

Lisa quickly averts her eyes. I don't know why I suddenly felt the urge to lie, but I don't want to drag Mum into that web. Luckily, my phone rings.

It's Harris, who hopefully has news for me on Sophie. After I obliterated every ethical line by spanking her over my desk, I really need him to tell me something that will deter me from falling any further down that rabbit hole.

"If you'll excuse me, I have to take this." I excuse myself and head to the bedroom before answering. "Harris, what have you got for me?"

"Not much about Sophie Rosen, I'm afraid. She lives alone, no pets. When she isn't at the office, she's either at home or at a boxing club in Shadwell."

"A boxing club?" I laugh at the unexpected intel. It suits her fiery attitude perfectly.

"Yes, she does Krav Maga," he clarifies. "She's par-ticularly close to one member of the group. A man called Baron Carson."

I tighten my grip on the phone, my body tensing.

"Are they hooking up?" I force the words out.

"No, I don't think so," Harris says, his words like music to my ears. "He's married with a kid, and they only ever seem to see each other at the gym."

"Good. What else?" I press.

"There's not much else to her. If you ask me, she's a pretty lonely woman. Her life mainly revolves around her job."

"What about a boyfriend?"

"Not to my knowledge. I've checked her mobile's call log. She's regularly texting a man called Gareth Hayes, and there's a bunch of missed calls from her father, but not much else."

A fleeting spark of something— sympathy, maybe— erupts in my chest. Sophie, sitting alone in her flat night after night. But the scene from the shop quickly snuffs it out. Just because she hasn't seen the copper since I've had Harris look into her doesn't mean they're not together. After all, I'm the one who's kept her at the office most nights working on the Windpower account.

"What about Harman?" I ask, wedging the phone between my ear and shoulder to pull on my joggers.

"He was her mentor for three years. They were close in that she'd go to his house for dinner with him and his wife."

"Any contact since?"

"No, nothing. She's tried calling him a couple of times, but the calls never connected. It appears that since the news broke of his scheme, he's been avoiding her."

Good.

"I've got the photos from the day at the golf club as well. I'll send them over after the call."

"Good," I confirm, pulling a T-shirt over my head. "Have you looked into her father? Anything that would help me take the bastard down?"

Harris snickers darkly before I hear him take a deep drag from his cigarette.

"Let's just say, when you've read what I found, you'll pay me a nice bonus."

"Let me be the judge of that. I'll stop by your office tomorrow evening, but send me the photos now."

"Alright, I'll look forward to my bonus." He snickers again, before he ends the call.

I head back to the living room to face Mum and Lisa. They've gone, but there's a note in Mum's ornate handwriting on the kitchen island.

> *We had to leave, but if you'd like me to change your room at St. James to a double, let me know.*
>
> *Love you, Mum*

I scrunch up the note and toss it in the bin. I shouldn't have told Lisa I was seeing someone. The rehearsal dinner is going to be a completely different kind of awkward now.

Pushing thoughts aside, I turn my attention to my phone. Harris has sent the photos from the golf club, showing Harman and the judge laughing on the patio. I flip through the rest, looking for pictures that weren't released in the papers. I find four with the two men in the foreground and people mingling in the back. Zooming in on the bystanders, I don't recognise any of them.

I lock my phone, relief flooding through me with the confirmation that Sophie wasn't there, that she wasn't involved in the scheme.

I settle into my usual evening ritual, the one thing in my day that still feels entirely mine.

Kettle on. Record spinning. Something old and rich, the kind of voice that smooths the edges off a long day.

Mrs Ruthers has left one of her casseroles warming in the oven. I slide it out, pour my tea, and finally sit at the dining table.

My fork hovers halfway to my mouth when the doorbell rings.

Apparently, tonight has decided I'm not allowed peace.

I push back from the table with a groan, muttering under my breath as I head for the door. "If this is another bloody relative barging in unannoun—"

The door flies open, and a wall of muscle charges into my hallway. A bloke—huge, with shoulders that could double as battering rams—barrels past me.

"What the fuck!"

He grips my arm, spins me around with alarming ease, and then something long and hard smacks across my arse. Square on. The sound cracks through the room like a gunshot.

"What the actual fuck!" I yelp, spinning back to face him as pain flares sharp and immediate.

The bloke's nostrils flare, bull-like. He's glaring at me, chest heaving, a wooden ruler held aloft like a weapon.

"Hurts, doesn't it?" he growls.

I blink. My brain scrambles to connect the dots. The ruler. The look in his eyes. Sophie.

Oh, bloody hell.

"How the fuck do you know about that?" I snap, hand instinctively rubbing the sting. "Who the hell are you?"

"Your worst nightmare," he bites out, stepping closer, "if you ever touch a hair on Sophie Rosen's head again."

He tosses the ruler onto my side console, the sound of it clattering like a warning, and turns for the door. And that's when it hits me. The build. The attitude. The way he says her name like he owns the right to defend it.

"Baron, right?" I call after him. "Baron Carson. Sophie's mate from the gym."

He stops and slowly turns back with a glare that could ignite fires.

"None of your damn business who I am." He pivots again, but I'm not letting this over-sized gorilla stroll into my penthouse, spank me, and just walk out.

"Does Sophie know you're here?" I taunt, voice low and deliberately casual.

He hesitates. His shoulders stiffen. No answer.

"Does your wife know," I add, "that you're out playing knight in shining armour for another woman?"

That gets his attention.

He spins on his heel, fury darkening his features, and charges. But this time I'm ready. He throws a punch that whistles past my head, and I duck beneath it. He stumbles forward, just in time for me to grab the ruler and bring it down on his arse. Hard.

The sound is beautiful. The reaction? Even better.

He howls like a castrated wolf serenading the moon and

clutches his backside.

I can't help it. I laugh. I actually laugh.

"It does hurt, doesn't it?" I mock, grinning. "Consider it poetic justice."

His jaw tightens, his fists clench, and for a second, I think he's going to come for me again. But then he breaks. The sound that rumbles out of him is a deep, genuine laugh.

"Fuck, man!" he wheezes between chuckles. "That was sly."

I straighten my T-shirt, smirk firmly in place. "It was," I agree, walking towards the living room. "You drink scotch?"

"As a matter of fact, I do."

He drops heavily onto my sofa, still rubbing his arse, while I pour two glasses. I hand him one, then settle into the armchair across from him.

We raise the glasses in a silent truce and take a sip.

"Ardbeg?" he asks, swirling the amber liquid.

"You know your scotch." I nod. "Tell me, what else do you know about today's events?"

He eyes me over the rim of his glass. If he thinks I'm playing gracious host, he's mistaken. I want to know who else Sophie has spoken to, what exactly she said, and how far this mess has spread.

"Sophie doesn't know," he finally says. "My wife told me. She bumped into her in the park."

"So, Sophie told your wife." I let that sink in. "She shouldn't have done that."

My stomach twists. If Sophie's talking, this could blow up.

Baron's expression hardens. "You're one narcissistic motherfucker."

I've been called worse.

I shrug. "Nothing wrong with wanting to protect my career."

He barks out a rough laugh. "Sure. Who cares if Sophie got hurt, right?"

My jaw tightens. "I don't know what your wife thinks she heard, but it was consensual."

He shakes his head, slamming his glass down. "No one's disputing that, mate. But you left her. You spanked her and then just... walked away."

I don't answer. Because he's not wrong.

"You don't just leave after something like that," he adds quietly.

"Even an arse like you should know that."

The silence stretches. His words hang in the air, heavier than they should. He's right, and that bothers me more than the sharp sting on my arse.

Baron leans back on my sofa, swirling his scotch like he owns the place. His eyes are on me with that lazy, knowing look men use when they've seen through another man's bullshit.

I hate that look.

He slowly exhales through his nose. "You've got it bad."

I take a slow sip, pretending I didn't hear him. "Excuse me?"

He smirks. "Sophie. You're not just her boss. You care."

My jaw works, but I keep my voice even. "She's an employee. A difficult one, at that."

"Bullshit." He laughs. "You say her name like it costs you something every time."

I scoff. "You're reading too much into it. I'm annoyed, not... whatever the hell you're implying."

Baron tilts his head, studying me the way a boxer sizes up his opponent before the bell rings.

"Right. Because you're just annoyed that you spanked her, manhandled her, and then walked out like some cold bastard. And now you're sitting here drinking scotch and listening to love songs on vinyl."

"I like soul music," I snap, maybe a little too fast.

He grins. "Yeah. Soul. Fitting."

I glare at him over the rim of my glass, but it's no use. He's enjoying this far too much.

"I've known a lot of men like you," he says. "The ones who think being in control means not giving a damn. You'd rather burn your own house down than admit you care about someone."

"I don't care," I bite out. "I'm responsible for her. That's it. Don't get the wrong idea."

He snorts. "Mate, I think you're the one with the wrong idea."

To my horror, I don't have a ready retort. The silence hums between us, the music crooning faintly from the record player.

Baron leans forward, elbows on his knees. "Let me give you a little advice, boss man. You keep pretending you don't feel something for her, you'll lose her in ways that sting worse than that ruler on your arse."

I narrow my eyes. "You finished?"

He grins. "Almost. You're going to apologise to her."

My head snaps up. "Excuse me?"

"You heard me." He swirls the scotch lazily. "You humiliated her. Whatever arrangement you two have going on, and don't bother denying it, you crossed a line. So, you fix it."

I stare him down, but he doesn't flinch. "You've got some nerve coming into my home, hitting me, drinking my scotch, and then ordering me around."

He shrugs. Fucking shrugs. "Someone's got to tell you when you're being a complete arse. Consider me that guy."

"You think I owe her an apology?" I raise a brow, feigning amusement.

If Sophie wasn't friends with him, I'd have kicked him out by now. But I'm too curious about what she sees in him.

"I don't think," he says evenly. "I know. And for the record, she's not the kind of woman who'll take this lying down. She might look soft, but that one's got steel under her skin. And she's not crying over you, if that's what you're wondering."

"I'm not wondering anything."

He snorts. "Sure, boss man. Whatever helps you sleep."

He sets his glass on the table with a dull clink, then looks at me like he's about to drop one last grenade. "You know, my wife mentioned Sophie has been trying to get a table at Nobu for weeks. Kept getting knocked back."

My brow furrows. "Nobu?"

Baron smirks knowingly. "Yeah. So, maybe if you weren't so busy scaring the life out of her, you'd know these things. Maybe you'd have offered to help. A man like you surely has connections."

The bastard is baiting me, and it's working.

I do have connections. The head chef sends me lunch when he tests new dishes. I could have gotten her a table in five minutes.

But she didn't ask.

That thought lands heavier than it should. Because maybe she didn't think she could. Maybe I've made myself that unreachable.

Baron watches me, reading every flicker on my face. "So, here's what's going to happen," he says, bringing me an inch away from grabbing him by the collar. "You're going to swallow that overgrown ego of yours and apologise over a nice dinner. Properly. None of that clipped 'sorry you feel that way' bullshit you corporate types love. You hurt her. Fix it."

"I don't take orders."

He grins. "You'll take this one."

He stands and smooths a hand over his jacket when curiosity gets a hold of me.

"How do you know where I live? And how did you get past the concierge?"

Just so I know who to get fired.

He simply shrugs. "You've got your connections, and I've got mine. Make things right with her, or you'll find out just how far my connections reach."

Oh, good. Cryptic threats. My favourite.

He strides towards the door like he owns the last word.

At the threshold, he pauses. "And for what it's worth—that ruler move? Still hurts like a bitch."

I laugh, but then the door clicks shut, and the penthouse suddenly feels cavernous. The music fills the silence again, slow, aching, and too damn fitting.

I drop back into the armchair, glass dangling loosely between my fingers. Baron's words echo in my head.

You've got it bad.

He's wrong. Sophie is just a complication. A reckless, infuriating complication who challenges my authority at every turn.

But the truth settles in, heavy and inescapable.

Every time she walks into my office, the air changes. Every time she bites back at me, my blood hums. And every time I cross that line with her, that blurred, dangerous line, I lose another piece of the control I've spent my entire life building.

I pinch the bridge of my nose, cursing under my breath.

Damn Baron Carson for being right.

Psychopath

Sophie

If anyone ever asks me what title I'd give yesterday, it would be Failure.

Not the cute, character-building kind, but the gut-punch, ego-shattering, I-wish-the-ground-would-swallow-me kind.

First, my most successful client meeting mutated into a complete disaster. Then, I had the biggest argument with my boss to date—the kind that scorches everything. And by the end of it, I'd agreed to a spanking. Agreed! My greatest humiliation, signed, sealed, and delivered with my own pen.

Next came the tears. Full snotty cry in the middle of the office. Congratulations, Sophie. Public breakdown: unlocked.

And to top it off, I confided in Lucy like a pathetic little girl. Father would be appalled if he'd knew. Rosens don't show weakness—ever.

So yes. I'm a failure.

But the plan was simple: keep my head down, work hard, and stay professional. But somehow, I turned that into the most personal debacle of my career.

If Harman knew, he'd be laughing himself breathless, saying Nothing is as bad as it looks. Translation: don't panic, Sophie. The mess can still be salvaged. Except it feels like I've already hit the iceberg. Twice.

I step out of the shower, grab the squeegee, and drag it across the fogged-up mirror. And there she is— the woman of the hour. My reflection sharpens into the face of someone halfway between unravelling and waking up. My hair clings damply to my neck; my eyes are swollen but defiant. The look of a woman who's been spun in a washing machine of emotions and somehow survived the cycle.

I allowed Carter to spank me. Allowed, like it would get me back into his good books. Let's face it, if such a book even exists, his is nothing more than a pamphlet, and my name has certainly never been in it.

Still, I can't shift this sadness gnawing at my insides. Carter was angry with me, and I hated it. Not because I saw my career threatened. No, that would be too logical. I hated it because, in some twisted way, I want Carter to be proud of me.

Well, if that doesn't call for three-hundred-pound-an-hour therapy sessions to unpack Daddy issues, I don't know what does.

Lucy reckons it's a natural response to a spanking. Weirdly, she knows an awful lot about that kind of stuff. She even gave me advice on tending to my sore backside and confirmed what I already knew—Carter shouldn't have walked out like that. He should have stayed. Said something.

And now, it's morning, and I'm still none the wiser on how to face Carter.

How do you look at a man who's humiliated you and still feel that pull? That slow, treacherous burn of attraction that coils low in your stomach and refuses to die?

Because when Carter spanked me, his words sharp, his strikes precise, I should have been terrified. Every smack stripped me bare, peeled back the thick layer of professionalism I'd wrapped myself in. I felt exposed. Small. And somehow, impossibly, liberated.

And then, when his hand wrapped around my throat, something in me short-circuited. The world tilted, and I was no longer the humiliated employee. I was a woman caught in a storm of her own making—a mess of defiance and desire.

It's absurd. Completely, certifiably absurd. I should have been trembling with anger, with fear even. But I was trembling for a whole different reason.

Because in that breathless, charged moment, I wanted him.

Clean, simple, and devastatingly real.

I wanted to fall to my knees—not out of submission, but out of some desperate need to show him I could make it right. That he could be proud of me.

It's twisted, I know. Every rational part of me is waving a red flag, screaming run. But there's this tiny, reckless part that can't help but crave him.

"No!" I tell my reflection with a firm nod. "No more over-thinking."

The only thing I can control right now is my work. And if I can't fix my dignity or my twisted attraction to my boss, I can damn well salvage the Ravens deal.

I pull on my cream blouse like it's a bulletproof vest. My pencil skirt follows. Hair up, lipstick on. Every layer another shield between me and yesterday. By the time I step out the door, I'm a polished lie of composure.

My destination: the golf club.

My mission: find Mrs Ravens.

My secret wish? That I don't bump into Carter any time soon. Because if I do, I'm not sure if I'll slap him, apologise to him, or worst of all—kiss him.

An hour later, the taxi stops outside the golf club—that monument to old money and self-importance. Sprawling greens, white stone arches, manicured hedges. Even the air smells expensive.

It's been almost three months since I was last here. The last time, everything started to unravel. Harman got disbarred, I plummeted from my pedestal, and Carter was brought in to turn my career into a personal case study in humiliation.

I inhale deeply. The past clings to me here. But now is not the time to wallow. I have a client to win.

I stride along the stone path, my hands swiping at my thighs in calming circles. The murmur of polite conversation grows louder as I round the corner to the back patio.

And there she is. Mrs Ravens.

She's seated beneath a white parasol, posture flawless, pearl earrings catching the sunlight.

I gather my composure and head her way.

"Mrs Ravens, may I have a word with you?" My voice is steady despite the nerves.

She looks up, expression unreadable.

"Miss Rosen, after our meeting yesterday, I wasn't sure you knew who I was."

I take the seat opposite her, my backside instantly burning. I ignore the reminder and launch in.

"I wanted to apologise for yesterday. If my behaviour was perceived as unprofessional, I'm truly sorry. It was never my intention to make you or your husband uncomfortable."

Mrs Ravens eyes me warily, her manicured nails tapping against her porcelain cup.

"Did you not flirt with my husband to win his business?" Her tone is sharp.

I swallow hard. "I apologise. It was unprofessional. But please believe me when I say it was never my intention to disrespect you or your marriage."

She studies me, then sighs softly.

"You're not the first woman to try that tactic with my husband, Miss Rosen. And you won't be the last."

Relief floods through me.

"I know it's no excuse, but in a male-dominated industry, it sometimes takes unconventional methods to get ahead."

She narrows her eyes slightly, taking a slow sip of tea.

"At least you're honest. It certainly isn't easy for a woman," she concedes, "but you must understand I cannot condone that behaviour."

"I understand completely," I say quickly. "And if you prefer, I will remove myself from your husband's account. What's important is that our firm secures his business."

"Very well, I will discuss it with my husband."

I feel relief wash over me as she gives me a small smile. I thank her before making my escape.

The taxi is still waiting. I slide into the back seat and give the driver the office address.

My phone pings.

> Gareth: Burger or burrito?
>
> Me: Neither. I prefer food that doesn't require a napkin strategy.
>
> Gareth: Napkins are half the fun. You're supposed to get messy.
>
> Me: That's exactly what I try to avoid. In meals and in life.

I huff at the irony.

"How did the meeting with Mrs Ravens go?" Millie's voice chimes the moment I reach her desk.

She hands me my mail and a blessedly steaming cup of coffee before falling into step behind me, clutching her notepad.

"Really good, actually," I reply, sinking into my chair and firing up my laptop. "Let's go over my schedule."

"You've got a couple of overlapping meetings," she begins. "Farm Valleys is scheduled for tomorrow at ten a.m., but Laren Automotives has requested the same time."

Of course they have.

"Ask Harry from Laren if he'd prefer dinner next Thursday instead. Seven p.m."

I can't cancel on Farm Valleys. It's my only shot at winning them back. Carter has already written them off, but that's exactly why I want them back. Just once, I'd like to walk into his office, drop the signed contract on his desk, and watch his smug expression crack.

"Consider it done," Millie says, flicking another page. "You've also got two dinner reservations for Wednesday at eight p.m. One is with your father."

Oh, what a joy.

Six emails from Baron. All of them titled something equally relentless—'Autumn Krav Maga Do- RSVP Required'. Apparently, kicking people in the ribs isn't enough. Now I'm expected to party with them too. Hard pass.

"And the other reservation?" I ask absently, distracted by my inbox.

Millie hesitates, twisting her pen between her fingers.

"It's... Mr Carter," she says softly.

I blink. "At eight p.m.?" That's a bit late for a meeting, even by his standards.

"I don't think it's a meeting," she murmurs. "He's booked a table at Nobu."

My brain flat-lines. Nobu. As in, that Nobu. As in sushi, dim lighting, and every rich man's attempt at a peace offering.

Is this his way of apologising? For the spanking? The choking?

I swallow hard, heat blooming beneath my skin as my thighs press together. The memory ambushes me—his hand firm around my throat, his voice low and unforgiving. The way my pulse had spiked, not in fear, but something dangerously close to arousal. Something happened in that moment, something I can't rationalise or name, but it's carved into me all the same.

He doesn't even like me. Whatever we had in those long hours working side by side, it was an illusion. A temporary truce between two ambitious people chasing the same goal. But when his fingers closed around my throat, when his eyes burned into mine, I saw something real. Something raw. Hate.

And now this? Dinner?

My laptop pings. It's an email from Ravens. He's attached an invitation to a luncheon. Thursday a couple of weeks from now, one p.m., with his wife and—

Shit.

"Sophie?" Millie's voice wavers with concern.

Before I can form an answer, the door flies open.

"Out!" The voice booms through the room like a thunderclap, deep and commanding.

The devil himself. Carter.

Millie flinches and scuttles out faster than I've ever seen her move.

The door slams shut behind her, and I'm left staring at the man who has stormed into my office like he owns it. And frighteningly so, he does.

"I specifically told you not to approach Ravens," he barks out, closing the distance to my desk with an accusing finger pointed at me.

Here we go. I suppose Nobu is off the table now. Shame.

"I didn't. I went to his wife," I respond, calm and casual. But inside, my heart is racing out of... Fear? Rage? Arousal? Who knows these days.

I put my focus back on my laptop to answer Baron's latest email. Even the GIF of a doe-eyed puppy can't persuade me to join their piss-up.

"You think you're being clever?" he asks with hands on his hips.

My hands hover over the keyboard, digging crescents into my palms while I take a deep breath. If I don't match his rage-fuelled attitude, this conversation might not escalate.

I give him my sweetest voice, shrugging innocently, "I told you I was going to salvage the deal."

To gain some distance from him, I round the desk and refill my glass with water. Anything that will prevent me from looking at him will help.

Why does he always have to yell at me? I never see him lose his shit with any of my colleagues.

"You'll see," I continue while keeping my back to him, "after that luncheon we'll have them."

"How so?" he says with an irritating lightness. "Are you

planning on hiding your tits?"

God, I want to punch him.

His footsteps draw closer but I refuse to turn towards him.

"Don't fool yourself Sophie," he says, standing so close now his minty breath ghosts my neck. My treacherous body reacts immediately, but I clench my thighs.

Oh please, not now!

"You only stand a chance of winning this account, if you spread your legs for him," he taunts me, bending my composure to near breaking-point. "And there's no fucking way in hell, I'll let you do that."

I swing around and throw the content of my glass in his face.

Fuck him, and fuck my job!

I'm done taking so much insolence from him.

Completely unperturbed by the water dripping off his face, he grabs my waist and pulls me towards his chest, sending the glass crashing to the ground.

"I should have spanked you harder," he snarls mere inches away from my face.

His pupils dilate, swallowing the soft grey of his irises. His aftershave hits my senses like a rogue wave. My knees weaken. My lungs forget their job.

What is this man doing to me?

I should be afraid. I should feel cornered, threatened, furious. But with his hard, muscled body pressed so tightly against mine, fear is the last thing my body remembers. I'm struck by this reckless thrill that sparks like fireworks in my veins.

His fingers tighten around my ribs, digging in just enough to remind me that he's not gentle. Not with his words, not with his touch, and certainly not with me. It's almost bruising, the pressure, as though he's trying to mould me into something I can't quite be, or crush me before I can slip through his grip.

I draw in a shaky breath. I'm certain now— he hates me. Truly, inexplicably hates me.

"What have I ever done to you?" The words fall out of me, trembling.

There's a flicker of something in his expression—Confusion? Surprise?—before it hardens again.

My instincts scream at me to step back. I shift my weight, but before I can take a single step, his hand shoots up and seizes my neck. His palm is hot against my skin, fingers firm, commanding. And then, he pushes.

The motion forces me backwards, my spine hitting the wall behind me with a dull thud.

Every nerve in my body is on fire, torn between the urge to fight him off and the aching, dangerous truth that I don't really want to.

"Every time you talk back at me," he murmurs, his voice chillingly calm, "I want to squeeze that tiny neck of yours until you can no longer utter a word."

Oh, he hates me.

"Every time you do something wrong, my fingers itch to give you a good hard spanking. Just imagining deep red welts on your arse makes me rock hard." His fingers twist into the hair at the nape of my neck, tugging firmly until my head arcs back.

Oh, he loathes me.

My inner voice is screaming at me to fight. But my body? It's frozen. I want this. I want him to tell me why he hates me. And why, regardless of his hatred, I'm still drawn to him.

"Every time I just see you," he growls in a low and gravelly tone, like he's tasting me on his tongue, "I want to rip those tight clothes off you until there's not a single inch of your body you can hide from me."

He fancies me?

His face is snarling, primal. I press myself further against the wall, accepting the sting on my butt to gain some space to breathe. But he's everywhere.

He leans closer, still, until there's nothing more than a breath between our lips. For a heartbeat, I think he's going to kiss me, but then a slow wicked smile dances across his lips and he whispers, "and I want to do it all while I thrust my cock into you."

He wants me!

His free hand moves to my butt and grabs it with a fervour that will leave me with bruises. I bite my tongue to suppress a whimper.

"Hate me if you must," I manage, my glare locking on his, "but I will never let you fuck me."

My voice doesn't shake, though my heart's doing gymnastics. I won't let him see the chaos he's causing inside me—the heat, the confusion, the terrifying, stupid ache. He can want me, hate me, or use me as target practice for all I care. But he will not own me.

He presses his hips into mine in answer, his erection speaking volumes. My pulse spikes again, half fury, half shame.

Fight. Fight, you idiot!

The tension on my hair suddenly eases. The aggression softens. His hand slides down, his fingers tracing the curve of my neck until his palm cups the base of my throat. Gently. Deliberately. His thumb glides across my collarbone in a way that's almost… reverent.

"I have many feelings for you, lioness," he murmurs, and the way he says it, low and thoughtful, vibrates straight through me. "But hate isn't one of them."

For a heartbeat, I forget how to stand. His gaze locks on mine, and there's something real there. Something that terrifies me more than his temper ever could. But then, just as suddenly, he steps back. The space between us floods with cold air, washing away the anger, the insane thrill. It leaves me hollow. Empty.

"You will let me fuck you, Sophie," he says with quiet conviction, as though he's already lived the moment in his head. "More than once."

I open my mouth to object but something hot and dangerous is holding me back— excitement.

He sees it too, because that arrogant, knowing smirk returns.

"You and me, it's a done deal. I'm your future, so you better get used to it."

He turns away and strides out of my office, leaving me standing there, frozen. Every rational thought has packed up and gone on holiday. He doesn't hate me. He wants me. But for what? To be his dirty little office secret? The man's a bloody psychopath! How dare he storm into my office and treat me like something he's already claimed?

The rage boils hot and fast, searing away the last of my paralysis. Before I can talk myself out of it, I storm after him. My heels hammer against the floor. Millie's startled yelp barely registers as I barrel straight into her. I knock her off balance but don't stop.

I fully understand his need to put his hands around my throat, because right now, mine are itching to choke the smug life out of
    him.

I catch up just as he's about to disappear into his office. He doesn't even look surprised.

The bastard.

No. He turns, curious, like I'm a fascinating experiment he's waiting to see explode. Ignoring the warning bells in my head, I march straight into his space and jab a finger at his chest.

"You're my boss, so fucking act like it!" My voice echoes through the corridor.

Somewhere behind me people gasp, but Carter doesn't even flinch. He just tilts his head, studying me like a lion amused by a particularly noisy gazelle.

His voice drops to a near-whisper, low and lethal. "There'll be consequences."

He turns and steps into his office, like the last ten seconds didn't happen, and closes his door right in my face.

"Sophie?" Ben's voice comes from behind me. "You... alright?"

I force a brittle smile. "Of course. Everything's peachy. If you'll excuse me, I have a meeting to get to."

Half the staff is staring. I sweep past them, head high, praying the ground will take pity on me and swallow me whole. Inside my office, I grab my coat and handbag.

"Miss Rosen?" Millie appears in the doorway; concern etched across her face. "Are you okay?"

"I'm sorry I knocked you over," I mutter. "I'm leaving early. Clear my schedule for today... and tomorrow." Because who knows, there might be a termination letter on my desk by the time I come back.

Millie hesitates. "What if the Ravens call?"

"Then direct them to Carter." I grab my phone and stride past her. "I have to go."

I make for the lifts, ignoring the stares, ignoring the whispers. I need air. I need distance. I need to remember who the hell I am before I let that man undo me completely.

The cold air bites at my cheeks as I burst out of the building. For a moment, I just stand there, trying to process the absolute train wreck I've just made of my life.

How dare he storm into my office and treat me like I belong to him? And how dare I let him get under my skin like that?

My heels click against the pavement as I start walking fast, aimless, trying to burn off the humiliation. I've officially lost it.

I shouted at Carter, the managing director, in front of half the office. How could I be so reckless? I might as well hand-deliver my own termination letter.

The city hums around me—too polished, too busy, too sure of itself—while I feel like a malfunctioning cog in the machine.

I turn a corner and power-walk down the next street, when my brain finally catches up to my legs and the irony slaps me square in the face. I realise where I've ended up.

Rosen & Smith. My father's firm.

The name gleams pretentiously in large gold lettering above the door. I stare at it, at the building that represents everything I've spent my adult life running from.

Maybe this is it, the sign I've been avoiding. Maybe it's time to swallow my pride, admit defeat, and ask my father for a job.

Well, congratulations, Sophie. You made it... straight into a public meltdown and possibly unemployment.

I hover on the step, torn between going in and throwing myself into the Thames. Then through the glass doors, I see Father leaning over the reception desk, his face twisted in anger as he berates the young receptionist, his finger jabbing the air like a weapon, and suddenly I'm twelve years old again, shrinking under his disappointment, forever his misbehaving child who can never meet his impossible standards.

My feet are moving backwards before my brain catches up, carrying me away from the building, away from trading one controlling man for another.

Boss

Medard

Fucking act like it. Like I'm not already trying. Like I'm not already bending every rule for her.

I gave her the most important case and kept her from being swamped with clients. I let her take the lead in the meeting with Ravens, and spared her the humiliation of her peers for losing not one but two accounts! I handpicked her assistant and gave her a fucking corner office. I've been a generous boss to her.

Yet, one word of truth and she throws it all right back into my face.

It reminds me of someone else who once demanded I prove myself worthy of her attention.

14 years ago, Medard, 21 years old

Law, Economics and Society: The Foundations of Capitalism. Shit!
If I want to take this module, I'll have to drop Ethics. Who the hell needs Ethics anyway? No one cares about Aristotle when you're drowning in corporate merger and acquisition clauses. But apparently, the dean does. He's been hammering it into us since the first week—Ethics looks good on paper. Firms want it. Firms love it. Firms hire you if you've got it.
So really, I'm screwed.
"Don't you want to get changed?" Maddie's voice floats out from the shoe box-sized bathroom of her dorm, muffled by the ancient door and the sound of Adam Levine trying to convince the world he's still got Moves Like Jagger.
I glance down at myself—light grey sweatpants, UCL hoodie, bare feet shoved under the covers of her bed.
"Why? What's wrong with my clothes?"
The huff she lets out is dramatic enough to rival an opera performance.
"Don't tell me you forgot," she whines, her head poking out of the

bathroom, eyes narrowed at me like I've just confessed to murder.

I shift my focus back to the laptop. My cursor blinks accusingly on the module enrolment page.

"Forgot what?"

"Dinner!" she throws her hands out like I should know exactly what she's on about. "Reservations. Tonight. That new Italian place around the corner. The one everyone's been raving about."

Right. Dinner. Romance. Being an attentive boyfriend. The list of things I should be doing but can't because fuck you, Ethics.

"Oh yeah," I mutter quickly, selecting the Ethics module before it gets snatched by some overachiever with better time management skills. "Mario's, right?"

Her jaw drops. "It's Luigi's!"

Close enough. Italian plumber, weird moustache, same bloody family tree.

"What time?" I ask, scrolling for my next choice. "I just need to book these modules before midnight."

"Are you serious right now?" she snaps, crossing the room in her little black dress that suddenly makes me feel like the world's shittiest boyfriend.

Before I can blink, she snaps my laptop shut.

"Hey! What the fuck, Maddie?"

"Medard," her voice is high, sharp, dripping with annoyance, "you promised me tonight. We haven't been on a proper date in a month!"

I pull the laptop back, open it again, my pulse already spiking with the pressure of missing out on classes I actually want.

"I've been busy. Uni doesn't exactly run itself. Besides, we see each other every day."

"That's not the same!" she fires back, louder than the music still playing from her tinny speakers.

Then—slam! She shuts my laptop again.

For fuck's sake.

The muscle in my jaw ticks. I pinch the bridge of my nose before I lose it. "Maddie, I have to book these modules tonight. We'll go tomorrow, I swear."

"No! Stop being such a narcissist!" Her arms fold across her chest like steel barricades. "Either we go tonight or we're done."

The ultimatum slams into me. Although, part of me wants to tell her where to shove it, I also know she's right. I've been prioritizing everything but her. Ambition. Grades. My own impossible standards. And though top marks matter, so does she.

With a sigh, I drop the laptop onto the bed and cross the room to pull her into my arms. "I'm sorry, baby. I don't want to lose you."

Her chin tilts up when I wrap my hand gently around her throat, lifting her gaze to mine. I kiss her hard and deep, showing her everything words can't seem to manage. Her lips curve into that smile—the one that makes my damn heart forget how to beat.

"Give me five minutes." I tug at a strand of her chocolate-brown curls. "I'll change, and then we'll head out."

She softens instantly and nods. I turn and grab my phone, when it rings. It's Alex.

"Hey man, you alright?"

"Med, I don't, I can't—" his voice cracks, torn apart by sobs, "he's gone!"

My blood runs cold.

"What happened? Talk to me!" I demand, stepping away from Maddie, from the bed, from everything except Alex's broken voice.

"My dad, he's dead." His words are raw, jagged, punctured with agony. "Miguel knows. He's home with abuela. But the little ones... they're still at school. I haven't told them yet. How do I... what do I even say?"

Fuck!

His brothers. Ten and twelve. Barely more than babies. Younger than Alex was when he lost his mum.

"Fuck," I breathe, my chest splitting open. "Deep breath, mate. One at a time."

I hear him inhale shakily, the line stretching silent before he whispers, "he had a heart attack at work. One second, he was fine, then he just... keeled over. Why does this world hate me?"

Tears burn behind my eyes. I didn't know his dad well, not really. He was always working, always providing. But I feel Alex's pain like it's my own. He's twenty-one and an orphan now.

"Babe? What's wrong?" Maddie's voice breaks through, but I don't turn. I can't.

"Go get Benito," I tell Alex firmly. "I'll pick up Samuel and meet you at your nan's."

He exhales shakily. "Thank you." Then the line clicks dead.

I shove my laptop and wallet into my bag and shove my feet into *my sliders, turning towards Maddie.*

"I've got to go. Alex's dad just passed away."

Her face pinches with something between disbelief and irritation. "What? Now? What about our reservations?"

I stare at her, dumbfounded. "I need to pick his little brother up from school. I'm sorry, baby." I lean in to kiss her, but she steps back.

"And yet again, you choose something else over me!"

I bristle. "Not something. My best friend."

The very same I rarely see these days because she demands all my attention. Even now, when the man has just lost everything.

I head for the door when her voice cuts sharp behind me. "Okay, fine, I get it. It's sad, but the guy is dead. What difference does it make if you see Alex today or tomorrow?"

Her words slice clean through me. Cruel. Cold. A truth I didn't want to face about her until now. I turn, eyes hard, my heart already retreating from hers.

"Fuck you. We're done."

The door slams behind me, rattling in its frame, final and absolute.

Sophie isn't Maddie. I know that. Maddie wanted me to abandon Alex. Sophie just wants... what? Respect? Professionalism? For me to stop treating her like she's mine?

But she is mine. She just doesn't know it yet.

I'm done with her defiance and downright ignorance. She wants me to act like a boss? I'll show her who's in charge.

Pressing the button on the intercom, I finally let go of the illusion that Sophie Rosen will ever be a model subordinate and focus on what truly matters.

"Janet, connect me to HR, to whoever is in charge of the Employee Relations team."

Antichrist

Sophie

"Sophie, heed my warning!" Father's voice snaps through the air, tight and clipped.

He shoves his hands into the pockets of his perfectly pressed coat; shoulders hunched with old-world fury as we stride across the marble floor. His shoes squeak with every step, like even the Italian leather disapproves of my life choices.

"Warning about what?" I snap back, stabbing the lift button.

"You know exactly what I'm talking about."

"I really don't—"

He cuts me off with the expression that's haunted my existence since age five: the disappointed patriarch. The one that says "you could cure cancer, Sophie, and I would still find a way to blame your tone of voice."

The doors slide open with a slow, sinister hiss, like even the building is dreading this conversation, and he steps inside first.

"Just heed it," he says over his shoulder. His voice echoes inside the small metal box, bouncing off the walls in waves of relentless authority.

I follow him in, arms crossed, already feeling that familiar itch of irritation crawl under my skin like a rash I can't scratch.

The lift hums to life. Then, without warning, it jerks, violently, dramatically, as if it's drunk and trying to remember how gravity works.

And that's when I hear it. A low, off-key hum.

I turn, and there is Richard, dressed as a clown. A full, multi-coloured monstrosity of red nose, painted grin, and a shirt that proudly declares Farm Valley across his chest like he's auditioning for the world's most tragic corporate mascot.

He's humming some tuneless nightmare that sounds like it was composed by Satan's kazoo.

"Do you mind?" I ask, dryly.

He doesn't even blink. Just keeps humming, louder, his painted smile a mockery of joy.

I press my fingers to my ears, but it's useless. The sound seeps in anyway, right through my skull, vibrating like bad decisions and cheap wine.

And then, like a ghost from my personal hell, Father's voice booms beside me. "Are you listening, Sophie? You have always misbehaved! Or do you not remember when you threw your Latin book into the fireplace?"

I groan internally. "Oh, my God."

He keeps going. "I had to send your nanny into the city that night to fetch another one. You were seven! Seven years old and already unruly!"

"Yes, well, Latin is dead, Father. I was just giving it a proper burial."

He ignores me, of course, because heaven forbid logic gets in the way of nostalgia for my moral failings.

And just when I think this ride couldn't possibly get weirder, the doors slide open again.

Enter: Mr Ravens, dressed, and I swear I'm not hallucinating this, as a fourteenth-century Romeo. Tights, puffy shorts, and a feathered hat that looks like it mugged a peacock.

"Miss Rosen," he purrs, stepping inside, "what a delight. Didn't expect to see you here. Or did I?"

I blink at him, then at the feather. "Mr Ravens. What on Earth are you doing here?"

He grins wider, eyes sparkling like he's just been hit by Cupid's arrow. "I missed you, my little dove. It's been far too long since I serenaded you by candlelight."

And then, because the universe apparently hates me, he blows me a kiss.

I turn to Father in desperate hope that he hasn't seen any of this, but no, he's still ranting about the time I dared to walk through the dining room in my pyjamas while he had investors over. I was eleven. The trauma, apparently, still haunts him.

"Miss Rosen, my rose," Ravens croons dramatically, producing a medieval lute—for the love of all things holy—from thin air.

And then he starts singing. Badly. Cat-in-a-blender badly.

"Ravens," I snap, clawing at my thighs. "Stop. Please. For the sake of my ears, just stop."

He doesn't. Neither does Richard the Clown, who is now humming louder, like he's competing for the world's worst duet.

"Everyone, just shut up!" I yell, shoving my fingers into my ears.

No one listens. Of course they don't. They never do. Their noise rises—a chorus of humming, crooning, and lecturing, until I'm one frayed nerve ending away from exploding.

And then, as if on cue from the gods of chaos, the lift pings again.

The doors part. And there he is—Carter.

Tall. Handsome. Trouble wrapped in a tailored suit and a smirk that can caress and obliterate in the same breath. He steps in, casual as sin, leans against the wall, and watches. Silent. Unbothered.

Father notices him immediately.

"That man!" he bellows, pointing at Carter like he's discovered the Antichrist in Armani. "That man is bad news!"

Of course, he acknowledges the one person I wish he wouldn't. Carter's smirk deepens—lazy, lethal, and unrepentantly amused.

"Do not trust him!" Father continues, spittle flying. "Stay away from him, Sophie!"

Each accusation makes Carter's expression more wicked, more entertained, like Father's outrage is a personal aphrodisiac.

Then Carter whistles a sharp, playful sound, the kind you'd use to call a dog.

My head jerks down automatically, scanning the floor for an actual animal, because at this point, why not?

But then instinct takes over before logic can protest. I move, fast, my heel catching on the lift's uneven flooring as I lunge straight towards him.

I stumble. He catches me. His arms close around me, solid and warm, holding me like he's been waiting to. I can feel his breath against my temple, calm and steady, even as chaos erupts around us. I turn in his arms, my back pressed against his chest, and watch the spectacle.

Father's head expands with each scream. Ravens hits a note so sharp, a string on his lute snaps. Richard starts juggling to accompany his creepy hums.

In the mirror behind my father's reddening face, I catch Carter's reflection. He smirks, darkly amused, and completely in control, like he's the only sane one in a lift full of lunatics.

Then the lift drops and we plunge with it.

My stomach lurches into my throat, and I cling to him instinctively. His grip tightens, anchoring me against his chest.

The others blur—Father popping like a balloon, Ravens vanishing mid-falsetto, Richard dissolving into confetti.

And then—silence. Serenity.
Carter looks down at me, that dimpled smile tugging at his lips.
"Are you okay?" he murmurs, brushing a loose strand of hair from my cheek.
Before I can answer, the doors slide open again and everything looks normal.
No clowns. No medieval stalkers. No fathers breathing fire. Just Carter, standing there, looking at me like I've lost my mind.
He raises a brow. "Do I have to be concerned?"
I spin towards the mirrored wall, expecting to see him still holding me, arms around me, chest pressed to my back, but there's no one there.
Just me. Arms wrapped tightly around myself.

There's a melody filtering through the fog of my sleep, and it's not my usual shrill, merciless alarm. It's something far more soothing.

Groaning, I roll over, half-asleep, and fumble blindly across my bedside table for my phone. My fingers graze the cord, yank, and suddenly I'm halfway strangled by the charging cable. I pry the cord off my neck and blink at the screen.

Millie. Calling. Nine a.m.

"Oh, bloody hell."

I lurch upright, my heart hammering. "No, no, no…" My voice is a croak of disbelief. I never oversleep. I'm the kind of woman who wakes up to her alarms. My body clock is German-efficient. But here I am—traitor to my own routine. That's what happens, when you bark at your boss in front of the entire department and then feel the need to spent the entire night scoping out the job market, just to realise that every other law firm in this city would be a downgrade of my career.

I jab the green button and hold the phone between my shoulder and ear while tripping into the bathroom. "Yes, hello?"

"Miss Rosen?" Millie's voice trembles like she's calling from the inside of a hostage situation.

"Yes, Millie," I mutter, slapping paste onto my toothbrush, "what can I do for you?"

"Well—" she hesitates, and I can already tell this is bad. Really bad. "Mr Carter was just here asking for you. He seemed… surprised that you weren't in yet."

I nearly choke on my toothbrush. Carter. Every molecule of blood in my body drains to my feet. For a split second, my consciousness zones out. My reflection in the mirror gapes back at me like a deer in headlights—headlights of Carter's very expensive Lexus, to be precise.

Gaslight, Sophie! There's no situation unless you make it one.

I spit, grab a towel, and feign nonchalance. "OK, and?"

"After yesterday, I wasn't sure if you're coming in today. So, I told him something about, uh, commuting times, efficiency, and that you'd decided to prepare for the Farm Valleys meeting from home," Millie rambles, each word tumbling out like she's being interrogated on the witness stand.

God bless her sweet, anxious soul.

"I know you said to clear your schedule but I thought you might still want to take that meeting."

"It's fine, Millie. You thought right. Sorry, I forgot to tell you to keep it." I try to calm her down while I zip up my skirt, wrestle my blouse into submission, and hop on one foot into my heels. "Did Carter say anything else? Was he annoyed?"

Was he waving a termination letter bearing my name?

There's a pause, then a nervous sigh. "No, he just left. He seemed... fine? I think. He's hard to read and kind of terrifying, if I'm honest."

Understatement of the year.

"Right," I mutter, stuffing my laptop into my bag and bolt out of my flat. "Thanks, Millie."

I hail a taxi and tumble in, still buttoning my sleeve. "The French Bistro on Regent Street, please. Fast as you can."

"Ah, Sophie!" Richard calls out, his arms open wide as I draw near his table. "Please, take a seat."

My steps falter for a second. Last night's dream crashes into my consciousness—Richard in a clown costume, humming like a swarm of bloody bees. My determination to set him straight sparks to new heights.

He gestures at the chair beside him, but I opt for the seat across from him, placing my handbag on the table. This conversation won't take long, and I have no intention of lingering any longer than necessary.

"I must admit, I was pleasantly surprised when you reached

out," he says with a smug grin, adjusting his gaudy golden tie. "I was beginning to think you had no interest in my business."

"On the contrary, I care deeply about Farm Valleys, and only Farm Valleys," I reply, flashing a smile as I prop my chin on my hands.

"Well, I didn't get this feeling when you kept cancelling my meeting requests." His brows furrow as he wipes the sweat from his forehead with a napkin.

It's barely twenty degrees in here and yet the man sweats like a pig in a Finnish sauna. The waiter approaches, but I dismiss him with a subtle shake of my head.

"Here's the deal, Richard. I'll overlook that you went to Carter behind my back, and in return, I'll be the best damn lawyer you've ever had," I assert, pouring water into a glass and push it towards him. "Need an investment secured? I'll make it happen. Facing a lawsuit from an employee? I'll take care of it."

His mouth splits into a sleazy grin, no doubt, loving the sound of my proposal. I take a moment to drink in his premature reaction, knowing that by the time I'm finished with him, I'll be the only person grinning at this table.

"But if you dare to request one more meeting just to bring a plus one to one of your pathetic gatherings, consider our agreement null and void," I state firmly, making sure there's no room for misinterpretation. "And I'll be filing charges for defamation and breach of fiduciary duties. Do I make myself clear?"

Richard, now crimson-faced and flustered, nods while nervously scanning the bistro for eavesdroppers.

"Good," I say with a grin and grab my handbag, "I expect your retraction of termination by the end of the day. Make sure Carter knows it was a grave error in judgement on your part and I'm, in fact, the best lawyer you've ever had."

He nods with a dismissive grunt as I round the table and pat his shoulder, "oh, and don't forget about the increase. A twenty-eight percent hike shouldn't be a problem for you, right?"

"You're not the woman I thought you were," he mutters, prompting a chuckle to escape my lips.

"Well, thank goodness for that!" I retort, my grin stretched wide.

I stride out of the bistro with a newfound sense of

empowerment. For the first time, I have proven myself a force to be reckoned with.

Tyrant

Sophie

Thirty minutes and a cab ride later, I'm at the office, and it's thriving on controlled chaos today. Phones bleating, the printer coughing up documents, every conference room filled with clients.

Millie glances up from a fortress of files, and I clock the disaster that's her ginger hair immediately—wild corkscrews springing free. The exhaustion is carved into her face.

"Hey, did I miss anything this morning?" I ask, rifling through today's mail. No HR letterhead.

Thank Christ.

"Nothing new," she says. Then she drops the bomb. "But you've just missed Mr Carter. He came by to check if you'd returned from your meeting."

My stomach plummets straight through the floor.

Shit. Double-shit.

This can't be good. Maybe he wants to personally sack me. Knowing him, he'd probably get off on it; get some sick, twisted satisfaction from watching me squirm before he axes my career. I can practically see him leaning back in that obscenely expensive leather chair, chin resting in his palm, grey eyes glittering with something dark and satisfied as he delivers the killing blow.

"Shall I let him know you're back?" Millie asks, already reaching for her phone.

"No!" The word cracks out too sharp.

Millie's hand freezes mid-air, her eyebrows climbing.

"I mean—" I force a smile. "No need. I have to give him an update on Farm Valleys anyway. I'll catch him later."

Smooth, Sophie. Really convincing.

Thankfully, Millie nods and disappears to wage war with the coffee machine, leaving me to face my inbox.

I power up my laptop and dive into emails with the fervour of someone trying to outrun their own thoughts. Meeting requests fly out rapid-fire. Contracts get reviewed. I answer every inane, mind-numbingly stupid question my clients can conjure.

The hour bleeds away. But then a notification pops up like a death omen.

Mrs Henderson from HR. Meeting request. Fifteen minutes.

I freeze completely. My heart stops, restarts, then takes off at a gallop.

Fifteen minutes? No subject line, no agenda. Just her signature: Head of Employee Relations.

Oh, no. Oh, God, no.

She deals with reports of insubordination. Disciplinary action. The nuclear option before termination.

My brain shifts into full-scale panic, sirens blaring, red lights flashing. At best, I'm being formally warned. At worst, I'm being sacked.

Fantastic odds. Really. I should take those to Vegas.

My chest constricts painfully. My hands move of their own accord, swiping down my thighs in vigorous, desperate strokes that do absolutely nothing to calm me. I can already hear Father's voice echoing in my skull, that particular tone of disappointment he's perfected over the years—*A Rosen does not make mistakes, Sophie. A Rosen excels. You are not excelling, Sophie.*

I down the dregs of my coffee, slam my laptop shut, and attempt to arrange my face into something competent.

The lift ride down feels like descending into corporate hell. I swipe my clammy palms down my thighs again and again until finally, mercifully, cruelly, the doors slide open.

Reality completely short-circuits.

Oh God. I've finally lost it. I'm certifiable.

Carter is standing right there.

They're going to cart me off to some facility where I can live out my days making friendship bracelets and talking to walls.

I dreamed this exact moment last night—same immaculate suit, same hallway, same devastating presence.

He arches one brow, a minute movement that somehow screams volumes. Those sharp eyes drag over me in slow, deliberate assessment. His stance is deceptively relaxed—hands tucked casually in his pockets—while mine are death-gripping my thighs.

Words? Completely gone.

Breathing? Apparently optional.

We move at precisely the same moment, me stepping out, him stepping in, and pass close enough that the air between us seems to crackle.

He doesn't look away. Not once. Neither do I. Those steel eyes stay locked on mine with an intensity that makes my nerve endings ignite.

My nails dig crescents into my thighs, desperate for some grounding proof that I'm actually awake and not trapped in some fever dream conjured by stress and sexual frustration.

Just as the lift doors begin their slow slide shut, his mouth curves into that rare, dimpled smirk.

"Good day, Miss Rosen." His voice is low and dark with an edge of something that makes my stomach drop and my thighs clench involuntarily.

The doors glide shut with finality, severing the connection but doing absolutely nothing to diminish the impact.

I stand there, pulse thundering. I drag in a shaky breath and force myself to turn.

Mrs Henderson's office. Right. My execution awaits.

I take exactly three steps before my foot catches on absolutely nothing and I pitch forward. My arms shoot out in a graceless windmill. I barely manage to get my hands out in time as my knees crack against the polished floor.

For a moment, I just kneel there, stunned.

I don't trip and fall. Ever. I've mastered the art of walking in heels since I was sixteen. Hell, I can run in these things if circumstances demand it. I can navigate cobblestones, grates, slick marble floors, but apparently, I cannot walk down a flat corridor that leads to my professional demise.

Brilliant. Just brilliant.

Heat floods my cheeks as I scramble to my feet. I frantically scan the corridor.

Thank God, no one witnessed my spectacular display. The hallway is mercifully empty. I adjust my skirt, lift my chin, and force my legs to carry me towards Mrs Henderson's office.

"Come in," she calls on the first knock.

"Miss Rosen, thank you for seeing me on such short notice," she greets me, smile professional and devoid of warmth. "Mr Carter was adamant to get things in order immediately."

Of course, he was. The absolute prick.

My jaw clenches. I force my face into professional composure.

"Of course," I manage, "So what's this meeting about exactly?"

"If you can just bear with me one minute." She turns back to her screen.

Take your time, Mrs Henderson. By all means. In the meantime, I'll just sit here and shred my thighs to ribbons while my career circles the drain.

I lower myself into the chair, trying to appear calm when really, I want to bolt.

My hands find their usual landing place, fingernails pressing hard into my thighs.

If Carter requested HR to speak to me, it can only mean one thing—he reported me for insubordination. I can't believe he has the sheer audacity after everything he's done and said over the past couple of days. The hypocrisy is staggering.

I should have reported him. Marched straight down here after he suggested spanking me. But I didn't.

Oh, no. I nodded like an obedient fool and leaned over his desk to have my dignity shredded by his ruler.

And yesterday? Same spectacle, because apparently, I'm too stubborn to learn my lesson. I had to handle it myself. Had to prove I could match him blow for blow.

Now it's too late. HR wouldn't believe me. They'd mark it down as retaliatory allegations. Classic corporate chess. He's played it perfectly, and I've walked straight into checkmate.

Mrs Henderson finally breaks the silence. "Right, sorry to keep you waiting. We're in the midst of finding interns."

She rummages through paperwork until she unearths a notepad and pen.

"So, in light of recent events, Mr Carter thought it best to let us know about the circumstances between you two."

There it is. I knew it. He did report me. The bastard actually did it.

White-hot anger flares in my chest.

"I understand," I interrupt, desperate to prove to her that I'm a rational woman. "But please let me explain how this all came about. There's context—"

"I don't need to know the details, Miss Rosen," she cuts me off. "All I need to know is whether you acted on your own accord, or if you feel that Mr Carter has in any way motivated you."

Motivated me?

His handsome, punchable face is reason enough. That smirk

alone should be classified as provocation. But none of his words or actions justifies my outburst.

"Surely his challenging character had something to do with it," I admit hesitantly. "But in the end, I had my reasons."

Her face remains completely impassive. A blank slate. She could be contemplating my termination or her shopping list, and I'd have no idea which.

"Do you think this could affect your work relationship with Mr Carter in the future?" She continues her questioning, her pen scratching across the notepad in undecipherable hieroglyphs that I'm certain spell out my professional demise.

"Absolutely not! I'm very professional in my endeavours. Please note that the situation between Mr Carter and myself is very unusual. An anomaly, really. And I'm doing my utmost not to have this affect the business."

She sighs.

My stomach sinks. She's going to write me up or fire me. I can see it in the way her pen moves, in the set of her shoulders.

Father can never know.

"Alright, that's all I needed to know," she says, setting down her pen. "I'll fill out the form and email it to you both for signing."

Wait. Just a form? I'm safe!

"There's a form to fill out?" I straighten up in my seat.

"Of course," she says, glancing at me over her thick-rimmed red glasses with something that might be surprise at my ignorance. "We need to record these things so we can't be held liable for any mishaps in the future. And given the positions you both hold within the firm, we must do our due diligence."

Both. She keeps saying both.

The realisation hits me like a freight train. This isn't just about me. Whatever form she's filling out involves him too.

"I understand," I manage. "Are there going to be any repercussions? Disciplinary action?"

Mrs Henderson looks up from her notes, brows furrowing. "No, Miss Rosen. It will simply be an entry in your employee file. Standard documentation."

Standard documentation. AKA—a black mark. A permanent record of my inability to keep my composure.

She dismisses me by returning to her laptop. I drag my feet out of her office, defeat weighing me down.

The office door clicks shut behind me.

My heels tap against the floor; every step heavier than it should be. My pulse races from the suffocating ten minutes I've just endured. Ten minutes of veiled corporate smiles and HR jargon that boil down to one humiliating truth: Sophie Rosen, you've been slapped with a neat little write-up for daring to grow a backbone in front of Medard bloody Carter.

Well, congratulations to me. Career highlight of the year.

The anger bubbles up now, hot and fierce, replacing the fear. I'm done bending to his outrageous rules. Done playing whatever twisted game he thinks we're engaged in.

I inhale sharply, waiting for the familiar sting in my thighs to ground me, and march towards the lift.

The mirrored doors part, and I step inside.

Except I'm not alone. Ben.

Shit. Of course.

His tie is slightly loosened. His familiar mop of short brown curls bounces as he glances up from his phone, startled.

"Soph? Leaving HR?" His voice is half question, half accusation.

I paste on a breezy smile, pressing the button for our floor.

"Fancy seeing you here," I say, deliberately ignoring his question while gesturing to the purple silk tie hanging around his neck. "Very luxe. Is it a rental or did you adopt it from a royal?"

He snorts. "Nice deflection. But I asked first. What the hell were you doing in HR?"

"Returning a stapler."

Ben stares at me. "A stapler."

"Yes. Silver. Pointy. Holds paper together."

He narrows his eyes, unconvinced. "You don't own a stapler?"

"Mine ran away."

"Staplers don't run away, Soph."

"Clearly, you've never met mine. It has commitment issues."

The corner of his mouth twitches, but he isn't letting this go. His gaze sweeps over me, assessing. He's waiting for me to crack.

"So," I say brightly, "tell me, how did Carter roast you for losing the Bradford account?"

That gets him. His expression shifts, frustration flickering. He sighs heavily. "You haven't heard?"

"No, I've been busy. Carter's been drowning me in work."

"Lucky you," he counters. "He stripped me of all acquisitions and handed them to Amina."

I wince, genuine sympathy blooming. "Ouch. That's brutal."

"Ouch is an understatement," he says, jaw tight. "Imagine watching every negotiation being funnelled straight into the arms of someone who already thinks she's God's gift to corporate law."

"Amina does have that effect," I agree.

"She's unbearable," Ben mutters darkly. "I swear she polishes her halo with client tears every morning before breakfast."

He's not wrong. Amina has perfected the art of being brilliant while completely intolerable.

"Anyway," he continues, his voice dropping, "what about you? You stood up to Carter yesterday. In front of the entire department. And now you're coming out of HR looking like you've been ordered to participate in mandatory team-building exercises."

I bristle, forcing a hollow laugh. "I love those."

I don't. There's nothing worse than having to argue with the incompetence of your peers while pretending collaboration is anything other than painful.

"No, you don't. You complained for three weeks after the last one." His eyes bore into mine. "What were you doing in HR, Soph?"

The lift glides to our floor. The doors slide open, but I don't move. Neither does he.

"Ben, drop it," I say firmly, stepping out into the corridor.

He follows. Persistent as a rash. "I can't drop it. Not when it's obvious something's going on. What did HR say to you?"

"Nothing," I hiss at him over my shoulder, not slowing my pace.

"Liar," he hisses back. "Are they writing you up?"

I stop dead and spin to face him, but my silence is answer enough.

His eyes widen, horror and outrage flashing across his features. "Jesus Christ, Soph," he breathes. "For what? Insubordination?"

"Keep your voice down," I hiss urgently.

The last thing I need is for this conversation to turn into another piece of juicy office gossip. It's bad enough that he knows. Bad enough, that I was even so stupid to blow up in front of my peers. Bad enough that it's now documented in official company records.

He steps closer, lowering his voice. "Tell me I'm wrong. Tell me you didn't just get written up because Carter's ego couldn't handle you calling him out."

My lips press into a thin, hard line. I don't confirm. I don't deny.

His jaw tightens. "Unbelievable! He's such a bastard."

"You're not wrong," I murmur, a bitter laugh escaping.

He studies me for a long moment, then his expression shifts. Concern etches itself across his features.

"Soph," he says slowly, voice dangerously gentle, "what you said to him yesterday—is there something going on between you and Carter?"

My world tilts.

I force a scoff. "What?"

"You heard me. And I don't mean work-related. I mean personal. Voluntary or not."

The implication makes my stomach twist violently. He's too close to the truth.

I laugh, too loudly, too fake. "That's absurd. You're being ridiculous."

"Am I?" he presses. "Because he treats you differently, Soph. Everyone can see it. And you let him. You let him get under your skin. With him, it's charged. There's tension when you two are in the same room."

Charged. Tension.

The words slice through me. Too accurate, too close to every truth I've been desperately trying to bury.

I force my chin up. "You're imagining things. Seeing patterns where there aren't any."

"I don't think I am."

"Well, maybe you should spend less time worrying about me and more time fixing the Bradford account," I retort sharply, striding away.

"Soph," he calls after me. "I'm not blind. And I'm not implying that you—"

"Stop," I snap, whirling around. "Just stop. There's nothing between Carter and me. Nothing voluntary. Nothing involuntary. Nothing at all. Got it?"

His eyes search mine, desperate for honesty. I give him nothing. Blank slate.

Finally, he exhales heavily, shaking his head. "Fine. Have it your way. But if he hurts you. If he's done something—"

"Don't!" I cut him off. "There's nothing going on. Nothing to worry about."

The tremor in my voice betrays me.

He doesn't argue. He doesn't push further. But the look he gives me says everything words can't. He doesn't believe me.

And worse, I don't believe me either.

Boyfriend

Medard

Just two hours ago, Sophie burst into my office for our Windpower meeting like a storm given human form—all determination, frustration, and barely contained fury. Instead of sulking on the comfy leather sofa like I half-expected, she claimed my desk like it was a hard-line boundary in hostile territory. It's as if she requires the cold, unyielding surface to hold herself apart from me, to maintain an impenetrable wall between us. Physical distance as psychological warfare.

Clever woman.

I'm not surprised she's pissed off. In fact, I expected her to come charging in here the minute her meeting with HR wrapped up, guns blazing and ready to eviscerate me with that sharp tongue. But instead, she locked herself away in her office like a woman possessed and worked through more than half her open tasks with single-minded determination, until she had no choice but to come to my office for our scheduled meeting.

I suppose she's still trying to come to terms with the new arrangement. The shift in our dynamic. That's fine by me. I'm not entirely unreasonable. I had a full day to sit with the idea, to let it marinate and settle into something I could accept. So, it's only fair I give her the same courtesy. The same space to process.

I just wish she wouldn't mull it over in complete, oppressive silence that feels like it's suffocating the air between us.

"I'd offer you a glass of wine," I say, unable to resist the smirk teasing the corners of my mouth as I hand her a glass of sparkling water, "but I like to spare my housekeeper a trip to the dry cleaners."

To my surprise, she takes it. Her fingers brush against mine in that brief exchange, and I can't help noticing that electric spark dancing between us. That current that seems to exist only when we touch, when our worlds collide.

Christ, even the smallest contact affects me.

"You don't have to worry about me," she finally speaks as I settle back down behind my desk, trying to appear relaxed when I'm anything but. "Message received loud and clear—don't mess with the boss." She huffs, fatigue clinging to her voice like an unwelcome shawl, weighing down the sharp edges I've come to expect.

She's trying desperately to keep her anger hidden, buried beneath layers of professionalism, but it slowly simmers to the surface anyway. Boils over in subtle ways—the set of her jaw, the tension in her shoulders, the way her fingers grip that glass just a fraction too tightly. She's really pissed off by my decisive handling of the situation, by the way I've manoeuvred us both onto this new playing field.

But it was her own request, wasn't it?

That I act according to my station, according to the rules she kept throwing in my face. And a boss is supposed to make tough calls, even when those decisions aren't agreeable. Even when they make beautiful, infuriating women glare at you with eyes that could set you on fire.

I ignore her attitude, or at least pretend to, determined to push forward as I sift through the paperwork stacked high on my desk. I methodically finalise my part of our strategy for the luncheon, running through talking points and client concerns with practised efficiency.

The hour stretches on, filled with the ambient sounds of typing and shuffling papers, a testament to our mutual concentration and stubborn refusal to acknowledge the elephant taking up residence in the room. Her fingers fly across the keyboard with impressive speed, occasionally pausing to adjust her hair, pulling it into an even tighter bun, and unconsciously showcasing that structured, controlled nature that defines her.

She never lets it down. Literally.

Everything about Sophie Rosen is meticulously arranged and carefully curated—the sleek up-dos that hug her face and expose the elegant column of her neck, her natural-looking manicure that probably costs more than most people's weekly food shop, her subtly painted pink lips that look effortlessly perfect. All of it complemented by dainty golden jewellery that catches the light when she moves.

I wonder how she looks when she sheds this polished exterior. When she's exposed and blissfully bare in the comfort of her home, with no one watching, no armour required. Does she let her hair down then? Does she wear old t-shirts and no makeup? Does she look soft and vulnerable, or does she maintain that rigid control even in solitude?

Would she let me see that version of her? Or would she keep those walls up even in intimacy, guarding herself against me the way she guards herself against the world?

I want to be the one she lets in. The only one.

The mental image is dangerously distracting.

"I noticed you've managed to get Farm Valleys back," I clear my throat, breaking the silence that's hung heavy between us for far too long. The tension is starting to feel oppressive.

"Yes, and before you complain that I've wasted my time," she snaps without missing a beat, her eyes still glued to the screen like she can't bear to look at me, "I got Richard to agree to a twenty-eight percent increase."

Impressive. Genuinely impressive.

Twenty-eight percent. Not thirty. Not twenty-five. She calculated exactly what she's worth. What she could get elsewhere. And made him pay it.

She's fucking brilliant.

I lean forward deliberately and push against her laptop until its screen turns black, cutting off her escape route. Her sharp gaze snaps to mine immediately, anger flashing in those blue eyes like lightning in a storm.

"You've done well," I say evenly, holding her stare. "And you should be proud of yourself."

There's a slight softening in her features, barely perceptible, but I've learnt to read her micro-expressions like a language only we speak. The icy demeanour warms just a fraction, thaws at the edges, but she stays frustratingly quiet.

The silence grates against my nerves.

"We should order dinner," I suggest.

I usually don't give a damn if someone is angry with me. I'm not here to please people or win popularity contests. But with Sophie, it's different. Irritatingly different. I can't stand that she won't speak to me beyond these clipped, professional exchanges. That she's thinking ill of me, painting me as some kind of villain in whatever narrative is running through that sharp mind of hers.

I hate it.

"No, thank you. I have no appetite." She shoots down my offer with surgical precision, retreating immediately behind the fortress of papers that now separates us like a barricade.

Her refusal is telling. Revealing.

"You're angry with me," I state the obvious, eyes narrowing slightly as the tension in the air is now almost suffocating.

Without lifting her gaze, she lets out a sigh heavy with meaning. "Why would I be angry? I asked you to act according to your station, and you did just that. You followed my instructions to the letter."

"And yet you're still upset about the outcome," I note, a frown creeping onto my face as I catch the way she chuckles at my words.

"Oh no, I love it. Who wouldn't?" Her question is laced with sarcasm, absolutely dripping with it.

Now she's actively provoking me. Pushing buttons, she knows will get a reaction. I can't stand it any longer.

I rise from my chair and approach her with purposeful strides, gathering the papers from her hands and dumping them haphazardly on the desk behind me. She opens her mouth to protest, but I cut her off.

"Sophie, I have no patience for your tantrum." I lean against the desk, arms crossed, my gaze unwavering. "You better tell me what's really bothering you. Now."

To my surprise, she leaps from her chair and gathers her belongings with frantic, jerky movements. Coat, bag, phone—she's preparing for a tactical retreat.

"Keep your patronising bile to yourself," she spits out, venom in every word. "If you're ready to talk about Windpower like actual professionals, you know where to find me."

No fucking chance, lioness.

In a swift motion fuelled by instinct and frustration, I grab her wrist and pull her against my chest. I refuse to tolerate her disobedience any longer. With the form submitted to HR, we're on the path to making this official. Once she signs, we'll be on solid ground. Until then, I just need to convince her this is right.

"What are you—" she gasps as she twists in my grip, trying to break free.

I pull at her wrist again, my other hand finding her waist as I yank her firmly into my arms, feeling the heat of her body against mine.

"Carter!" she gasps again, and there's something in her voice.

It's half arousal, half... shock?

Her handbag and coat tumble to the floor. The scent of her perfume engulfs me like a tidal wave of bluebells and something uniquely her that drowns out every rational thought I might have had. My body sways closer, drawn by this insatiable need for her that I've stopped trying to deny.

"Let go of me!" she protests, her voice weak but resolute as she pulls against my hold.

I lean down, my mouth brushing the shell of her ear and whisper, "Watch your attitude, lioness, or you might chip a claw."

Anger flares in her eyes when there should be arousal.

Something doesn't add up here. Something's wrong beyond the obvious.

Despite the all-consuming need to hold her close to my chest, to feel her heart hammering against my skin, I do release her.

She stumbles backwards, catching herself on the backrest of the sofa, breathing hard.

"I don't want to fight," I say, forcing my voice to remain calm. "So, tell me what's actually bothering you."

So, we can finally get to the nicer part of this new arrangement. The part where we stop pretending.

"Are you serious?" Her head rears back, disbelief flashing across her features like neon. "You attacked me in my office, and just because I had the balls to call you out on it, you went straight to HR like a tattletale!"

Wait. What?

Something really doesn't add up here. Why would she still be upset about my cornering her in her office? She confirmed my report to HR. Mrs Henderson said she acknowledged everything.

"What do you think I reported to HR?" I ask carefully, a sinking feeling starting in my gut.

"Insubordination, of course," she mutters, like it's the most obvious thing in the world.

What the fuck?

What did they tell her?

Are there only complete imbeciles working at this firm?

"Sophie," I huff, my hand finding the bridge of my nose as I try to process this spectacular miscommunication. "I didn't report insubordination. I thought I made myself abundantly clear yesterday."

I pick up her coat and handbag from the floor, and carefully place them on the chair as confusion blooms across her beautiful face like ink in water.

"Then what was the meeting with HR about?" Her voice is smaller now, uncertain.

I lean back against the desk and spin my laptop around, showing her the subject line of my email request to HR. She approaches the screen tentatively, as though the illuminated words hold her fate in their digital glow.

And in a way, they do.

As recognition dawns on her, she stumbles back on a resounding gasp that echoes through the office.

"A consensual relationship agreement?" Her voice cuts through the air, sharp and unyielding. "You're not my boyfriend. We're not a couple. This is insane!"

Her thighs hit the back of the sofa. She struggles to steady herself as the weight of that email crashes down around us, heavy and relentless like falling debris.

"After I was honest with you about my intentions," I say, crossing my arms to fight the overwhelming urge to reach for her again, "I wanted to give you time to accept these feelings between us. To process what this is."

I pause, watching her face.

"But then you bared your claws for all to see, demanding the right to undermine my superior position. You wanted me to act like your boss? Fine. I'm acting like your boss."

"You... you gave me no choice!" she stammers, her head shaking in disbelief, hair starting to escape that perfect bun. "You overstepped the line! You cornered me!"

"I acknowledged that the line is bullshit," I say, forcing the words out with measured calmness I don't entirely feel. "And you agreed by barking in my face in front of the entire department. So now I'm levelling the playing field. You want to yell at me? Please, go ahead. But you'll be doing it as my girlfriend, not my subordinate."

Her eyes flash with defiance, her finger pointing at the laptop like she's trying to stab it through sheer force of will.

"Are you listening to yourself? You're completely deranged if you think I'll sign this."

Not deranged, lioness. Just finally honest with myself.

I take a measured step towards her, hands tucked safely in my suit pants, partly to appear non-threatening, partly because I simply don't trust myself around her anymore. Not when every instinct is screaming at me to claim her in every way possible.

"Would it really be so absurd for us to be together?" I ask, my voice low and vulnerable, slipping out like a confession I didn't mean to make.

The words hang in the space between us, painfully impossible to ignore. I know she feels it too, this attraction between us, this pull that defies logic and professional boundaries. We're drawn to each other despite every rational thought demanding the opposite.

"You—" she begins, then falters, the words dying on those perfect lips.

Her gaze drifts over my face, searching, studying, as though she sees the fleeting vulnerability that flickers in my eyes before I can mask it. I puff out my chest instinctively, trying to reclaim my composure, to hide the uncertainty threatening to spill over and expose me completely.

"You're my boss," she finally says, voice steady but edged with something unspoken. Fear, maybe. Or hope.

"That's not what I asked," I reply, stepping closer, feeling the weight of this moment pressing down on us.

Her eyes flicker with intrigue, with longing, with the unspoken question of what this could be if we let it. She can fool herself all she wants, but I know the truth. Despite my reckless behaviour, she's silently begging me to take her, to feed that hunger buried beneath her defiance and professionalism.

I close the remaining distance between us, my gaze locking onto hers with an intensity that makes the air crackle.

"I know you liked when I—"

"But that's all that matters," she cuts me off sharply. "That, and that you stay behind the ethical line."

There it is. The classic Sophie Rosen response—stubborn, defiant, and wilfully ignorant towards her true feelings.

My voice drops to a whisper as I lean close to her ear, close enough that I can feel the heat radiating off her skin. "Is that really what you want?"

Her hands subtly rub her thighs, fingers brushing over the fabric of her skirt in that unconscious gesture I've come to recognise. The sight of her being flustered around me is so endearing, I have to fight the urge to grin like an idiot.

"I saw how you looked at me in our first Windpower meeting," I continue softly, my breath warm against her ear. "How you blushed and got nervous. Tell me, did you imagine us fucking on all that paperwork spread across the coffee table? Because I did. Multiple times."

Her breath stutters, catching in her throat. Her nails dig into her thighs, desperate for grounding. Her body tenses as if physically fighting the flood of arousal I'm deliberately stirring in her.

"I noticed how you leaned into me when I held you by your delicate neck," I whisper, voice thick with the memory. "I was desperate to capture that first big breath when you gasped, to taste that moment when I finally released my hold on you."

"Stop it," she pleads, her voice barely audible, almost lost beneath the hum of the air conditioning. But I hear her. And I know she's fighting herself more than she's fighting me.

"Tell me I'm wrong," I challenge her softly, giving her an out if she really wants it. "Tell me you don't feel this pull between us. This gravity."

I want her to look at me, really look at me, but her gaze remains stubbornly fixed on something behind my shoulder. I want to grab her chin, force her to face me when she lies, or finally admits what I already know is true. But I hold back, knowing I can't rush her. Can't force this.

Instead, I ball my fists in my pockets and wait. Patience has never been my strong suit, but for her, I'll try.

"I don't," she finally whispers, her words small but her eyes betraying her completely.

There's a hurricane swirling within those blue irises, a mix of uncertainty and longing and fear. She doesn't know how to escape it. Doesn't know which direction safety lies anymore.

"Kiss me," I whisper, and it's almost a plea, though my voice leaves no room for confusion about what I'm asking.

Surprise flickers across her face, widening her eyes. But she doesn't pull away. Doesn't run. She studies me instead, as if weighing the moment, calculating the cost. The hum of the air conditioning and our breathing become the only melody—anticipation, hope, doubt, all mixing together, and dragging each second that she remains perfectly still.

"Sophie," I whisper her name like a prayer just before our lips meet.

Her kiss is soft and sweet, like a gentle caress that immediately dispels every ounce of tension in my body. I lean into her, my hands finding her waist, the nape of her neck. She feels divine melted into me. I coax my tongue into her mouth, tasting her, wanting more. She responds with a soft whimper that goes straight to my cock, her hand rising to my chest, her fingers slipping between the buttons of my shirt and grazing my bare skin.

Fuck. Nothing else has ever felt this good.

I want more. I need more of her.

With our lips fused together, I lift her onto the backrest of the sofa. My beautiful, perfect lioness opens her legs instinctively to invite me in, and the sight nearly undoes me. She pulls me closer with her legs, wrapping around my waist, and Christ, the feel of her wanting me—actively wanting me—is intoxicating beyond measure.

My hand slips beneath her skirt, massaging her thigh gently, eliciting quiet moans that challenge every ounce of restraint I possess not to strip her of every piece of fabric that separates us.

Everything about her feels impossibly perfect. From her plump lips, her creamy thighs that are softer than I imagined, her warm centre pressed against my crotch, to her perfume that gets me rock-hard every goddamn time I'm near her.

I kiss her neck, feeling her pulse race frantically beneath my lips, and to my surprise, it calms the usual urge to chase a quick release.

I don't want fast and meaningless. I want to lose myself in Sophie. I want to drown myself in her bright blue eyes, feel her arms wrapped around me, while I sink into her until there's not an inch of space between us anymore. Until I don't know where I end and she begins.

"You see, lioness," I whisper between kisses trailing down her collarbone, "you belong to me."

The words are out before I can stop them. A confession. A claim. A truth I've been holding back.

She gasps, but then a sudden jarring impact hits my shoulders, her hands shoving hard. I stumble back, dazed and confused, my brain struggling to catch up.

She stands abruptly, her face marred with incredulity and something darker.

"You're the worst!" she snaps, her voice trembling as she adjusts her skirt with shaking hands. "You condemn Harman for influence peddling, yet you're as unethical as they come. You're a hypocrite!"

The accusation stings more than I expect.

"Call me unethical for taking what I want," I say, voice steady even though inside I'm battling complete chaos, trying to understand what just happened. "But don't forget, lioness, you want me too. You just kissed me. You moaned for me."

Why is she pushing me away? What did I do wrong?

Her eyes flash with that infuriating, beautiful defiance that makes me want to kiss her and throttle her in equal measure.

"Never!" she seethes, yanking her coat and bag off the chair and bolting out of the office like it's on fire.

My gaze remains fixed on the open doorway, wondering if she might storm back in here. Half-hoping she will. But the minutes slip by with excruciating slowness, leaving me alone with my reeling thoughts.

I take a seat on the sofa, pinching the bridge of my nose in an effort to slow the chaos in my head.

"You belong to me." The words echo in my head. Why did that set her off? She was kissing me. She wanted it. Wanted me.

She's fighting the idea of us more fiercely than I expected. More desperately.

Her perfume invades my senses, still clinging to the air, to my clothes, to my skin. She still lingers on my lips. Warmth spreads through my body, travelling south until I'm half-hard again just from the memory.

She kissed me. My defiant lioness cracked and kissed me. A smile tugs at my lips despite everything.

Soon, there will be so many cracks in her defences that she'll fall apart right underneath me. And then she'll be mine completely.

If she doesn't break me first.

Satan

Sophie

I kissed Carter.

The thought loops through my head like a broken record that won't quit, scratching the same groove over and over until I'm certain it's carved permanently into my consciousness. It's been there since the second I bolted out of his office last night, pounding behind every heartbeat, whispering into every quiet breath, haunting every moment of attempted normalcy.

Even the mindless drone of late-night TV couldn't drown it out. Not the news. Not the quiz show I half remember watching. Not even the true crime documentary that usually holds my attention like a vice.

And certainly not when my hand slid between my thighs in the darkness of my bedroom, chasing the ghost of his lips like I could somehow kiss him again through memory alone. Like I could recreate that feeling—that devastating, world-tilting feeling—through sheer force of will and imagination.

And when release hit, crashing over me in waves that left me gasping his name into my pillow, the guilt came right on its heels. Swift and merciless.

His name. I said his name. Not some fantasy, not a faceless lover, but Carter. Medard Carter. My boss. The man I'm supposed to resist.

I'm so fucked.

I clawed at my thighs until they were red-raw, until the sting was enough to ground me back in reality, until the physical pain could eclipse the emotional chaos.

It's getting worse. I know it's getting worse. The scratches last longer now, hurt more, take more to satisfy. But I can't stop. Won't stop. It's the only thing that feels like control.

I broke my own promise. Shattered it completely.

I let those piercing greys lure me into the depth of professional damnation, where I danced with the devil himself.

But it felt good. He felt so good. His mouth moved over mine with a tenderness that shouldn't have belonged to him, confident but not arrogant, commanding but caring. He touched me like I was something he'd been waiting his entire life to find.

Until he ruined it. "You belong to me." Like I'm property. Like I'm something to be claimed rather than chosen. That's when I knew I had to run.

But I kissed him anyway.

Heat pulses through me again, a wave that starts in my chest and dives straight between my legs. My thighs press together automatically, as if I can trap the arousal there before it gives me away.

This cannot happen again.

Kissing Carter is wrong, ethically wrong. It's so wrong, it would be my professional suicide.

I swipe my palms down my thighs to scrub away the need, the want, the everything.

Focus, Sophie. Work. Breathe. Gaslight until he forgets.

That's the plan. If Carter brings it up, I'll blink in confusion, smile politely, and gaslight the hell out of him. Nothing happened last night. There was no kiss. No hands. No whispered promises. No line crossed that could ruin me. I'll bury it beneath deadlines and caffeine.

The chaos in my inbox has become my sanctuary, and I cling to it like it's my personal salvation. I'm half through finalising another contract, when Ben's voice slices through the silence and I jerk, blinking up at him.

"Earth to Sophie!"

How long has he been standing there?

He grins, waving a to-go cup in front of me. "You want it or not?"

"Want what?" I ask blankly.

"The pumpkin spice latte I got you. Extra caffeine, no poison disguised as sugar." He sets it on my desk, rotating it so I can see the name scribbled on the side. Bombshell.

I snort. "Subtle."

He shrugs, flopping into the chair opposite me. "Thought you could use a pick-me-up. After the slap on the wrist, I mean."

I shush him, eyeing the slightly open office door. "Keep your voice down. And it wasn't a warning, just... a misunderstanding."

A monumental misunderstanding.

I can't believe Carter went to Mrs Henderson and told her we're a couple. The sheer arrogance. And I don't even want to think about my own meeting with Mrs Henderson. God, I tried to explain myself. No wonder she looked at me like I had grown two heads. Who wants to hear about stolen kisses between meetings, or worse, inappropriate shenanigans in the supply closet? The fantasy shoots straight to my cheeks but I snuff it out before Ben can see me squirming in my seat.

His brow arches, full of nosey curiosity. "Oh really? What kind of misunderstanding?"

"The kind I don't have time to explain," I shoot back quickly, squeezing my thighs for good measure.

The last thing I need is to spin some tale that doesn't involve the CRA that HR kindly sent me this morning.

I read it. Of course I read it. Every clause, every implication. "Consensual Relationship Agreement between Medard Carter, Managing Director, and Sophie Rosen, Junior Partner." Like we're a done deal. Like my signature is a formality.

Like I've already agreed to be his.

They can wait for hell to freeze over, and for Carter to be metaphorically locked in it, before I sign the damn thing.

He studies me for a moment, that annoyingly perceptive glint in his eyes. But then he sighs and leans back. "Lunch later?"

"Sure," I say, grateful for the subject change. "One o'clock. Lobby."

"It's a date," he says with a smile, "and don't you dare bail on me. It's been too long."

"Pinky promise."

He hooks his little finger around mine, then leaves, leaving me to dive back into the contract I was working on when my laptop pings with a new message.

> Medard Carter: We need to talk.

Great. No greeting. No context. Just four words that might as well say *You can't hide from me.*

I stare at the message as though it might self-destruct. Then, summoning what's left of my professional dignity, I type.

> Sophie Rosen: Of course, Mr Carter. I'll check my calendar and let you know when I'm available.

Professional. Civil, and thoroughly gaslighted. Except my heart's hammering like I've just committed a felony.

I take a steadying breath. I can do this. I can face a day of work and pretend last night didn't happen, that I didn't... No. Not going there. That entire episode is now archived under 'Classified Work blunders– Do Not Revisit.'

The morning drags by in slow motion. No follow-up from Carter, thank God. Just endless paperwork and the occasional caffeine refill from Millie. For a couple of blessed hours, I almost convince myself I imagined him, imagined the whole damn thing.
Then, another message pings.

> Medard Carter: Miss Rosen, your calendar appears fuller than this morning. I assume you'll still find five minutes of your precious time for me?

Oh, for crying out loud!

> Sophie Rosen: My apologies. I'm sure I'll be able to squeeze you in sometime next week.

> Medard Carter: Today.

I type, delete, retype, and delete again. No, I'm not answering. This conversation is pointless.
If he wanted to, he could order me into his office immediately, and I'd have no valid grounds to deny him. Unless I'd want to chance my luck at getting an actual warning for insubordination.
My focus shifts back to work, the safe cocoon of routine. Even when Father calls twice, I mute my phone. It works, for a while. Until a new message pops up.

> Medard Carter: Lioness, my patience is wearing thin.

Oh my god.
He just wrote this hideous pet name into the company messenger.
I ball my fists to calm the panic raising inside me, but there's none. To my dismay, I feel my cheeks heat like I'm some lovesick fool who actually likes the stupid endearment. I push back from my desk, as though his message is radioactive, as though I need to physically distance myself from his words.
The three little dots appear, indicating he's typing again. I tentatively lean forward, my hands gripping the edge of the seat.

> Medard Carter: I'm heading to your office now.

I nearly fall off my chair as I lunge for the keyboard, fingers flying, typing the first words that come to mind.

> Sophie Rosen: Catch me if you can

> Medard Carter: ?

Catch me if you can? How old am I? Twelve?

> Sophie Rosen: Like I said, I'm very busy today. But if you can catch me in between appointments, you'll have my attention.

There. Dignity restored.
I know how to make myself busy. He won't get a chance to get a word in.

> Medard Carter: Sounds enticing, but what's to stop me from ordering you into my office, or simply coming to yours?

Of course, he plays the boss-card, but I can still beat him with his own weapons. I square my shoulders, and with a wicked grin, I reply.

> Sophie Rosen: A level playing field.

The phrase tastes like victory in my mouth. He wanted to level the playing field by making me his girlfriend. Fine. I'll level it by making him chase me.
Two can play power games.
I wait with bated breath for his response. The three little dots appear and disappear a few times, but then he finally responds.

> Medard Carter: Game on.

Perfect.
Now I just have to stay in my office for the rest of the day, and sneak to lunch and back. I can do that. It's only a short walk to the lifts.
The plan works for all of thirty minutes until my bladder, the traitor, decides it can't hold more than two cups of coffee. I ignore the urge, squeeze my legs, bounce my knees. I even consider peeing into my Ficus. I last five more minutes before I surrender

and dart into the corridor.

It's quiet. Safe. Millie's at her desk, typing like a saint. I make it halfway to the restrooms when I see him at the far end of the corridor—suit perfect, phone in hand, eyes locked on me like a hawk spotting prey. The corners of his mouth curve into something lethal.

Oh, no. Not today, Satan.

I speed-walk, fast, but not enough to draw attention. He mirrors me, long strides closing the gap with terrifying grace. The air between us crackles. Every step feels like a countdown.

I dart into the women's restroom, heart pounding, seconds before the door swings open behind me.

He wouldn't dare, would he?

"Uh, Mr Carter?" Ben's voice floats from outside. "That's the women's restroom."

Bless you, Ben, my accidental knight.

"My mistake," Carter replies smoothly before the door clicks shut again.

I sag against the tiled wall, laughing quietly into my palms. I can't believe this is my life now. Playing tag with my boss. Father would be mortified if he'd knew I'm spending my working hours sneaking down hallways and sprinting into restrooms.

The thought kills my amusement in an instant.

I shouldn't fool around like this. I should focus on my work and keep Carter well and truly on a professional distance.

But I don't want to. That's the problem. I don't want professional distance. I want his hands on me. I want to be caught.

I want exactly what I shouldn't have.

I push off the wall and use the bathroom, determined to get back behind my desk. I peek out into the corridor, and to my delight, the coast is clear. I hurry back towards my office. Millie is still engrossed in something on her screen. I fire up my laptop again. No new message from Carter. I sigh in relief, and ignore the hollow feeling in my chest that feels dangerously close to disappointment.

I wanted him to chase me. I wanted to run. I wanted the thrill of being caught.

What's wrong with me?

Ten to one p.m.- Show-time.

I put on my coat, and stash my phone and purse into its pockets. This way, I won't struggle with the strap of my bag if I have to run from Carter again. Millie is away from her desk on her own lunch break. Stealing myself as discreetly as possible, I walk towards the lifts. The corridor is empty, bar the cleaning lady who's heading for the restrooms. She gives me a polite nod, but then her attention snags on something behind me. A low whistle rings out, stopping me cold. Carter stands outside my office, that lethal grin curving his mouth.

"Damn it," I whisper, and when he starts moving towards me, I don't think for another second. I power-walk as fast as I can towards the lifts. I'd bolt if I could, but like Carter, I can't look like a crazy person running through a law firm like it's the Olympics.

A glance over my shoulder confirms he's still on my heels, and he's closing in. My heart's racing, adrenaline flooding my veins.

This is insane and immature. This is... completely thrilling.

The lift doors are still closed. Of course, they are.

I jab the button. Nothing. The display above shows the car stuck three floors down. There's no time. I veer right and shove through the stairwell door. The heavy metal slams behind me, echoing through the concrete space. My heels are traitorous, slowing me down. I yank them off mid-run, clutching them to my chest, and start flying down the stairs. I'm adamant to outrun my boss, but not to break my neck in the process.

The sound of the door above banging open tells me he's followed. His footsteps are steady at first, controlled and measured. Then faster. Closer.

I hit the landing between the sixth and fifth floors and grab the railing to spin myself down the next flight. My lungs are on fire, but I can't stop grinning.

God help me, part of me loves this.

The chase. The thrill.

Another floor down, and he's gaining. His footsteps echo louder and faster. I risk a glance over my shoulder. He's right there, his suit still impeccable, but his hair slightly dishevelled. He's got that predatory glint in his eyes that is enough to buckle my knees.

I push harder.

One more landing. Then another. The lobby is close, and Ben, my safety net.

And then it happens.

His chest collides with my back with enough force to knock the breath from my lungs. My heels clatter to the ground while his arm snakes around my waist, pulling me against him in one swift, effortless motion. His other hand shoots out to brace us against the wall, caging me in.

The sound that leaves me is half gasp, half squeal, my heart hammering so loud it could echo through the stairwell.

"Got you," he pants, his breath hot against my ear.

The words vibrate through me, triumphant and deliciously dangerous. His chest rises and falls against my back, the rhythm syncing with mine until I can't tell which heartbeat belongs to whom.

It shouldn't feel this exhilarating, but by God, ever since he ordered me into that corner, I've been wondering what it feels like to have Carter pressed against my back. I never thought I'd feel this excited to be captured by a tall, strong man.

This is the fantasy I've been fighting. The one I tell myself I don't want. Being caught. Being claimed. Being overwhelmed by someone stronger.

And Carter knows it. He's always known it.

Slowly, I turn in his hold and press my back to the wall. The concrete is cold. He's not. We both start laughing softly, because this is absurd. Because we're adults playing cat and mouse in a stairwell. Because every line we're supposed to keep between us is slowly burning to ash.

"Do you make a habit of chasing your employees, Mr Carter?" I manage, breath still short.

"Only the ones worth catching," he murmurs.

This is wrong. So wrong. He shouldn't say these things to me, yet my stomach flips.

He reaches up, loosening his tie with one hand, popping open the top two buttons of his shirt. The movement is slow and sinful. A bead of sweat slides down his neck, and my eyes follow it like it's a drop of the sweetest wine. I want it.

I want him.

"Carter—" I warn, though my voice wavers, betraying my resolve.

He steps closer, his intoxicating scent enveloping me until I can't think straight.

"Kiss me," he whispers.

My pulse spikes. "No."

I want to, with every fibre of my being and against every rational thought left in my desire-stricken mind.

"Yes," he presses, low and coaxing. "Kiss me, lioness."

That pet name, spoken in that husky tone, unravels me. My eyes drop to the hollow of his throat, watching the rise and fall of his chest, the twitch of his jaw as he waits. In the dim light of the stairwell, the amber flecks in his irises look larger, making his eyes appear darker and much warmer.

God, this man is truly beautiful.

Before reason can catch up, I rise on my toes and lean into him, my lips almost touching his neck.

His neck. Where his pulse beats. Where I could taste his sweat, his skin, his vulnerability. I'm going for the one place that would make this equal—where I could make him as undone as he makes me.

My lips graze his skin, but then the sound of a door creaking open above jolts me back.

Footsteps echo down the stairwell—real life, real consequences.

I slip under his arm and scramble for my shoes, but he grips my wrist and pulls me back into his arms. His mouth slams onto mine, his hand wrapping around my neck and tugging the hair at my nape. My mouth parts on a soft gasp and he uses the moment to sweep his tongue through my mouth.

"Carter," I mumble between kisses, the footsteps above pounding louder, faster.

He stills, chest heaving, eyes blazing. He slowly releases his hold on me.

My legs tremble as I stumble back, grab my heels, and sprint down the stairs without daring to look back.

When I reach the bottom floor, I hear his calm and composed voice, already masking the chaos between us as he greets whoever just walked down.

I slip out into the lobby, pulse racing, the ghost of Carter's lips still lingering on mine, and one terrifying, undeniable truth pounding in my chest—I kissed Carter.

Again.

The Accused

Medard

The door slams below, the echo of her footsteps fading into the lobby. I stay exactly where I am, one hand braced against the cool concrete wall, the other pinching the bridge of my nose. I'm still catching my breath, not from the chase, but from her. The taste of her lingers on my tongue, that faint trace of her perfume hanging in the stale stairwell air like she's branded the entire bloody building.

And I've got a problem. A very visible one. I glance down, and sigh

Christ.

The one time I decide to act like a rational adult and let her go, I'm standing here with a hard-on that could violate several company health and safety policies. I drag in a deep breath and pull myself upright, trying to steady the storm raging inside me. Just as I start to recompose myself, the footsteps approach from above, growing louder with each passing second.

Perfect timing.

I shrug out of my jacket, sling it over my forearm in what I hope looks casual, and take a slow step back from the wall, strategically masking the very inconvenient evidence of my current state.

Muhammad appears on the landing, flushed but smiling, her ponytail swinging as she jogs the last few steps.

"Oh! Mr Carter," she says, surprised but clearly thrilled.

I adjust the jacket slightly lower. "Mrs Muhammad."

She beams, visibly pleased. "You're taking the stairs too? I started doing this after my maternity leave. Trying to shift the baby weight, you know. Saves me the gym, and I can spend that time working instead."

"That's... commendable," I say smoothly. "Efficiency is a valuable habit."

Her smile widens.

"Exactly! More time for the firm, less wasted on treadmills."

It's almost endearing, until my mind twists the thought—more time for work means less time for her children. The thought of Sophie ever saying something like that, of her prioritising depositions over bedtime stories, feels fundamentally wrong.

No, when Sophie and I have a baby—

Jesus Christ.

Where the hell did that come from?

I blink, my brain grinding its gears like a faulty transmission as Muhammad waves cheerfully and continues downstairs. I mutter something that sounds vaguely like "Keep up the good work," and wait for her footsteps to fade before I allow myself to groan quietly.

A baby? With Sophie? We haven't even had a proper date yet.

Hell, we can barely have a conversation without her trying to murder me or me trying to kiss her.

I rake a hand through my hair. Maybe walking slowly might help redirect blood flow to somewhere other than my crotch. Maybe the physical exertion will knock some sense back into me, too.

But it doesn't.

Because all I can think about is Sophie. Her soft gasps, her mouth, her stubborn refusal to make this easy. The way she looks at me like I'm both the storm and the shelter.

I hit the next flight of stairs, shaking my head, half-amused, half-exasperated with myself.

I don't do this. I don't fantasise about shared futures, about permanence, about domestic bliss and Sunday mornings. I've never been the man who dreams of white picket fences.

Until her.

Focus, Medard.

There's a plan—bring the firm back up, knock Sophie's father off his pedestal, reach the peak of my career.

Another landing. Another breath.

God, I love her laugh. That uninhibited, genuine sound that lights up her entire face. The way her cheeks flush when she's caught between indignation and arousal. The way she looks at me when she thinks I'm not watching, like she's imagining all the dirty things I could do to her, that I want to do to her.

Yeah, there's no universe where that woman isn't part of my future.

Sure, she's running from me today, pretending she can outrun this thing between us.

She can't.

I reach the fourth landing and my legs are starting to feel the burn, but at least my dick is finally calming down. Small mercies.

I'll convince her to sign that damn CRA. Henderson has been pestering me all day about it. I've already signed mine; Sophie's still "reviewing." Which is Sophie-code for H*ell no, Carter.*

Fine. I'll chase her.

Then, once she's admitted we're inevitable, and she will, there'll be—

A wedding.

Why the hell not? It makes perfect sense. Not in some sappy, romantic way, but as a strategic alliance. A contractual agreement that solidifies exactly what I've already decided—she's mine. Permanently.

And there's the added bonus of tax benefits. Alex will be thrilled I'm finally thinking about optimising my net income. Sure, he'll be mortified about the circumstances surrounding the marriage, but he'll perk right up when I let him invest the surplus in derivatives.

It makes sense to marry Sophie. It's practical. Efficient. Logical.

She'll fight me on it, of course. She'll claim we haven't even been on proper dates yet, that this is all too fast, completely insane. That's fine. She can have her dates during cake tastings and wine pairings. Two birds, one stone.

And then, a year from now—maybe sooner if I have my way—she'll carry my child.

I stop mid-step, pressing my palm against the stairwell wall.

When did I become this person? The man who fantasises about babies and weddings with a woman who won't even sign a relationship agreement?

The man whose never wanted forever with anyone is now mentally picking out venues.

Christ.

I've lost it completely.

Still, there's no way I'd miss out on a little Carter. A child half Sophie, half me would be nothing but perfection. Strong genes, sharp mind, impeccable bone structure. A child that would carry on my legacy.

Sophie will be my beautiful lioness, devoted mother and—

I pause mid-step, my own thoughts grinding to a halt.

Housewife?

Christ, what century am I living in?

Sophie would castrate me if she heard that thought. And she'd be right to.

No, scratch that. Sophie will be a devoted mother and a brilliant lawyer, my fierce partner, and probably still argue with me about everything. The woman thrives on conflict. She'd be bored senseless without it.

It's all very logical, really. Very practical. Not emotional in the slightest.

I reach our floor, my pulse finally steady, my body returning to something resembling professional composure. I adjust my tie, roll back my shoulders, and walk through the office doors with purpose.

She will stop running. She will see what I see—this perfect life we could build together.

I cross the threshold into my office with one final thought lodged deep and certain in my mind: It's not a matter of *if*. It's a matter of *when*.

Sophie Rosen will be by my side. And God help anyone who tries to tell me otherwise.

"Carter, Miss Rosen won't accompany you," Buckman says, strolling into my office.

"Excuse me?" I growl.

Buckman halts mid-stride, clearly surprised by my tone. "I've thought about this, and after the initial meeting with Ravens didn't pan out, I think it would make a better impression if you and I handle the luncheon next week. Senior leadership only."

The luncheon. Windpower.

Get a fucking grip, Medard!

"Buckman," I huff, pinching the bridge of my nose, "I appreciate your support, but Miss Rosen and I have it handled."

"With all due respect, you still haven't explained what happened with Ravens. We were practically shaking hands on that deal."

Christ's sake.

For the amount of money I've invested into this firm, I should have requested he walk around with a ball gag.

I shuffle the papers on my desk. "Ravens simply wasn't aligned with our approach."

He frowns, leaning forward. "Carter, we were a shoo-in. What happened in that meeting?"

"I said," I repeat slowly, enunciating each word like I'm speaking to a particularly dim child, "he wasn't aligned."

Buckman squints at me, clearly debating whether to push further. "Right," he mutters finally. "You're the boss."

"Glad we're clear on that."

He opens his mouth again, but mercifully, my phone starts buzzing.

Sweet salvation.

I glance at the screen. Mrs Henderson from HR.

More like bitter salvation.

"If you'll excuse me," I say. I wait for Buckman to leave before I pick up. "Mrs Henderson."

"Mr Carter," she says, her voice carrying that syrupy politeness only HR professionals can weaponise. "I just wanted to confirm that the CRA is no longer required. Miss Rosen told me you two discussed the matter, and agreed to shelve it for now."

I close my eyes briefly, counting to three.

"It's still required," I say evenly. "Miss Rosen will sign it. Just leave it with me. I'll chase her down myself."

There's a pause. I can hear her typing, probably documenting this entire conversation for some future tribunal.

"I understand, Mr Carter," Henderson continues. "Also, your request for the CRA prompted me to review our overall compliance schedule, and it appears we haven't conducted a harassment, diversity, and inclusion refresher in... oh, about five years."

I drag a hand down my face. "That so?"

"Yes," she says brightly. "The former managing director kept postponing them. I imagine, given recent events, it would be appropriate to hold a session sooner rather than later."

"Recent events," I echo. "You mean the CRA."

"Among other things," she says, far too casually.

I pace towards the window. HR ethics training, the three words most likely to kill my libido and my will to live.

"Mrs Henderson," I say carefully, "it's nearly the end of the quarter. People are buried in casework. Let's look at scheduling something for the new year."

"That won't do," she replies immediately. "Given the nature of your request and the recent redundancies, it's imperative we address workplace boundaries now. In fact—"

"In fact," I cut in, making an executive decision, "I'm giving you one hour to put something together. One hour. Do it this afternoon."

As annoying as the old woman can be, she's got a valid point. Not about the CRA. The boundaries between Sophie and me are quite clear—there are none. But about the potential effects of the redundancies.

"You're serious?"

"Deadly."

"Well—" She sounds genuinely pleased now. "Thank you, Mr Carter. This is exactly the kind of proactive leadership we need."

"Good," I say. "Then we're done here."

"Excellent," she says sweetly. "I'll see you in an hour for the session. You might want to prepare a few words. As managing director, your presence is essential."

The line goes dead before I can protest. I drop into my chair and yank open my laptop. For thirty seconds, I stare blankly at a spreadsheet. Then, like my fingers have a mind of their own, I type *wedding venues London countryside* into the browser.

I scroll past a castle. Too obvious. A vineyard. Too French. A barn with string lights—

"Christ, pull yourself together," I mutter, slamming the laptop shut.

The phone buzzes again. Henderson: HR session in Conference Room Two. Four p.m.

Just what every self-respecting MD wants on a Friday afternoon—a forced seminar on how not to want your employee.

Pinching the bridge of my nose, I reopen my laptop. I've got one hour to be productive before I have to sit through corporate torture.

Gratefully, the hour slips by faster than expected. By the time I've finished the financial projections and responded to three emails, Janet pokes her head in to remind me about the seminar.

I roll back my chair and straighten my tie. If I survive today without either choking someone or confessing that I want to put a ring on Sophie Rosen's finger, I'll consider it a win.

Ready to fake professionalism like it's a goddamn art form, I march out of the office.

Conference Room Two is already filling up with faces of boredom. Friday afternoon may not have been the best choice to guarantee an enthusiastic audience. But that's exactly why I chose it.

Henderson stands at the front, beaming beside a PowerPoint titled "Creating Safe and Respectful Workplaces" in a font so cheerful it's borderline offensive.

I take a seat in the front row for leadership visibility. Appear engaged, appear ethical, appear like I don't currently spend the majority of my waking hours chasing my employee to accept me as her lover.

Buckman strides in, greeting Henderson with both hands.

"These sessions are vital, absolutely vital," he says.

Buckman, the man who couldn't persuade the former MD to approve a single HR initiative in five years, now wants credit for progress he had no hand in creating.

He drops into the seat opposite me, flashing a smug grin that probably worked wonders back in 1986.

And then she walks in. Sophie.

Laughing, head tilted back, blue eyes bright. Ben Reynolds is beside her, grinning. The sound of her laughter slices through the dull corporate buzz, straight through every defence I've built.

My gut tightens, but not with jealousy. Reynolds is harmless. He's got that protective older-brother energy, and I'm certain he's as straight as a roundabout. Not that I mind. Quite the opposite. It makes him safe, and she's comfortable around him in a way that's entirely platonic.

Her gaze finally meets mine, and it's like an electric current snaps between us.

I tilt my head towards the empty chair beside me like an unspoken order.

She shakes her head slightly.

I arch a brow. *Try me.*

Her lips twitch, and for a second, I think she'll defy me. But then she sighs, murmurs something to Reynolds, and takes the seat next to me.

My beautiful lioness, for once, obedient.

Reynolds claims the seat on her other side, shooting me a brief nod that clearly says *I'm watching you, boss-man.*

Fair enough.

Muhammad walks up to Henderson, explaining how to work the pointer. She's always the eager beaver.

"Good afternoon, Mr Carter," she chirps, settling beside Buckman.

I nod politely, and she beams.

Henderson claps her hands. "Alright, everyone, thank you for joining us. Today we'll be discussing harassment, inclusion, and diversity."

Kill me now.

She gestures towards me. "But first, our managing director, Mr Carter, will share a few opening words."

Of course I will.

I stand, tug my jacket straight, and plaster on my professional smile. "Thank you, Mrs Henderson. These sessions are indeed crucial. We have a duty to ensure that every employee feels safe, respected, and valued. The success of this firm depends fundamentally on trust and shared responsibility to maintain professionalism at all times."

From the corner of my eye, I catch Sophie biting her lip, shoulders shaking as she tries not to laugh.

I continue, voice steady. "And in the shared responsibility, we all have to maintain professionalism at all times, regardless of the circumstances."

She disguises a giggle as a cough.

I wrap up the speech and sit down.

Leaning closer, I murmur, "You might want to school your reactions better, Miss Rosen, or everyone will suspect there's something going on between us."

She doesn't even look at me, just mutters, "You're insufferable."

"Only with you."

Her elbow brushes mine, and I nearly forget what century I'm living in.

Henderson starts clicking through slides. "Let's begin with harassment. What constitutes inappropriate behaviour in the workplace?"

Muhammad's hand shoots up before anyone else can even breathe. "Comments about someone's appearance."

A few nods ripple around the room.

"Good example," Henderson says.

"Cornering people in their office," Sophie says, her voice clear and pointed.

I fight the urge to smirk.

"Very true," Henderson replies. "Can anyone think of more subtle forms?"

Buckman clears his throat importantly. "Unwanted personal questions. Enquiring about someone's private life when they haven't invited that level of familiarity."

"I fully agree," Sophie chimes in, gesturing towards Buckman like he's the corporate messiah. "Personal boundaries are incredibly important."

Muhammad adds, "Standing too close. Invading someone's personal space."

Sophie tilts her head, eyes flicking briefly to me. "Would threatening someone to do something be harassment... or coercion?"

Oh, she's playing now.

Reynolds chimes in. "Depends on the threat. Could be blackmail."

Muhammad nods. "If there's pressure involved, that would definitely count."

I clench my fists under the table as the CRA is publicly scrutinised by everyone for potential misconduct, unaware that their very own boss is the accused who's currently standing trial.

Henderson nods. "Exactly right. If the acting party uses their position of power to pressure the other person, it absolutely constitutes harassment."

Sophie, eyes still on me, says sweetly, "Would repeatedly asking someone to do something count as applying pressure?"

I lean forward slightly, voice perfectly calm. "It would depend entirely on the intent. I'd call it thorough follow-up. Ensuring clarity."

A few snickers scatter through the room.

Henderson smiles diplomatically. "Perhaps it could be seen that way, unless the persistence causes genuine distress. Excellent discussion, Mr Carter, Miss Rosen. It's wonderful to see such engagement with these topics."

"Oh, of course we're engaged," I say with a slight smirk. "When it comes to such an important topic."

Sophie's blush could power the entire projector.

The next twenty minutes blur. Sophie's phone keeps buzzing. She glances down repeatedly, a small smile playing at her lips.

I lean over. "Who's that?"

"Work," she lies as her screen lights up. I catch the name. Gareth.

The bloody copper.

That'll have to change. Immediately.

I snatch her phone before she can react. She gasps.

"Carter, give it back," she whispers urgently.

"Shh," I say calmly, scrolling through messages. Gareth's tedious little this-or-that game.

> Gareth: Comedy or horror?

> I type: Documentary. I prefer facts to feelings.

Sophie leans forward, strategically blocking the view.

"Stop that right now," she hisses.

> Gareth: Tattoos or clean skin?

> I type: Clean skin. Commitment belongs on contracts, not arms.

Her hand shoots under the table, trying to grab her phone. I catch her wrist, then twine our fingers together. She freezes, eyes darting to my face.

Her skin is warm against mine, soft and trembling. I stroke my thumb over her knuckles.

"Relax," I murmur. "I'm just helping with your correspondence."

> Gareth: Music loud or soft?

> I type: Soft. If I can't hear my own thoughts, it's not relaxation.

Sophie hums disapprovingly. "You're wrong there. I like heavy metal music."

"No, you don't." I fight the urge to grin, to draw attention to us. "You're fierce on the outside, but soft in the middle. More Adele than Korn."

"Corn?" she asks, twisting her little ear stud. "As in sweetcorn?"

I can't help but laugh. She's utterly adorable when she's

confused.

"The band. K-O-R-N."

Her lips twitch. "You're impossible."

Henderson's voice cuts through. "Miss Rosen, what are your thoughts on how diversity contributes to workplace productivity?"

Sophie startles. "Uh—"

I squeeze her hand, keeping my face composed. "Miss Rosen was just telling me that diversity strengthens innovation through varied perspectives."

Henderson nods approvingly. "Excellent contribution."

"See, lioness. Our engagement is HR-approved," I tease.

"Let go of me," she hisses.

"Not a chance."

I trace lazy circles on her hand with my thumb. Henderson drones on, and all I can think about is how Sophie's pulse beats against my palm.

After an eternity, Sophie mumbles, "I need to use the ladies'."

I release her hand reluctantly, watching her slip out. The moment she's gone, the air feels thinner.

Buckman's pretending to be enthralled by Henderson's slide on Active Bystandership, nodding along like he still has a wrung on the career ladder to climb. Muhammad is scribbling notes like her life hangs in the balance. I glance her way out of polite obligation. She beams, waves her pen slightly in acknowledgement. I nod back. Her grin widens to concerning proportions.

Christ.

Reynolds catches me looking and smirks, shaking his head as if I'm the class clown caught passing notes. Then, bizarrely, he looks away with theatrical annoyance, like I've personally offended him. Whatever that's about, I don't have the patience to decode.

Henderson starts handing out leaflets. I shuffle through pages, eyes snagging on the Sexual Harassment leaflet:

Non-verbal: Looking a person's body up and down.
Verbal/Written: Remarks of a sexual nature.
Physical: Impeding movement, unwanted touching.
Visual: Sharing suggestive images.

I stare at the list.

Non-verbal? Guilty.
Verbal? Multiple counts.
Physical? Define 'unwanted'.

Christ. I'm a bloody case study.
Then my eyes land on Visual. Not guilty.
It's a small, pathetic victory, but I'll take it. Still, the rest of it hits harder than it should.

What the hell am I doing? Since Sophie Rosen walked into my life, I've been reduced to this—a grown man counting his workplace infractions like confessions in a booth.

But she hasn't said no. Not really. Not definitively. She's shelved the CRA, not rejected it outright. I take that as a form of ongoing consent under review, however shaky that logic might be.

Henderson is now deep in a tangent about dress code policies and self-expression in the workplace, which Reynolds appears to be very passionate about.

Sophie returns, and I quickly shuffle the harassment leaflet to the bottom, drawing her attention to the diversity one.

"Did you know," I whisper, "that inclusive workplaces are thirty percent more innovative?"

I hold out my hand under the table, palm up.

"No, I didn't," she whispers back, confused.

And then, without thinking, she slips her hand into mine.

Her eyes widen, but it's too late. I curl my fingers around hers.

For the next half hour, I don't hear a word Henderson says. All I know is the warmth of Sophie's hand in mine.

When the seminar ends, Sophie pulls free immediately and bolts with Reynolds.

Buckman claps my shoulder. "Good show, Carter."

I force a smile.

Then I'm alone with empty chairs and the echo of Sophie's laughter.

I loosen my tie, sinking back into the chair, letting the silence wash over me.

She thinks she's clever, testing me in plain sight. But she doesn't realise—every test she throws, I'll pass. Every challenge, I'll meet.

The projector clicks off. I glance around and catch a glimpse of movement through the glass. The staff are filtering out, heading home for the weekend.

Except me.

I'm still sitting here with a head full of her voice. I push up from the chair, loosening the tie that suddenly feels like a noose around my neck.

Thunder rolls somewhere in the distance, deep and warning. A heartbeat later, a flash of lightning slashes across the darkening clouds. Then comes the rain. Torrential.

My eyes flick back to the corridor just in time to see Sophie dart past, tugging her coat tight.

I'm on my feet before conscious thought catches up. I try to catch up with her, but moments later she's in the lift.

The indicator shows ground floor—lobby, not car park.

Of course. She takes the bloody tube. In this weather.

A plan forms.

If she won't talk about the CRA in the office, I'll make sure she doesn't avoid it outside either.

Logical. Efficient. Completely unprofessional. But perfect.

I grab my coat and laptop, ignoring reason.

By the time I hit the car park, the storm's in full swing. I slide into the driver's seat and speed out.

Two minutes later, I'm driving down the street, watching the pavement.

And then I spot her.

Her brolly flips inside out, fighting her. Her bag slips off her shoulder. She looks small and furious and completely irresistible.

I ease the car forward until I'm beside her, and lower the window.

"Get in," I call out.

She stops, water dripping off her nose. "You've got to be kidding me."

"Do I look like I'm kidding?"

The car behind me honks.

She folds her arms. "I'm fine. I don't need—"

Another honk.

I arch a brow. "You're causing a traffic jam, lioness."

She mutters something like "unbelievable," but pulls open the door and slides in, slamming it behind her.

Water splashes everywhere—across the seat, the dashboard, my arm. My leather seats are now officially collateral damage, but I couldn't care less.

"Good evening to you, too."

She shoots me a look. "There's a word for what you're doing right now."

"Chivalry?"

"Harassment," she says sweetly.

I glance at her, pulling into traffic. "We're really doing this again?"

She smirks. "You should have taken better notes in the seminar."

"I was busy watching someone giggle through my speech."

Her eyes flick to me, the faintest blush colouring her cheeks. "You made yourself an easy target."

I start driving properly now, merging into the flow of Friday evening traffic. "I'll take that as a compliment."

"Of course, you will."

Silence settles, just the rain drumming and windscreen wipers swishing.

She crosses her legs, glancing out the window. "That seminar should have been your personal intervention."

"Excuse me?"

"You ticked off half of Mrs Henderson's slides. Cornering someone? Check. Unwanted touching? Check. Using authority to pressure someone—"

"—like signing a mutually beneficial agreement?" I cut in.

Her eyes narrow. "You really can't help yourself."

I grin. "Not when it comes to you."

"That's not something to be proud of."

"Depends who you ask."

Her sigh is half frustration, half disbelief, entirely Sophie. "You honestly don't see how bad that sounds?"

"Actually," I say, voice dropping lower, "I think you like how it sounds."

She twists towards me, fire igniting in those blue eyes. "You are—"

"—right?"

She groans. "Impossible."

"And yet, still your favourite form of transport."

That earns me a fierce glare. I laugh.

But the laughter dies when she says quietly, "This isn't funny, Carter. You're the one pushing. The one holding all the power."

She's right. I am the one with power. I'm her boss. I control her career. Every interaction is coloured by that imbalance. But offering her the choice to decline—that levels it, doesn't it?

I grip the steering wheel tighter. "Then decline the CRA."

Her mouth opens. Closes. No words come out.

Exactly.

My gaze stays on the road, on the red taillights ahead blurring in the rain. "You can't, can you? Because that would mean ending this."

"This isn't anything," she snaps, but her voice wavers and fingers are pressing into her thighs.

"Then say it." I risk a glance at her. "Say you don't want this."

Her silence is louder than the thunder.

I exhale slowly. "It's Gareth, isn't it?"

She turns, incredulous. "What about him?"

"He's why you won't sign. You're waiting to see who wins." The words taste bitter on my tongue.

Her laugh is sharp and humourless. "You think every decision I make revolves around you?"

"In this case, yes."

She shakes her head, wet strands clinging to her jaw, her neck. "You're arrogant, Carter. You actually believe I'd choose you over Gareth?"

"I don't believe it," I say quietly, but with absolute certainty. "I know it."

"You're impossible."

"You're blushing."

"Because you're infuriating."

"Because you're thinking about the stairwell," I counter, remembering the taste of her, the way she melted against me.

She glares ahead, refusing to answer. But she squeezes her thighs together, and that tells me everything.

"Don't you even want to know where I live so you can stop stalking me?" she says suddenly.

"Don't need to."

Her eyes flick to the dashboard navigation system, then widen when she sees her own address on the screen.

"You looked up my address?"

I shrug. "Had to make sure my employees get home safely. Responsible management."

"That's not compliance, that's creepy."

"Semantics."

It probably is creepy. Definitely is. But I don't care. I need to know she's safe. Need to know where she is. Need to know everything about her.

When did I become the man who looks up addresses?

She huffs, crossing her arms, and stares out the window like I'm the last person on Earth she wants to look at. Which is rich, given how hard she's breathing.

The rest of the drive hums with loaded silence. Tense and electric.

When I pull up near her building, rain still hammering down, she moves to open the door. But I'm already out, rounding the car.

I hold my coat above us as we sprint for the door, both laughing despite ourselves.

"You're insane!" she calls.

"Persistent. There's a difference."

We reach her front steps, both breathless, both dripping. She fumbles with her keys.

Then I catch it. That quick glance—down my soaked shirt, across my chest, lingering at my throat before snapping back up to my face.

Her pupils darken. Just slightly. But I see it. I see everything when it comes to her.

For one suspended second, I think she might say *Come in.*

But she doesn't.

"Thank you for the ride," she murmurs, stepping inside, creating distance between us with painful efficiency.

I nod, rainwater dripping from my hair. "Anytime."

The door clicks shut, and I'm left standing in the rain, soaked through, my heart pounding harder than it has any right to, harder than logical reason should demand.

I run back to the car and sit in the dark for a moment.

She will sign that CRA. She will stop running. And when she finally admits what we both already know—that this is inevitable—I'll be right here.

Waiting. Always waiting.

I start the engine and pull away, her building disappearing in the rear-view mirror. But the taste of her, the memory of her hand in mine, the look in her eyes just before she closed the door?

Those stay with me all the way home.

Devil

Sophie

Anytime, he said.
Anytime, but not today.
"No, not today. Not today. Not today," I repeat the words like a mantra, hurrying up the stairs. My legs feel like jelly, my brain foggy with arousal, and between my thighs? Wet, like a broken dam that's finally given up the fight.

He's arrogant, insufferable, downright obnoxious, and I'm so incredibly turned on I feel like a fourteen-year-old discovering her clitoris for the first time.

My hands are shaking when I try to slot the key into the door, and I'm certain it's not because I'm drenched from the torrential rain. I'm hot in all the wrong ways possible—feverish, desperate, absolutely losing my mind. I fly through the door and let myself fall back against it, panting from the race up the stairs and from Carter's twisted effect on me.

The way he was towering over me with those intense grey eyes, those damn amber flecks sparking like the thunder rolling in the background. Rain dropping off the tips of his hair, droplets catching on his jawline before sliding down his neck and creating a path I wanted to trace with my tongue. His shirt drenched, clinging to his broad chest like a second skin, pronouncing every single muscle like an anatomy lesson I desperately want to study with my hands. And mouth. And possibly my entire body.

My bag drops from my shoulder with a dull thud as my hand slides under the waistband of my skirt. Before I can reason with myself about how utterly wrong this is, how unprofessional, how completely insane, I'm drawing small, desperate circles over my clit.

I've never been so aroused in my life. So needy that I had to use every ounce of willpower I possess to not grab him by that soaked shirt and drag him up to my flat, propriety and professional boundaries be damned.

But by God, that crisp ocean scent that should have been washed away by the rain but was somehow more potent than ever. His perfectly shaped lips that were silently beckoning to be kissed until neither of us could remember our own names.

My fingers move faster over my bundle of nerves, but it's not enough. Not nearly enough. I want his fingers on me, rougher, more demanding. His mouth, hot and commanding. His cock sliding over it while he tells me in that deep, authoritative voice exactly what he wants to do to me, how he wants to take me apart piece by piece until I shatter completely under one epic orgasm.

It's wrong, so utterly wrong, but that deep, confident tone saying *anytime* nearly broke my resolve. That one single word held so much dominance, so much dark promise about the things he would do to me if only I'd let him into my flat. The way his eyes had held mine, unflinching, absolutely certain, like he already knew every fantasy playing through my head and was more than willing to make them reality.

I push my hips off the door, my movements becoming more frantic, more desperate. Moans spill out without permission in raw and needy sounds I barely recognise as my own. I stifle them with my free hand, pressing hard against my mouth as though shielding the universe from my reckless, all-consuming obsession with my boss.

My orgasm is close, building like a storm inside me. Close enough to barrel through me like Carter's relentless insistence that I sign myself over to him.

I press my hand harder against my mouth and pinch my nose until my body screams for air, and I can pretend for one minuscule, perfect moment that it's Carter's hand wrapped around my throat.

The orgasm crashes over me harder and more intense than anything I've ever felt before, tearing through me like the lightning through the clouds outside. I'm shaking and gasping. I gulp for breath, my lungs burning as oxygen floods back in.

I stand there for what feels like an eternity, my hand still in my knickers, slick and dripping, my head pressed against the cool door. My legs are trembling, my heart hammering so hard I can feel it in my throat.

I wait until I can finally breathe steadily again, until the room stops spinning, until the cold from my wet clothes starts seeping into my overheated skin like reality checking back in.

I peel myself from the door and finally pull my hand out.

My fingers are slick with red.

Period red.

Oh God.

So much for being wetter than I've ever been before. I've got my bloody period. Three days early. That never happens.

If that isn't a monumental sign from a higher power that masturbating to the image of Carter, the devil himself, is a professional sin of the highest order, I don't know what is. The universe is literally telling me to stop.

I drag myself to the bathroom to wash the evidence of my embarrassing lapse in judgement off my hands, scrubbing like Lady Macbeth trying to remove a particularly stubborn stain. Then I peel my wet clothes off piece by piece, and throw my knickers directly into the bin. They're definitely beyond saving, both literally and as a metaphor for my dignity.

My teeth chatter from the cold as I step into the steaming hot shower, letting the water pound against my skin. I'm a mess between my legs, and I can't help but shake my head at the sight, at the absurdity of it all.

I need to get my head straight. I can't let Carter keep pushing the boundaries past our professional relationship.

Stalking me outside the office after looking up my address just so he could drive me home? Unbelievable.

Insisting we hold hands under the table like a couple of teenagers hiding from the teacher? Unprofessional.

Chasing me down a stairwell and then kissing me like I'm oxygen and he's drowning? Completely unacceptable.

And yet, every time he touches me, it's like he's branding me for eternity.

I can still taste him on my lips. Still feel the ghost of his hand in mine, on my throat, my thigh. Still hear that single word, *anytime*, playing on loop in my head like some sort of erotic audiobook I didn't ask for but apparently downloaded anyway.

I need to establish boundaries. Clear, professional, legally-binding-if-possible boundaries.

I need to remind myself that I worked too hard to get where I am to throw it away for a man.

But I held his hand today. During the seminar. Without thinking. My hand just... found his. Like it belonged there.

Like I belonged with him.

No. Absolutely not.

I need to focus on my career, my goals, my perfectly planned future that doesn't include being anyone's "anytime."

The water pounds against my skin, washing away the rain, the arousal and blood, and hopefully some of the insanity that's taken up residence in my brain. By the time I step out, wrapped in my fluffiest towel, I've made a decision: I need perspective. Normalcy.

A reminder that there are other men in the world. Men who don't make me feel like I'm constantly teetering on the edge of either an orgasm or a nervous breakdown.

Men like Gareth.

I grab my phone from where I abandoned it with my bag and pull up his contact before I can second-guess myself.

He answers on the second ring, his voice warm and easy in that uncomplicated way that feels like a balm on my frayed nerves.

"Sophie? This is a surprise. I didn't think you were allowed to use phones during working hours. Thought your boss might have banned those alongside evening entertainment outside of the office."

I laugh, remembering Gareth's unfazed expression when Carter approached us in the shop. I pad into my bedroom to find dry clothes.

"It's seven p.m. on a Friday night. I don't work that late," I lie, because there's been plenty of times when I actually have done that. "And no, he hasn't quite achieved that level of dictatorship yet. Give him time."

"So, what's up? Everything okay?"

"Yeah, fine. I just—" I pause, pulling on the matching set of chocolate brown cotton pyjamas I wear once a month for shark week. They're safe and comfy. "I was wondering if you wanted to grab coffee sometime? Maybe next Saturday?"

"Next weekend?" His surprise is evident. "That's pretty short notice for you. I thought your diary was booked solid weeks in advance."

"It usually is," I admit, sitting on my bed and towelling my hair dry. "But I could use some normal human interaction that doesn't involve clauses or complaining clients. And besides, you gave me thirty minutes' notice for our first date, so I figure turnabout's more than fair."

He laughs in his typical warm and genuine way. "Fair point.

And here I was thinking you'd forgotten about that disaster of a date."

"Your reality check after our... blunder? Hard to forget."

"Yeah, sorry about that. I can sometimes be a bit upfront."

"It's fine. I should apologise. This really wasn't what I had planned." I wince, remembering how kind Gareth was, despite realising that my mind wasn't on him while we had sex. "I owe you a coffee, at least."

"Fair enough." He's grinning now, I can hear it in his voice. "So next Saturday then. Is there a decent café near you? Since it's the weekend, no point trekking to the city."

"There's one about five minutes from my flat," I say, grateful he's thinking practically. "And it does good coffee and allegedly edible pastries."

"Allegedly?"

"I've never had one, but given your fable for heavy carbs, you should be fine."

He laughs. "Perfect. Ten o'clock. It's a—" He pauses, and I can hear the question forming. "Is this a date-date, or—?"

And there it is. The clarification I shouldn't have to make. The boundary I shouldn't need to establish, because I am a single woman and Gareth is a decent man who's worth a shot.

"As friends," I say, "just... friends grabbing coffee."

The words taste painfully right in my mouth, and I hate that I feel the urge to say them. Hate that I'm drawing lines with Gareth so not to wrong Carter. I should be free to date whoever I want because I shouldn't be anything with Carter except his employee.

But apparently, I'm setting boundaries with the wrong man.

I'm clarifying my intentions with someone who deserves clarity, while letting another man drive me home, hijack my text conversations, and chase me down stairwells like he has every right to. The realisation sits heavy in my chest.

"Friends," Gareth confirms, and if he's disappointed, he hides it well. "That actually sounds perfect. No pressure, just coffee."

"Exactly."

We chat for a few more minutes about nothing important—the TV show he's currently watching, whether the weather will finally improve, his theory about London funding bonuses for the top brass at the Met by excessively installing speed cameras everywhere.

"And those this-or-that questions I sent you," he says, his voice brightening. "Your answers totally took me by surprise. I guessed you like soft music, but I did see you more as a comedy-kinda-girl rather than boring documentaries."

I freeze mid-towel-scrunch, my stomach dropping like it's struggling to digest a heavy rock.

Those weren't my answers. Those were Carter's answers. Carter, who apparently thinks he knows me better than I know myself. Carter, who hijacked my phone and my text conversation like the controlling, presumptuous freak he is, and answered every single question correctly.

Documentaries. Soft music. Clean skin. He knows I'm fierce on the outside but soft in the middle. He knows I need facts, not feelings, to process the world. He knows I want commitment to mean something permanent—on contracts, on skin, on everything.

He knows me. Really knows me. And that terrifies me more than anything else he's done.

What would he have answered for himself?

The thought intrudes before I can stop it, curiosity blooming despite my best efforts to crush it. Does he prefer comedy or horror? What does he do when he's not terrorising his employees? What kind of music does he listen to when he's alone? Does he have hobbies, or is "acquiring law firms and ruining lives" a full-time occupation?

I hate that I want to know. Hate that my brain is now cataloguing questions I have no business asking. Hate that I'm more interested in what makes Medard Carter tick than I am in the perfectly nice, uncomplicated man on the other end of this phone call.

"Sophie? You still there?"

I snap back to attention, mortified by where my thoughts wandered. "Yeah, sorry. Just...yes. Very me."

The lie tastes bitter, but what am I supposed to say? Actually, those were answered by my boss who stole my phone during an HR seminar and apparently knows me better than people I've actually been on dates with?

"You okay?" Gareth asks, genuine concern in his voice. "You sound distracted."

"Just tired," I manage, forcing brightness into my tone. "Long week."

"Then coffee next week is definitely happening. You need a break from that place."

We say our goodbyes, and I end the call, tossing my phone onto the duvet like it might burn me.

I just friend-zoned a good man to preserve... what? A relationship that doesn't exist? A professional boundary that's already been demolished? A future with someone who thinks stalking and hand-snatching are acceptable courtship rituals?

I'm protecting Carter from Gareth. When it should be the other way around.

The flat feels too quiet now. The kind of silence that lets thoughts creep in, dangerous thoughts about grey eyes and commanding voices and hands that know exactly where to grip to make you feel both terrified and safe.

No. Absolutely not.

I need a distraction. Something violent and satisfying that doesn't involve masturbating to my boss in the entryway like some sort of depraved welcome mat.

I pad to the living room, flop onto the sofa, and pull up my streaming queue. True crime documentaries. Perfect. Nothing puts life in perspective quite like watching other people make catastrophically bad decisions.

I scroll through the options and land on one with a particularly promising title: Till Death Do Us Part: Women Who Killed Their Husbands.

Perfect.

I hit play, pull a blanket over my legs, and settle in for an evening of learning creative ways to dispose of problematic men. Not that I'm planning anything. But it never hurts to be prepared.

Especially if Carter has now decided to overstep every ethical line outside of the office too.

The documentary opens with ominous music and a woman's voice describing how she poisoned her husband's coffee over the course of six months.

"Amateur," I mutter, reaching for the remote to turn up the volume.

If I were going to do it, I'd be far more efficient, like bashing Carter's head in with that pretentious pencil holder he keeps on his desk.

Not that I'm thinking about it. Not at all.

My phone buzzes on the cushion beside me. A text from an unknown number.

        Unknown: Sleep well, lioness. Dream of me.

My heart stops. Then races. Then does something complicated that feels like a cardiac event.

There's only one person who calls me that.

I should be angry. Furious, even. He's crossed yet another line, somehow got my personal mobile number, which I definitely didn't give him.

But instead, I'm staring at those words like they're written in some ancient language I'm trying to decode.

Dream of me.

As if I have a choice.

As if I've been dreaming about anything else since the moment he walked into my life and turned it completely upside down.

I won't respond. I won't give him the satisfaction.

But I also don't delete the message, and instead, save his number to my contacts under AP. Arrogant Prick.

When I finally drift off an hour later, the documentary still playing in the background, my dreams are full of intense grey eyes, commanding voices, and a single word that feels like both a promise and a threat.

Anytime.

Saviour

Medard

The quarterly financial report sits in front of me, pages of numbers and projections that should have my full attention.

They don't.

I'm staring at the same column of figures I've been pretending to review for the past ten minutes, my mind somewhere else entirely.

Specifically, on one certain stubborn junior partner who's no doubt buried in contract work, avoiding me with impressive dedication.

A week. It's been a full bloody week since the rain, since I stood outside her building and offered her everything. Well, everything within the confines of a legally binding agreement, and she's been treating me like I'm radioactive.

She arrives with the crowd. Leaves with the crowd. Takes lunch at her desk. Routes all communication through her assistant like she's some sort of human firewall. The few times I've managed to catch a glimpse of her in the corridor, she's perfected the art of being urgently needed elsewhere.

It's driving me insane.

"Carter? You listening?"

I look up to find Buckman watching me from across my desk, his expression carefully neutral. He's perched on the edge of one of my office chairs, suit pressed, tie perfectly knotted. Everything about him screams corporate lifer coasting towards retirement.

"I'm listening," I say, which is a lie.

"Really? Because I just asked you the same question twice." He shifts uncomfortably. "The board meeting yesterday... there were some concerns raised."

"What concerns?"

"The marketing budget." He clears his throat. "You approved a fifteen percent increase without review. A few people noticed."

I lean back in my chair and pinch the bridge of my nose. "The budget was acceptable."

"Perhaps, but—" He trails off, clearly weighing how far he can push. "You've seemed preoccupied this week. I'm not criticising, just concerned. The firm can't afford any... instability. Not after everything we've been through the last few weeks."

Everything we've been through. As if Buckman has anything to do with salvaging this place from the smoking wreckage of influence peddling and criminal charges that nearly destroyed it.

The problem with Buckman is that he's been here for thirty years. Watched the firm rise, watched it nearly collapse when the former MD was disbarred, and decided his best strategy is to stay exactly where he is—second in command, comfortable and safe, until he can collect his pension and disappear to whatever golf course retirement he's been fantasising about.

He doesn't fight to save this place. He doesn't take risks. He just... stays, and keeps his head down. Which is why I was brought in. To do the actual work of rebuilding while he counts down the days to retirement.

That's why I'll never respect him.

"Everything's fine," I say, my tone clipped. "I've just been handling multiple priorities at once. It's called management."

"Of course." He nods quickly, backing down as he always does. "I just wanted to ensure everything is... under control."

"It is."

He doesn't look convinced, but he knows better than to push further. Buckman might be cautious to the point of cowardice, but he's not stupid. He knows I'm the only thing standing between this firm and complete collapse. That gives me a certain amount of leverage he can't afford to challenge.

"The Windpower luncheon—" My phone rings, cutting him off.

I glance at the screen. Mum.

Perfect. Exactly what I need right now.

I decline the call, but ten seconds later she's ringing again. I haven't spoken to her since she dropped by my place with Lisa a couple of weeks ago. I should pick up, keep the peace.

But Christ, I've got other things on my mind right now.

My phone rings again, and this time I answer. "What?"

"Medard." Her voice is tight, controlled in that particular way that means she's about to say something I don't want to hear. "I need to speak with you about Theo's wedding."

My jaw clenches at the mention of my brother's name. I glance at Buckman, who's pretending to examine his fingernails but is clearly listening.

"I'm in the middle of something," I say, keeping my tone neutral.

"This won't take long. James, you remember James, Theo's best friend, his father had a stroke. He's flying to the States tonight, which means that Theo no longer has a best man."

I can see exactly where this is going, and I want no part of it.

"That's unfortunate," I say flatly.

"Medard, you need to step in."

"No."

"He's your brother—"

"I'm aware." My voice drops, carefully controlled despite the anger simmering beneath. "The answer is still no."

"You're being unreasonable. I don't understand why you won't—"

"I have my reasons," I cut her off before she can say anything else. Anything that might reveal too much to Buckman's attentive ears. "Reasons we're not discussing now."

"Medard—"

"I said no. Theo can find someone else. I'm sure he has plenty of friends who'd be honoured to stand up with him."

"But you're family."

"I couldn't care less." The words come out harder than I mean them to, frustration bleeding through despite my best efforts. "I'll attend the ceremony. That's all I'm offering. Stop pushing."

"You're being childish about this."

"I'm being clear. Now, I have work to do. Goodbye." I hang up before she can respond, frustration coiling tight in my chest.

Buckman is staring at me with an expression I can't quite read. Shock, maybe. Or disapproval.

"What?" I snap.

He shakes his head slowly. "That's how you speak to your mother?"

"My mother is perfectly capable of handling direct communication."

"That wasn't direct. That was—" He trails off, clearly thinking better of finishing that sentence.

"Was what?"

"Nothing." He stands, hands raised in a placating gesture. "Not my business."

"You're right. It's not."

The office falls into silence. Buckman shifts his weight, clearly debating whether to continue this conversation or make a strategic retreat.

"I didn't know you had a brother," he says carefully.

"There's a lot you don't know about me, Buckman. We work together. That doesn't make us friends."

His expression tightens slightly, but he nods. "Of course. I just meant... whatever personal matters you're dealing with, they seem to be affecting your focus."

"My focus is fine."

"Is it?" The question is gentle, but there's frustration underneath. "Because a couple of board members pulled me aside yesterday. Asked if there were health concerns. Wanted to know if they should be preparing contingency plans."

My hand tightens around the pen I'm holding. "They need to mind their own bloody business."

Though I suppose from the outside, the signs look concerning. Weight loss from skipped meals. Dark circles from sleepless nights. Distraction, irritability, obsessive focus on one junior partner.

"They own twenty percent of this firm. Their business is our business." Buckman takes a breath, choosing his next words carefully. "Look, I'm not trying to overstep. But I've got significant capital invested here. And right now, you're the only one who can safe this firm."

There it is. The real concern. Not about me, not about the firm's reputation or employee morale. About his pension. His comfortable exit strategy.

Classic Buckman.

"The firm will be fine," I say coldly.

"Then prove it." He moves towards the door, then pauses. "Whatever is occupying your head, whether it's family matters or something else, you need to resolve it. Quickly. Because if you're distracted, if you make the wrong call on Windpower, everything I've built with Harman, everything you've been rebuilding, comes crashing down."

"Your concern is noted."

"I'm serious, Carter. I stayed with this firm through the scandal because I believed it could be salvaged, that you could be the saviour. You've done brilliant work so far. But it's still fragile. One major misstep, and the board loses confidence. Clients will start looking elsewhere again. Partners start jumping ship." He meets my eyes. "I can't afford that. None of us can."

"Are you finished?"

"For now." He opens the door. "Just... sort out whatever this is. Before it becomes a problem we can't fix."

The door closes behind him and I sit in the silence he leaves behind, his words echoing in my head. As much as I hate to admit it, he's right. I'm distracted. Unfocused. Behaving like someone I don't recognise.

All because of a stubborn woman who won't sign a simple agreement.

I grab my phone, pulling up the unsigned CRA on my screen. I sent her another copy the day after the HR seminar, and it's been sitting in her inbox ever since. Untouched. Unacknowledged. Not declined. Just... ignored. Like if she doesn't acknowledge it, it ceases to exist.

Which is worse than a refusal. At least a 'no' is definitive. This is purgatory.

My thumb hovers over her contact. I could call her. Demand an explanation. Order her to my office this instant and refuse to let her leave until she signs the bloody thing.

But that's not how this works. That's not how she works.

Sophie Rosen doesn't respond to demands. She digs in her heels, lifts that stubborn chin, and fights back twice as hard. I learnt that the first day I met her.

Which means I need a different strategy.

I lean back in my chair, staring at the ceiling. She won't come to me. That much is clear. She's avoiding me, hiding behind work and distance and all the professional boundaries she thinks will keep her safe.

The quarterly report sits on my desk, demanding attention. But all I can think about is her. About blue eyes and bluebells, and that stubborn tilt to her chin. About the way she looked in the rain, water dripping off her long eyelashes, desire and defiance warring in her expression.

About how I let her walk away. Let her close the door between us. Let her retreat behind walls I helped her build.

I should have kissed her again. Should have pushed harder. Should have made her admit what we both know is true.

About the fact that she won't sign the bloody agreement, and I'm running out of patience.

And when my patience runs out, I stop playing by rules. Stop waiting. Stop being reasonable.

She thinks she's won by avoiding me. She hasn't. She's just delayed the inevitable.

Batman

Sophie

After spending the entire week dodging Carter with the dedication of a woman fleeing a particularly persistent debt collector, the café is exactly the kind of place I need this morning. It's small and unassuming, tucked between a florist and a charity shop on a quiet side street. The kind of place filled with the comforting hum of Saturday morning chatter, the hiss of the espresso machine, and the rich aroma of freshly ground coffee. No one from the firm would be caught dead here. It's too ordinary, too far from the city, too blissfully free of networking opportunities. It's the perfect place to focus on my life outside of work and a certain someone.

I arrive early, claim a table by the window where weak autumn sunlight filters through, and order for us both. A flat white for me, a pot of English Breakfast for Gareth. He's not a coffee drinker. Something I learnt on our disastrous first date.

Gareth appears exactly on time, spotting me through the window and waving before pushing through the door. A small bell chimes overhead. He's dressed casually in jeans and a beige jumper that matches his brown hair impossibly well, and when he slides into the seat across from me, that easy smile spreads across his face.

"You ordered already?" He spots the teapot and grins. "And you remembered. I'm impressed."

"It's nothing," I brush him off with a smile.

It really isn't, compared to the effort he went through on our first date and how spectacularly I thanked him for it. It ranks somewhere between the stomach bug that made five-year-old me vomit on Father's lap during a client call, and my recent, monumentally poor judgement with Harman at the golf club in my list of life's lowlights.

"It's appreciated nonetheless," he says, pouring himself a cup, steam curling between us.

He settles back into his chair, looking relaxed and easy-going. Everything Carter isn't.

Stop thinking about him.

"So," Gareth begins, wrapping his hands around his cup, "I have news. Big news, actually."

"Good news, I hope?"

"The best." He leans forward slightly, enthusiasm creeping into his voice. "I'm transferring from Roads Policing to the Drug Unit."

My jaw drops. "That's a big change, right? When did this happen?"

"Official confirmation came through yesterday. I've been angling for it for months, but the Met works at a glacial pace with endless bureaucracy." He takes a sip of his tea, grinning. "But it finally came through."

"Congratulations," I say, meaning it. "That's what you wanted, right? More investigative work?"

"Exactly. Don't get me wrong, traffic was fine, but I joined the force to actually investigate crimes, not just chase down speeders and drunk drivers." His expression shifts, becoming more serious. "The Drug Unit is different. Deeper cases, more complex networks. It's going to be challenging."

I nod at Gareth's words, but my attention drifts to the table next to us where a toddler is crying. She's just hit herself with her doll, and her mother is consoling her with kisses and cuddles. I wonder if my mother ever cradled me like that when she wasn't high on whatever trip she was taking.

Probably not.

Where Father's only focus was creating a mini-version of himself, she was too self-absorbed to even notice I existed.

Maybe that's why Carter's attention grips me the way it does. He's someone who finally, openly admits he wants me, regardless of how blunt and controlling he's being about it.

I shouldn't be thinking about Carter. Not now. Not while Gareth sits across from me being the perfect gentleman.

"Challenging how?" I ask, cradling my cup between both hands.

He exhales, considering. "Well, for starters, the learning curve is steep. Different legislation, different tactics. Surveillance work, undercover operations sometimes. And the hours are unpredictable. You can't exactly schedule when drug dealers decide to conduct business."

"Sounds familiar. Billable hours wait for no one." I smile.

"See? We're both gluttons for punishment." He grins, then continues. "But the real challenge is going to be earning respect.

The Drug Unit guys are tight-knit. They've been working together for years. I'm the new bloke coming in. So, I'll have to prove myself all over again."

"You'll be brilliant," I say with certainty. "You're observant, methodical, and you don't give up easily. They'd be idiots not to see that."

His smile warms. "Thanks, Sophie. That actually means—"

My phone buzzes on the table between us, the vibration loud against the wooden surface. I glance down instinctively.

> AP: Tonight, 8pm, your place. We'll discuss the CRA.

My stomach drops. All week, he's been texting me good morning and good night. It was annoying at first, but after a few days, I found myself looking forward to the texts. But this? This isn't a simple *good morning* or *good night, lioness*. It's an invasion.

"Everything okay?" Gareth asks, noticing my expression.

"Yes, fine," I say too quickly, my fingers already flying across the screen. "Just a client with terrible timing."

> Me: Absolutely not.

I set the phone face-down on the table, trying to refocus on Gareth. The espresso machine hisses behind the counter, and someone's cup clatters against a saucer. "Sorry, you were saying about earning respect?"

"Right, yeah. So, the thing is—"

My phone buzzes again.

> AP: That wasn't a question.

My jaw tightens. Of course, it wasn't. Nothing with Carter is ever a question. It's all declarations and demands and that insufferable certainty that the world will bend to his will.

Gareth's watching me, curiosity flickering behind his eyes. "Demanding client?"

"You have no idea," I mutter, typing back furiously.

> Me: And mine wasn't a suggestion. There's nothing to discuss. Certainly nothing that requires my BOSS stepping foot into my home.

I emphasise the word boss like it might remind him, or me, of the professional boundaries he seems determined to obliterate.

"So, the Drug Unit," I say, forcing brightness into my voice as I set my phone down again. "Will you need additional training?"

"Actually, yes. There's an eight-week intensive course starting right after my trip to Gibraltar. Surveillance techniques, informant handling, evidence preservation for drug cases. Should be interesting."

My phone buzzes.

> AP: Happy to do it at my place.

I stare at the screen, my traitorous mind immediately conjuring images of Carter's home. What does it look like? Modern and minimalist, all clean lines and expensive furnishings? Or something older with character and history? Does he have artwork on the walls? Books? What does a man like that surround himself with when no one's watching?

Stop it.

"Sophie?"

I blink, realising Gareth's been talking and I've heard approximately none of it. "Sorry, what?"

"I asked if you've ever considered criminal law. You'd be good at it."

"Oh. No, corporate law is enough drama for me, trust me."

My fingers move across the screen almost of their own accord.

> Me: No.

Short and definitive.

Gareth takes another sip of his tea, his eyes never leaving my face. The café door opens with another cheerful chime, letting in a gust of cool air and two women with yoga mats.

"Must be some client to have you this distracted on a Saturday morning."

"She's persistent," I lie smoothly. "Wants to meet this weekend to discuss a contract dispute. Apparently, waiting until Monday is unconscionable."

"She sounds delightful."

"She's a nightmare," I say, which isn't entirely a lie if I just swap the pronouns.

My phone buzzes again.

> AP: 8pm, lioness.

The pet name sends an unwelcome shiver up my spine. I hate that he calls me that. Hate how it makes me feel flustered. Hate that some treacherous part of me likes it.

"You know," Gareth says carefully, "if you need to take that call—"

"No, absolutely not. He can wait." The word slips out before I can catch it.

Gareth's eyebrows rise. "He?"

Shit.

"She, I meant she," I correct quickly, feeling heat creep up my neck. "She's the client, but he's her assistant who handles her scheduling. They're both a nightmare."

Gareth doesn't look entirely convinced, but he lets it slide with a knowing smile. "Right. Her assistant."

I grab my coffee cup, taking a long sip even though it's gone lukewarm. Outside the window, Saturday morning shoppers pass by—a man with a stack of newspapers under his arm, teenagers in over-sized hoodies, a woman being pulled along by an overeager spaniel.

I type back quickly, my annoyance bleeding through into the message.

> Me: Enjoy the view of my front door, because I won't be opening it.

There. Clear enough even for his arrogant, boundary-stomping brain.

I shove my phone to the far side of the table like physical distance might help. "Tell me more about Gibraltar. When do you leave?"

Gareth's face lights up. "Not for another couple of weeks, but I'm counting down. I can't wait to explore the Rock, do some hiking, take a lot of photos. No morning alarm, no paperwork, just sun and freedom."

"Sounds perfect," I say, genuinely envious.

When was the last time I took a proper holiday? One that didn't involve my laptop and a constant stream of emails?

"You should take some time off too," he says, reading my mind. "You look exhausted."

"Flatterer."

"I mean it. When was the last time you did something just for yourself? Something that had nothing to do with work or obligations?"

I open my mouth to answer, but my phone buzzes before I can

form the words.

> AP: We'll see about that.

One sentence that carries the weight of absolute certainty, of a challenge accepted, of a man who's never encountered a door he couldn't eventually walk through.

My mind immediately spirals into increasingly absurd scenarios.

He'll pick the lock. Does he know how to pick locks?

He'll charm the building manager into giving him a spare key.

He'll scale the bloody building and come through the window like some sort of corporate Batman.

Nothing feels too far-fetched when it comes to Medard Carter.

My fingers fly across the screen, desperation making me reckless.

> Me: I won't be home.

I stare at the message after I send it, mortification flooding through me. How pathetic. I'm basically telling him that I'll be hiding out somewhere to avoid him. That he's got enough influence over me to change my Saturday evening plans. That he matters enough to make me flee my own flat.

"Sophie?" Gareth's voice pulls me back. "You're doing it again."

"Doing what?"

"Going somewhere else entirely." His expression is gentle but knowing. "Want to talk about it?"

"No, I—" I start, but my phone buzzes again.

> AP: Please don't make this harder than it already is. I'll see you at eight.

The air leaves my lungs.

Please. Carter said please.

The word sits there on the screen like a crack in his otherwise impenetrable armour, a glimpse of something underneath all that commanding certainty. Vulnerability. Or exhaustion. Or something I don't have a name for but can feel echoing in my own chest.

It makes everything worse.

I could handle the demands, the arrogance, the relentless boundary-pushing. But this? This small concession that maybe, just maybe, he's struggling with whatever this is between us too?

That's dangerous territory.

"Sophie."

I look up to find Gareth watching me with that steady detective's gaze, the one that misses nothing.

"Sorry," I say quietly, setting my phone down with finality. "You're right. My head's been somewhere else. That's not fair to you."

"It's your boss again, isn't it?" he says, smiling at me in a kind and understanding way. "Billy Big Bollocks from the shop."

I don't confirm or deny it, but my silence is answer enough.

He leans back in his chair, the wood creaking slightly, studying me over the rim of his teacup. "You know, in my line of work, we're trained to spot patterns. And the pattern I'm seeing is that every time you think about him, you look like you're preparing for battle."

"That's because I am," I admit, surprising myself with the honesty.

"And yet you're still thinking about him."

"Unfortunately."

He's quiet for a moment, then offers a small smile. "For what it's worth, I don't think it's unfortunate. I think it's human."

"Human and stupid aren't mutually exclusive."

"No," he agrees, "but neither are reasoning and longing."

We sit in companionable silence for a moment, the café bustling around us. The morning sun has shifted, casting longer shadows across our table. Eventually, I drain the last of my coffee and check the time on my phone.

"I should go," I say reluctantly. "Let you enjoy the rest of your Saturday without my pathetic drama."

"It's not pathetic," he says, standing when I do. "It's just complicated."

We walk to the door together, the bell chiming cheerfully as we step out onto the pavement. The florist next door is setting out buckets of chrysanthemums, their autumnal colours bright against the grey stone. Gareth pulls me into a brief, friendly hug.

"Have fun in Gibraltar," I say into his shoulder. "Send photos of the monkeys."

He pulls back, laughing. "Gibraltar? Sophie, I'm not leaving for another couple of weeks. I literally just told you that ten minutes ago."

I blink. "You did?"

"Your head has clearly been somewhere else entirely." His smile is understanding, despite having endured yet another date where I've been anything but present. "Go deal with whatever you need to deal with. But maybe try to be honest with yourself about what that actually is."

He gives me a final wave and heads off down the street, hands in his pockets, leaving me standing there on the pavement. I watch him turn the corner, disappearing behind a group of tourists studying a map.

Then I pull out my phone, Carter's message burning a hole in my consciousness.

AP: Please don't make this harder than it already is.

I stare at the words, thumb hovering over the keyboard. Part of me wants to type *Fine*. To give in, to stop fighting this thing between us.

Because he has a point, doesn't he? We need to discuss the CRA. That's legitimate. Professional.

Except we both know the moment I let him through that door, the moment we're alone in my flat with no colleagues, no witnesses, no professional distance to hide behind, everything changes. We'll cross a line there's no coming back from, and I'll be exactly what I swore I'd never be again—a woman compromising her career for a man.

My finger hovers. Wavering.

I lock my phone without responding and shove it deep into my coat pocket.

Let him sit with his own *Please* for a while.

I turn towards home, trying not to count down the minutes until eight p.m. Trying not to acknowledge that I still haven't said no.

I pace my flat, the floorboards creaking under my restless feet. Would he actually come over?

The thought leaves me with goosebumps, exhilarating and terrifying all at once. This is insane. I'm acting like some Victorian maiden waiting for a scandalous caller to ruin her reputation.

And this particular scandal could destroy everything I've worked for.

If Carter comes over tonight, if we cross whatever ethical line we've been tap-dancing around for weeks, I'll be exactly what my father accused me of. His words from that disastrous dinner echo—*You were Harman's little pet. I do not know what happened between you two, but if it could compromise your integrity—*

Nothing happened with Harman. Nothing. But if something happens with Carter? If I let my boss into my flat, into my bed?

Father will never believe it started after my promotion. He'll assume I've been sleeping my way up the ladder all along. That every achievement, every case I've won, was earned on my back instead of through my brain.

The thought makes me physically ill.

The worst part is that Carter initiated that bloody CRA. He went to HR and formally requested permission to pursue a relationship with me. Like I'm some corporate acquisition to be processed through the proper channels.

The arrogance makes my blood boil.

I grab cleaning supplies and attack the kitchen counter like it hasn't been cleaned in a decade. Scrubbing in furious circles, the sharp scent of lemon cleaner burning my nostrils.

What if I just don't answer the door? Except he knows I'm home. My silence was basically a neon sign flashing 'I'm home and panicking!'

I move to the floors, then the bathroom, scrubbing until my knees ache and my hands smell like bleach and desperation.

But none of it helps.

Because underneath all the panic and rationalisation, there's something else simmering.

Want.

Raw, undeniable, absolutely inconvenient want that refuses to be scrubbed away.

I want to know what would happen if I let him in. If I stopped fighting and just surrendered.

The thought terrifies me more than anything else. Because I can picture it too clearly. Carter walking through that door, and everything around us exploding as we tear our clothes from each other's bodies.

The shower beckons, and I surrender. Hot water pounds against my tense muscles. When I finally step out, I pull on my light-blue silk robe, then pour myself a generous glass of wine. Chardonnay. Dutch courage.

Forty minutes til eight o'clock.

I stare at my phone, waiting for a reprieve that won't come. The minutes crawl by with agonising slowness.

If I let him in, my life will be irrevocably changed and my career in tatters.

Every late night, every sacrifice, every bloody thing I've given up will crumble because I can't control myself around my boss.

My boss.

The man who has the power to destroy my reputation, to confirm every terrible thing Father has ever thought about me.

I can't let that happen.

Restless, I grab my phone and type:

> Me: No need to come over. I've made my decision. I'm not signing it.

I hit send. Eighteen minutes. He still has eighteen minutes to turn around.

"It'll be fine," I whisper to my empty flat. "He'll see the text. He'll respect my decision."

The words sound hollow even to my own ears.

I sink onto the sofa, wine glass clutched between both hands, trying to steady my breathing. He's a professional. Surely, he wouldn't just show up after I explicitly told him not to.

Would he?

The doorbell rings, slicing through the silence like a knife. I freeze. Wine sloshes in my glass. My heart just fainted momentarily. The doorbell chimes again, echoing with ominous finality.

He's here. He came anyway.

Of course, he bloody did.

I force myself to stand on trembling legs. Fear and something far more dangerous intertwine inside me. I set my glass down and cross the room, each step feeling both too fast and too slow.

This is it. The moment everything changes or stays the same.

My hand hovers over the handle, every instinct screaming contradictory instructions—open it, don't open it, run away, let him in, kiss him.

I can't bring myself to open it.

There's a gentle knock, and I'm sure I can feel the warmth of his body radiating through the door.

"Open up, lioness. I know you're there." His voice filters through, low and certain, making my stomach flip.

I press my ear to the door, waiting, hoping for his footsteps to retreat.

He huffs a sound of frustration and maybe amusement.

"I just want to talk. To make you understand," he finally says with that same vulnerable undertone he had when he asked if it was absurd for us to be together.

I want to understand. God, I've been wanting to understand whatever this is since I first laid eyes on him.

Before the warning bells can go off, before Father's voice and my own common sense can have their screaming match, I step back and open the door.

He leans with one arm against the door frame, head dipped, gaze travelling up the length of my body. His presence is magnetic, overwhelming, filling the doorway and somehow the entire stairwell beyond like he's bending space and time through sheer force of will. His lips curve into a slow smile, his eyes locking onto mine with an intensity that steals whatever breath I'd managed to gather.

"You shouldn't have come here." My voice comes out steadier than I feel, which is a small miracle. "I texted you not to."

He slowly strides past me, and I make no effort to stop him, stepping aside like he has some sort of right to be here. He claims my space with the same confidence he claims everything else—boardrooms, cases, apparently my sanity. His presence fills my small living room, making it feel even smaller, the air thicker and harder to breathe. The scent of him fills the room, my senses.

I never should have opened that door.

"I saw the text," he says, his voice rich and commanding, sending goosebumps erupting across my skin despite my best efforts to remain unaffected. "But I still think we should discuss this."

I close the door, sealing us in, sealing my fate, and follow him deeper into my flat. My heart thuds wildly against my ribs as I struggle to process the fact that my boss, the man who infuriates and intimidates and arouses me in equal mind-bending measures, is currently standing in my personal sanctuary.

"There's nothing to discuss," I manage, though my words tremble slightly.

He steps closer, and I force myself not to retreat, but to hold my ground even though every survival instinct I have is screaming at me to put more space between us. His eyes narrow, studying me like I'm a case he's trying to crack.

"You and I both know that's not true." His voice drops lower, more intimate, vibrating through the small space between us. "You want me."

"Egotistic much?" I scoff, crossing my arms defensively even though the gesture feels hollow. My racing heartbeat betrays every word, every pretence of indifference.

He laughs, entirely too knowing, like he can hear my pulse from where he stands. He closes the distance between us before I can process the movement or prepare myself. In one swift motion, his hand grips my arm and he pulls me against his chest with surprising gentleness. His other arm snakes around my waist, palm pressing flat against my lower back, anchoring me to him in an embrace that threatens to turn every defence I've carefully constructed to ash.

The silk of my robe is thin, far too thin. The heat of him bleeds through the fabric as I can feel every plane of his body against mine.

"In denial much?" he counters, his voice a rumble that vibrates through his chest.

Any semblance of composure—any pretence that this isn't affecting me exactly the way he knows it is—is wavering with each passing second.

"There's nothing to deny. You are my boss, nothing more."

I try to pull away, to reclaim some space, some dignity, but he holds me tighter. I can feel his heart beating against my chest, steady and strong, while mine races out of control.

God, it feels so good to be close to him. So dangerously good.

"Yet here I am on a Saturday night in your flat." His breath is warm against my ear, sending shivers up my spine. "Tell me, after we kissed in my office, in the stairwell, did you run straight to him to confess?"

"What?"

"The copper, lioness. Did you finally ditch him?"

Unbelievable.

So much for wanting to discuss, for wanting to make me understand. He's only here to stake his claim again, to command that I bend to his will.

The sheer arrogance.

What gives him the right to think he's so much better than Gareth? To assume I'd just... what? Drop everything for him? He's got nothing on Gareth. Certainly not kindness. Certainly not respect for boundaries. And certainly not the basic human decency to acknowledge that I might have agency in this situation.

"Don't flatter yourself, Carter," I fire back, putting as much conviction as I can muster into the words even as my body betrays me by leaning into him. "Yes, I kissed you, but don't mistake those moments for mutual affection. I merely did what I felt I had no choice in. But I draw the line from here on out. I want nothing from you but your professionalism."

The words come out stronger than I expected, and something shifts in the air between us. Something important.

The realisation crystallises cold and sharp in my chest. Regardless of what I feel for him—this confusing, overwhelming attraction that won't quit—he has no right to make assumptions about my feelings. No right to corner me, to push me, to presume that I'll just fall into his arms because he's decided that's how this story goes.

I might want him, God knows my traitorous body makes that obvious, but that doesn't give him carte blanche to override my explicitly stated boundaries.

Something flickers across his face. Pain, maybe. Or recognition. His jaw tightens, and for a moment, I think he might actually hear me. Might understand what I'm saying about power and choice and all the ways this is wrong.

But then it's gone, replaced by that infuriating certainty.

His laughter rings out and he finally releases me. I stumble back, caught between relief and an aching sense of loss, like my body is mourning the contact even as my mind celebrates the space.

He swipes a hand over his mouth, jaw tight, those hooded, sinfully enticing eyes fixed on mine.

"Fair enough, lioness." The pet name falls from his lips, and I instantly know he's not accepting the boundaries I've just demanded. "I'll leave you to your many thoughts and denials."

He turns towards the door, and rage flares hot in my chest. Some irrational part of my brain screams that I can't let him leave like this, can't let this end with him dismissing my clearly stated boundaries like they're nothing but amusing obstacles.

"But know this," he continues, pausing in the hallway, and turning on his heels to pin me in place with his glare. "I don't care how long I have to play this game of push and pull with you. I will savour every kiss, every touch you grant me, until you finally accept that you're mine."

The promise hangs in the air between us, heavy with certainty that infuriates me.

Mine. Like I'm property. Like I'm something to be won or claimed or conquered.

He strides towards the door with purpose, reaching for the handle, when the words finally tumble from my mouth, sharp and furious. "I will never sign that form, and I will never be your sordid office fling."

The words barely leave my lips when he spins around. Two large strides close the distance between us, and then his hand is on my throat with enough pressure to make breathing suddenly require conscious effort, to make my pulse jump frantically beneath his palm.

"You ignorant woman," he grates through his teeth, his face inches from mine. Close enough that I can see the amber flecks in his eyes, feel his breath on my lips. "You won't be some meaningless fling I fuck over my desk between board meetings."

My eyelids flutter as the loss of air creates a fog across my vision, softening the edges of everything. But I'm determined to hold his gaze, to not look away, to not give him the satisfaction.

"Then who will I be?" I gasp between small intakes of breath, my heart pumping frantically to deliver oxygen to my buckling legs.

"You'll be my *wife*."

My eyes widen. I'm certain I'm going to pass out, if not from lack of air, then from the sheer weight of his declaration hitting me like a punch to my chest.

Wife. Not girlfriend. Not partner. Wife.

He's not talking about dating. About seeing where this goes. He's talking about forever. About marriage. About making this permanent before we've even had a proper conversation about what 'this' is.

And he says it like it's already decided. Like my opinion is a formality he'll collect later.

It's not a promise or a proposal or even a question. It's a fact, spoken with such unwavering conviction that I can already feel the phantom weight of a wedding band branding my ring finger. I can taste his name on my tongue. Sophie Carter—a woman already in the making, forged in the heat of this moment.

But his hand is still on my throat. He's declaring his intention to marry me while cutting off my air supply. The symbolism isn't lost on me—this is what marriage to Carter would be. Beautiful and suffocating.

He finally loosens his grip, and air rushes back into my lungs in a desperate, gasping gulp that burns.

Then his lips crash onto mine.

He kisses me like he's been waiting years for this moment, like I'm his oxygen and he's been suffocating without me. I kiss him back like I've completely lost my mind. Because I have.

I just told him I felt I had no choice in our previous kisses. And now I'm kissing him back with abandon. Proving him right. Proving myself a liar.

Every rational thought, every professional boundary, every promise I made to myself, it all evaporates under the scorching heat of his mouth on mine.

I'm panting hard, my lungs working overtime to regulate my breathing, and my heart pounds wildly in sync, a rhythm that feels dangerously close to surrender. My body feels like it's about to implode when his tongue sweeps through my mouth, claiming, demanding, leaving no room for doubt about what he wants.

My body sways towards him. I want him like I've never wanted a man before, and with an intensity that frightens and exhilarates me in equal measure. My hands reach for his collar, fingers curling into the fabric, desperate to pull him closer, to deepen this kiss into something even more catastrophic, to fall completely and see where I land.

But painfully, agonisingly, he pulls away.

His hands leave my body, the loss of contact almost painful. He takes a step back, then another, putting space between us that feels like miles.

He storms out of my flat without another word, without looking back, leaving me standing there in my thin silk robe with my lips swollen, my throat aching where his hand had been, and caught somewhere between desire and destruction.

Lunatic

Medard

I lost control.
That's the thought circling through my mind as I drive towards the Argentinian restaurant where I'm meant to meet Alex. Except I've passed the turn-off three times now, circling the block like I'm lost in my own city.
I'm not lost. I'm... processing.
What the fuck did I do last night?
I showed up at her flat uninvited. Accused her of wanting me there. Grabbed her when she denied it. Then, when she had the audacity to call herself my "sordid office fling," I wrapped my hand around her throat and declared—not asked, declared—that she'd be my wife. Then I kissed her like a man possessed and walked out.
Christ, when I lay it out like that, I sound completely unhinged.
My wife. The conviction behind those words wasn't fuelled by logical reasoning, the kind I can justify in a boardroom. No, it was driven by something far more dangerous—the hurt in her voice when she thought she couldn't be more than a fleeting novelty.
Like she was disposable. Temporary. Something I'd use and discard between meetings.
The thought made something violent twist in my chest. My hand was around her throat before conscious thought caught up, and the words came pouring out with a force that startled even me.
I don't know what this thing between us is. But I know it surpasses basic attraction. It's more than wanting to fuck her senseless, though God knows I want that too.
It's the way she stood there calling me egotistic while her pulse hammered against my palm. The way she fights me even when her body has already surrendered. The way she looked at me with equal parts fury and desire in those impossible blue eyes.
And when I told her she'd be my wife—watching her eyes go wide with shock, feeling her breath catch beneath my hand—it felt right.
Which is precisely what terrifies me now.

Because the truth, staring back at me in the rear-view mirror is that I don't love Sophie.

At least, not yet.

So, who the hell am I to make such an audacious claim when my heart has yet to fully embrace hers? When I've spent years building walls so high that nothing gets through?

Love has burned me before. Left me bleeding out in ways that had nothing to do with physical wounds and everything to do with trust shattered beyond repair.

So no, I don't love her. I won't let myself. Not yet. Maybe not ever.

But I feel something undeniable.

There's something compelling about our connection, like an electric current pulling me towards her even when every instinct screams to maintain distance. I've never felt compelled to claim someone like this before, to wrap my hand around their throat and promise them forever like it's already decided.

It's not love. Love is weakness. Love is giving someone the power to destroy you and hoping they won't use it.

This? This is different. This is practical. Strategic.

She's brilliant, ambitious, challenges me at every turn. We're compatible in ways that make perfect sense. Strong genes, sharp minds, undeniable chemistry. A partnership built on solid foundations rather than fleeting emotions that fade with time.

The fact that I couldn't stand her calling herself a meaningless fling? Territorial instinct. Basic male biology.

The fact that I had to kiss her after saying it? Physical need. Sexual compatibility. Nothing more.

The fact that I had to leave immediately after, before I pushed her against that wall? Restraint. Self-control.

It's all very logical when I break it down like this.

Except.

Except there's this unnamed, uncharted territory between logic and lust. The way my hand fit perfectly around her throat. The way saying *you'll be my wife* felt more right than any carefully planned strategy ever has. The way her gasp of *then who will I be* revealed her ignorance to believe how much she means to me. It nearly broke something in me I didn't know could break.

It's not love. I won't call it that. I can't afford to.

But it's something.

Something that made me grab her throat and stake my claim like a barbarian. Something that made me promise her forever without thinking twice. Something that made me kiss her like I'd die if I didn't, then leave before I could do something even more reckless. Something—

I'm full of shit.

The thought hits me as I realise, I've just passed the restaurant for the fourth time.

I'm lying to myself. Constructing elaborate logical frameworks to avoid the simple, terrifying truth that's been staring me in the face since she walked into my office that first day.

But I can't admit that. Not yet. Maybe not ever.

Because admitting I'm falling for her, that I might already be completely gone, means giving her the power to destroy me. And I've been destroyed before. I know exactly what it costs.

So. I'll keep calling it logic. Strategy. Territorial instinct and sexual compatibility.

And I'll ignore the way my heart nearly stopped when she asked who she'd be. The way those words came out without hesitation—*You'll be my wife.* The way kissing her felt less like satisfying desire and more like coming home to something I didn't know I'd been missing.

I'll ignore all of it.

Because the alternative—admitting I'm in love with Sophie Rosen—is too dangerous to even consider.

I finally force myself to pull into the car park on the fifth pass.

Enough. I've made my decision. Declared it, actually, with my hand around her throat and absolute certainty in my voice.

Sophie will be my wife. I told her as much last night, and I don't make empty promises.

I straighten my collar and check my reflection in the rear-view mirror. Composed. Controlled. Completely rational.

Time to make this official.

The warm, fragrant air of charred meat and chimichurri envelops me as I step inside the restaurant. To my surprise, Alex isn't here yet, and neither is Aletha standing at her usual post by the front desk. I stride over to our usual table and settle into my seat, letting my mind arrange itself into some semblance of order.

Just as the waiter brings a pot of tea, the door swings open. Alex strides in a mere thirty minutes late, his expression a mixture of bemusement and irritation that's distinctly him.

"Is your calendar broke? You're three days early," he calls out, brows furrowing as he scans for the chaos only I could orchestrate. "We don't meet until Wednesday."

I can't help the faint smile that slips through, smoothing the edges of my otherwise composed demeanour.

"And you're thirty minutes late," I reply, checking my watch for emphasis.

"Well, some of us have hobbies," he says with a playful shrug, sliding into the seat across from me with that easy grace he's always had.

"My apologies," I say, placing a hand theatrically over my heart, feigning deep concern for his precious time. "Am I keeping you from your ballet class?"

He snorts, amusement lacing his voice as laughter breaks free. "Fuck you. And unlike you, ugly bastard, I'd look hot in a tutu."

I chuckle, enjoying the familiar rhythm of our banter. It grounds me, pulls me back from the edge of whatever spiral I was caught in outside.

"So, what did you want to talk to me about?" His tone shifts slightly, curiosity bleeding through the casual bravado as he leans back in his chair. "Must be important if you're calling emergency meetings."

"Couple of things," I begin, leaning back just enough to emphasise my nonchalance, or at least the appearance of it. "There's a penthouse on the market right now that I want to acquire. Dunbar Wharf. I'll send you the details later. Check the figures and let me know what you think."

His brows knit together, confusion wrenching at his features. "I'm sure you can afford it. But why move? I thought you liked your place?"

"I'm starting to outgrow it," I reply, waving off his concerns with a dismissive gesture, "I need more space for what's coming."

Alex's eyes narrow with apprehension, and I can see a flicker of unease dance across his features as he processes my ominous words.

"Alright—" he trails off, clearly wanting to press but holding back.

Before he can dig deeper, I catch sight of Aletha watching us from across the room, her expression tight. A different kind of tension sparks in my stomach, the kind that comes from unfinished business and conversations I should have handled better.

Ignoring the warning bells in my head, I rise from my seat, the undeniable urge to confront this head-on pulling at me.

Alex huffs behind me, a protest muffled beneath his breath.

"Come on, not again!" he groans, his voice laced with equal parts disbelief and exasperation.

Undeterred, I stride towards her, catching up as she attempts to evade yet another conversation by disappearing into the back.

"Aletha, wait!"

She halts, spinning to face me with dramatic suddenness, her dark eyes flashing.

"What do you want?" she snaps, arms crossing defensively over her chest.

"I just want to know if you're all right," I say, keeping my voice steady, though I can see confusion carving lines into her forehead.

"Why? Because I banged my head against the door or because you choked me?" Her words drip with sarcasm, a shield against the vulnerability flickering behind her eyes.

Christ, when she puts it like that, I sound like a complete psychopath.

"I'm sorry you got hurt," I respond, and the sincerity is actually there, buried beneath layers of poorly executed sexual encounters. "But I did promise you a hard fuck."

Probably not my finest moment of sensitivity.

Her indignation flares like a match struck in darkness.

"You're unbelievable!" she retorts, spinning on her heel. But her resolve wavers, compelling her to face me once more, anger and hurt warring on her face.

The intensity of it catches me off guard.

"You know what? You're a fucking arsehole! I've served you your food for over two years, and you knew I liked you, and you couldn't even bring yourself to show me a shred of kindness!"

The accusation lands heavier than I expect. She's not wrong. I've treated her like convenient relief—available, willing, and ultimately disposable.

"I'm sorry I hurt you," I say as she turns away, and I mean it. "What else do you want me to say?"

Her incredulous gasp resonates in the space between us. She stares at me as if I'm a riddle she can't quite crack, a puzzle with missing pieces she'll never find.

"What is wrong with you? Why did you choke me?"

I shrug, keeping my expression neutral beneath her bewildered gaze. "It's just what I do."

It's a shit answer. I know it even as the words leave my mouth. But what am I supposed to say? That I have preferences that require explicit consent and proper communication? That I should have established boundaries before taking her against the bathroom door?

Her expression shifts into pure disbelief. She shakes her head, stepping backward as if physical distance could shield her from my presence.

"That's not normal. You're not normal. Stay away from me, you lunatic!" she seethes, then bolts into the staff room.

I watch the door swing shut, oddly unbothered. People fear what they don't understand. And I've long since stopped trying to make people understand me.

Calmly, I straighten my cuffs and make my way back to the table. Alex's head is already shaking, disbelief carved into every line of his face.

"Unreal," he mutters, exhaustion bleeding through the single word.

I take my seat, steady and composed as if I didn't just get called a lunatic by the woman I casually used for sex. "So, where were we?"

Alex theatrically exhales through his nose. "Don't tell me you've done it again. I actually like the steak they do here. If we get banned, I'm holding you personally responsible."

I reach for the teapot, filling my cup with deliberate care. A smile tugs at the corner of my mouth because the absurdity of it all is almost charming in its dysfunction.

"I didn't fuck her," I say, stirring the tea once before setting the spoon down with a soft clink. "Not today, anyway."

I pause, letting the words hang for a beat, savouring the moment before I drop the bomb.

"I've met someone."

Alex chokes mid-sip, tea spurting in wild arcs across the table, speckling my shirt with careless abandon. I fix him with an exaggerated glare, the kind that says *really?*

"Come again? You've met a woman?" His eyes widen in genuine disbelief before morphing into that infuriating grin he always wears when he thinks he's caught me out. "An actual woman? With a pulse and everything?"

He waves me off like I'm some lost cause, sliding back into his seat with a theatrical sigh.

"I get it now! But I hate to tell you, mate, your blow-up doll doesn't exactly count as a stable relationship."

Unfazed, I dip my napkin into his water glass, blotting the damp spots on my shirt with practised ease. I offer a brittle laugh before snapping back to my usual no-nonsense self.

"Fuck you."

He leans forward, eyes sparkling with curiosity that borders on glee.

"Vale, who's this woman who's finally made you fall in love?" he asks, his fingers flicking in that signature *tell me more* gesture that lets his Spanish roots shine through.

I shake my head with what I hope looks like a mischievous grin, tossing the napkin aside like a card I'm done playing. Raising the teacup to my lips, I take a slow sip, savouring the moment before I correct him.

"Don't get ahead of yourself. No one's talking about love."

His brows knit together, confusion and intrigue battling for dominance on his face.

"Then what are we talking about?"

I lean in, voice lowering to something almost conspiratorial, letting the weight of what I'm about to say settle between us.

"That's actually the other thing I wanted to talk to you about." I pause, holding his gaze. "Do you want to be my best man?"

His reaction is instantaneous and explosive, a laugh that sends more tea flying across the table, the mess now comical in its excess. I chuckle despite myself, my shirt officially a lost cause.

"Now who's getting ahead of himself?" he manages between guffaws, wiping tea from his chin with the back of his hand.

"Will you do it or not?" I ask, voice steady, letting him see I'm completely serious. "If not, I'll ask Theo."

He scoffs, shaking his head with that knowing look. "Número uno: you would never ask your brother. Número dos: hell yeah, I'll be your best man! No one throws a better stag do than me."

His enthusiasm is infectious, genuinely warming something in my chest that I didn't realise had gone cold. I recline, feeling tension ease from my shoulders for the first time since I left Sophie's flat last night.

"Good. It's sorted then."

My mind drifts. Sophie in a gown, white as winter snow, studded with thousands of tiny diamonds that catch every stray beam of light. Once she's mine, properly and legally mine, I'll have her dripping in jewels. Not because of love or some sappy nonsense, but because my wife will deserve nothing less than perfection. Because she'll be a reflection of me, of us, of what we're building together.

"So, when am I meeting her? When's the big day?" Alex presses, his excitement thick in the air between us.

I swirl the dregs of tea in my cup, weighing how much truth to spill without drowning him in the full insanity of the situation. I settle on water-boarding him.

"Nothing's planned yet. I only told her last night that we're getting married. In fact, I'm still working on her accepting me as her partner."

The silence that follows is deafening.

His disbelief is palpable like a physical weight pressing down on the table. He throws his arms up in an exaggerated gesture that's almost endearing in its drama.

"Puto carajo! You've gone completely nuts." He leans forward, voice dropping to something between concern and exasperation. "I know women haven't exactly been your strong suit, but fuck me, Med, you can't seriously think that's how you win over a woman."

A slow smirk curls the corners of my mouth as I drain the last of my tea, adrenaline buzzing pleasantly in my veins. The same certainty that filled me last night when I had my hand around her throat floods back.

"You know me." I set the cup down with quiet finality. "I always get what I want."

And I want her. With every fibre of my being, with every calculated move I make, with every logical argument I can construct.

Whether she's ready for it or not. Whether I'm ready to admit why or not.

Husband

Sophie

I bolt upright, drenched in sweat and panic, my heart hammering like I've just ran a marathon. I spent the entire night tossing and turning—tangled in sheets and self-doubt and scenarios my brain had no business constructing—until sleep finally found me around four a.m.

And what did it gift me? A dream that's still haunting me in broad daylight, clinging to my consciousness like a bad smell.

In this surreal nightmare, I was gliding down the aisle of an enchanting church, sunlight streaming through stained glass windows, illuminating everything with a golden, ethereal glow. My heart was bursting, actually bursting, with happiness and love, with all those emotions I've spent years convincing myself I don't need. And then I turned to face my groom, ready for my happily ever after.

But it wasn't Carter standing there in a tux.

It was Father.

His eyes filled with that familiar mix of condescension and disappointment, looking at me like I'd just confirmed every terrible thing he's ever thought about me. That expression that says *I knew you'd fail eventually.*

That wedding, Carter's twisted delusion of what my life should be, would be the funeral of my career. Of everything I've worked for. Of me.

Even now, hours later in the harsh light of a new day, the aftershock of Carter's words is still reverberating inside my skull like a gong someone won't stop hitting. *You'll be my wife.* Like it's the most logical sentence in the English language. Like it's no different from *Pass me the deposition* or *File this by Friday.*

I lie in bed for a while, staring at the ceiling, watching dust motes dance in the sunlight filtering through my curtains, trying to decide whether to laugh or cry, or possibly check myself into a psychiatric facility.

Eventually, I do two of the three—an unhinged giggle that rolls right into a sigh so heavy it makes my ribs ache. The tears come next, hot and frustrating, and my hands automatically claw at my thighs to seek that sharp anchor of pain that brings clarity.

And then, because this is how I cope when I'm too humiliated to face Baron at the gym, I fling off the duvet with theatrical force and decide that today will be dedicated to more cleaning. Not because my flat needs it, God knows, I've already scrubbed it to within an inch of its life yesterday, but because I need the distraction. Scrubbing grout is infinitely better than replaying the scene at my door on an endless, masochistic loop.

Except cleaning doesn't silence the reel in my head. It just provides a soundtrack.

With every sweep of the mop, there he is—Carter, standing tall in my doorway, that imperious tone tolerating absolutely no argument. With every flick of the duster, there's his gaze, sharp and assessing, burning with intensity, and impossible to look away from.

My boss. My very inconveniently, devastatingly sexy boss who apparently thinks marriage proposals are delivered via choking and declarations.

God, how I wish he looked like a hideous little goblin. Some twisted creature from a fairy tale that would make this attraction physically impossible.

Who am I kidding? My libido would still weep under his magnetic pull. I'd probably find the goblin version weirdly attractive too because apparently my taste in men is as broken as my sense of self-preservation.

I grab the bottle of stainless-steel cleaner and scrub at my extractor fan. Not that it needs it. I rarely cook, and almost never with any grease. But tempting domestic accidents by standing precariously on my dining chair with one foot propped up on the counter is infinitely better than listening to the thoughts in my brain. My very stupid brain who apparently is a masochist with unlimited creative capacity, because it doesn't just replay what happened. Oh no. That would be too simple, too merciful.

It invents.

By the time I've finished cleaning the windows until they're a death trap for the pigeons, I'm already married to him in my head.

In one version, it's perfect—Carter in a tailored tux that probably costs more than my yearly salary, me in a dress that makes me look like a million pounds. He kisses me like the world might end if he doesn't, and I let him, because why the hell wouldn't I? We live happily ever after in some impossible dream. He probably even does the dishes. We have two perfect children and a dog named something pretentious like Hemingway.

By the time I'm polishing the cutlery with aggressive, pointed strokes, the fantasy has shifted into something darker.

This time I say yes to his insane proposal, and within a week I'm trapped in some soulless penthouse with ceilings so high they make me dizzy and furniture so expensive I'm afraid to sit on it. Except in this version, he's not the man who pulls late nights with me over case files, whose rare smile makes my stomach flip and my brain malfunction. He's my boss, squared. My husband and my employer. Which means I can't breathe, can't think, can't exist without him reminding me whose name is on my pay check and my marriage certificate. I end up suffocated under the crushing weight of his authority, a decorative wife in a gilded cage.

My flat is absolutely spotless by now, smelling of lemon and bleach and my own desperation, but my mind is still reeling. The usual satisfaction I get from my flat being sterile is nowhere to be found.

Christ, this is hopeless.

I let myself collapse onto the sofa, breathless and defeated, my gaze travelling over the shelves of books that line my wall. Re-organising might be the answer. A new project. A fresh distraction.

I pull stacks of books out with perhaps more force than necessary, and decide to embrace the trend of colour-coding them. Who cares if they live happily within their proper genres? It's aesthetics that count. Visual harmony over literary logic.

Ten minutes later, I've built multiple precarious stacks for each colour, creating a rainbow disaster zone across my living room floor when the worst version creeps in uninvited—I tell him no. A firm and professional no. He doesn't take it well. Monday morning I'm escorted out of the office by security, cardboard box in hand, my colleagues watching with a mix of pity and schadenfreude. No job, no income, no references. Give it a few weeks and I'm living under a bridge somewhere, trading legal advice for Wi-Fi access at coffee shops. The pigeons don't even respect me. Father was right about everything.

Mid-afternoon, and I'm exhausted—less from the cleaning and organising, more from living fifty-seven different lifetimes with Carter inside my head. My flat is sparkling, my books sorted by colour like some sort of Instagram fever dream, my laundry folded with military precision that would make Father proud, and I still don't know whether to laugh, cry, or book a one-way ticket to a country without extradition treaties.

I collapse onto the sofa with a generous glass of wine and pull my knees to my chest as my uterus kindly reminds me that it's still cheerfully shredding its lining. The silence of the flat presses in around me, heavy and suffocating.

I turn on the telly in hopes it'll drown out my thoughts. I land on a travel show about Rome. Cobblestone streets, ancient ruins, the Trevi Fountain sparkling in the Italian sun.

Despite my best efforts, despite every bit of common sense I possess, I can't help but picture Carter and me honeymooning there. Walking hand in hand through the Colosseum. Sharing gelato. Him pulling me into shadowed alcoves to kiss me passionately while tourists walk past.

"You're completely mental," I mutter to myself, drain my wine glass in one long swallow, before checking how much flights to Rome cost these days.

The alarm goes off at seven a.m., shrill and unforgiving. I don't move. I just lie there, blinking at the ceiling, listening to the piercing tone until it grates against my nerves enough that I roll over and slap at my phone with enough violence to probably crack the screen.

Blessed silence returns. But it doesn't fix the hollow, restless ache in my chest. The dread sitting in my stomach like a stone.

The thought of walking into the office today and facing Carter after Saturday night, after *you'll be my wife*, makes my stomach twist into complicated knots. The idea of pretending like nothing happened, like he didn't fundamentally alter the fabric of reality with those words?

Impossible. Absolutely impossible.

I do the only rational, professional, absolutely mature thing a junior partner can do—I call in to take an emergency day.

Buckman picks up after two rings, his voice already tired. "Sophie?"

"Yes, it's me," I say, keeping my voice steady, adding a slight rasp for authenticity. "I need today off."

There's a pause, heavy enough that I imagine him straightening his tie, weighing whether to pry. "Is everything alright?"

"Yes, nothing to worry about," I reply quickly, keeping my tone clipped and neutral and definitely not suspicious. "I just... need the day. Personal matter."

Another beat of silence that stretches uncomfortably, then he says with resignation, "Understood. We'll manage without you."

I hang up, guilt needling at me like tiny knives. But only for about thirty seconds. Then I picture Carter's face when he realises, I'm not there, that I'm actively avoiding him, and the guilt is washed away by a delicious, rebellious thrill that makes me smile despite everything.

I make coffee, strong enough to wake the dead, curl up on the sofa, turn on the telly, and try desperately not to think about him.

It lasts all of four seconds. Because of course, in some cosmic joke at my expense, the first channel I land on is about couples getting married at first sight. Actual strangers agreeing to marry each other based on nothing, and I immediately think about him. About how the producers should have asked him to participate. He'd have a ring on every woman's finger in three seconds flat with that commanding voice and those grey eyes, and I would absolutely hate it with the fire of a thousand suns.

My phone buzzes.

>AP: Are you alright?

Of course, I'm alright. I get demanding marriage proposals every other week.

The nerve!

I groan, pulling the blanket over my head like it's a shield against my conflicting emotions and questionable life choices.

"You're pathetic," I mutter into the fabric, and fling my phone across the sofa where it bounces off a cushion, lands on the floor with a thud, and starts ringing.

I kick off the blanket, ready to bark at Carter that he's legally not allowed to contact me on my day off. But when I flip the phone over, it's Baron's name flashing across the screen.

"Morning, sunshine," he drawls, far too cheerful for someone calling before nine a.m. "What time are we picking you up?"

"Who is we? And where are we going?" I ask, pulling the blanket up to my chin.

Baron snorts. "The autumn do, remember? It's tonight. Lucy and I will pick you up. Eight sharp."

"I don't know—" I hesitate. The thought of socialising when I'm busy actively avoiding my boss and having a minor existential crisis, feels reckless at best.

"Yes," Baron insists, his tone brooking no argument. "No excuses. Lucy wants to dance, Gareth's going to be there, and you—" he pauses, and I can practically hear his knowing grin through the line, "—need to get away from work and have some fun before you go completely mental."

"I'm the embodiment of fun," I protest weakly. "As long as it's not on a school night."

I'm never the embodiment of fun. I'm the embodiment of billable hours and anxiety.

"You're not," he says bluntly. "Pick you up at eight."

"No, you won't," I warn, flinging the blanket off me for added emphasis. "I mean it, Baron. I won't open the door, so don't waste your time."

Seriously, what is wrong with men these days? Do I need to put a sign on my door under the 'No junk mail' notice that says 'No unsolicited male callers'? Or possibly 'Beware: Emotionally unstable woman with wine and poor impulse control'?

"Alright," he mumbles, but I can hear the calculation in his voice. "But if you change your mind, and I really hope you do, just let me know."

"Bye, Baron," I say, hanging up before he can guilt-trip me into it with stories about Lucy being desperate for adult-interactions, or some other emotional manipulation tactic.

I drop my phone onto the cushion beside me and spend the next nine hours ignoring it while I binge-watch the entire series of couples getting married to strangers, eating my way through an entire punnet of grapes, and trying not to think about one particular handsome man.

By the time six p.m. rolls around, I've transformed into a proper sofa gremlin. My hair is knotted into something resembling a bird's nest, my pyjama top is stained with coffee, and I have a serious case of body odour that I'm surprisingly not bothered about. I unlock my phone to read the barrage of text messages I've been avoiding all day.

> AP: Buckman mentioned you needed an emergency day. If there's anything the firm can provide to support you, let me know.

How about a boss that doesn't drive me insane in every way possible?

> AP: I understand if you need space, just let me know you're safe.

I'm safe. Not so sure about my sanity.

> AP: Just one word so I know you're alright.

> AP: If this is about Saturday night, I'm sorry for leaving the way I did. We should discuss this properly.

I know how these discussions end—with him making demands, and me being more confused than before. No, thank you.

> AP: I meant what I said. Every word.

I believe you, and that's what I'm afraid of.

AP: You don't have to respond if you're not ready. But I need you to know I'm here when you are.

AP: Please.

I wish you were.

My thumbs hover over the keyboard. I could tell him I'm fine. Could thank him for checking. Could acknowledge the texts.

But what would I say? 'Thanks for the marriage proposal. Very thoughtful. I'll get back to you with an answer by end of business Wednesday'?

I lock the phone without typing anything.

I wish he were here, and that's the problem.

That's the thought that makes me want to throw my phone at the wall.

I wish he were here, sitting on my sofa, filling my space with that commanding presence, looking at me with those grey eyes that see too much.

It's a big problem. Possibly the biggest problem I've ever had.

Because no matter how fiercely I remind myself that he's my boss, that it's wrong, that it's dangerous, that it could destroy everything I've worked for, my chest still tightens when I think of him. When I remember how close we sit during late nights at the office, knees almost touching sitting next to each other, how perfect my hand fits in his. How he calls me lioness, like he sees something in me no one else does. Like I'm not just another employee or another conquest, but something rare and worth claiming.

As infuriating as he is, as impossible and arrogant and boundary-stomping as he is, I want to be around him. I want to argue with him about case strategy. I want to watch him work, all focused intensity and sharp intelligence. I want to know what he's thinking when he looks at me like I'm the only person in the room.

The doorbell rings, pulling me from my self-pity.

"Please don't let this be Carter," I whisper the words on repeat like a prayer, shuffling to the front door while frantically trying to smooth my hair into something resembling respectability.

There are faint noises outside the door, like the rustle of fabric and the soft clearing of a throat. It stops me dead in my tracks.

Don't make the same mistake twice. Don't open the door. Learn from your errors.

But then there's a knock, polite and nonthreatening, and a voice rings out.

"Hello, Sophie? Are you home?"

Gareth?

I yank open the door, and lo and behold, Gareth stands in my door frame, looking unfairly put-together in dark jeans, a tight-fitted white t-shirt, and a black leather jacket and boots that make him look like he walked off the set of a motorcycle ad.

"Hey, what are you doing here?" I ask, very aware of my dishevelled state and eau de sofa gremlin.

"Baron asked me to pick you up," he says with an apologetic smile.

"Did he now?" I huff, unable to stop the eye-roll that could probably be seen from space. I step aside to let Gareth in because apparently, I haven't learnt anything about letting uninvited men into my flat. "I told him I wasn't in the mood to go out tonight."

Gareth rubs the back of his neck in a nervous gesture that makes him look boyish and harmless. "Yeah, he reckoned you'd say as much. He also told me to use these in case you resist."

He pulls out a pair of handcuffs from his back pocket and dangles them on one finger between us, the metal glinting under the ceiling light.

"Baron has no right to make such threats," I say with a laugh that sounds slightly unhinged, turning away and walking back to the sofa.

Gareth follows but instead of taking a seat next to me, he stands cross-armed in front of me, blocking my view onto the telly like some sort of attractive bouncer. "He also reckoned you'd say that. And he told me if you resist, he'll give you a good tanning at the next sparring session."

Tanning.

My eyes bug at the word, memories slamming into me with brutal force. Carter spanking me with his ruler. The first time he put his hand around my throat. The burn, the ache, the way my body betrayed me by responding.

"Sophie? You okay?" Gareth frowns, immediately squatting down in front of me and squeezing my shoulder with concern. "I'm sure it was just a joke."

"Of course it was," I brush him off, plastering on a breezy smile that probably looks manic, and bolt towards the bathroom.

"Give me five minutes. I'll just freshen up. Then we can go."

Maybe drowning out my thoughts with loud music and alcohol isn't such a bad idea after all. It's certainly better than the endless spiral I've been caught in since Saturday night, living multiple hypothetical lives inside my head while my real life falls apart.

I quickly run through my routine—shower that's more like a controlled drowning, blow-dry that creates acceptable hair, lipstick that makes me look less like a cave dweller. Then I head into the bedroom.

At least my period has already decided to leave me in peace. My uterus must have thought it couldn't handle the menstrual cramps for much longer, given the near asphyxiation and the emotional chaos of the past couple of days. Even my body has limits.

Ten minutes later, I emerge looking like something resembling a functional human being—pale blue dress that hugs every curve, heels that guarantee blisters but also legs for days, and a little extra perfume to mask any lingering sofa gremlin essence.

When I check my reflection in the hallway mirror, I don't look like a woman hiding from her boss after he declared his intention to marry her. I look like a woman about to make questionable choices involving vodka. Not that I plan to get drunk. Never have been. Never will. But a couple of drinks with friends will do me good.

Stalker

Medard

She's not here.

The realisation hits me the moment I peek into her office. Nothing. Her desk sits empty, the chair tucked in with military precision, no coffee cup, no scattered files, no sign she's been here at all. My jaw tightens.

I stride towards her assistant's desk. "Where is she? Where's Miss Rosen?"

The girl looks up, eyes widening. "I... I don't know, Mr Carter. She hasn't come in yet."

"What do you mean you don't know? You're her assistant. Surely, she informed you if she wasn't coming in today."

Her face pales. "I... I don't know, sir."

"Has she called? Sent an email?"

"No, Mr Carter. Nothing."

Before I can respond, Buckman appears at my elbow.

"Carter, a word?" He guides me away from her desk. "I was about to notify Millie. Sophie just called me. She's taken an emergency day."

The words hit differently than they should. Emergency. My chest tightens.

"Is she alright?" The question comes out before I can stop it.

Buckman's brows rise slightly. "She didn't say. Just that she needed the day for a personal matter."

Personal matter. Which could mean anything from a doctor's appointment to actively avoiding me after I told her she'd be my wife, then kissed her and walked out like a bloody coward.

"Right," I say, schooling my features. "Thank you for letting me know."

I turn to head towards my office.

"Carter?" he calls after me. "If there's anything the firm can do to support her—"

"I'll handle it," I say without turning around, then immediately regret the possessive edge in my tone.

I make it ten feet before Muhammad falls into step beside me.

"Mr Carter, although my client list is full, and I'm overseeing

Mr Reynold's acquisitions, I'd be happy to support you while Miss Rosen is out."

"Why are you overseeing Reynolds' work?" I interrupt, stopping mid-stride.

She blinks. "Because you told me to after he lost the Bradford account."

Right. The potato debacle.

I turn and head directly towards Reynold's office. Muhammad follows, now looking slightly concerned, which is fair given I'm currently operating on approximately two hours of sleep and a dangerous amount of caffeine.

I stick my head in without knocking.

"You're off the hook," I say without preamble. "Muhammad's oversight. You don't need it anymore. Don't fuck up again."

Relief floods his features. "Thank you, Mr Carter."

I withdraw, leaving Muhammad looking bewildered.

"But her accounts—" she starts.

"Will be managed," I cut her off. "I'll take care of them myself."

I don't wait for her response, just continue to my office and slam the door. I drop into my chair and pull out my phone.

> Me: Are you alright?

I stare at the message before hitting send. Concerned employer checking on an absent employee. Perfectly appropriate.

The message delivers. Read receipt shows she's seen it. No response.

I force myself to focus on work. Twenty minutes pass. I check my phone. Nothing.

I type another message.

> Me: Buckman mentioned you needed an emergency day. If there's anything the firm can provide to support you, let me know.

Send. Delivered. Still nothing.

An hour drags by. I've read the same paragraph of a contract five times and retained none of it. My phone sits on my desk like a silent judge of my pathetic state.

> Me: I hope everything's okay.

Delete. Too personal.

> Me: Just checking in.

Delete. Too casual.

> Me: We should talk.

Delete, delete, delete.
By eleven, I've given up any pretence of working.

> Me: I understand if you need space, just let me know you're safe.

Send. Delivered. Then nothing.
Noon arrives. I've accomplished approximately nothing productive.

> Me: Just one word so I know you're alright.

Send. Delivered. Nothing.
I lean back, dragging both hands through my hair. This is ridiculous.
One o'clock. I try a different approach.

> Me: If this is about Saturday night, I'm sorry for leaving the way I did. We should   discuss this properly.

Nothing.
She's not reading them. That stings more than her defiance ever could.
Two o'clock. I'm in a meeting with a client and barely paying attention. I check my phone under the table like a bloody schoolboy. Nothing.

> Me: I meant what I said. Every word.

Send before I can reconsider. Delivered. Still nothing.
Three o'clock. I've sent six messages now. Six. I'm officially that person—the one who can't take a hint, who keeps texting into the void hoping for a response that clearly isn't coming.

> Me: You don't have to respond if you're not ready. But I need you to know I'm here when you are.

Still nothing.
I'm on the cusp of throwing my phone out the window, or drive to her flat and kick in the door.
Four o'clock. The office feels oppressive, every minute

stretching into an hour. I try to focus on work but Sophie's absence is a physical thing, a weight pressing on my chest.

    Me: Please.

One desperate, pathetic word.
Delivered. Read! My breath catches.
Then nothing.
By six o'clock, I've sent eight messages total and received exactly zero responses.
I grab my coat and head out, Janet calling something about tomorrow's schedule that I acknowledge with a grunt. The drive home should be simple.
Except I don't go home.
I tell myself I'm not going to her flat. That would be stalking, crossing a line I've already crossed one too many times, the behaviour of a man who's completely lost the plot. I'm just driving. Thinking. Processing.
But somehow, I find myself outside her building.
Her flat is dark. Every window is black.
She's not home.
The relief is immediate and short-lived, quickly replaced by a different kind of concern. Where is she? Is she alright? Is she avoiding me specifically, or is something actually wrong?
I sit in my car like a complete stalker, engine idling, telling myself to leave. To go home and stop this madness. I pull out my phone and do something I'm definitely not proud of—I look her up on social media.
All her accounts are sparse. Nothing recent. Nothing that tells me where she might be.
I'm about to give up when a thought occurs to me.
The gym. She does Krav Maga.
I search for Krav Maga clubs in her area, and find the one in Shadwell. I click through to their social media page. And there it is: Join us tonight for our Annual Autumn Do at White Russian! Eight PM.
White Russian. Cian's club.
I sit back, a slow smile spreading across my face.
She's not hiding. She's out. At Cian's club. Which means I know exactly where to find her.
I pull away and head towards Alex's house. I need backup for this.

He opens the door, eyebrows shooting up when he sees me. "Med? What are you—"

"Can I come in?" I'm already pushing past him before he can answer.

He closes the door slowly, following me into his living space with obvious confusion. "Everything alright?"

"Everything's fine," I say, which is a blatant lie, but he doesn't need to know that.

He studies me for a moment, then shrugs and heads back to his dining room where I seem to have interrupted his dinner of some sort of pastry on a plate and... what the actual fuck? Is he crafting?

There's a ton of colourful ribbons and wires on his table, and a glue gun plugged into the wall behind him with its cable stretched across the room.

"What the fuck is this?" I laugh, picking up a bright pink ribbon. "Are you Martha fucking Stewart now, or what?"

He snatches the ribbon from my hand and shoves it with the others to the far corner of the table.

"Never you mind," he mumbles, clearly embarrassed by his new-found hobby.

I let it slide with more important matters pressing on my mind. He sits back down, picks up the pastry, and brings it halfway to his mouth. Then he catches sight of my face. The expression I'm wearing, the one I can feel pulling at my features in equal parts mischief, determination and barely contained chaos. He stops mid-bite, pastry hovering in the air, his eyes narrowing.

"No," he says flatly.

"I haven't said anything yet."

"You don't need to. I know that face." He sets the pastry down with exaggerated care. "That's your 'I'm about to do something monumentally stupid and I need you to enable me' face."

"I prefer to think of it as my 'I have a brilliant plan' face."

"It's the same face, and the answer is no." He crosses his arms. "Absolutely not. Whatever you're planning, I want no part of it."

"You fancy paying Cian a visit tonight?"

He stares at me. Then drops his head into his hands with a groan. "Dios mío. You're going to get us killed."

"Is that a yes?"

"That's a 'you're insane and I should have better friends.'" He looks up, resignation already settling into his features. "What time?"

"Starts at eight, but I'd like to get there asap."

"And why, exactly, are we visiting Cian's club on a Monday night?"

"Does it matter?"

"Yes, because the last time you dragged me somewhere without explanation, I ended up holding your jacket while you punched a man for looking at your car wrong."

"He wasn't just looking at it. He sat on the bonnet taking pictures, pretending it was his car."

"Still, punching him was overkill."

I wave him off. "This is completely different. This is... pure observation."

"Observation," he repeats, completely deadpan. "Observing what?"

"Does it matter?"

He studies me, and I can see the exact second he figures it out.

"This is about the woman. The one you're supposedly marrying despite her not accepting you."

"She will accept me. I just need to get my hands on her to make her see sense."

"Which is why she's not answering your calls."

"She's not answering my texts. I haven't called."

"Because that would be too sane." He sighs. "Fine. Give me thirty minutes."

"Twenty."

"Thirty, or I'm not going."

"Twenty-five."

He glares at me. "You're impossible."

"So I've been told. Recently, in fact. By the woman we're going to see tonight."

"We're not seeing anyone," he corrects. "We're coincidentally visiting Cian's club."

"Exactly."

"You're going to end up in prison," he mutters, heading towards his bedroom. "And I'm going to end up visiting you there, wondering where I went wrong in my life."

I pull out my phone one more time.

Nothing. But that's fine.

In a couple of hours, I'll be able to see for myself that she's alright.

Forty minutes later, the bass pulses through our chests. The volume is deafening.

The interior screams aristocracy meets grunge with its black damask walls paired with multi-coloured chandeliers. Bodies writhe on the dance floor, neon strobes slice through the air, and the scent of alcohol clings to everything.

Alex's arms fly up and he thrusts his hips to the beat. Unlike me, he knows how to dance and pulls the attention of a few women around us.

Show-off.

But to my surprise, he doesn't acknowledge them as he'd usually does.

We make our way to the main bar. Cian is serving some girl a cocktail disguised as a rainbow. She hands him a twenty, and he returns her change along with his business card and a wink that's probably got a ninety-five percent success rate. It's so blunt and unsophisticated, but it works for him every time. This is his playground, after all, and he has spent years perfecting exactly how to play on it.

"I'll go say 'hi' to Cian," Alex shouts into my ear, "you coming?"

I shake my head, already scanning the crowd. "I'll catch up with you later!"

Before he can respond, I prowl towards a blond mane that's bopping wildly to the music. I'm almost able to reach her, when she turns and I realise it's not Sophie.

For the next half hour, I tap shoulders, circle the dance floor four times and even stand outside the ladies restroom long enough that security requests I stop creeping out female guests.

I'm almost resigning myself to not finding her, when my eyes finally land on her beautiful face, and my blood begins to boil.

She's standing at a bar table, and next to her is none other than Gareth fucking Hayes. I barely take in her other companions—Baron Carson and another woman who I assume must be his wife. No, my focus is on Sophie and that stupid copper. He playfully bumps his shoulder against hers and both are laughing like they're on some bloody double-date. My feet propel me forward, ready to drag her away from her company and over my lap.

I make it halfway across the room when she gets up and walks straight towards me. For a moment, I think she's spotted me but when she's barely three feet away, her eyes lock with mine. Surprise has her stumble back but I reach out and grab her hand, steadying her before she pulls her arm out of my hold.

Her gaze travels the length of my body, taking in the all-black outfit of shirt, jeans and Chelsea boots—courtesy of Alex's wardrobe.

Yes, baby! It's all yours.

She frowns and says something, but the music is too loud to make out a single word. Her hands find my shoulders, and she leans up on her toes to bring her mouth close to my ear.

"I said, are you stalking me now?" She tries to pull away, but I circle my arm around her waist and press her against my chest.

Fuck, I've missed her.

"You didn't answer any of my texts!"

She rolls her eyes and attempts to push me away, but I yank her back. She can't expect me to sit idly by while she keeps dating that prick. I've made my intentions more than clear now.

She pulls against my hold once more, then opts to intertwine her fingers with mine. I let her guide me out of the dance hall and into the corridors. We take a few turns until we're tucked away in a far corner where the corridor ends. There's nothing more but an emergency exit and the vibrations of the music bouncing off the walls.

"What are you doing here, Carter?" she says with an exasperated huff.

Finally, away from the chaos inside, I take a moment to drink her in. Her hair is pinned up. So even on a night out, she won't allow herself to literally let her hair down. Her dress is a pale blue silk tube dress that barely stops below her arse. The matching heels are an inch higher than she wears at the office. She looks hot, too damn hot to be out and around other men. The fucking copper, no less.

"I've come to make sure you get home safe."

She snorts, pointing her tiny strapless handbag at me, and I realise we're still holding hands.

"Gareth is taking me home, and regardless, I can take care of myself."

She starts to turn away, but I pull her back and press her against the wall, holding her captive between my arms.

"I told you, you'll be my wife," I bite out, "so stop this jealousy-bullshit, and finally get rid of him, or I'll do it for you."

"Just who the fuck do you think you are?" she asks, voice soaked in incredulity.

Her foul language takes me by surprise, but then I smell the booze on her breath. She's plenty tipsy.

"I'm the man you've been avoiding since he proposed to you."

"Proposed?" she says, laughter bouncing off the walls, "I must have missed the part where you went down on one knee and asked the question."

"Is that what you want, lioness?" I whisper, leaning forward so our lips are almost touching. "You want me to fall to my knees and beg you for the inevitable?"

"That's not what I—" she gasps as my mouth captures hers, my tongue darting out to taste her.

She instantly melts into me, moans spilling from her.

"Carter, what are you doing?" she pants, her head lolling back as I kiss her neck. "Someone might see us."

My hand glides up the back of her soft thigh before hooking her leg around my hip. I kiss a path down her body, inhaling that sweet scent of her skin. She smells divine, like a meadow of bluebells and Sunday morning cuddles in bed. I curl my fingers around the top edge of her dress and bra, and tug until her breasts spill out.

Fuck, the sight of her is testing my restraint. My balls tingle, my cock is twitching violently at the mere sight of the two dark pink bullets, I'm desperate to pull between my teeth.

"Don't worry, lioness. This won't take long," I whisper against her nipple before my mouth latches onto it.

I gently suck on the sensitive peak before releasing it with a pop. Sophie's moans swirl around me as I give the same attention to her other nipple.

My kisses travel further down her body, as her fingers find my head and run through my hair, eliciting the most toe-curling sensation to shoot up my spine. I slide the hem of her dress over that delectable arse, that I've admired so many god-damn times and wished to sink my teeth in.

My knees hit the floor, and I feel the strain of the jeans against my solid cock.

Fuck, I'm dying to feel her on it. Her hands, mouth, pussy—any will do as long as it's hers.

I hook her leg over my shoulder. Her dress hikes up further by the movement, and exposes her panties—a skimpy piece of pale blue lace, that's adorned with a dark patch. A devilish grin pulls at the corners of my lips. She's sopping wet and ready for me.

"Carter—" Her gasp pulls me out of my momentary trance.

I look up over the soft swell of her breasts. Her gaze is sultry, her hips swaying forward in a silent plea.

Victory curses through my veins as I hook my finger under her panties and pull them aside. Her heady scent invades my senses.

Fuck.

Whatever it is that makes a pussy beautiful—Sophie's got it. And she's mine. This pussy is mine.

Another gasp draws my attention to her face, her eyes widening in horror, clarity flooding her.

"Wait, Carter, I don't think—" she starts, but her words dissolve into a moan as I swipe my tongue through her pussy.

Her knees buckle, one hand flies to her mouth, the other slides along the wall for purchase.

I devour her with fervour, lapping at her sweet juices. She tastes incredible, better than the best scotch I've ever had.

"Oh god, Carter!" Sophie cries out at another firm sweep of my tongue. I drag up the little hood until her bundle of nerves is fully exposed, and then I go in for the kill. I suck on her pearl like it's holding the key to her heart.

The pleasure ripples through her body. Her hand presses harder against her mouth, but her muffled whimpers still shoot straight to my cock.

"That's it, lioness," I mumble between nibs and sucks. "See how good I can make you feel?"

She whimpers a quiet "yes" as her legs start to tremble.

"Accept us, and you'll have this for the rest of your life. Marry me!"

She gasps just before I can feel her flutter against my lips. One more suck, and she'll come undone. But before I can close my mouth on her again, she lifts her leg off my shoulder and shoves. Her heel digs into my flesh, my knees lift off the floor, and before I can find my balance, I fall right onto my arse, stunned.

What the fuck?

"Screw you!" she yells, nostrils flaring with indignity as she re-adjusts her dress.

"Sophie!" Her name rips from my throat as she shoves through the emergency exit.

The door crashes against the wall.

Fuck!

I scramble to my feet and push out into the dark. The night air bites at my lungs as I search frantically, and then I see her. She's storming down the narrow alley. But then my chest flares with rage.

Some pissed bastard stumbles into her path and grabs her elbow.

"Come on, sweetheart." His voice is thick, repulsive. He cups his dick through his jeans. "You look like you're up for a little fun on my cock."

"No," Sophie snaps. "I said get your filthy hands off me."

My blood roars. My fists clench. I take off towards them, ready to rip him apart, but Sophie beats me to it.

She jerks her arm free, grabs him by the shoulders, and her knee drives up hard into his gut. The sound he makes is grotesque, a strangled grunt that bounces off the walls as he doubles over. Against his better judgement or sheer stupidity, he tries to grab her neck. But my lioness? She doesn't falter.

Christ! Even her rage is glorious. Enough to drop men to their knees. Enough to make me want to drop to mine, again.

She deflects him like he's nothing more than a mosquito, her arms pushing his away with sharp precision before her palm shoots up. It collides with his chin, snapping his head back as though he's suddenly enamoured with the starless sky above.

"You fucking bitch!" he bellows, staggering forward.

Her hand whips out, clamps his arm, and spins him like he's a rag doll. His body arches as she yanks him back by his hair, bending him so far, I feel the pull in my own damn spine.

My gaze follows her every move in awe of her strength, her beauty. Even amidst the ugliest of circumstances, she truly is a force to be reckoned with.

Then, in the final blow, she jumps—Jumps!—in those killer heels and slams her elbow into his chest. The thud echoes through the alley. The piece-of-shit hits the ground hard, weeping with pain as he curls up.

And Sophie? She doesn't flinch. Doesn't break a sweat. Doesn't even smudge her lipstick. She steps over him, adjusts her dress, picks up her handbag, and marches towards me. Her eyes blaze when she reaches me, but her stride doesn't falter.

"I told you I can protect myself!" she snaps, every word a bullet.

Her heels hammer against the cobblestone, the sharp rhythm echoing through the alley, syncing with the relentless pounding of my heart.

Holy. Fucking. Shit!

I knew she was strong. But this? Seeing her unleash herself completely untamed, breaking down someone twice her size—it's the hottest proof that she wants me.

She could easily fight me off, but chooses not to. She lets me overpower her, lets me dominate her, because deep down she knows she belongs with me. Wants me. Needs me.

"Carajo!" The word slices through my thoughts.

Alex is standing behind me, slack-jawed and starry-eyed.

"What a woman!" His voice is thick with awe. "You don't want to mess with her."

I turn back to her, watching as she reaches the end of the alley, strides onto the high street, and disappears around the corner. I swallow, my chest tight, my cock harder than granite, my heart thundering.

"Meet Sophie," I say, my voice raw, "my future wife."

Alex's grin splits wide as he claps my shoulder. "Of course, she is."

Tosser

Sophie

Marry me EXCLAMATION MARK! Like a bloody demand, not a sincere, heartfelt offering wrapped up in a humble question. God forbid, the prick has to actually ask for something for once in his entitled life!

I'm livid, absolutely seething. My heels pound against the cobblestones like tiny hammers of fury, carrying me further away from this arrogant tosser with his magical lips and his complete inability to understand basic proposal etiquette.

I feel the adrenaline drain out of me, and the effect of the vodka swirling through my body stronger than before. I think I'm slightly more drunk than I thought. But I'm still good. Still in control of my body and mind. I don't understand why people struggle with it so much. Being drunk is easy. Dealing with Carter? Now that's a challenge far more difficult than walking in a straight line.

I pop into the first corner shop I pass, the fluorescent lights making me squint as I grab a bottle of Chardonnay from the shelf, not even looking at the price because I'm having a crisis and crises don't have budgets. I pay the bewildered cashier, and step back out onto the high street.

One big swig later, straight from the bottle like some sort of classy wine connoisseur, and I instantly feel the hum of booze flare through my senses like liquid confidence.

God, his lips though! They felt so bloody good on my clit, his hands so perfect on my body, all commanding and sure and absolutely obliterating to my sanity. I was so riled up, so ready to come all over his handsome face while he knelt there looking like some sort of sex god making offerings at the altar of my—

"Hey, sexy!"

"Fuck off, you absolute twat!" I yell, flipping the bird with my free hand to some guy standing outside a pub, my clutch tucked under my arm, my wine bottle clutched in the other hand like a weapon I'm not afraid to use.

He stumbles backwards, hands up in surrender, and I keep walking because I'm on a mission. A drunk, angry, sexually frustrated mission.

That demand. That bloody demand ripped me right out of my wanton stupor like someone had thrown a bucket of ice water on my lady parts.

I can't believe he thought I would accept that pathetic excuse for a proposal. It wasn't a proposal, not now in the club, not back in my flat when he had his hand around my throat. It was nothing more than Carter dangling his fucking superiority over my head like I'm some sort of corporate acquisition he's decided to merge with.

Another swig. The wine's not even cold anymore, but I don't care. It's wet and alcoholic and that's all that matters.

I feel the booze pumping through my veins harsher than before as the crisp midnight air fills my lungs and bites at my bare shoulders.

Shit!

I left my coat at the club. And Gareth. Double shit! Triple shit! All the shits!

I fumble with my phone, squinting at the screen because when did phones get so bloody bright? I shoot him a quick message with fingers that suddenly don't want to cooperate.

> Me: Hey, somethinf come up had to go homf but fotgit my cost.

I stare at the message. That's not... that's not how words work. But send. Done. No takesies backsies.

There's absolutely no way I'm going back to that club. Gareth's a good guy though, a nice guy. He'll pick up my coat despite my ditching him without explanation. Unlike Carter, who'd probably hold it hostage and demand I sign something in triplicate for its safe return. Or worse, use it to blackmail me into another round of whatever the hell that was in the club.

Na-uh! Not gonna happen!

I take another defiant swig.

It doesn't matter that he kissed me with a ferocity that puts all my past kisses to absolute shame, making every other man I've ever kissed feel like a practise round for the main event. Or that his amber-flecked eyes devoured me with an intensity that made me feel like the sexiest woman on this entire planet, possibly in this solar system. Or that a single touch from him sets my entire body ablaze and I know, I just know, that only he can extinguish this raging desire that's consuming me from the inside out.

God, I'm so sick of fighting off his advances. So sick of fighting against my treacherous, traitorous libido that keeps insisting he's exactly what I need.

I stop mid-stride, nearly tripping over my own feet, and with flailing arms that nearly send my wine bottle flying, I look down at the primary source of my betrayal.

"Get on fucking board!" I announce to my crotch, pointing at it accusingly with the hand holding my phone. "You can't have him! We've discussed this! Multiple times!"

A woman walking her dog crosses to the other side of the street.

I start walking again, trying to maintain my dignity while ignoring the fact that my soaked knickers are squelching with each step like some sort of perverted tally counter keeping count of my humiliations. A few people watch me with confused expressions, probably wondering if they should call someone.

"What?" I bark at a couple who've stopped to stare. "Have you never seen a woman have a rational discussion with her own vagina? It's called self-reflection!"

Their heads immediately whip away, faces flushed with either embarrassment or genuine concern that they're about to be attacked by a raging lunatic with a wine bottle and questionable decision-making skills.

Let them worry. I couldn't care less about anyone's opinion tonight. I need to put a stop to this excruciating mind-fuck that is Medard Carter. I need to cleanse myself of him. Exorcise him from my system like a demon that's taken up residence in my knickers.

I take another swig of wine, definitely warm now, possibly terrible to begin with, and nearly walk into a lamppost.

"Excuse you!" I tell the lamppost, which has the audacity to just stand there. "Some of us are trying to walk here!"

My phone buzzes. Gareth.

> Gareth: Are you okay? That message was concerning. Also, I think you meant 'coat.' Do you need me to come get you?

Sweet Gareth. Lovely, uncomplicated Gareth.

> Me: Im FINE im walkibg im FINE the wine is helping

Gareth: What wine? Where are you?

I squint at my phone, trying to remember where I am. There's a... street. Buildings. Some sort of bin that's judging me.

Me: streets. Tehres streets. Many of yhem

Gareth: I'm coming to find you. Stay put. I have your coat.

Stay put? I'm on a mission! A drunk mission of self-discovery and Carter-removal!
Another text comes through. Baron this time.

Baron: Gaz says you left early. You good?

Me: briiiiiiiiiiiiillll!!+

Baron: Where are you?

Me: bench. Its a good bemch

Baron Carson: Don't move. What street?

I look around for a street sign. Everything's a bit blurry but I manage to make out enough letters.

Me: the one with the nane on it

Baron: Sophie!

Me: FINE dean street ma ybe

Baron: Stay there.

"I don't need rescuing!" I announce to my phone, then realise I haven't actually sent that as a text. I jab at the screen with force, spelling every word out loud.

Me: IM FINE IM A INDEP ENDENT WOMAN

Beyoncé would be so proud of me right now. Or possibly concerned. It's hard to tell.
I spot a bench. Wait, I'm already on a bench. This bench. The one I just texted about.
I'm so efficient.

I collapse further into it with less grace than intended, clutching my wine bottle like it's the only friend I have left in this world. Which, let's be honest, at this moment it might be because I ditched my friends for Carter.

"Stupid Carter," I mutter to the bottle. "With his stupid face and his stupid eyes and his stupid tongue and his stupid... stupidness."

The wine doesn't respond, but I feel like it understands me on a deep level.

"He can't just demand I marry him," I continue, because apparently, I'm having a full conversation with alcohol now. "That's not how proposals work. There should be... I don't know... romance? A question? Maybe not having his face buried between my thighs at the time?"

A man walking past gives me a very wide berth.

"ALTHOUGH," I call after him, because why not make this worse, "THE THIGH PART WAS QUITE GOOD. JUST POOR TIMING!"

He breaks into a light jog.

I slump back against the bench, staring up at the sky that's spinning slightly. Or maybe I'm spinning. Hard to tell.

My phone buzzes again.

> Gareth: Can't find you. Baron says he's close to you. Stay where you are.

> Baron: I see you. Don't move.

I try to take another sip of wine but miss my mouth slightly, dribbling down my chin like some sort of sophisticated lady of the evening.

"This is fine," I tell the universe. "Everything is fine. I'm just a successful lawyer having a small breakdown on a public bench while arguing with my rep-rerop-reproductive system. Totally normal Sunday night behaviour."

It's not Sunday. I think. What day is it?

"Sophie Rosen." Baron's voice cuts through my wine-induced philosophical musings.

I look up to find him standing in front of me, arms crossed, expression somewhere between amused and concerned.

"Baron!" I announce with far too much enthusiasm, my voice echoing off nearby buildings. "You found me! Not that I was lost. I knew exactly where I was. On a bench. This bench. Very specific location."

He drops onto the bench beside me, eyeing the wine bottle dangling from my fingers. "How much have you had?"

I hold up the bottle proudly. It's mostly empty. When the hell did that happen?

"Not enough to forget that Carter stalked me."

Baron's brows shoot up. "He what now?"

"Stalked!" I wave my arms dramatically, nearly clocking him with the bottle. "Venit, vidit, vicit!"

"He came, he saw, he conquered?" Baron translates, and my jaw drops.

"You speak Latin!?" I throw my arms up in astonishment. The bottle goes flying and lands with a soft thunk on the grass behind me. "And yes, he conquered all right. Right between my thighs. But I shoved him off because I'm an in-indepedentet woman who makes her own decisions, thank you very much."

There's a beat of stunned silence.

Then Baron starts laughing in a deep, genuine laughter that makes his shoulders shake.

"The man has balls," he manages between guffaws. "I'll give him that."

"It's *not* funny!" I protest, but I'm giggling too because his laughter is infectious and also everything's kind of hilarious when you're this drunk. "He thinks he can just demand we be a couple!"

"The absolute cheek," Baron says, still grinning like a loon.

"Right?" I pause, squinting at him suspiciously. "Wait. Are you siding with him? Why are you grinning? I was right to push him off mid-orgasm and legging it."

Baron whistles low. "Brutal."

"He deserved it!" I insist, then immediately deflate. "Didn't he? He deserved it, right?"

"Come on." Baron stands, offering his hand. "Let's get you home before you pass out on this bench and someone mistakes you for a very well-dressed homeless person."

I let him haul me up, wobbling like a newborn giraffe. "This is all your fault. Yours and Lucy's. You two filled me up with vodka like I'm some sort of Russian nesting doll."

"I know," Baron sighs, steering me down the street with one hand firmly on my elbow. "If it makes you feel better, Lucy isn't feeling so clever either. You women can't hold your liquor."

"Sexist," I mumble. "Is she alright? Where is she?"

"Gaz's taking her home."

"Good old Gareth. Saint Gareth."

Baron chuckles, keeping me vertical as we navigate the pavement. I lean into him heavily because apparently walking in heels while drunk is harder than ice-skating with only one leg.

"You really pushed him off?" Baron asks after a moment, curiosity threading through his voice.

"Yeah. He thinks—" I pause, searching for words through the booze fog. There's no way I'm telling Baron about the proposal. "He thinks he can decide my future without consulting me first."

"And how do you feel about that?"

I stop walking, swaying dangerously. "I feel like... like he's an arrogant arse who thinks he can just steamroll over my life. But also—" I hiccup. "Also, his mouth is bloody magic and I might be in love with him, and I hate it. I hate it so much."

Baron's expression softens. "Yeah. I figured."

"You did?"

"Sophie, you've been talking about him all night. Everyone's figured it out except maybe you and Carter."

"Huh, you stupid," I laugh through another bout of hiccups.

He hails a taxi, and I practically fall into the back seat. It feels like a cloud. Baron's shoulder is solid and warm when I slump against it. My eyelids are suddenly made of lead, and I let them close. Just for a moment.

"Sophie?" Baron's voice floats from somewhere far away. "Water's on your nightstand. Paracetamol too. You're going to need them."

"Mmph," is all I manage, snuggling deeper into something soft that smells like home.

The light clicks off, plunging everything into blessed darkness.

"Sleep it off," Baron says quietly, and I feel a blanket settle over me. "Tomorrow's going to be interesting."

Git

Sophie

I wake to my mouth tasting like I've licked a pub floor, and my skull pounding like it's been used as a football. The air reeks of stale vodka and something sickly sweet—probably the perfume I bathed in last night.

I groan, peel one eye open, and immediately wish I hadn't.

"Oh, bloody hell."

Through my bedroom door, I've got a front-row view of carnage. My flat looks like it's been through a riot. The vase that used to sit primly on the side table is now in five hundred glittering pieces across my rug. Cushions gutted with their stuffing scattered like some demented snowfall. My books, my poor books, are face-down and spine-up, casualties of war.

Someone's been in here.

My pulse spikes. Panic floods my veins faster than last night's vodka ever did. I scramble for my phone, following its charging cable stretched across the room like a tripwire. My thumb hovers over Gareth's name. Sensible, dependable Gareth, who'll know exactly what to do.

But I pause.

Work.

I might be having a crisis, but Carter made it crystal clear last night that he doesn't do "absences." He does expectations. And consequences. And with my flat looking like a crime scene, I'm hardly going to waltz into the office and draw up contracts like nothing happened.

I dial Ben first.

"Morning, Soph!" His voice is aggressively cheerful and over-caffeinated.

"Ben," I croak. "Cover for me at the office. I've had a break-in."

"A what?"

"I'll explain later. Just... please?"

A pause. Then a sigh. "Fine. But you owe me lunch. And pudding."

"Deal. Just make sure Carter doesn't find out."

He chuckles. "Done. Take care, yeah?"

I hang up and finally call Gareth.

He answers on the second ring. "Sophie? You alive?"

"Debatable." My voice sounds like I've swallowed gravel. "My flat's destroyed. I think someone broke in."

Silence. Then a low curse. "Stay put. Don't touch anything. I'll be there in ten minutes. Twenty, tops."

I flop back onto the bed, heart hammering, thighs burning. Gareth's on his way. I should feel better. But my brain won't shut up about one persistent question—Why the hell am I wearing my graduation gown?

The doorbell rings.

Bloody hell, he's quick. It's been barely ten minutes since I hung up with Gareth.

I yank off the gown, swap it for a modest light grey loungewear set of sweater and trousers, and tie my hair up in a quick, messy bun. Then, while carefully avoiding ceramic shrapnel, I shuffle towards the door and open it, ready to collapse into Gareth's reassuring presence.

Except it's not Gareth.

It's Carter.

With hands in his pockets, he's leaning against the door frame like he's posing for GQ—dark suit immaculate, eyes the colour of a gathering storm fixed on me with unnerving intensity. He looks ready to dominate a boardroom, not check on an employee who may or may not still be drunk.

"Lioness." His voice is low and smooth as whiskey. "You're alright."

I blink at him. "What... why... how are you..." Words abandon me. I sound like a malfunctioning robot.

"I was worried." His gaze slides past me, taking in the disaster zone. His jaw tightens. "Clearly, with good reason."

"How do you even know about this?"

I'm going to murder Ben.

Carter doesn't answer. He simply steps forward, like he's been granted permanent access to my life. I plant my hand against his chest to stop him, and the heat radiating through his shirt slams right into me, dragging me back to the club. His hands. His mouth. His—

Damn you, libido.

He walks further into my flat, forcing me backwards, and shuts the door with his foot.

"What happened last night, lioness?" There's dark amusement threading through his words.

Does he mean the disaster in my flat or the moment we shared at the club? Before I can ask, another knock rattles the door.

"Morning!" Gareth's cheerful voice filters through. "Open up before your neighbours think I'm here to arrest you."

Carter's expression shifts, subtle, but I catch it. His jaw hardens. His eyes darken.

Well, isn't that just great.

I shove at him, then swing the door wide.

Gareth steps in wearing full police kit, hair slicked back, eyes scanning the chaos instantly. He's all business, until he spots Carter.

"Oh." The word comes out slowly. "Didn't realise you had company."

Carter's smile doesn't reach his eyes. "We've met."

"At the shop. You're her *boss*."

I want the floor to swallow me whole.

"Brought this for you." Gareth hands me my coat. "Glad Baron found you."

The coat weighs heavy in my hands, as the memory slams into me again—Carter's mouth on mine, on my breasts, between my thighs, before he demanded I'd marry him and I stormed out. Heat floods my cheeks.

"Thanks," I mumble, unable to meet Gareth's eyes, but Carter's smirk says he's reliving the exact same memory.

The bastard.

Gareth clears his throat. "So... what was the emergency?"

"Pardon?" I stammer, clutching the coat tighter.

"You texted me last night to pick up your coat. Said something came up."

I want to hide under the bloody thing.

"I... it's complicated."

Carter's smirk deepens. I glare at him, which only makes him look smugger.

Git.

"Right." Gareth breaks the silence. "Let me make you tea first."

He heads to the kitchen. Carter watches me for another beat before prowling after him like a predator claiming territory.

"She doesn't drink tea," he says smoothly.

My head snaps round. "Excuse me?"

"She drinks coffee." He continues like I haven't spoken. "Splash of milk. No sugar."

Gareth glances at Carter, then me, sugar pot in hand. He sets it back on the counter with deliberate care. "I know that."

The air thickens. Testosterone practically crackles. I half expect them to whip out measuring tapes.

"I'll check the locks," Gareth says, sliding past Carter and clapping his shoulder. "Tea for me. One sugar, thanks."

He doesn't wait for a response, disappearing into the living room—which I'm glad about because he misses Carter's sneer.

With Gareth inspecting for forced entry and Carter occupied with drinks, I resign myself to sitting at the kitchen table.

"You didn't have to come," I mumble, hyper-aware of Gareth nearby and how things ended with Carter last night, after I defended myself against that drunken tosser. Krav Maga really paid off. Though, if only I could bring myself to use those skills to disarm the particularly stubborn specimen of a man currently standing in my kitchen.

"I wanted to." He leans against the counter while the kettle and coffee machine work. "I care about you."

His Adam's apple bobs, and for a fleeting moment he almost looks vulnerable. But then he turns away, continuing with the drinks like the last five seconds didn't happen.

I ignore the sudden ache in my heart. The morning is surreal enough as it is. I pull my legs to my chest, arms wrapped around them, trying to process last night.

The club. Baron and Lucy ordering vodka like it's going out of fashion. Gareth attempting a deflection move and landing on his arse. Lucy mentioning something about belts and whips. Then Carter. The heated moment, his mouth everywhere. He proposed in his own twisted way, and I bolted straight into that disgusting man's arms. I fought him off and left. I remember walking down the main road with a wine bottle. God knows how I got that. Then everything's foggy. Baron was there. Took me home. I remember lying in bed, the room spinning, and then waking up this morning.

"Soph? Have you always left the keys in the windows?" Gareth calls from the living room.

"Yes," I call back, voice cracking.

Carter places coffee beside me. I whisper "thanks", trying to clear my throat. To my surprise, he crouches in front of me, eyes roaming my face. I retreat behind my knees. I hate when he looks at me like that, like I'm a puzzle he's determined to solve.

"Did you wreck your place?" he asks out of the blue. "Did you do this because I proposed?"

"Keep your voice down." I hiss, eyes darting towards the open door. "Why would I wreck my own flat?"

He shrugs, a smile tugging at his lips. "You tell me. Maybe your subconsciousness is trying to break you out of that mould you're hiding in, so you can finally accept us."

That's ridiculous. I'm not confined in some mould. I'm just... me.

Before I can respond, he straightens and pours Gareth's tea. He adds milk and a teaspoon of sugar, but then he pauses, sugar pot and spoon still in hand. His lips curve into that devilish smirk, mischief dancing in his eyes.

"Carter, don't." I warn, barely breathing, eyes shooting towards the open door again. Gareth's boots are still thudding in the hallway. "You're being petty."

Carter doesn't even flinch. Of course, he doesn't. The man has the audacity of a cat in church, unbothered, smug, and somehow infuriatingly magnetic while doing it.

He shrugs casually, that sinful smile widening, and proceeds to shovel three more spoons of sugar into Gareth's cup.

"You call it petty," he says, stirring slowly. "I call it territorial."

I blink. "Territorial?" My voice pitches higher. "I'm not some—"

I stop myself before saying trophy, possession, or God forbid, territory to mark. Because that's exactly the sort of thing Carter would twist into something indecent just to watch me blush.

Before I can properly scold him, Gareth strides into the kitchen, his tall frame filling the doorway.

"The lock on your front door and all the windows look fine," he says, scanning the room before his gaze lands on the cup. "No tampering. Is that mine?"

"Sure is." Carter's lips twitch as he barely hides a grin behind his tiny espresso cup.

Gareth takes a generous gulp. The reaction is immediate. His face scrunches like he's just licked the inside of a sugar bowl.

"Jeez, that's sweet." He coughs, wiping his mouth. "You sure you only put one in?"

Carter's smirk is pure sin.

"If you don't like it," he says, shrugging one broad shoulder, "should have made your own."

I glare at him, but it's useless. He knows exactly what he's done, and he's bloody enjoying it.

Smug bastard.

And still, my pulse is doing that ridiculous fluttering thing again, the one that says I should be furious. But part of me—God help me—likes watching him claim the space like he owns it.

I lean back against the wall, tucking my legs tighter against my chest to stop myself from clawing at my thighs. My nerves are shredded, my head pounding, and the two men in my kitchen are circling like rival lions.

"So, any enemies I should know about?" Gareth takes another sip in a silent challenge to Carter. "Preferably ones with a key?"

I laugh weakly. "No one's got my key."

"No one? What if there's an emergency?" Genuine concern laces Gareth's voice, but all I hear is the pity underneath. *Poor little Sophie, all alone.*

Carter's jaw ticks. "That'll change."

Gareth glances at Carter, then refocuses on me. "If you like, I can keep a spare—"

"I'll keep a spare at the office." Carter interrupts, downing the rest of his espresso. "Makes the most sense."

The words are possessive, protective, and wildly inappropriate coming from my employer. Gareth nearly chokes on his tea.

"No," I say automatically. "That's not—"

Carter's eyes meet mine, and the look silences me. It's not threatening. It's... claiming. Like the decision's already been made and I'm just catching up.

"We'll discuss it later," he says, which means we won't discuss it at all. He'll just show up one day with a copy.

And then it hits me, clear as daylight.

The vase. The cushions. The books.

I did this.

The realisation creeps in like an unwelcome guest. Still drunk and furious, I woke in the middle of the night, still fuming about Carter, still buzzing from vodka, and tore through my own flat like a hurricane.

My stomach twists with shame.

This is worse than the scratching. Worse than clawing at my thighs until they bleed. This is destruction beyond my body—I'm destroying my home now. My safe space. The only place that's supposed to be mine.

And they're both standing here treating me like I need protecting, when the real threat is me.

"I'm fine, guys." The lie tastes bitter. I force brightness into my voice and turn to Gareth. "Anyway, you probably need to get to work now."

Gareth's eyes narrow slightly. If he knows I'm deflecting, he's decided not to push. That's the difference between him and Carter. Gareth respects boundaries. Carter bulldozes straight through them like they're made of tissue paper.

"Yeah, sure," Gareth says slowly, setting his disgustingly sweet tea on the counter. "But I'm checking in later. And Sophie?" His voice drops, serious now. "If you need anything, and I mean anything, you call me. Yeah?"

The sincerity in his eyes makes my chest ache. He's a good friend. The best, really.

"I will. Promise."

I walk him to the door, hyper-aware of Carter's presence burning into my back like a brand. The tension is thick enough to choke on.

At the threshold, I hug Gareth gratefully, as much for the buffer he's provided as anything else. When I pull away, something shifts in his expression, and before I can stop him, he cups my face with both hands. The gesture is far more intimate than our newly established friendship warrants. He presses a slow, deliberate kiss to my cheek, his lips lingering there just long enough to make it look like something it isn't.

"Take care, Soph," he murmurs loud enough for Carter to hear. "Call me later, yeah?"

The cheeky bugger.

He pulls back with an innocent smile, then glances over my shoulder. Whatever he sees on Carter's face makes his grin widen. "Mr Carter."

"Gareth," Carter returns, voice like ice.

Gareth gives me one last squeeze on the shoulder, before

heading down the hallway, whistling.

I'm going to kill him. Slowly.

I close the door and lean against it, squeezing my eyes shut. I need a second. Just one bloody second before I turn around and face—

"How long have you been seeing him?" Carter's voice is measured, controlled. Too controlled.

My eyes fly open, and I turn slowly.

He's standing in the middle of my hallway, hands in his pockets, his jaw tight. His glare is dark, fixed on me with an intensity that makes my pulse spike.

"It's—" I swallow, my hangover making coherent thoughts difficult. "It's been a few dates."

It's as close to the truth as I can manage. We have been on dates. Just not the romantic kind.

Carter's expression doesn't change, but something shifts in his eyes. "Then it won't be difficult to end it."

It's not a question.

My brain, foggy and pounding, struggles to form a response. But before I can, he continues.

"I meant what I said, Sophie." His voice drops lower, darker. "I'm dead serious about the proposal. And I'm not in the habit of sharing my woman."

My woman.

The words feel like shackles around my wrists, sending heat straight through me despite my exhaustion. I should argue. Should tell him he's being ridiculous, possessive. That I'm not his woman. I should remind him about workplace policies and professional boundaries, and the fact that he can't just stake a claim on me like I'm territory to conquer.

But I don't.

My head is pounding. My mouth tastes like regret. Every bone in my body aches, and I'm still trying to process the fact that I destroyed my own flat in a drunken rage. I'm too hungover, too exhausted, too emotionally wrung out to enter into a debate with him.

Especially when part of me—a traitorous, reckless part—likes hearing him call me his.

The silence stretches between us.

His eyes search mine, looking for resistance, for a fight. When he doesn't find one, satisfaction curves his mouth.

"Get back to bed," he says, voice dropping to that commanding tone that does things to me I refuse to examine right now. "You're taking the day off."

It's not a suggestion. It never is with him.

I should refuse. Just for the sake of it. But I feel like crap, and can really do with some more sleep. So, I just nod and do as I've been told.

His eyes darken with something that looks dangerously like triumph, but I'm too tired to even care. I walk to my bed and snuggle into my duvet. My eyelids feel heavy, but I force myself to stay awake until Carter has left. Only, he doesn't. I can hear him in the kitchen opening drawers and cupboards, and turning on the tap. But then everything goes quiet, and sleep pulls me under.

Smug Man

Sophie

I'm on autopilot as I push through the door of the coffee shop, the familiar bell chiming overhead. The queue is mercifully short this morning, and within minutes I'm ordering my usual—a flat white, extra shot, because I'm going to need all the caffeine I can legally consume to get through today.

My mind is elsewhere, still processing the spectacular disaster that was two nights ago. My first time being properly drunk, and what a roaring success that turned out to be.

Note to self: never again. Ever.

The hangover alone was punishment enough—head pounding, stomach rebelling, every light feeling like a personal attack from the sun itself.

But worse than the physical aftermath? The results of my drunk spree. Wrecking my own flat like some sort of vodka-fuelled maniac. Gareth and Carter showing up at my door like rival suitors in some twisted daily soap. The pair of them in my kitchen, testosterone crackling while I sat there nursing coffee and mortification in equal measure.

That particular nightmare will haunt me for a very, very long time.

At least Carter told me to take the day. Well, ordered me to in his typical arrogant, "I've-decided-this-for-you" way that just infuriates and... no. Just infuriates. That's it.

Right?

But when I woke up yesterday afternoon, groggy and disoriented, I couldn't believe my eyes. The broken vase—gone, swept into the bin. My books—neatly stacked along the bookcase. The shredded cushions—disposed of entirely.

While I slept, Carter had tidied my flat.

Actually tidied it. Like some sort of corporate fairy godmother with a fetish for control.

I want to be angry about it. Want to rage about the presumption, the invasion of privacy, the sheer audacity of letting himself stay while I was unconscious and vulnerable.

But I can't. Because as much as I try to find fault in the gesture, to twist it into something manipulative or controlling, I genuinely can't. It was... kind. Thoughtful, even.

And that side of Carter is somehow more terrifying than his fury.

"Sophie?"

I blink, realising Lewis, the barista, is waving a hand in front of my face, my coffee held out between us like an offering.

"Sorry!" I grab the cup, cheeks heating. "Miles away."

"Must have been somewhere nice." His smile is warm. "You were grinning from ear to ear."

Oh God.

Mortification floods through me like a tsunami. Was I smiling? While thinking about Carter cleaning my flat? About him being... decent?

"Just thinking about... work," I lie badly, already backing towards the door. "Big case. Very exciting. Lots of... legal... things."

Lewis's grin widens like he knows exactly what I'm lying about, but thankfully lets me escape without further interrogation.

I practically flee onto the pavement, coffee clutched like a shield.

This is fine. Everything's fine. I'm absolutely not developing feelings for my impossible, infuriating, occasionally-kind-when-you-least-expect-it boss.

Not at all.

I force my thoughts into safer waters for the remainder of my commute—need to message Gareth and thank him for his help yesterday, get new sofa cushions on my way home, ask Baron when he wants to train this week, make an appointment with the GP for my contraceptive injection.

The injection that's always been just a precaution, but might actually be necessary now. Because now there's a man in my life who's made it abundantly clear he wants to sleep with me.

And God, the way this man can kiss and pleasure a woman with just his mouth—I can only imagine how phenomenal the actual sex would be.

Christ's sake, Sophie.

Stop thinking about him.

I shake off the mental image of Carter's smouldering gaze, step out of the lift, and turn down the corridor when I spot Ben making a decidedly suspicious beeline for the cleaning cupboard. His eyes meet mine for a split second before he ducks inside like he's dodging sniper fire.

Oh no you don't.

I follow him in, pulling the door shut behind us. The space is cramped, smelling of bleach and wet mop.

"Sophie, I can explain—" he starts, but I'm already stabbing my finger into his shoulder.

"Traitor!"

"Ow!" he winces like I'd stepped onto a puppy's tail.

"How did Carter find out?" I demand, punctuating each word with another jab. "You promised you wouldn't tell him about the break-in!"

"I didn't tell him!" Ben throws his hands up defensively, backing into a bucket. "I told Millie, and Carter overheard. He cornered me, Sophie. What was I supposed to do?"

"Not tell him?"

"Have you *met* Carter?" His voice pitches higher. "He doesn't corner you and accept 'no comment' as an answer. He backed me into my own bloody desk and used his scary corporate lawyer voice until I cracked like a cheap biscuit!"

Despite my anger, I feel a twinge of sympathy. Carter in intimidation mode is formidable. I've been on the receiving end enough times to know.

"You're a wuss," I mutter, but there's less heat in it now.

"Maybe." Ben slumps against the shelf of cleaning supplies, looking genuinely miserable. "But Soph, no one dares crossing Carter. No one except you."

"That's not—"

"You've got balls of steel." He continues like I haven't spoken. "And Carter? He would never let anyone else get away with half the stuff you pull. Anyone else would be jobless, but you're untouchable."

I open my mouth, but nothing comes out.

Because what am I supposed to say to that? That Carter's not different with me, when he clearly is? This is the exact situation I've been trying to avoid all along. The narrative, I've pleaded with Carter not to create.

"I never asked for any of this," I admit quietly.

"Did you get in trouble?" Ben asks, his expression softening into genuine concern.

"No." The word comes out quieter than I want it to. "He was just... concerned. Wanted to make sure I was alright."

Ben's hands clap together in a weird overly theatrical way.

He catches my expression and shrugs. "Well, if everything's fine between you two, then this whole conversation is pointless, isn't it?"

"I suppose so," I agree slowly, because Ben has no idea that Carter showed up at my flat.

What it meant that he did, and that he stayed. That he literally cleaned up my mess while I slept. That he can be gentle and thoughtful and impossibly kind when I least expect it.

Without my permission, my body deflates on the spot—head dropping, shoulders sagging. Fighting off Carter's advances is becoming increasingly difficult. More than that. It's becoming exhausting. Like swimming against a current that's slowly, irrevocably pulling me under. And part of me is starting to wonder why I'm still swimming at all.

"Is there something you're not telling me?" Ben's gaze cuts through me, but then I notice a tiny bit of glitter on his collar, catching the fluorescent light.

"Is that glitter?"

His hand flies to his collar, brushing at it dismissively. "Crafting session with my niece."

"Isn't your niece fourteen? You told me she's only into boys and playing grown-up now."

His expression shutters. "Well, maybe she's got multiple interests. Did you ever think of that?"

"I'm sorry," I say, raising my hands in surrender at his sudden defensiveness. "What's your prob—"

"You know what? I'm done with this interrogation." He pushes past me towards the door. "Some of us have actual work to do."

What the heck? What's got him so hot and bothered?

"Ben!" I call after him, but he waves me off without looking back.

Fair enough. Let him cool off. I'll catch him in the staff kitchen sooner or later.

"You owe me lunch and pudding!" I call over my shoulder as a parting gift, then turn to head in the opposite direction, and crash straight into a solid wall of muscle.

My arms whirl outward in a desperate attempt to save my

coffee from disaster. I stumble back. My heel slips. But before my backside gets a chance to kiss the floor, a strong arm wraps around my waist and pulls me back against a very firm, very warm chest.

"Good morning, lioness," Carter's lips curl in amusement.

I immediately step back, hyper-aware that anyone could walk by and see us. My heart does a somersault I absolutely did not authorise.

"Shall I get another CRA form for you and Reynolds?" he asks, nodding over my shoulder to where Ben stormed off.

"Pardon?"

So apparently, he's jealous when it comes to Gareth, but perfectly fine with Ben. Can someone please explain this man to me?

"I just saw you both coming out of the cleaning cupboard. Isn't that where people conduct their sordid office—"

"I know what you meant," I cut him off before—God forbid—he can remind me of his first 'proposal', which I'm now thinking about anyway. "If you'll excuse me, I've got a call with Farm Valleys in five minutes."

I move to walk around him, but he stops me with his arm, blocking my path like a very attractive roadblock.

"No, you don't. I just told your assistant to cancel it. We've got urgent matters to take care off." He manoeuvres me around, and before I can protest, we're walking in tandem away from my office. "And take these."

He holds out two pills and produces a bottle of water from his suit jacket like some sort of pharmaceutical magician.

"Is this your new tactic?" I can't help but mock him. "If so, you should know that you usually don't tell people that you're drugging them."

Carter doesn't bite, but he throws me a look that screams *oh, please.*

"They're electrolytes, lioness. They'll help your kidneys after your little adventure," he says with a devilish grin and a wink that belongs in a wall calendar of London's most hunkiest bachelors.

Smug bas...man. That's actually quite sweet of him.

I take the pills, and wash them down with my coffee, ignoring the disapproving shake of his head.

"Very counterproductive, lioness."

"Stop calling me that," I hiss as we pass Buckman coming out of his office.

Carter and I give him a polite nod as he thoughtfully strokes his beard. We turn a corner, and I realise that we're heading towards Carter's office.

"Would you rather I call you fiancée?" he grins, showing off those sexy dimples.

I want to punch him for being so effortlessly handsome. No human being deserves to be this beautiful. No wonder he believes the world will bend to his will. It probably mostly does.

"You're impossible," I mumble, because frankly, my mind has gone elsewhere—specifically to the dampness between my thighs that I'm desperately trying to ignore.

We finally reach his office, and to my surprise, Janet's not behind her desk.

"I gave her the day off." Carter reads my mind, holding the door open for me like a gentleman who's about to do very ungentlemanly things.

The second I walk through, I spot the mountain of cake boxes on his desk. The sugary scents waft over, tempting and indulgent.

"That's a lot of cake. What's the occasion?" I ask, forcing levity into my tone despite the knots forming in my stomach.

"Our wedding," he deadpans.

The words hang in the air between us, taunting me with their casualness.

"Of course," I reply, hiding the tumult swirling inside me. "So, you're really holding onto your delusions."

"My delusions are your denial." He shrugs with infuriating confidence, opening the first box and breaking off a piece with a cake fork. "Here, try this."

The way he speaks with such certainty is alarming. He's clearly lost the plot. It's one thing to entertain this ridiculous idea of us getting married. But it's an entirely different, far more unhinged thing to actually go out and order wedding cake samples.

"I don't eat cake," I say, crossing my arms with defiance thrumming through my veins.

"Everyone eats cakes."

"I don't—ever."

"Well, today, you are. Now eat." His tone leaves no room for argument, and my gut tells me I shouldn't argue with a man who's clearly severed all ties with reality.

I huff, but round his desk anyway, letting him feed me a piece because apparently, I've lost control of my own life.

"Not bad," I concede, trying to mask how it feels like I'm giving in, like I'm stepping closer to a precipice I shouldn't even be near.

"What's that one?" He's curious, playful, and I pick up the little card despite myself.

"Triple chocolate with coffee liquor ganache." My voice sounds distant, as if I'm watching this unfold from outside my own body.

"Feed me a piece." His eyes twinkle with that playful glint that sends shivers racing down my spine and heat pooling in places it shouldn't.

Should I be annoyed or amused by his insistent charm?

I raise a brow, but don't move. He leans in closer, his hand brushing my back and sending electric sparks through my entire nervous system. I take a step back, trying to shield myself from the warmth radiating between us.

"Here." I break off a piece with my fork, feeding him despite the internal battle raging inside me.

"Too heavy. What do you think?"

I try a piece and feel instantly assaulted by the overly sweet taste. "You're right. Maybe the lemon?"

He breaks off a piece and feeds it to me, his eyes never leaving mine.

"Too sharp." I scrunch my nose.

"The copper, you have twenty-four hours to break things off with him," he says so casually while closing and opening cake boxes that I almost miss what he's demanding. "What's that one?"

"Yeah right, boss." I pick up the card while swallowing the profanities clawing up my throat. "Carrot cake with walnuts and Irish cream ganache."

"I'm serious, Sophie. Break things off, or I'll do it for you."

I drop the card on his desk, and move my hands to my hips to keep them under control. So, I won't scratch my thighs or—God forbid—slap him across the face.

"And what are you going to do if I don't? Kill him?" I laugh like he's just told me a particularly bad joke, but the glimmer in his eyes tells me he's not joking at all.

"I'm a man of the law, not a criminal."

"So is he," I retort, annoyance bubbling under my skin.

He chuckles, dark and low, drawing closer, "If anything, he's a dirty cop like they all are. But by all means, try me. I'll show you exactly how good I am at my job. I'll find the dirt and get him behind bars."

His voice is gravelly and seductive, leaving me breathless despite my best efforts to remain annoyed. I shouldn't let him threaten Gareth like this, but Christ, Carter going all alpha male is disintegrating my knickers.

I break off a piece of the carrot cake and feed it to him, watching as his eyes widen in delight.

"That's a good one! You've got to try it!" His hand finds my lower back as he leans over to break off another piece.

I want to protest, to push his hand away, but it feels dangerously comforting. I let him feed me, let him make me lose myself in the moment. "That's the one! Wow! It sounds awful but—"

"—tastes like heaven."

His gaze captures mine, and the air seems to shift, charged with a magnetism that pulls me closer against my better judgement. He inches forward, his intentions crystal clear, but at the last moment, I snap out of the trance. I turn away to escape, to reclaim some sense of control, but he's too quick. He grabs my waist and spins me back, catching me in an embrace that sends fireworks erupting behind my closed eyelids.

"Stop fighting me, lioness." His voice is a low growl, vibrating through me, pushing every limit of reason I possess.

"Never," I protest, but it comes out in a weak whisper, and my pull against his hold is only half-hearted at best.

He drags a single digit down the column of my throat, like he's tracing an invisible path that leads to my collar bone.

"No more running. No more avoiding this," he says in a low and gravelly tone, like he's tasting me on his tongue.

"I'm not running."

His eyes snap up to mine, and my breath stutters as my mind drags me back to the first day we met here in his office. His gaze was just as intimidating back then, but now I understand why. Carter sees right through me. He sees the war waging inside me, the battle between wanting him and wanting to preserve my integrity. But he doesn't understand it, and he never will, because I can never tell him what I did when Harman was still here. So, I have to keep running, hoping that soon, he'll get tired of the chase.

"You still owe me an orgasm from the last time you ran away."

"I owe you a slap across the face," I say, but it's an empty threat.

"Feisty. I make you a deal. I'll let you slap me—" He chuckles, his hand finding the back of my thigh. "—while I thrust my cock into you."

"This is highly unprofessional." I manage to exhale, though my heart quickens at the thought.

He cocks his head, wearing that sinister smile that chills yet ignites me. "And yet, you love the idea."

His fingers glide upward, dipping underneath my skirt and moving dangerously close to my soaking knickers.

I tremble, pushing weakly against his hold, but he shakes his head.

"Tell me you don't want this, and I will let you go," he rasps, his finger nudging at the edge of the lace fabric.

I don't want this. I don't want to get entangled with my boss. I don't want this to threaten everything I've worked for. But I want him, despite his arrogance and his controlling ways. I want him to ravish me. I want to lose myself in him while he utterly corrupts me. Even if it destroys me in the process.

"I can't," I sigh in defeat, but the breath gets cut off.

Carter drags his finger up my seam and applies perfect pressure to my clit. My head falls forward, resting against his shoulder as he continues to circle that sensitive bundle of nerves.

I should push him off. Tell him how inappropriate it is. That someone could burst into his office at any moment. I glance over his shoulder—at least the blinds are drawn. Someone would actually have to come in here to witness the spectacle. Still, I should tell him to stop, before—

"Oh, God," I whimper, his finger dipping into my wetness.

"Soon-to-be-husband would suffice," he mumbles, tugging at my chin to move his mouth onto mine.

He tastes delicious. Like cake and coffee, and just him. My whole body is buzzing. Primed for whatever dirty things he wants to do to me. But we're in the office. We shouldn't, but I desperately want him to. Just one more minute. I'll let him have his way with me for one more minute, and then I'll push him off and read him his rights.

A second finger plunges into me, pumping with slow,

deliberate thrusts between firm swipes over my clit. I cling to his shoulders, trying desperately to stifle my moans.

"That's my lioness," he mumbles, and then, to my surprise, he kisses the top of my head in a slow and reverent way that makes my chest ache. "My fierce woman."

The words wash over me—soothing, grounding, absolutely pride-inducing. My resolve shatters completely. My hand moves around his neck and pulls him down onto my mouth. His fingers plunge in deeper as he returns the kiss with earnest need. The minute is long over, my orgasm is building to dizzying heights, and I'm so close to coming on his fingers when a knock on the door suddenly breaks the spell.

I break our kiss, my eyes frantically searching his to find them blazing with fury at the interruption. He slowly pulls his fingers out of me, and takes a deep breath to school his expression into something professional.

"You good?" he asks softly, tucking a stray lock of hair behind my ear while I adjust my clothes and lipstick with trembling hands.

"Do I look good?" I still pant from his kiss.

"Always, lioness," he says, giving me a brief smile before his face morphs into the usual no-nonsense-director expression.

"Come in," he calls out.

Amina strides in with a bright smile plastered across her face.

Until she spots me, and her smile drops.

I want to scratch her eyeballs out.

Groom

Medard

For. Fuck's. Sake!

Is this some fucking cosmic joke? No one ever dares to drop by my office unannounced. No one, but my lioness who I. Just. Want. To. Fucking. Orgasm.

The door swings open, and in glides Amina Muhammad—composed, immaculate, and newly rewarded with the shittiest client on our books.

"Mr Carter. Sophie." Her voice is polite but crisp. Her gaze sweeps over the chaos of half-eaten cakes. "What's going on here?"

For half a second, I'm caught—then instinct kicks in. I straighten, let that commanding tone I've perfected slide into place like a weapon I've mastered.

"Ah," I say smoothly, the faintest smirk tugging at my lips as I pick up a cake fork. "We're conducting a little... market research."

Sophie's eyes flick to mine for just a moment—I catch the flash of something there. Amusement. Maybe admiration. She's impressed by the quick thinking, even if she'll never admit it.

"Market research?" Amina echoes, scepticism practically filing a motion for discovery.

"For a potential new client," I say easily. "A boutique bakery chain seeking to expand commercial contracts. They sent samples."

It's a complete fabrication, but I deliver it with the same conviction I'd use in a courtroom. The trick isn't in the lie—it's in the certainty with which you tell it.

"Yes," Sophie adds quickly, picking up the thread beautifully. "They're called—" Her eyes flick to the nearest box. "Smug Temptation."

My mouth twitches. I don't look at her—because if I do, we'll both lose composure, and I need to maintain this charade a little longer.

Muhammad's brows furrow. "Smug Temptation?"

"Catchy, isn't it?" I say without missing a beat. "We're evaluating their branding and product quality. Due diligence."

Sophie's watching me work, and I can practically feel her trying not to be impressed. There's something deeply satisfying about performing under pressure when she's the audience.

"I wasn't aware of any new client," Muhammad says coolly.

I offer her that polite, measured smile that usually works wonders with her. "Not everything crosses your desk, Amina."

My tone is smooth, professional. But I notice the way Sophie's posture shifts. The way her jaw tightens almost imperceptibly. The way her fingers grip her fork just a fraction tighter.

Interesting.

"I just like to stay informed," Muhammad replies.

"I know," I say, voice warm and approving because it's true—Muhammad is excellent at her job. "It's one of your best qualities."

Sophie stabs her fork into a slice of cake with more force than necessary.

Oh, this is delicious. And I'm not talking about the desserts.

"Yes," Sophie says, her voice dripping with false sweetness. "She's the very definition of diligence. If we ever need to sue someone for being too prepared, we'll call Amina as expert witness."

I hide my grin behind a careful expression of professional neutrality. My lioness has claws, and she's just extended them.

Good.

Let her see for herself how soul-crushing jealousy can be. Breaking ties with the copper wasn't an idle threat. I'm not standing by while he tries to take whatever this thing is between them to the next level. A couple of dates was already too much. She's my woman. Period.

Muhammad steps closer, inspecting the cakes. "These look rather indulgent."

"They are," Sophie replies, matching her calm perfectly. "We're testing which flavour aligns best with their brand identity."

Muhammad's head tilts. "And what exactly does cake have to do with legal branding?"

Sophie meets her gaze without flinching. "Everything. Clients associate emotion with experience. Smug Temptation wants to be perceived as confident, rebellious, and subtly addictive."

I cough discreetly to hide a laugh. Subtly addictive. If she only knew how well that description applies to her.

"And which one best represents that?" Muhammad asks.

"Carrot cake," I say immediately, because why not commit to the absurdity.

Sophie turns to me. "Carrot cake?"

I meet her eyes, letting mischief show. "Classic. Reliable. No surprises."

There's a message in that, and I know she catches it. She always does.

Muhammad hums. "I'd say the firm has a bit more zest."

"Maybe lemon, then," I suggest.

"Too sharp," Sophie says automatically, defensively, and I catch that slip with satisfaction.

Muhammad's brows rise slightly. Sophie plasters on a polite smile. "Too sharp for broad appeal. Carrot's safe."

Oh, she's definitely jealous. The knowledge settles in my chest with smug satisfaction. She doesn't want to be, probably hates herself for it, but she is.

Good.

Muhammad studies us both, and I can see the suspicion forming. She's sharp enough to sense something's shifted in this room, even if she can't quite put her finger on what.

"Would you like to try one, Amina?" I offer smoothly, because I'm curious how far I can push this before Sophie actually breaks that fork. "Your opinion's always valuable."

Sophie's smile looks painful. "Yes, *Amina*. Give us your professional insight on crumb texture."

I'm enjoying this far too much.

Muhammad takes a bite, considering. "This one's... heavy," she says finally.

"Good observation," I say, genuinely appreciative of her analytical mind.

Sophie's jaw clenches. I notice everything about her—every micro-expression, every tell. She's absolutely seething, and trying desperately to hide it.

"Well," Muhammad says briskly, setting her fork down. "I'll let you get back to it."

"Of course," I say, gracious in victory.

"Yes," Sophie adds with sugar-sweet poison. "We'll circulate the tasting notes."

Muhammad blinks, clearly deciding this entire firm has lost

its mind, and leaves.

The door closes, and I let the laughter loose.

It booms through the room, deep and genuine, because the absurdity of what we just pulled off is too good. Sophie joins in.

Oh, that sound. It warms my chest.

"Smug Temptation?" I manage between chuckles. "You actually said that."

"You're welcome," she says, wiping tears from her eyes. "You froze. I saved you."

"I didn't freeze."

"You absolutely did."

I grin at her, at this brilliant, infuriating woman who keeps me on my toes. "You're something else, Lioness."

The pet name's second nature now. I use it to watch her react—or pretend not to. She's getting better at hiding it, but I know she likes it.

When the laughter fades, I let my eyes linger on her. Let the corner of my mouth lift in that way that always gets under her skin.

"You were jealous."

"Excuse me?"

I let my smirk grow, because this is too perfect. "When I complimented Muhammad. You almost snapped your fork in half."

"Oh, so now we're back to formalities," she scoffs, crossing her arms defensively. "I was frustrated by the sugar content."

"Right." I take a slow step closer. "Because you always stab pastries when you're concerned about nutrition."

She glares, but I'm enjoying this far too much—watching her try to deny what we both know is true.

"Don't flatter yourself, Carter."

"Oh, I'm not." I tilt my head, studying her. "I'm just saying, it's nice to have proof my lioness does, in fact, growl when someone else gets my attention."

"Growl?" She echoes, incredulous. "I didn't growl."

"You did," I say, grinning because she absolutely did. "Quietly. But you did."

She shakes her head, biting back a laugh. "You're egotistical beyond repair."

"And yet," I murmur, stepping closer still, closing the space between us, "you keep feeding the ego."

She rolls her eyes. "Only because it's occasionally entertaining."

I laugh softly. "Admit it, Sophie. You like this."

"This?"

"Us," I say simply, laying it out there. "The back-and-forth. The pretending you don't want to throttle me one second and kiss me the next."

She tries to scoff, but her throat's too tight. I can see it in the way she swallows.

"Delusional," she mutters finally.

I grin, that self-assured grin I know drives her mad. "Maybe. But I bet you've already considered the idea of me being your husband. You thought about what your life would be like as my wife. Tell me I'm wrong."

She opens her mouth—and nothing comes out.

Victory tastes sweeter than any of those bloody cakes.

Because somewhere between the lies, the laughter, and the jealousy she can't quite hide, she knows I'm right.

I swipe my fingers through the cream on the carrot cake and bring them to my mouth. Sophie's eyes widen as my lips close around the two digits, and I slowly drag them out. It tastes utterly divine—whipped cream cheese frosting mixed with my woman's essence.

"Can't wait for our wedding night when I'll lick this frosting off your hot slit."

Sophie's jaw drops, her cheeks flush, and then she bolts out of my office. I can't help but snicker, because I'd bet my shares in this firm, that I've just soaked her panties.

Conniving Dick

Sophie

I stumble down the corridor, mortified by every squelching step. Those words. Carter's words. I want them to become reality.

God, I want him to lick me out like he's the devil starving.

I fall into my office where Millie intercepts me before I can even set my bag down.

"Miss Rosen! Are you alright? I heard about the break-in—"

"False alarm," I cut her off, forcing a bright smile while I subtly clench my thighs. "Everything's fine."

"Are you sure? Because Mr Reynolds said—"

"Really, Millie. It's fine." I slide past her and take my seat, hoping she'll take the hint.

She doesn't. She follows my lead and lets herself drop into the opposite chair, launching into a stream of client updates that I try desperately to focus on while my phone buzzes in my pocket.

"—and the Laren contract needs your signature by Friday, and Pharma called about the clause amendments, and—Miss Rosen, are you listening?"

"Mmm, absolutely." I'm not. I'm reading Gareth's text.

> Gareth: hey, you alright?

I type back quickly while Millie's still talking.

> Me: All good. Survived the hangover. Thanks again for yesterday.

"—so, I told them you'd review it by tomorrow, is that alright?"

"Yes, fine, perfect." I have no idea what I've just agreed to.

Millie gives me a look that says she knows I'm not paying attention but is too polite to call me out. "I'll leave these files on your desk, then."

"Great, thanks Millie."

She finally leaves, and I immediately return to my phone.

> Gareth: no big deal. Did you manage to get some rest, or did billy big bollocks drag you straight to work?

A smile tugs at my lips, thinking of Carter performing domestic duties.

> Me: Actually, he let me take the day off.

> Gareth: Two days in a row? Billy must really like you.

My stomach does something complicated between a drop and a flip. This thing with Carter needs to come to an end before I completely lose myself in it.

The thought lands like a heavy rock on my chest. In a different dimension—one where he isn't my boss and I don't have to navigate risky waters to keep my job—I'd have loved to explore our feelings.

I vigorously swipe my thighs to dispel the lingering sense of sadness. Carter is, and always will be, an arrogant prick. He has to be, or my resolve will shatter.

> Me: He doesn't. And I don't like him.

The lie tastes bitter, but I swish it down with a gulp of coffee.

> Gareth: Sure. Let's just ignore everything you said at the club about how handsome and magnetic he is.

Oh God. Did I actually say that? Out loud? While drunk?

> Me: I admit that I had a crush on my boss, but don't hold me accountable for what happened that night. You're just as guilty for filling me up with vodka as Lucy and Baron are.

There. Better. Nicely gaslighted myself. Father would be proud.

> Gareth: what happened that night? Why did you bolt?

My fingers hover over the keyboard. Carter showing up. Dropping to his knees between my thighs. Marry me.

> Me: Nothing.

> Gareth: Fair enough. Just be careful Soph. I saw how he looked at me when I kissed your cheek. Before you know it, you're not signing a client contract but a prenup to protect his assets.

I choke on my coffee, the liquid burning my throat as I cough violently. My eyes water.

Because Gareth doesn't know. He has no idea that Carter has already proposed. Twice. That the prenup joke is frighteningly, horrifyingly not far-fetched at all.

When I can breathe again, I type back.

>Me: Prenups aren't legally binding in the UK.

>Gareth: That's what you took from my message? Jeez, you've got it bad.

I stare at the screen, my thumb hovering over the keyboard. But I can't think of a single response that wouldn't be either a lie or a confession I simply can't make.

So, I don't respond at all.

Because terrifyingly, he's absolutely right.

I've got it bad.

I set my phone down and lean forward, pressing my cheek against the cool glass of my desk.

The little grains of dust are swirling in circles, round and round, until they take flight, propelled upward by the gust of air-conditioning, before settling down once more. My cheek feels cool and comforting against the glass as I watch the little dance of my waning focus.

I'm screwed. I've let this spin out of control.

In the span of a mere few weeks, I've gone from being ignored to being his fiancée.

I have to face the hard truth that the ethical line is no longer just blurred or shifted. It's been completely obliterated by Carter.

My fingers itch to claw at my thighs, to ground myself through the sharp sting of pain. But instead of trying to expel the thoughts with vigorous swipes, I let myself bathe in the feeling.

I deserve every ounce of it.

My phone sparks to life, Father's name illuminating the screen before it goes black again as the call disconnects. If he knew the magnitude of my failings, his lips would be forever stuck behind that greying goatee.

I swore to myself I would never get entangled like this again. But something about Carter shifts my morals into the abyss, like a murder justified by self-preservation.

I tap my phone, navigate to my contacts, and dial Harman's number before I can second-guess myself. It rings, the sound buzzing against my ear before travelling through the glass desk.

Then it disconnects.

I don't even know what I'm hoping to achieve by calling him. Harman—a man who's danced in the darkness of immorality and paid the price for it. Maybe I'm hoping he could give me a reason to accept Carter's reality. Or warn me away from it.

But the fact that he won't answer should serve as a sign from a higher power. Whatever I feel for Carter, I have to snuff it out before it destroys me.

I jolt upright, yanking open my drawer and pulling out the pack of cleaning wipes. Then I attack my desk with vigorous, punishing strokes, scrubbing away dust and doubt in equal measure. If only Carter could be erased as easily.

Laughter erupts behind my door, followed by Carter's voice, stopping me in my tracks. I cautiously walk towards the sound and press my ear against the door.

"I can't recommend the Macallan 25 from the Sherry Oak series. With its lofty price tag, I expect more subtle citrus notes that don't leave me with acid reflux. A much better choice would be the 15-year-old from the double cask. It's matured in both American and European oak, giving it a much sweeter taste. But if you like to try the 25-er, I've got a bottle in my office."

"Absolutely, if you don't mind," another male voice replies to Carter, turning the blood in my veins to ice.

I yank the door open, heart pounding, and come face to face with one of my worst nightmares. Baron stands there, looking as composed and calm as ever.

"Baron," I squeak, "what are you doing here?"

Both men freeze, surprise flickering across their faces. I clear my throat, trying to inject some casualness into the moment. "I mean, did we have plans?"

Baron chuckles in a low, warm sound as though he's just caught me with my hand in the cookie jar, and then leans in to press a quick kiss to my cheek.

"No, no plans. After our night out, I thought I'd stop by, check you're alright."

Before I can respond, Carter pipes up, his voice smooth and just a little too smug. "I should apologise. I dragged Sophie away from you guys on her night-out."

"I'm aware." Baron raises a thick eyebrow, glancing at me with a grin.

"I, you—" My voice falters. My eyes dart between the two of them, confusion and panic swirling in my chest.

This can't be happening. I need to get Carter out of my personal life, not have him slip into my circle of friends.

"You do? Then you know we had something important to discuss," Carter says with a gleam, flashing Baron his stupid, captivating dimples.

"Oh, I know," the traitor chuckles.

He doesn't. Not the proposal. And he never will.

"Well, do you fancy grabbing dinner tonight?" The traitor has the audacity to ask me.

"She can't," Carter interrupts sharply, and I bite back a groan as the pain from my nails digging into my thighs intensifies. "We already have dinner plans."

"We have?" I splutter, utterly bewildered.

"Yes, I've booked us a table at Nobu."

Baron's face lights up like the sky on bloody Bonfire Night, clapping his hands with a boyish grin. "That's great! You've been trying to get a table there for months!"

I will lynch him, and the next sparring session? Definitely without the pad.

"Yeah, great," I force out, plastering on a smile before pulling Baron into my office. I turn to Carter, voice tight. "If you'll excuse us, there's something we need to discuss in private."

I slam the door right in his grinning face.

"Well, well, well," Baron says, leaning casually against the bookcase, eyes twinkling with mischief, "looks like you two are making progress."

"You traitorous little weasel!" I hiss under my breath as I jab my finger at him like it's a weapon. "You're supposed to be on my side. Not swap advice on whiskey, or bloody grin at every word he says."

Baron doesn't even flinch. Doesn't cower. Doesn't apologise.

No. He just shrugs, all casual indifference, like invading my space at the office and detonating my professional relationship to my boss is the sort of thing he does between push-ups and protein shakes.

"I was just friendly with your boss," he says, tone smug, lips curving into a smirk that I want to slap right off his face. "And you, little Missy on her high horse, sang a completely different tune couple of nights ago." His eyes gleam, devilish, daring me to combust.

"Besides, Gareth's a good guy, sure, but you two? No spark. None. Flat as yesterday's beer. But you and Medard—"

Medard!?

My jaw drops so far it nearly unhinges. "Are you bloody kidding me right now?" I screech. "Have you completely forgotten everything I told you about that controlling maniac?"

Baron shrugs again. Shrugs!

The audacity.

I want to launch myself at him and aim straight for those broad, cocky shoulders. But without gloves, I'll probably break a nail or sprain a wrist, and he'll just laugh at me.

"You call it controlling," he says with a sly grin, "I call it caring."

Caring. I actually choke on my own outrage. I stalk across the room, pacing like a woman on the brink of setting fire to the world. My arms flail in frustration because there are not enough words in the English language to express just how deranged this conversation is.

"Am I—" I spin, glaring at him like he's grown two heads, "—am I surrounded by Neanderthals? Since when is Carter the knight in shining bloody armour? He's the dragon! He eats knights for breakfast! He's not the kind of man you get involved with!"

Baron raises a brow, folding his arms across his chest like he's some kind of Greek statue come to life. Only Greek statues don't usually look this smug. His eyes glitter with challenge.

"Right," he drawls, "so you're definitely not interested in him?"

Of course, I'm interested in him! Just this morning, the man had his fingers inside me. I'm not an idiot, and I know I can pretend all day that I hate him, but it won't change the truth—I'm falling for Medard Carter, faster than I can wrap my head around it. But I can't allow myself those feelings. It would destroy my career, everything I've built for myself, and fought tooth and nail to keep.

"Absolutely not!" I shout with enough vehemence to shake the walls. To really drive it home, I shake my head so hard I might give myself whiplash. "Not. Interested."

And because the universe hates me today, the door creaks open just then. Millie breezes in, all sunshine and obliviousness, holding a plate in her hands. A small cake. A very familiar small cake.

"Miss Rosen?" she chirps, confused but trying to hide it. "Mr Carter wanted you to have this. He said it's from the cake testing for your wedding?"

The room tilts. My eyes bug out. My jaw falls open. And there it is—the half-demolished carrot cake of doom.

That conniving dick.

Baron bursts into laughter, loud and unrestrained, doubling over like he's watching the best comedy sketch of his life.

"I can explain!" My voice cracks embarrassingly, a whine bubbling through.

But before I can start, Millie swipes a finger through the thick cream topping and lifts it towards her lips.

"Don't," I yelp, lunging forward with the kind of desperation reserved for people about to defuse bombs.

Because it is a bomb. A nuclear memory detonates in my head—Carter's fingers dipping into that cake after he had them ... inside me!

My stomach knots. My thighs clench. My sanity? Gone.

"Don't eat that!" I cry out, smacking her hand down so hard the cream splatters.

Panicked, I swipe the frosting away myself, scrubbing it from her skin like it's toxic waste. Which, in a way, it is.

Millie stares at me, eyes wide, like she's just witnessed the unmasking of a lunatic. She thrusts the plate at me as though handing over contraband to the authorities.

"Believe me," I say, my voice verging on manic as I fling the cake straight into the bin like it's possessed, "you do not want to eat that!"

Silence descends. Baron is wheezing with laughter, tears streaming down his face. Millie is frozen, gaping at me like she's seriously considering calling HR.

Think, Sophie. Think!

I turn to Millie and Baron who are now looking at me like I belong in a padded room.

"Reynolds had a piece this morning," I say smoothly, flicking my hand with fake nonchalance, "and it gave him terrible diarrhoea."

Millie blanches. Perfect.

I latch onto her elbow and usher her towards the door like a woman on a mission. "Anyhow, thanks for your service, I'll be out in a second."

I shut the door firmly behind her, press my forehead to it for a long beat, and exhale like I've just survived war. When I finally turn, Baron takes a seat at my desk, grinning like a cat that's just eaten the canary and saved the feathers to taunt me with later.

"You were saying?" he prompts, leaning back in my chair like he owns the place, smug as hell.

"Shut up," I mutter.

Arrogant Bastard

Medard

I take the two flights of stairs with a quickened pace, the takeout bags from Nobu swaying at my side. The unmistakable notes of soul music drift into the stairwell.

Sophie has impeccable taste.

I rap against the wood. Floorboards creak beyond the door, and then she's there, pulling it open. Surprise—raw and almost defensive—etches itself across her features.

"No!" she blurts fiercely.

She tries to shut the door, but I'm faster. My foot wedges the gap, my shoulder nudges forward, and suddenly I'm in her space. "Honey, I'm home," I tease, my fingers reaching for her cheek, but she swats my hand away.

God, defiance suits her far too well.

"What are you doing here, Carter?" she demands, cinching her robe tighter, as if silk could save her from me.

The sight wrecks me. Creamy thighs peek out, the fabric barely clinging to curves I've already memorised. Tonight, I have every intention of winning her over.

"You didn't come for your food, so I brought it to you," I lift the bags, trying for casual when everything in me is wound tight with hope and desperation.

"Believe me, the food is the last thing that kept me away."

Her boldness pulls a laugh from my chest. After this morning in my office, I was certain she'd come around, that she'd accept my dinner invitation without a second thought. But give this woman enough time, and she'll invent a thousand reasons why I'm the devil she needs to resist. Well, the devil has run out of patience.

"Careful, lioness. I'm beginning to think our quarrels are just foreplay in disguise."

I walk into her living room, unsurprised to find everything immaculate—new cushions, replaced vase, reorganised books, even a new blanket for the sofa. Can't wait to spend the evenings cuddled up in it with her—naked.

She's put herself back together with meticulous care. But I remember her undone, and I want her that way again.

"You should leave," she insists, arms folded across her chest.

The posture only serves to press her breasts higher, and my breath falters.

I shrug out of my coat with deliberate leisure, rolling my sleeves up. "You passed on Nobu for this?" I pluck the miserable salad from her coffee table. I waited nearly an hour at the restaurant before accepting she wasn't coming.

"Hey! There's nothing wrong with it!" She lunges to snatch the box.

"You deserve better." I cross to her kitchen and toss it in the bin. "Proper sustenance, not this rabbit food."

I rummage through her cupboards, finding chopsticks and plates.

"Sit! Eat with me," I say, arranging the dishes across the coffee table.

She hovers, caught between her desire to throw me out and her curiosity. Then her feigned indifference cracks just enough to betray her hunger.

She finally lowers herself onto the cushion, maintaining careful distance.

My defiant lioness.

"How did you even get this? They don't do takeaways."

I shrug, passing her a plate loaded with gyozas. "I know the chef. Try these."

She hesitates, then bites. Her eyes flutter shut, her face softening with pleasure before she catches herself.

"They're... fine."

"You should tell your face that." My smirk earns me a stifled giggle.

Fuck, that laugh. It settles in my bones like good scotch.

"Okay, fine. They're delicious."

"Did you get the cake?" I ask.

She snorts. "You're the devil, you know? I looked insane swatting it out of Millie's hands."

The image floors me. I double over with laughter, and she joins me, her musical giggles mixing with my deeper rumble.

"Don't laugh! Poor Millie almost ate the damn thing!"

God help me, I want a lifetime of moments exactly like this.

The laughter fades gradually, leaving something heavier in its wake. Her fingers trace anxious patterns on her thigh, and I want to still them with my own.

"It was delicious," I murmur, my voice coming out rougher than I mean it to.

Her cheeks flush. She rises, muttering about wine, about water, and I watch her retreat.

I pinch the bridge of my nose to gather my thoughts. I want to break through her barriers. But whenever my hands draw closer, she withdraws like a tide pulling back from shore. This endless push and pull is driving me mad.

She returns with bottles and glasses. I move without thought, taking them from her hands, letting my fingers brush hers.

We pour. We sip. We talk about everything except what matters—Krav Maga, soul music, her allergy to cats, her dreams of travelling through Asia. I collect every detail like precious pearls.

We pretend the chemistry thrumming through us doesn't exist, even though it's so thick I could reach out and touch it.

"To a long and happy life," I toast, raising my glass.

She clinks hers against mine. "To a long and happy life."

"Together," I add deliberately.

She rolls her eyes, giggling despite herself. "Before you get lost in your delusions, I'm not interested in marriage."

"Why is that?"

She shrugs. "I'd rather focus on my career than waste time nurturing a relationship."

"If that isn't the perfect excuse for your boss." I try to laugh, but the sound falls flat.

"What about the copper, then? You prioritised him that night." I push because I always push.

The words taste bitter. There's still hurt over her ignoring my calls, choosing him over me.

"That was different." Her tone lacks conviction.

"How was it different?"

"It doesn't matter. You'll be pleased to know that I've learnt my lesson." As though to prove a point, she snatches her phone from the coffee table.

I slide closer and pluck it from her hands. "No work tonight. Just you and me, two normal people enjoying each other's company."

I place it on the table and cage her against the sofa, my arm draped along the backrest. She doesn't move away.

"Who says I'm enjoying myself?"

"You did. The wine gave you away," I say with a glance at my watch, "and the fact I've been here for two hours and you haven't thrown me out yet."

"My father taught me manners, Mr Carter."

"Forget your father. Show me your true self."

Her gaze sharpens, something flickering in those beautiful eyes. She pulls her legs up, her knees brushing against my shin.

"What do you think would happen if I did?"

Her nails graze her thigh in a slow drag I'm desperate to feel on my skin.

"You'd finally admit this thing between us is real."

"It's not a matter of admission," she whispers, her eyes travelling the length of my chest with deliberate slowness. "But acceptance."

The moment stretches, charged and dangerous, our lips brushing the edge of contact—

Her phone buzzes.

Gareth Hayes.

The fucking copper.

"Don't answer it." Irritation bleeds through my voice.

She hesitates, then leans away and answers. "Hey."

His drawl filters through. "Hey, are you free right now? Thought I could stop by for a drink."

Her smile is innocent. "I can't right now."

I clear my throat loud enough for him to hear.

"Alright, got friends over?"

"Something like that. Let's talk tomorrow." She hangs up.

I'm something like a friend?

Fuck that!

She clearly hasn't broken things off with him like I told her to.

"You didn't listen." I grate through my teeth, pinching the bridge of my nose hard enough that it aches. "I told you to end it."

Her chin lifts, defiance flashing. "I heard you loud and clear. But no one gets to decide who I date but me."

She turns away, gathering dishes and taking them to the sink like she can escape this conversation through mundane tasks.

Her words spark the darker part of me. I rise, closing the distance, and when I grasp her wrist, pulling her against me, I know I'm crossing into dangerous territory.

"Have you slept with him?"

"That's none of your business," she seethes, but makes no attempt to pull away from me.

"Answer me!" I roar.

Her eyes burn with defiance, but beneath the fire there's something else—embarrassment, guilt, a flicker of vulnerability she cannot quite smother. It's enough.

"You have," I whisper, the words feeling like a blade twisting in my chest.

Her silence is damning.

"We're not a couple. I don't have to justify myself to you," she says with a defiant raise of her chin.

I'm warring with myself, caught between wanting to cradle her face and admit how much I'm hurting, and slamming my fist into her kitchen cupboard for making me lose control.

"How many times?" My hand cups her chin, forcing her gaze to mine.

"Carter, please." She tries to turn away.

"How many times have you let him fuck you?" I bark through the pain, yanking her arm harder than I should.

Her eyes flick to my hand, then back to my face. Something shifts in her expression, the guilt morphing into anger.

"Once," she bites out, pulling against my hold.

The admission douses my rage with cold clarity. Once. Only once. But even that feels like more than I can bear.

"He was that bad?" I try to laugh, to twist the pain into mockery as I step back to give her space.

"No," she retorts. "He just doesn't force himself on me. He's a gentleman."

Her insinuation knocks the breath right out of my lungs.

I always gave her a choice. She could have said no at any point. Yet she allowed me to taste her, to touch her. And now she's throwing it back in my face like I took something she didn't offer.

I can't stop her from lying to herself, but I won't let her make me the villain of her cowardice.

"Message received. Don't mess with the staff," I fire back, then walk to the living room for my coat.

"You don't get to be hurt now!" she charges after me. "You knew the ethical line existed!"

"Fuck the ethical line!" I shout back. "This is nothing but your pathetic excuse so you don't have to admit you're drawn to me."

"That's not true," she counters but her words falter as I close the distance again, pulled by an invisible thread I can't seem to cut.

Why won't she just admit it? The chemistry between us is so blatantly obvious, so painfully all-consuming that I know she feels it too.

"Tell me the truth, Sophie." My voice drops low as I cradle her face. "If I wasn't your boss, if there were no lines to cross... would I have a chance? Would you want me?"

Her hands rub her thighs nervously. Her eyes glisten with unshed tears as the silence stretches.

Then, softly, painfully, "It doesn't matter."

"It does." My thumbs graze her cheeks. "Please, answer this one question."

"I wish you weren't my boss."

The confession tears through me, ripping away my restraint. My lips crash onto hers with desperate hunger. I walk her backwards through the flat until the back of her knees collide with the bed.

"Carter, what are you doing?"

"Call me Medard," I murmur.

"But you are my—"

"When I was thirteen, I gave my crush a rose from my mother's garden." The words tumble out as I lick a trail along her neck. "She crushed my heart the same way she crushed that rose."

"That's awful," she pants. "But why are you telling me this?"

"It's just you and me, lioness. Two people who want to guard their hearts." I pull the belt from her robe. "Just Sophie and Medard."

With one guiding push, I ease her down onto the bed, and she goes willingly.

I kick off my shoes, unbutton my shirt, leaving it to hang loose. My hands reach for the belt buckle, and her body tenses.

"I'll only give you what you want," I promise, despite the doubt I'll be able to rein myself in once I start.

"I would have loved it if you'd given me a rose," she says softly.

That innocent confession nearly undoes me completely.

I unbuckle my belt, letting my slacks glide down. Dressed in boxers and open shirt, I capture her lips again. The mattress dips as I cage her between my knees. I rock her higher up on the bed, my hands roaming her thighs, spreading them slowly. Her robe slides down her shoulders, revealing soft breasts and white lace panties that make my mouth water. I drag my mouth across her shoulder, inhaling her scent, imprinting her on my memory.

"Carter," she gasps.

"Medard," I correct, voice rough with need.

Her head tips back, her lips parting on a shaky exhale. "This is wrong," she whispers, but her body arches into me.

"Then tell me to leave."

Her fingers curl into my shirt, clutching instead of pushing. I take it for what it is—Permission.

The kiss I press to her lips is slower, deeper, weighted with obsession. She tastes like defiance and surrender.

She fists my hair, tugging hard enough to make me groan.

"You're impossible," she sighs.

"And you're mine," I growl, gliding my crotch along her lace-clad pussy.

She exhales hard, her eyes rolling back.

My forehead drops to hers, chest heaving as I fight the urge to devour her completely, to take everything she's offering and more.

"You're infuriating," she whispers, breathless at another sweep of my boxer-clad groin over her sensitive spot.

"And you're perfect."

Her lips part in protest, but I silence it with my mouth—fierce, consuming, all teeth and desperation and need. She pushes at my chest, nails catching on my shirt, but her mouth fights back with equal heat, feeding me and denying me all at once.

My lips trail down her throat. My hand glides along her thigh, then slips beneath to her arse. Her skin is so soft, so warm.

"Stop," she gasps, but there's no conviction.

Her hands splay against me, not pushing, just hovering. Trembling.

"Do you want me to?" I murmur against her jaw, giving her the choice even though it might kill me if she says yes.

She shudders, and her silence is answer enough.

"You love it," I continue, my teeth grazing her collarbone.

"Love isn't the word I'd use."

"Want, then."

Her eyes flash with defiance even as her chest rises, heavy and fast. "You think you can just show up with overpriced gyozas and I'll fall at your feet?"

"Worked, didn't it?" I smirk, brushing my thumb across her bottom lip. "You're here. You're looking at me like you want to bite and beg in the same breath."

She snaps her teeth at my thumb, biting down just enough to make my cock twitch with bated anticipation. "Arrogant bastard."

"And yet," I murmur, tugging her closer, "you don't stop me."

"Medard." It's barely a whisper. A warning. A plea.

Hearing my name on her lips like that undoes me completely.

I glide my hands down her body, thumbs strumming her nipples through the delicate lace, fingers pressing into her ribs, hands gripping her hips before I settle between her legs.

Her eyes widen. For a suspended second, I think she'll tell me to stop, but then she opens her legs wider—barely an inch, but enough.

I hook my thumbs under her panties, and she lifts her hips, allowing me to peel the lace down her legs.

"Fucking perfect," I rasp, inhaling the heady scent of her pussy.

My mouth waters. My cock pulses, begging me to throw caution to the wind and just thrust into her.

Well, the bastard will have to wait.

My lioness still owes me a taste of her orgasm.

I pull her lips apart gently, revealing her pink clit, and she yelps, eyes slamming shut.

I blow softly across her exposed flesh, pulling a quiver from her legs.

"Medard—" she whimpers.

Slowly, deliberately, I push a finger inside, coaxing her closer to surrender. She scoots back instinctively, uncertainty battling with hunger on her face. A second finger joins the first, and her body yields as I pump slowly. My breath ghosts across her clit, making her shudder once more.

Her hands pull at the sheets desperately. I move my thumb to her clit, slowly circling around it as I continue to drag my two digits in and out of her tight opening.

Desperation grips her as she bucks her hips, trying to move herself onto my thumb, but I tut and pull my hand away.

"No, please!"

I straighten on my knees, rubbing my shaft through my boxers, but it barely calms the fucker down. I'm so painfully hard for her, I just want to rip my boxers off and shove inside her until I'm balls-deep.

"Fuck, lioness, I can't get enough of you" I grate through my teeth with another firm squeeze to my cock.

"Then don't—" The tiny words leave her lips. "Don't stop."

Finally, lioness.

I snake my arms around her thighs and pull her onto my mouth. She gasps, melodic moans spilling from her lips. I devour her hungrily, sucking her clit while my tongue delves deep.

Her hips rise against me, rhythm building as she fists the sheets hard enough to pull them free.

I glide my palms over her body. I want her to crave my hands, to thrum with anticipation whenever I reach for her.

Her breath quickens, her climax approaching. Two fingers pump while I suck on her clit.

"Medard," she mewls, tugging my hair.

But then, out of nowhere, she suddenly pushes against my head, fighting the orgasm from slamming into her. I'm not letting her escape this again—not from pleasure, not from us.

With a firm pull on her thighs, she falls against the mattress. I hook my arms across her stomach to pin her, thumb pulling at her little hood. I suck hard, and when my teeth latch onto her in the tiniest nibble, she comes undone.

"Oh god, yes!" she cries out, body convulsing, pussy fluttering against my lips as she finally lets herself fall.

I keep lapping at her, drawing out every last tremor until her breathing has calmed. I lean back to admire my beautiful, sated lioness.

But before I can catch more than a glimpse, she's off the bed, wrapping her robe around herself.

"You should leave," she mumbles, storming out of the bedroom.

Defeat grips my heart, but I have no fight left in me. I take a few deep breaths. I've given everything I have, and she keeps running.

I button up my shirt and get dressed with a calm I do not feel before joining her in the living room. She's standing by the window, gazing out at the city lights like an ethereal figure caught in turmoil. I reach out, tucking a stray tendril behind her ear.

She turns her head away, rejecting even that small touch.

Enough.

I'm done playing by her rules.

"Stop fighting this, lioness. Our future has already been written."

She laughs quietly, but there's no light to it.

Whatever is keeping her from me, it's not the copper. He's just another excuse.

I slide my hand down her arm until it hits her pulse point. Her eyes land on mine, confusion flickering. I twine our fingers together and bring our hands to my mouth.

"No more excuses." I kiss her knuckles, my voice dropping low enough for her to understand this as a command. "Tomorrow, I'll pick you up and we'll secure the Windpower account together. Then we'll go back to my place and celebrate with champagne and my cock between your thighs."

She visibly swallows, her cheeks flushing.

"And the next day, you'll sign that CRA, because I'm not hiding my fiancée." I pull her against my chest and seal my words with a kiss.

"I can't—"

"This isn't a discussion. This will be done my way. "

Period.

Her brows furrow as irritation begins to simmer underneath her skin. But I'm not backing down.

"I meant everything I said. This isn't a fling—it's the beginning of a lifetime. You will be my wife. This is non-negotiable."

"You're out of line," she warns, anger swirling in her eyes as she half-heartedly pulls at our joined hands.

I pull in the opposite direction, yanking her against my chest. My hand wraps around her throat, not squeezing but holding, and force her chin up.

"Oh, lioness. From here on out, I'm the one drawing the line," I grate through my teeth, "right under your defiance."

I pull out the folder I hid under my coat and thrust it against her chest. She holds onto it with one shaking hand while the other instinctively moves to her throat.

"Read this." I lift my chin towards the folder. "And know that I may not give you a choice, but I do it with the intention of giving you a happy life."

With those final words, I leave her flat, letting the door slam.

Hope flares that this parting gift will finally break down her walls. But beneath it, something harder settles—determination.

I'm done asking.

From now on, she'll learn what it means to belong to Medard Carter.

Protector

Sophie

The door slams shut behind him. I stand frozen, barely breathing. My thoughts spin so fast they blur—anger, confusion, arousal, fear, excitement, indignation—all swirl together until one emotion cuts through the chaos: relief.

Relief.

A laugh bubbles up from my chest, quiet at first then louder, building until it spills from me in waves I can't control. It's hysterical, almost manic. I press my hand to my mouth as if I can contain it. Despite his aggressive delivery, I'm genuinely relieved he's making the choice for me. He's decided for both of us what I've been too terrified to take for myself.

The folder slips from my trembling fingers and lands on the floor with a soft thud. Papers scatter at my feet, but I can't stop laughing—laughing so hard that tears stream down my cheeks, hot and relentless, blurring my vision.

"Mrs Carter," I say aloud to the empty room, my voice caught somewhere between acceptance and self-mockery, testing how the name feels on my tongue. I picture it—the perfect life he's promising with such arrogant certainty. Not hiding what we are. No more pretending I don't crave him with an intensity that terrifies me.

I see lazy Sunday mornings with coffee and his rare, genuine smiles. Business dinners—his hand on my lower back, claiming me in front of everyone. Coming home to him instead of an empty flat and wilted salads. His intensity focused entirely on me.

The image shouldn't feel as intoxicating as it does.

The hysteria settles gradually, leaving me breathless and shaky, my ribs aching from the force of it. I wipe my eyes with the back of my hand, mascara probably smeared across my cheeks like war paint, and my gaze drops to the papers scattered across the floor.

My heart stops.

Court transcripts.

The words jump out at me in cold, official typeface, and beneath them, my parents' names, impossible and damning.

The laughter dies in my throat, replaced by something cold and sharp that steals my breath more effectively than Carter's kiss ever could.

I drop to my knees, hands trembling violently as I gather the pages with desperate fingers, and start reading. Each word feels like a punch to the gut, unravelling everything I thought I knew. My breath hitches, shock tenses my body as the truth suffocates me with an unapologetic force. I scan page after page, the words sending me deeper into a twilight zone of an alternative past I never dared to imagine. Betrayal surges through my chest and blurs my vision all over again as the tears fall like a never-ending hailstorm. A sense of panic sets in, prompting me to reach for my phone and call the only person who can calm me down.

"I need you," I sob uncontrollably into the speaker. "He lied to me, my own father!"

"I'm on my way," his raspy voice reassures me before the line goes dead.

My thoughts are reeling, trying to fathom the reality that I've been lied to my entire life. Everything I am, everything I've done, was to appease a man who couldn't even let me have a good memory of my own mother. I keep flipping through the pages, hoping for a shred of information that could justify everything that happened, but there's nothing.

A knock on my front door jolts me out of my stupor. I run towards it, open it and let myself fall into his embrace.

"Hey, what happened?" Baron's concerned face greets me with the warmth I've been missing my entire childhood, and it sets another bout of tears free.

"Honey, talk to us," Lucy's calm voice rings out behind him, and I beckon them to come inside.

Both settle into the sofa as I gather all the papers from the floor and dump them on the coffee table.

"He lied to me! He told me she died of an overdose!" My cries break over the sobs. "He made out that she was some heroin addict who didn't care for me. But none of it is true!"

"Honey, why don't you sit down and take a deep breath? I understand this is a lot to take in, but—" Lucy tries to reason with me, but I cut her off.

"You don't understand. My own father betrayed me!"

She nods, exchanging a fleeting glance with her husband before she calmly responds. "Believe me, I know exactly how you're feeling."

"I know it sounds impossible, but Lucy has been through something similar." Baron clears his throat, indicating I should take a seat.

"How could someone possibly be so cruel?" I cry out, letting myself fall into the armchair, and dropping my hands into my palms.

I feel so betrayed, so worthless. I thought yearning for my father's love was painful, but this hurts so much more.

"Sadly, people can, especially your own family. So, you're saying that your mother wasn't an addict at all?" she asks, confusion edging across her face.

I've never told either of them anything about my past, other than my mother being dead. It was too embarrassing to admit my family had to battle drug abuse. A chuckle escapes my lips at the realisation that I carried this shame for years, when Father could have just told me the truth.

"No, she wasn't," I confirm, pulling out the relevant documents. "She was an ordinary woman who worked as an accountant at my father's firm. They married, bought a house, and eventually she got pregnant with me. That's when things went downhill."

"How so?" Baron asks, scanning the paperwork.

"There's a record listing countless doctors' appointments, indicating the pregnancy was tough on her. When she finally gave birth, she fell into a depression."

"Oh, Jesus," Lucy huffs, her hand instinctively finding her stomach.

It wasn't too long ago when she gave birth to their beautiful baby, so I assume she can empathise with how difficult new motherhood can be.

"Did she get any professional help?" she asks.

"No, and I'm sure my father is the reason why she didn't," I ball my fists at the memory of his disdainful attitude towards my sessions with Mrs Saunders. "When he realised, she wasn't getting any better on her own, he filed for divorce and sole custody. He claimed that she wasn't fit to be a mother."

The tears threaten to bubble up again, but I swallow them down.

"And let me guess, it was granted," Baron looks up to me, anger swirling through his bright blue eyes.

I nod, reading the transcript of the court hearing for the umpteenth time.

"The worst thing is that she fought him at every turn. She wanted to take care of me and even said that she'd be willing to go to therapy."

"And he still got custody of you?" Lucy's brows furrow in disbelief.

"Of course he did. A man with his station, a lawyer nonetheless, knows how to sway the courts in his favour."

"Wow, what an arsehole," she gasps at Baron's explanation. "Sorry, hun. I shouldn't have said that. He's still your father."

Her apology pulls a snicker from me, but there's no lightness to it. "But you're right. He's a major arsehole. He had all visitation rights removed from her, which ultimately drove her to commit suicide."

The room falls silent for a moment as all three of us try to comprehend how a single man could possess so much evil. I always knew Father to be a dominant and controlling narcissist, but I never thought he would hurt someone he's supposed to love so gravely.

"Sophie," Baron's voice cuts through the silence, "how did you get your hands on all of this? The files were sealed." He points at the red stamp that adorns almost every single page.

"Carter," I hesitantly admit.

"He handed them to you over dinner?" Baron's face falls at my admission.

"No, I didn't go to the dinner," I avert my gaze, embarrassment seeping out of my pores at the memory of letting him eat me out like a starved lion, and after I swore to Baron that I would never let him touch me again.

"He was here." Lucy's eyes lock with mine, an unspoken understanding conveyed between us. "You've let him into your home."

With her long brown curls and dainty features, she looks like a naive little deer, but she's far from it. She keeps her wisdom and strength hidden but strikes when she has to.

"How do you know?" Her husband looks at us, puzzled, our gaze never breaking.

"Have a sniff. Her entire flat smells of expensive cologne, and I mean three-hundred pounds a bottle expensive—the kind, reserved for power-craving, domineering men."

He sniffs the air, causing me to retreat in my seat, but then he simply shrugs his shoulders. "My cologne isn't cheap, but I'm not—"

"Rest my case," Lucy interrupts him with a gentle tap on his knee and a broad smile.

I've always been happy for them to have found pure, unbridled love in each other, but it's never been something I sought for myself. Maybe it's because my career always took priority, or maybe I never thought someone could love me so unconditionally. Yet, seeing them now, I suddenly feel a pang of jealousy.

"So, you've slept with him," Baron states matter-of-factly.

"Baron! You shouldn't be so upfront," Lucy scolds him, but then turns to me in anticipation of an answer.

I rub my thighs nervously, feeling like a tiny organism under their microscope.

"Something like that."

"What do you mean?" Lucy shoots back, earning a reprimanding tut from Baron. "What? You've started it. Now I want to know."

I huff, trying to find the right words without sounding like a woman of the night. "We got intimate, but not to that extent."

"Alright, and did you like it? Have you changed your mind about staying away from the steely-eyed wanker?" she grins mischievously.

"Baron!" My face heats up.

So, he's told his wife absolutely everything about my problems with Carter.

"I feel very uncomfortable right now," he murmurs, his large frame retreating into the sofa cushions.

"Oh, come on, Soph. You know, I only let him train with you so much because he gives me the juicy details afterwards. Take a little pity on me. With the little one, I barely get to leave the house now. I need entertainment."

"I'm glad my life is so entertaining to you," I scowl at her, but then her chocolate-coloured, doe eyes pull a giggle from me.

"I want to be with him," I admit aloud for the first time. "But I'm afraid that once he knows the truth about me, he'll no longer want me."

"Because of your involvement with Harman?" Lucy asks.

I nod, the shame still coursing through my veins.

I'm not even surprised that Baron told her about the biggest mistake of my professional career. Maybe even my entire life.

"There's only one way to find out," Baron says.

"But I could lose my job!" I interject.

"Maybe," Lucy counters with a shrug, "but any other option that guarantees your job involves either a relationship built on a big fat lie, or a confession. So, which one will it be?"

Benefactor

Medard

10 years ago, Medard, 25 years old

We're short again this month. By 183.65 pounds, to be exact. The weight of the numbers presses down on me, exhaustion burning behind my eyes as I study the bank statements and bills splayed across the small kitchen table. After ten long hours at the office, a hot shower and my bed are calling my name, yet a gnawing sense of dread twists inside me—existential anxiety that refuses to let go. I feel the shame bloom in my chest, heavy and unwelcome, but I pick up my phone anyway, my fingers trembling slightly as I dial Mum's number.

"Medard, darling. How are you? How is Freya?"

"Good, we're good," I manage, though my voice sounds flat even to me.

"That's good. Oh, hang on, your brother wants to speak to you."

"Theo's home?"

"Yes, Lisa's back from uni, so he decided to stay for the weekend."

My heart warms at the mentioning of Theo's and my old friend. Growing up next to each other, the three of us were inseparable.

"Yo! Any chance I can be your plus one for the trip?" Theo pulls me from my trip down memory lane.

"What trip?"

"You know, the one Mum and Dad gifted you for your graduation. Duh! You probably want to take Freya, but if she's busy, I'm free. For real, man, I need a break from this place, from college."

That trip. I haven't even told Freya about it. I know she'd jump at the chance to spend a week abroad, paid for by my parents. It does sound tempting, but I can't afford to be away that long. I just started at this tiny law firm in Shadwell and I've got a lot to prove.

"I don't know yet," I brush him off, more urgent matters pressing on my mind. "Can you put Mum back on?"

"Yeah, yeah. But think about it. You and me, hitting the town. It'd be fun."

There's a rustling on the other end of the line as Theo hands the phone back to Mum.

"Your brother seems desperate to get away for a few days. He's been talking non-stop about it. He even tried to convince your dad to give him his trip early, before he's even graduated."

I swallow hard, feeling the weight of my own worries. "Listen, I have a favour to ask you."

"What is it, darling?"

I take a deep breath to gather my courage, my eyes darting across the kitchen ceiling. The black mould has spread, trailing from the window over to the extractor fan.

"Could I borrow another couple of hundred pounds?"

"Has this month been tight again?" she asks with an undercurrent of concern.

"Yeah, I'm sorry. I'll pay you back once I'm earning a bit more money," I promise her, regardless of the never-leaving doubt that Freya and I will ever get out of this financial hole.

"It's alright, darling. I know you're doing your best. I'll transfer it right away."

"Thanks, Mum."

"Oh, wait! Your dad wants to speak with you."

Dad's voice filters through the receiver before I can stop her.

"What's going on, son? You know your mum and I are always here for you, but I've got to ask—why are you struggling so much? I thought I taught you how to handle your finances."

"You have, and I'm handling them. I've just had a few unexpected expenses."

"Like what? Handbags?"

I stay quiet, unsure how much to say, unwilling to lie or embarrass Freya in front of them.

"Theo showed me her insta-thingy account—shopping trips to Selfridges and cocktails almost every weekend."

"She only meets her girlfriends when I'm working on weekends," I defend her quickly.

"I rest my case, Medard. You're working yourself to the bone to build a future, and she's out having fun, splurging with money neither of you really has. You should ask yourself if this is really a partnership, or if you're simply her benefactor."

"She's not, I'm not," I argue back, even though I know Dad is right.

I push away from the table, the sound of the chair scraping along the flimsy linoleum floor piercing at my resolve to get us out of this dilapidated flat.

But still, I defend Freya's spending habits as I head to the cabinets to make myself a cup of tea.

"You've got it all wrong, Dad. Freya is doing her best. She's even working a couple more shifts at the gallery—"

My words catch in my throat. I glance at the battered kettle on the counter. It's tiny, barely enough for two cups. The white paint has yellowed with age, lime scale creeping along the inside.

We broke our kettle a few nights ago, and this morning I left Freya thirty quid to buy a new one. She doesn't drink tea, not really, but she knows how much I rely on that simple comfort after a long day. She knows how important it is to me. Yet, the five-pound charity shop kettle she bought shows how little she cares.

"Son, are you still there?" Dad's voice pulls me back.

"Yes, I am. Sorry, I—" I choke out the words as realisation slams into my chest.

I'm exhausted from the long shifts, the over-time for a bit more money that's never enough anyway. I'm mentally drained from trying to hold on to her, to us, while she pleads ignorance. For almost two years, I've been fighting to keep this relationship, and now it all boils down to this pathetic piece of plastic.

"Dad, can you get Theo on the phone again?"

"Sure, son."

Moments later, my little brother's familiar 'yo' crackles through.

"Pack your bags. We're going to Italy. I always wanted to see Rome."

I end the call, cutting off his cheers. Then I start packing my belongings and leave a note for Freya. I write five words on a sticky note and press it to the kettle: 'I'm done being your benefactor.' Then I walk out, and finally close the door behind me for the last time.

Idiot

Medard

The moment Sophie opens the door, anticipation seizes me by the throat. Her delicate hands nervously rub her thighs, and there's an apprehensive look painted across her features. She's dressed impeccably—a knee-length emerald green skirt that flows like water around her legs, paired with a fitted white blouse that hugs her curves just right. Not too much, but enough to steal the breath from my lungs. For the first time since I've known her, she's wearing her hair down, and the soft curls fall well past her breasts, cascading much longer than I expected. She looks breathtaking.

"We good?" I ask, leaning against the door frame to appear calm and controlled when I'm anything but.

I don't know if she's read the file or not, if it had the effect I was aiming for, or if she now believes me to be as bad and ruthless as her father. But I hope with every ounce of hope I possess that she's finally seeing sense.

She nods slowly, her lips curling into a small smile that looks uncertain, perhaps even forced.

Well, I'll be damned.

No rebuttal. No defiance. No claws.

She gathers her coat and handbag with slow, calculated movements, as though she's bracing herself for the car ride with me—the close proximity that allows for no escape.

"Come here, lioness," I tell her with a beckoning gesture, feeling brave but also wanting her to know that I'm here for her.

Whatever has stirred in her through our confrontation or the file I gave her, she's not alone in it. We're a team now, which means whatever pains or troubles her concerns me, too.

She closes the gap between us, and I can't resist the urge to touch her. Cupping her cheek, I lean in, taking the risk of a kiss to test the waters. The moment our lips meet, a rush of euphoria courses through me, igniting every nerve ending. She's not pushing me away—instead, she melts into the kiss.

She's finally accepting what I've been trying to tell her all along: I'm serious about us.

"Are you ready to close this deal?" I ask against her mouth, my heart racing with excitement.

She nods, and I steal another kiss, because I finally can. We make our way to my car, and though her silence feels off, her hand in mine is reassuring. As we drive towards the golf club, I rest my hand atop hers, where it's anxiously rubbing her thigh.

She's probably nervous about the luncheon. Frightened, she'll mess up again. But this time, I'm prepared. I will lead this meeting, so that everything will beautifully fall into place.

"How did you get the file?" she asks, her voice quiet but laced with curiosity.

I exhale sharply, feeling the need to protect her swirling in my chest. "I had a PI look into it."

"Why?"

"Due diligence, lioness. I wanted to know where the woman comes from that's going to bear my children," I say with a smirk, expecting her to lash out, to tell me I've completely lost my mind talking about children.

But she doesn't.

She falls silent, her gaze focused ahead. But her fingers entwine with mine, squeezing tightly as if sealing a pact between us.

All along, I wanted her to comply and accept us. But now that she's doing exactly that, something feels distinctly off.

"You're not going to kick off over my 'delusions' of having children with you?"

"It makes sense, doesn't it?" She shrugs, keeping her eyes fixed forward. "Naturally, that's the next step after the wedding."

She's right, but I don't like the way she says it—like she's resigned herself to her fate rather than being excited about building a future together.

We arrive at the golf club, but before she can make a move to step out, I gently tug at our joined hands to get her attention.

"I know you have a lot to process, but I'm here for you, lioness. I want to take care of you, and I want you to be happy—with me."

"I want that too," she admits quietly, and there's something in her tone that makes my chest tighten. "But there are a few things we should talk about."

"And we will," I assure her, bringing her knuckles to my lips. "As soon as we've secured Windpower."

I hop out of the car and open the door for her, my palm finding its natural place at the small of her back as we walk towards the club entrance.

At the threshold, she suddenly stills and turns towards me, that small smile curling her lips again. And then she kisses me like the world might end, like she's memorising the taste of me.

"What was that for?" I grin from ear to ear like a lovesick fool.

"Does a woman need a reason to kiss her fiancé?" She smiles over her shoulder as she walks into the club, and my heart damn near stops.

I follow her inside, but as soon as I spot the Ravens across the room, my happiness feels like it's been doused in gasoline and set on fire. Andrew Rosen—Sophie's father—is shaking hands with them, sealing something before leaving their table. Before I can fully compute their exchange, he heads directly towards us with purposeful strides.

"What the fuck is going on?" I demand, bewildered.

"I... I don't know," Sophie stammers, and I can hear the genuine confusion in her voice.

Her father approaches us, and I ball my fists, ready to put one through his smug face.

"Sophie, don't be late for our weekly dinner tonight," he says, his voice light and chipper, but leaving no room for questions or explanations.

I turn to her, my expression clouded with suspicion and something darker. "What have you done?"

The question bursts out, urgent and raw, but I don't wait for her to respond. I storm towards the Ravens, dread coiling tight in my gut with every step.

"Ah, Medard!" Gerald grins, his tone dripping with condescension that makes my teeth grind. "I'm afraid you're too late. I've just been offered a deal I simply couldn't pass on."

"Gerald, we had a deal." My voice is steady, but inside I'm fraying at the edges, unravelling.

"That we had, but it seems you're not the only one who suspected the lawsuit was coming."

The words slice through me. The enormity of it hits hard, and all my plans for the firm and my career collapse like a house of cards in a strong wind.

"So, you haven't sent the official tender out yet?" I ask, desperation clawing at my throat.

"No, and it appears I no longer have to." His eyes gleam with triumph, and my heart sinks further into chaos.

"Mrs Ravens, I implore you," Sophie interrupts, stepping forward with urgency. "Please, let us at least give you our proposal."

For a moment, watching her fight for this—for us—doubt flickers. She looks desperate, genuine. But I crush it down. Too much evidence. Too many coincidences.

Mrs Ravens shows no mercy, shrugging Sophie off with practised nonchalance. "I'm sorry, my dear. It's my husband's company, so the decision lies with him."

"Have a good day," Gerald ends the discussion with a smile as they take their leave, and I feel the ground shifting beneath my feet.

I storm off, the weight of betrayal clinging like a cold shadow, but Sophie is quick to follow.

Once outside, I pivot sharply, capturing her in my glare as my frustration is boiling over. "What the fuck have you done?"

"What? I haven't done anything!" she fires back, her voice sharp and defensive.

"Then how does your father know about Windpower?" I challenge, my heart racing with fear and betrayal.

"I don't know! I didn't tell him anything!" she insists, her eyes wide with what looks like genuine panic.

"Are you sure about that? You meet him for dinner every week. Maybe you slipped up." My voice rises despite my efforts to control it. "So, God help me, Sophie, if I find out you sabotaged this deal—"

"Screw you!" she snaps, pointing her finger at me defiantly. "I've seen my father once since you approached me about the account, and I know I didn't slip up. I wouldn't be so stupid, let alone stab you in the back like this!"

"I don't believe you." Scepticism drips from my words like venom. "You said 'I can't.'"

"What?"

"Last night," I bite out, closing the distance between us. My hand rises towards her throat before I remember we're in public. I ball my fist, leaving only my index finger out to point at her accusingly. "I told you about my plans of sharing a future together, and you said you can't—not won't. Can't! That's why you've been pushing me back all this time, isn't it? You've been scheming behind my back, lying to me, knowing full well that I'd find out eventually when you handed the account to your father on a fucking silver platter!"

She has the audacity to snort with incredulity, as though the idea that she's been scheming with her father is so far-fetched. She has weekly dinners with him, and up until last night, she didn't know how much of a piece-of-shit he truly is. It makes complete sense, and it explains why she's been off ever since I picked her up. Why, there's guilt clearly seeping out of her right now.

"I pushed back because you forced yourself on me, and now you want to hold that against me?"

Oh, no. Don't even try that pathetic excuse with me.

"You made sure I caught your attention so you could get your hands on a big account," I accuse. The words taste bitter, but painfully logical.

"That's not true." She shakes her head vehemently, but I wave her off, the frustration clawing at my insides.

"Get in the car," I call over my shoulder, the finality of it pouring from my lips as dark clouds of betrayal rally within me.

I don't know who to believe anymore, but with every passing second, the walls around my heart grow thicker—fortified by doubt and hurt.

The next thirty-seven minutes are dragging on, the weight of betrayal festering in my chest. My thoughts ricochet like an old pinball machine, crashing from Sophie's total disloyalty to her fervent commitment to the firm—perhaps even to me—before looping back to the incomprehensible scheme I find myself caught in. It's gnawing at me, this endless cycle of doubt and fury.

Sophie, silent as a grave, is sitting beside me with an unsettling calm. I want to reach out to offer her a hand as an olive branch of trust, but I also have the primal urge to slam her head against the dashboard for deceiving me so gravely.

The questions churn in my mind: How does her father know about Windpower?

My gut twists. My suspicions loom over Sophie again, but if there's the faintest possibility that she's innocent, I have to find out who the real traitor is at the firm.

Surely, it can't be Buckman. He risks it all if the firm falters—the value of his shares plummeting along with his cushy retirement plans.

Sophie's assistant? No, that timid girl wouldn't dare set foot into Rosen's office.

My own assistant, Janet? Absolutely not, loyalty runs thick in her veins.

My mind spirals back to Sophie again, to that achingly beautiful portrait of confusion and mistrust sitting beside me.

I glance sideways to find her absorbed in the scenery passing outside the window, her fingers twisting her earring. She doesn't fidget, though, doesn't rub her thighs. She looks calm, secure in her position, probably because she has her father's firm to fall back on.

My grip tightens around the steering wheel, knuckles stark white against the dark leather.

I'm an idiot. I fell for her charms, although I knew deep down that she was keeping secrets, despite knowing she could hurt me—and she did.

I pull onto the gravel path leading up to St. James, each crunch under the tyres like thunder in the silence, amplifying the heaviness that hangs between us.

"Where are we?" Sophie's voice slices through the air, her eyes surveying the intricacies of the old, haunting hotel with its ivy-covered walls.

"It's my brother's wedding rehearsal. I have to show my face for an hour. You can stay in the car or tag along. Up to you." The indifference in my tone is deliberate, a shield against the scrutiny of my emotions.

I planned to skip the rehearsal and head straight back to my place after securing Windpower. To make good on the promises I made last night. Now she can endure my family's hospitality. Let her wallow in guilt.

Without waiting for a reply, I swing open the car door and head to the wide terrace at the back, dread curling in my stomach as old memories of a broken heart flood in. Sophie follows closely, her presence almost an echo of my own turmoil.

"Medard, darling!" Mum's voice pierces the murmur of conversations, her energy pulling every eye towards us. She sweeps over, enveloping me in a hug before fixating on Sophie with undisguised curiosity. "And who have we got here?"

"This is Sophie, a colleague," I say tersely before turning away, desperate to drown myself in a drink. I find my father seated with Theo and Lisa at the bar, and I make a beeline for the scotch.

The hours drip away slowly, entangled in conversations with relatives and old friends from my childhood as dusk settles in. Laughter and well-wishes swirl around me, but I fixate on the warmth beginning to stir in my chest, fuelled by the scotch I'm repeatedly pouring down my throat. I planned to stay for an hour, but that quickly turned into two, then three. I keep telling myself it's because I enjoy the company, but the cold, hard truth is that I dread the ride home with Sophie.

"Thank you for coming," Lisa says, drifting up beside me with a flute of champagne in hand. "I know it means a lot to your brother."

Her engagement ring catches the light of the garden torches, sparkling like it's in on some cosmic joke. I once thought she was the best thing I'd ever have, but ironically, she hurt me the most—not because she betrayed me, but because she was supposed to be safe. A childhood friend and confidante who knew me before I built my walls and still chose to climb over them just to wreck what was left. She killed my foolish belief that love could ever be unconditional.

And then Sophie came along. I thought she was the antidote, but she was just the second dose of the same poison.

Some weaknesses are hard to lose, and mine just happen to wear lipstick and lie.

"I didn't have much of a choice with Mum's pestering," I reply dryly, my eyes flitting over the crowd.

"The pretty blond woman standing over there by the lavender bushes, is she with you? I don't recognise her."

I follow her gaze, landing on Sophie, now engrossed in conversation with Aunt Carol. A flicker of satisfaction jolts through me. She'll have to endure Carol's never-ending tales of her 'spiritual awakening' in Africa—all three hours' worth. The guilt must be gnawing at her, or maybe she's just that good an actress.

"If she was, what's it to you? You're marrying my brother." My voice is edged with bitterness, and I can feel the tension in the air shift palpably.

Typical Lisa—first she crushed my heart, and then she decided my brother might not have been her best choice after all. They deserve each other. Her, for hurting me. He, for never noticing how much she meant to me.

Lisa's expression morphs into disbelief. "I was just curious if she's the one you mentioned in your home the other day."

"Oh, come on." My frustration bubbles over, spilling out before I can contain it. "I'm fed up seeing the regret on your face, like you've made the greatest mistake choosing my brother."

"What on earth are you talking about? The greatest mistake?" Her voice rises slightly. "I don't regret choosing your brother. I love him."

I want to scoff, to dismiss her words as more lies, but something in her tone makes me pause. The confusion in her eyes doesn't look like acting, doesn't have that calculated quality I've come to expect. Still, I'm done playing her games.

"Right," I mutter. "Then explain the looks. The glimmers of hope every time we talk. What's that, Lisa?"

"Jesus, Medard! You have no idea, do you?" She's nearly exasperated as she looks at me, pleading for understanding I'm not sure I can give.

"When I stood right over there," she says, gesturing towards the entrance of the patio, "and your brother finally told me he loved me, I saw you standing behind that oak tree with flowers in hand. Knowing I wanted Theo, I never should have strung you along with secret dates and promises I never intended to uphold. But I did." Her voice softens with something that sounds like genuine remorse. "I gave you false hope."

I swallow hard, her words penetrating my defences like arrows finding their marks. There's no venom in them, just a brutal honesty that strips the anger right out of me.

"I was so ashamed afterwards," she continues quietly, and I can hear the weight of years in her voice. "So, I let you believe you'd imagined it all, that we were just fooling around. The regret you've seen on my face? It's guilt, Medard. And that glimmer of hope? It's me wishing you'd finally let go and find someone who makes you happy."

"What about your disdain for my brother's lack of achievements?" I challenge, though the sharpness in my words is reflected in the pain I see in her eyes.

"You mean your constant jabs at him?" she counters softly, and the gentle rebuke lands harder than any shout could. "The way you talk him down when he admires you more than anyone?"

Her words slice through me, clean and deep, cutting through years of resentment I've carried like armour. Guilt swells in my chest, twisting sharp and ugly. I grip my tumbler tighter, watching the amber liquid swirl as if it can drown the shame rising in my throat.

"I'm sorry," I mutter, forcing the words out past the knot of emotion. "I was a dick."

Lisa's lips curve into a faint smile. "And I'm sorry I hurt you back then."

There's no heat in her eyes now, only genuine affection—but it's for my brother, not me. It's real. It always has been. I just never wanted to see it.

I step back, nodding once before turning towards Theo. He's laughing with Dad, completely unaware of the storm that just passed between us, and I feel something shift in my chest. I cross the garden, and when he turns, surprise flashes in his eyes as I pull him into a tight hug.

"Congratulations, little brother," I say quietly, meaning every word for the first time in years. "I'm proud of you."

Madman

Sophie

The nerve!

I can't believe Carter actually thinks I'm somehow scheming with my father—my father, of all people! The notion gnaws at me, relentless and bitter.

It's close to midnight, and we're still at his brother's wedding rehearsal, like some casual, happy couple when we're anything but. We're not a couple—nowhere near it, despite his declarations last night about how I no longer have a choice, how I'm going to be his wife whether I like it or not.

The man's completely unhinged!

I've just had to endure hours of his relatives' interrogations, tales of weird spiritual trips to Africa, and endless anecdotes from his childhood.

I want to vomit.

I want to. Bloody. Go. Home.

But apparently, I'm not allowed to because every time I dare to speak to the lunatic, he tells me 'soon'. Well, soon ended hours ago.

I signal the waiter to pour me another glass of wine.

Scheming with Father—the absolute cheek! He knows about my complicated relationship with him—hell, he gave me a file detailing exactly how complicated it is—and yet he has so little trust in me.

I pinch the stem of my wine glass and scan the crowd until I spot him across the room. He sits composed in a leather armchair, swirling whiskey, looking every inch the controlled businessman.

What cuts deeper than anything is that after talking to Baron and Lucy last night, after reading that file, I allowed myself a glimpse of the feelings I've been trying so hard to bury. I dared to believe his promise of taking care of me.

I take another sip, hoping to swallow down the lump in my throat.

It took one second. One moment of adversity, for him to turn me into the antagonist without a second thought, without even giving me the benefit of the doubt.

I feel like a fool for falling for him when he clearly has so little faith in me.

My gaze shifts back to him just in time to see his father approach, murmuring something. Carter's hooded eyes rise slowly, landing squarely upon mine, and for a fleeting moment, I'm held captive by his stare.

"It was Sophie, right?" Carter's mother steps in, breaking the spell.

"Yes, it is," I swallow hard, recalling Carter's words from earlier, his casual declaration of me as his colleague.

There were countless times when I insisted, we were nothing more than that, throwing the professional boundary between us like a shield. But the moment he labelled me that way himself, reducing me to just another employee, it cut deeper than any bad word he'd ever said.

"Thank you for having me today, despite my barging in unannounced," I add with the politeness Father instilled in me.

Her expression softens. "Oh, don't worry, my dear. I'm always intrigued by a rare gem."

"I'm afraid I don't follow." I force a smile.

"There's something about you that has captured my son's attention completely," she observes, her eyes sparkling with pride. "So, you must be quite special."

I giggle uncomfortably. "I'm afraid you've got it all wrong."

Her brow furrows.

"I'm only here because we had a meeting with a potential client earlier, and your son's party was on the way home."

She lets out a soft chuckle, glancing at Carter. "If that's your view, then it appears that you've got it all wrong, not me."

Before I can voice my curiosity, she sighs. "You really are special, my dear, and I'm looking forward to getting to know you. Enjoy the rest of your evening."

Her gentle squeeze on my shoulder is both reassuring and unnerving as she leaves, and I'm left standing there feeling more confused than ever.

I've spent hours with his family tonight, and everyone has been kind and welcoming, especially his parents. It's hard to believe that he grew up surrounded by so much love and warmth, and yet here he stands, casting shadows of suspicion and doubt over me, ready to believe the worst without question.

The guilt twists in my stomach, sharp and unrelenting. I didn't scheme with my father—I would never. But I am guilty of something, and his name is Harman.

My gaze falls on Carter once more. Finishing my wine in one long swallow, I clutch my purse and brace myself for his scrutiny, for whatever comes next in this twisted game we're playing.

"It's late. I want to go home," I murmur, stepping up to him with apprehension.

A knowing smile plays on his lips as he retrieves the car keys from his pocket.

"Fair enough, let's go. But you'll have to drive. One too many of these," he admits, extending the keys towards me.

My eyes widen in disbelief, and I'm pretty sure my soul just left my body.

"I can't drive your car," I protest, feeling panic rise.

His laughter fills the room. "You'll be fine. It's an automatic. Think of it as a very expensive toy car. Two pedals, that's all."

With a casual wave, he heads for the exit.

Frantically running after him, I implore, "Carter, you don't understand. I can't drive your car or any car for that matter."

His reaction is unexpected as he comes to a sudden stop, and I nearly crash into his back. The exasperation rolling off him is practically visible.

"How do you not have a license?" He turns to face me, looking like I've just confessed to never having seen the ocean.

"I don't need one," I shrug, trying for nonchalant but probably landing somewhere around defensive, "I'm quicker taking the tube or a cab."

"Fine, looks like we'll be staying here," he concedes, heading to the reception desk.

Determined not to spend another moment in this place, I call after him, "I'm calling a cab."

His cynical response cuts through the tension, "Good luck with that. Small town. Taxi company shuts at nine p.m."

The absurdity leaves me dumbfounded as I swiftly fall into step beside him.

He requests two rooms, his voice steady with that hint of authority that would be attractive if it weren't so bloody infuriating. He accepts the keys, then strides ahead, leading me towards an antiquated lift that looks like it hasn't been updated since the Victorian era.

His expression remains stoic as the silence wraps around us thick and charged as neither of us makes a move to break the suffocating quiet.

We arrive at our floor, and as we pause in front of our separate doors, I shoot him one last indignant glare—an unspoken challenge that hangs between us like a gauntlet thrown down.

The door slams behind, the echo of my frustration bouncing off the walls of this godforsaken hotel room. In the dim light, I grip the edge of the bedside table as though it's the only thing keeping me tethered to sanity, staring at the intricate floral wallpaper like it might hold the answers to all of Carter's inexplicably irritating behaviour.

Does he really believe I'm responsible for losing Windpower?

And dragging me to a family gathering unannounced? Talk about adding insult to injury.

As if that wasn't enough, he drank too much, because apparently, self-control is optional when you're an arrogant git.

Last night was a mistake. I never should have allowed him to touch me, to cross that line...again!

With a huff that would put a petulant teenager to shame, I stomp into the bathroom, seeking solace and perhaps higher ground from this disaster. I scan the space and find a thin cotton dressing gown hanging on the door. Peeling off my clothes until I'm down to just my underwear, I slip into the gown, which feels about as substantial as tissue paper.

Making my way back to the bedroom, the temperature feels uncomfortably cold, so I reach for the thermostat, determined to find some semblance of comfort in this nightmare.

I crank it up without a second thought, watching the needle climb higher until it's gone way past normal and straight into 'tropical rainforest' territory.

"Oh, come on!" I press the button to lower it, only for it to jam stubbornly.

Abandoning the crappy piece of plastic masquerading as climate control, I try my luck with the window. But the old-fashioned sash panel won't budge because they've locked the damn thing!

I groan, accepting my fate as the room transforms into a sauna. I toss and turn in bed, unable to find relief, feeling like I'm slowly being cooked alive, like I'm in the depths of hell—Carter's personal brand of hell, to be precise.

Desperation kicks in. I reach for the phone, only to be met with the sound of absolutely nothing.

I can't take it any longer.

I grab my clothes and march to Carter's door, my knuckles rapping sharply against the wood.

It takes a few moments before the door finally swings open, and there he stands, wearing nothing but his boxers.

My breath catches, and for a split second, I'm stunned and acutely aware of the taut muscles rippling beneath his skin like he's been personally sculpted by some very talented and very unfair deity.

"What do you want?" His voice snaps, rubbing the sleep from his eyes as he does a quick perusal of my outfit, or lack thereof.

I clear my throat. "The thermostat is broken. I cranked it too high, and now it's stuck. Reception won't answer, and I can't sleep like this."

He pinches the bridge of his nose. "Reception shuts at midnight. I'm sure they'll sort it out in the morning."

"In the morning?" I exclaim. "Carter, I'll be marinated in my own sweat by then!"

A flash of humour crosses his features.

"Sounds like the perfect environment for you," he teases, arms crossed.

"Very funny. Now switch rooms with me."

"Hell, no! You broke the damn thing," he shrugs.

"And you're the reason I have to stay in this godforsaken hotel tonight!" I counter.

"Fine, looks like we'll be sharing a bed then," he says, walking back to the bed.

A flicker of hesitation washes over me, but then I find myself sighing as I close the door behind me and walk to the empty side of the bed.

How much worse can it get?

He's already had a taste of me in my bed. So, sleeping next to each other seems rather harmless.

"You'd better stay on your side of the bed," I warm him, refusing to acknowledge the warmth pooling low in my abdomen.

He's been in this room less than an hour, yet it's already

saturated with his signature scent. It's something crisp, masculine and expensive, that makes my traitorous body respond in ways I absolutely cannot afford right now.

He chuckles. "Don't worry, I have no intention of forcing myself on you. After all, why would I want to shag a traitor?"

The biting tone stings, but I refuse to let him see how much it hurts.

"I've already told you, I had nothing to do with it," I fire back.

He simply shakes his head.

"Sure, your father just happened to be at the golf club with a fully fletched plan. Don't take me for a fool," he mutters as he slides under the duvet.

I carefully slip into the bed, ensuring my back is turned away from him. "Think what you want, but without actual proof, you have no cause to get rid of me."

"So, you admit you went behind my back," he accuses, pouncing on my words like the lawyer he is, looking for a loophole.

"No!" I snap, turning to look at him over my shoulder with enough force to potentially cause whiplash. "I'm saying that if you try to get me fired, I won't stand for it."

"Good luck with that. Don't forget, I'm your boss," he laughs darkly, the sound sending an unwelcome shiver up my spine.

"Buckman won't allow it," I argue, sitting up to find the typical smirk playing on his lips like he's just won a game I didn't know we were playing.

"Buckman has lost his credibility, hence why he hired me," he retorts. "He will do exactly as I say."

His words hit me like a punch to the gut. With a sudden burst of determination, I jump out of bed, throw off the gown, and grab for my skirt.

"Screw you! I've done nothing wrong," I declare, my voice trembling.

I refuse to let him push me around, to let him dictate my fate like I'm some powerless pawn in his corporate chess game.

He sits up in bed, his frustration evident as he pinches the bridge of his nose.

"Get back into bed. There's nowhere for you to go tonight," he huffs.

"I'd rather hitchhike back to London than spend another second with you in this room," I retort, struggling with the zipper of my skirt like it's personally betraying me.

In one swift move, he jumps up and rounds the bed, his eyes ablaze with a determination that makes my pulse quicken for all the wrong reasons.

"No, you won't," he growls, his fingers wrapping firmly around my wrist.

As my skirt cascades to the floor, I fight to break free.

"Let go of me!" I shout, but his demeanour remains frustratingly impassive as he stands his ground like an immovable force.

In a moment of pure impulse, my hand flies out. It connects with his cheek in a slap that echoes through the room. His expression darkens, anger simmering just beneath the surface that threatens to incinerate me where I stand.

"Lioness," he rasps.

The endearment rolls off his tongue like a warning, a promise wrapped in velvet threat. With surprising gentleness, he pulls me close. His hands frame my face as he captures my lips in a kiss that tastes of punishment and promise.

But as the kiss deepens and threatens to drown me in a sea of sensation, as his tongue sweeps possessively through my mouth like he's marking his territory, a wave of clarity washes over me.

I can't let him do this.

With both hands flat against his chest, I push him away and deliver another sharp slap. The sound rings out like a battle cry, a declaration of war.

He grasps my throat and crashes his mouth onto mine once more—hard and unforgiving like a brutal claiming that leaves no room for protest. His tongue is invasive as it sweeps through my mouth, demanding submission. A whimper rises from my throat as his teeth clamp down on my lower lip.

I push him away again, fighting against the pull he has over me. I can't let him wreak havoc with my feelings when he's already holding all the power over my career, over my very existence.

As I turn away from him, desperate to put distance between us, his arm snakes around my waist like a steel band, and he lifts me clean off the ground. My feet kick out, my hands clawing at his forearm.

"Put me down!" I scream, my voice cracking with frustration and something dangerously close to excitement. My arms and legs flail wildly as I fight against his iron grip.

He grants my wish seconds later, but not in the way I expected. He drops me face-down onto the bed, the mattress bouncing slightly under my weight. I try to scramble onto my knees, but before my cheek can even lift off the sheets, he's sitting on the bed with my legs locked between his strong thighs. He reaches for my wrists, pulling them behind my back.

"This stops right now!" he roars, holding my wrists in one hand, freeing his other to deliver a sharp, stinging slap to my left butt cheek.

The impact sends fire racing across my skin, that makes me gasp into the bedding. But I have no time to process before my right cheek meets the same fate. I frantically wiggle beneath him, but he continues the relentless onslaught, alternating strikes with methodical precision, ensuring both cheeks will bear the same shade of crimson.

Exhaustion grips me, and my frantic struggles slow to weak tremors. I thought being disciplined by his ruler was humiliating, but this feels a thousand times more intense.

I squeeze my eyes shut and try to drown out all coherent thoughts. Instead, I focus on the symphony of sounds that fill the room—the sharp cracks of his hand, and my own sobs.

"You can disobey me," he gasps between ragged breaths, "you can fight me, and throw the fucking china at me, but you will never—" another stinging slap punctuates his words, "—push me away again when I show you my affection!"

He finally eases off, and I feel the gentle pressure of his palm rubbing my sore, tender skin.

"My heart can't take it anymore," he whispers. His hand squeezes my right cheek firmly, bringing his fingers dangerously close to the apex of my thighs.

A whimper escapes at the biting pressure, but then I become acutely aware of the dampness soaking through my knickers. A new wave of humiliation crashes over me. Despite every logical thought, I find myself arching slightly, silently begging him to continue.

Instead, he releases my wrists and widens his thighs, allowing me to slip from the mattress until my knees meet the carpet.

Kneeling between Carter's legs, my bottom spanked, my head bowed, and my eyes filled with tears, I should be horrified. Yet there's an unexpected calm that settles over me, leaving me with nothing but the insistent desire between my legs.

His hands cup my face, thumbs sweeping away tears. He encourages me to look up, and when I do, I see something that looks remarkably like admiration.

"My strong and brave lioness," he murmurs, "you're the most sensational woman I've ever met."

He captures my lips in a slow kiss that feels like worship, sparking the need between my thighs to dizzying heights, and making my entire body hum with want. I want him with a desperation that frightens me. I want to taste every inch of him, feel every ripple of his strong muscles as he bends my body to his will.

Gently guiding his hands to either side of his thighs, I begin to leave a trail of kisses down his body—from his neck, down his chest, over his stomach, to the waistband of his boxers.

He lifts himself, allowing me to drag the fabric down his powerful thighs. His thick length springs free, standing proud and imposing between his sculpted abdomen and my watering mouth. He's magnificent, longer and thicker than I had even imagined, with prominent veins that map his length like rivers.

I find myself compelled to part my lips and taste the pearl of moisture at his tip, and when I do, his head falls back on a low growl.

His hand tangles in my hair, and with deliberate force, he guides me forward, thrusting deep into my throat. I splutter around his impressive girth, tears blurring my vision. He grants me a brief gulp of breath before driving deep into my throat again.

My body responds despite my mind's protests to hold onto any semblance of agency.

My clit pulses, begging for relief. Unable to resist, I slide my hand between my thighs and begin to rub the swollen bundle over my knickers. My other hand glides up his torso, pressing against his chest in a futile attempt to gain some distance to breathe properly. But his firm grip on my hair keeps me exactly where he wants me.

I feel my arousal building to impossible heights with each powerful thrust, each sharp pull at my hair, each frantic circle of my fingers. I'm certain I'm dripping onto the carpet, making me feel utterly filthy and submissive, and somehow complete.

"Fuck, lioness!" Carter roars, pulling me off until my lips barely kiss the swollen head.

I hollow my cheeks instinctively, sucking the drops from his cock. His reaction is immediate as he pushes me back down, filling my eager mouth. His dominance over my body is intoxicating, addictive in a way that terrifies and thrills me all at once.

Driven by the all-consuming need I've never felt so strong before, I bunch my knickers into a tight fist and yank them upwards to feel the lace scrape across my most sensitive spot. The friction sends shockwaves through my entire system.

"Jesus Christ, Sophie!" he bites out, his gaze falling to where my fist grips the delicate fabric. "When we get back to the city, I'm going to put a fucking ring on your finger!"

My impending climax dies a sudden, brutal death as his words penetrate the fog.

He still believes he can simply bulldoze his way into my life. He thinks he can stake his claim, but I won't let him.

With every ounce of strength, I push against his grip, my nails dragging down his chest, and leaving angry red scratches. He releases my hair instantly. My lungs expand, the oxygen feeding the fury building inside me.

He snarls at the marks I've left, his eyes snapping to meet mine with deadly intensity. My legs quiver at the predatory look in his eyes. I wouldn't be surprised if he'd reach for his belt to deliver a punishment that will leave me unable to sit for a week. The thought sends a thrill of dark excitement through me, but I force myself to push it away, to focus on my anger instead.

I wipe the spit from my mouth as I slowly rise to my feet. I watch as a challenging gleam sparks in his eyes.

"I will never give myself willingly to you," I protest, taking a deliberate step towards him. "So, if you truly want me, you'll have to take me by force."

A slow, mischievous smirk plays at his mouth, and the sight propels me into action. I shove him backwards onto the bed and launch myself at him like a wildcat, my hands wrapping around his throat. But instead of surprise, he continues to grin up at me.

I want to squeeze the life out of him, to show him I refuse to let him conquer me without a fight.

His breath hitches slightly, but then his hands grip my hips with bruising force. In one smooth motion, he positions himself beneath me and slides his hard cock along the soaked lace of my knickers, re-igniting the delicious friction against my swollen clit.

My grip on his throat loosens involuntarily, and he takes immediate advantage by spinning us around until I'm pinned beneath him. He captures my wrists, stretching my arms above my head.

"You don't stand a chance of winning this fight, lioness," he growls in my ear. His teeth latch onto the tender spot where my neck and shoulder meet, biting down with enough force to mark me.

I cry out as the sharp pain shoots through my veins.

"I've already dug my claws into you. It's only a matter of time before I rip you apart completely, and then you'll be all mine." He punctuates his promise with another deliberate roll of his hips, his rigid cock dragging harshly across my aching pussy.

Despite the overwhelming pleasure, I keep fighting back.

Wedging my knees between our bodies, I thrash against his chest until I manage to hook my feet over his broad shoulders. My legs wind around his neck, and using every muscle in my core, I manage to twist him onto his back.

With quick, desperate fingers, I tear my knickers to the side, finally freeing my throbbing core. I grab fistfuls of his hair and push his mouth right onto my swollen clit. His tongue immediately dances across my sensitive folds, sending me spiralling.

He devours me with a hunger that sets my entire body ablaze, his tongue darting and teasing with expert precision, driving me relentlessly closer to the precipice of madness. I grind myself harder against his talented mouth, deliberately robbing him of precious air.

When his arms shoot up and encircle my thighs in an effort to pull me away for breath, a soft, triumphant laugh escapes me.

"Watch your arrogance, lion," I manage to gasp out, throwing his own words back at him, "or you might chip a claw."

But Carter has never been one to be outdone. With deft precision, he thrusts his thumb deep into my slick heat before sliding it upwards to breach the tight ring of muscle I never expected him to touch. My body jolts violently, and he uses that moment to surge upward, easily dislodging me.

I tumble backwards between his legs, but my stubborn pride

refuses to let me submit.

I scramble on my hands and knees towards the foot of the bed. But Carter is faster. He grabs my knickers and tears them down my legs, the rough action scratching my thighs and causing me to stumble forward, tangled in my own underwear.

His hands find my hips, and before I can comprehend, he yanks me back onto my knees and delivers a hard slap to my already tender backside. The painful sting reignites the lingering burn.

Carter's laughter rings out behind me, dark and sinister. He strikes me again, and I bite down on the sheets. But my traitorous legs begin to quiver as my arousal shamelessly trickles down my inner thighs.

He grips my burning cheeks before moving his thumbs to my lips, pulling them apart, opening me up to his hungry gaze.

"Oh, lioness," he purrs with dark satisfaction. "You can fool yourself with all that self-righteous bullshit, but I know exactly who you truly are. You love how I dominate you." He punctuates his words with another stinging slap that makes me cry out around the sheet clutched in my mouth.

He drives two thick fingers deep into my pussy, the obscene squelching sound undeniable proof of my shameful desire.

"You want to tell yourself that you can fight me on this," he rasps, slowly thrusting his digits in and out. His other hand maintains its punishing grip on my tender flesh, keeping me balanced on that razor's edge between pleasure and pain. "But deep down in that stubborn head of yours, you know you've always been mine for the taking."

He suddenly stills and drags out his fingers, and I can't suppress the whimper of disappointment that escapes my lips. His warm chest presses against my back as he snakes a hand around my throat, pulling me upright against him.

"Last chance to give yourself to me willingly," he growls in my ear, positioning himself behind me. I feel the broad head of his cock pressing against my wet opening. "Beg me to fuck you before I completely rip you apart."

My teeth clamp down on my lower lip, but my mouth stretches into a wide, almost manic grin.

"Never!" I laugh, the sound carrying a wild, unhinged tone that surprises me.

"Your choice," he growls so deep and dangerous, I'm certain

I've just signed my soul over to the devil himself.

He releases my throat, causing me to fall forward onto my hands. With surprising gentleness, he glides his hands down my spine towards my hips, where he takes a firm grip. And then, without warning, he rams into me with one powerful thrust.

My entire body ignites like I've been struck by lightning, and I hungrily meet his punishing rhythm as my hands fist the sheets.

"Carter!" I cry out his name as he plunges even deeper.

He twists his fist around my hair and uses the leverage to yank me upright against his chest.

"Do you have any idea how long I've wanted to do this to you?" he bites out against my ear.

My head falls back against his shoulder, completely surrendering as his free hand finds my aching clit. With his cock buried to the hilt, he suddenly stills, leaving me writhing.

"Answer me!" he demands, his fingers pinching my sensitive nub.

"My office," I whimper. "When you cornered me."

"Wrong!" he declares, his hands yanking down my bra cups. He pinches the hardened peaks, pulling another pleading whimper from my lips.

My hands desperately seek purchase, moving to his outer thighs where I claw at him.

"Fuck!" he hisses when my nails draw thin lines. His cock twitches violently, and then he pushes me back down onto the mattress and slams into me with renewed fury.

His thrusts become relentless, each powerful push sending shockwaves through my core until my entire body hums in ecstasy. His balls slap against my clit, creating a rhythm that threatens to push me completely over the edge.

"It took one look, MISS. Fucking. Rosen!" he pants with each thrust. "One fucking glance at you to make me crave you like an absolute madman!"

His confession barely registers through the tsunami of euphoria. Every muscle coils tight, the tension building until I can no longer contain it. I cry out as my orgasm surges through me like an earthquake. My body collapses forward, but he holds me upright by my waist, his powerful thrusts unrelenting.

I'm completely spent. As the orgasm fades, I immediately feel the soreness between my thighs. But I revel in the beautiful ache.

I bathe in this moment of complete surrender, this overwhelming feeling of belonging.

With a final thrust, he bottoms out, stretching my tender walls around his girth. His roar shakes the walls as he fills me completely, and I shamelessly gyrate my hips to milk every last drop.

His hand finds my neck, gently guiding me back up against his chest, where he captures my lips in a slow, deliberate kiss. His tongue brushes against mine with languid intimacy, as he cups me gently between my thighs.

He chuckles as my head rolls back against his shoulder, and for the first time since our battle between the sheets began, I feel truly comforted and cherished by the rich sound.

"My feisty lioness," he murmurs against my lips, "all tamed, all mine."

Executioner

Sophie

Something feels hot and heavy resting against my midriff. I force my eyes to adjust to the darkness in the room, and then I see him. Carter. His leg and arm drape lazily over me in a beautiful tangle of limbs, like a child snuggled up to his favourite blanket, lost in peaceful slumber. For the first time since I've known him, I catch a glimpse of him completely unguarded.

His features look softer in sleep, almost tender, and there's a vulnerability to him that draws me in. His eyelashes flutter slightly, long and ridiculously flirtatious as they rest splayed across those high cheekbones, casting delicate shadows that make him look both fierce and angelic all at once. The contrast is utterly intoxicating.

During the day, he's all sharp angles and commanding presence, a god-like figure who could make the sun itself bow in respect with just a look. But here, in this hazy twilight, he looks almost... human. It's a revelation that sends my heart racing and my thoughts swirling in a dizzying dance of awe and want.

I carefully disentangle myself from his warmth, each movement deliberate so as not to wake him. I tiptoe to the bathroom, a shiver of excitement coursing through me as I turn on the shower, letting the sound of cascading water fill the space like a soothing backdrop to my chaotic thoughts. His intoxicating scent clings to my skin—a blend of danger and desire that has my chest thrumming with warmth. But the stickiness between my thighs reminds me of the aftermath of last night, urging me to step under the hot stream.

After we fell into the sheets last night, our bodies spent and our desires finally quenched, he pulled me into his arms and cuddled me until we both fell asleep.

We didn't discuss the Windpower account again, but I hold onto a flicker of hope, that whatever this thing blooming between us is, it will outgrow any accusations or mistrust.

It will have to, because I know now that despite my professional reservations and all my careful boundaries,

I can no longer ignore the connection between us—even if it

means I have to confess everything and start living within the morally grey shadows.

I step out of the shower and with droplets still clinging to my skin, I dare a peak into the mirror. What I see, knocks the breath right out of my chest.

There are bruises on my wrists and hips. My butt looks almost normal, bar the slightest tint of red, and it feels tender and hot to touch. The worst mark is on my neck where Carter bit me—a large dark purple bruise adorned by a circle of tiny red dots where his teeth broke my skin. I gently stroke over the discoloured patch, feeling a sense of pride rush through me that I probably shouldn't feel. He's marked me. I belong to Medard Carter.

I surrendered to him. Gave myself over to the very man I feared would tear off the mask I had meticulously curated over the years, and he did just that. He pulled down the mask, burrowed his claws into me, and then tore me into a million little pieces until there was nothing left but my uninhibited and submissive true self—a side of me, I didn't even know existed. I've never felt more alive, more authentic than when I let him bend me to his will.

Still, these newfound feelings could have disastrous consequences for my career, and yet I fasten the towel around my body, drown out any worrying thoughts, and instead focus my attention on the handsome man waiting for me on the other side of the bathroom door.

Only, when I step back into the bedroom, Carter is already up and dressed.

"It's 10 o'clock, already," he says, his words clipped and businesslike while he's fastening his watch. He averts his gaze, but I still catch it—the spark in his eyes has dimmed, like nothing happened last night, like we're still on opposing sides of this thing between us. "Let's head back to the city."

He grabs his phone and keys, striding towards the door with purposeful steps that feel like rejection.

"I'll wait for you down in the lobby," he says over his shoulder without looking at me. "Don't take too long."

Before I can get a single word out, the door clicks shut.

Windpower. He must still think I'm responsible.

Despite last night, despite me surrendering to him, despite everything we shared in this bed, he still doesn't trust me.

I bite my bottom lip and dig my nails into my thighs, hoping the pain will stop me from welling up.

I want to be angry, to charge after him and tell him what a major arsehole he is. But all I feel is hurt—and guilt.

My hands tremble as I pick up my clothes off the floor and quickly slip into them, my heart beating with a newfound anxiety that threatens to choke me.

A few minutes later, I step out of the lift to find him pacing the lobby, phoned pressed to his ear, hissing into the receiver with barely contained fury. He's angry but doesn't want me to know the reason for it, as he cuts the call short the second he sees me approaching.

"Is everything alright?" I ask tentatively, falling into step with him as he heads towards the car.

"Why? Is there something you want to tell me?" He looks at me over the roof of his car, and my chest tightens at the accusation threading through his words.

I'm guilty. Just not in the way you think I am. I've done something—or more precisely, didn't do something I should have done. That's what I want to tell him, yet the words refuse to come.

"No, I—"

"Didn't think so," he cuts me off sharply and gets into the car.

Shit.

I should just tell him everything. But what good would it do? He doesn't know about Harman yet. He just thinks I schemed with my father. Telling him now would only make things worse, pile another betrayal on top of what he already believes. He has to believe me about the Windpower account first, before I can confess my actual sin.

I slide into the passenger seat, resigning myself to endure his silence.

The drive back into the city is thick with tension, an invisible wall between us that neither of us acknowledges. He remains silent, lost in a labyrinth of thoughts.

A call comes through, Buckman's name flashing on the screen between us. Carter abruptly stops on the side of the road, ignoring the honking cars as they swerve around us with angry gestures. Adrenaline ignites my courage, and I finally manage to find my voice again.

"Can we talk?"

"I have to take this," he murmurs, steps out of the car, and slams the door shut behind him with enough force to make me flinch. The call disconnects from the car's system and seconds later, Carter appears in the rear-view mirror. The phone glued to his ear, his posture is rigid with frustration. Maybe something happened at the office he can't talk about. Maybe he found out who told my father about Windpower. But who?

He flails his arm looking for something to anchor his gaze on, and when it lands on mine in the rear-view mirror, his stare says more than a thousand words ever could.

The knot in my stomach tightens. I'm the reason for his anger.

I break the eye contact, retreating into the seat with frantic swipes over my thighs.

Did I slip up with Father? I'm sure I didn't. But the way Carter just looked at me, like I've committed a cardinal sin, like I've betrayed him in the worst possible way, I must have done something terrible.

I dare another glance into the rear-view mirror, but the door on the driver side opens and Carter is already sliding back into his seat. He starts the engine and pulls back into traffic without sparing me a single look.

"Cart—Medard."

"Not now, Sophie," he cuts me off sharply, the leather creaking under his palms as they fist around the steering wheel.

Sophie. Not lioness.

I swallow the lump in my throat. Something's horribly wrong, and I don't know what. Don't know how to get him to talk to me.

London whirs past outside the window, and before I realise the familiarity of the route, he pulls up outside my flat.

He huffs, pinching the bridge of his nose, before he gets out of the car and rounds it to open the passenger door.

My heart races as I get out and stand before him, battling the palpable shift in the atmosphere between us.

"Would you like to come up for a moment?" I ask cautiously, my voice barely a whisper in the distance between us.

How could everything have changed so drastically? One moment, we were wrapped in warmth inside that hotel room; the next, he's this cold stranger who won't even look at me.

"No. Our journey ends here," he replies, his tone flat and devoid of the passion that swirled between us just hours ago.

Confusion flares in my mind, deepening as he pulls his phone from his suit jacket, and shows me a photo with a gesture that feels like a death sentence. My hands are unsteady, trembling as I catch a glimpse of the very thing I've been dreading, captured in vivid colour.

"That's you, isn't it?" His words pin me in place as he zooms in on a woman in the photo, standing alongside Harman and the judge on the patio of the golf club. Only half of her is visible— the arm and hand holding the glass of wine, and half her back that's exposed by the cut of her dress.

"I recognised the larger mole on your back this morning when you walked into the bathroom," he continues, the edge of his voice slicing through me.

"Carter, I can explain." My voice comes out frantic, desperate. I want to reach him, to pull him back from the abyss of hurt spiralling in his eyes.

This cannot be happening. Not like this. Not after the crazy day and the even crazier night we've had. There's something between us that surpasses basic intrigue or attraction. I don't want to lose it. I don't want to lose him.

He laughs, but it's devoid of joy, a sound dripping with sorrow. "I never noticed it before because I was so desperate to taste you, to have you, that I never took the time to take off your bloody bra."

His gaze is heavy, disappointment mixing with betrayal, each word a nail driven into the coffin of our connection.

"Carter, please let me explain," I plead once more, but the guilt is suffocating me. I can see it in his eyes—the hurt I've caused, the trust I've shattered. It's a storm unleashed because of my choices.

"I didn't know—" I begin, but fury ignites in his eyes, blasting through my words and silencing me with its heat.

"In light of this discovery and yesterday's outcome with Windpower, there's probable cause that you broke the non-disclosure agreement." His voice is clinical now, detached, like he's reading from a script. "As of this morning, you've been suspended pending further investigation into your involvement with Charles Harman as well as Rosen & Smith. All access to your phone, laptop, files, and the firm's offices has been revoked. You are not to contact any client or current employee of Carter & Buckman. Should it come to light that you have, your employment will be terminated with immediate effect."

"No, no, no, please! Carter, don't do this!" Panic surges inside me, a tidal wave of despair crashing against the very fragments of my walls that he broke down last night. My knees buckle as the world explodes into oblivion around me. My job, my life, and him—all of it shrapnel tearing at my insides, leaving me ravaged and stripped bare.

Tears blur my vision, and I stumble forward, reaching for his shoulders desperately. But he moves away from my touch as if I'm nothing more than an unwanted stain on his impeccable white shirt.

"I'm removing myself from all matters concerning you. The investigation will be handled by an unbiased independent body who hasn't been involved with you," he wields his words like a sword, the executioner who kills hope of a shared future.

Before I can gather more words, more pleas, anything that might make him stay, he turns and walks away. The car door slams shut, and he drives off without looking back.

My world spins out of control and thrusts me into a blur of heartbreak and hopelessness. I recoil, overwhelmed, as I stumble up the steps to my flat, each stride heavy with the weight of everything I am about to lose.

Moron

Medard

I'm a fucking moron!

I slam my foot onto the accelerator, weaving through the tightly packed streets with reckless abandon, honking and shouting at anybody stupid enough to step into my path.

I don't give a fuck.

I swore to myself that I would never get fooled by a woman again. Yet here I am, entangled in a web spun by none other than Sophie Rosen. She didn't just fool me—she deceived me. From the very first moment, when she defied me with that relentless spark in her eyes, I was hooked. I let her mess up the meeting with Ravens, blindsided by that fiery attitude and a great arse, while she was scheming with her father behind my back to steal the account right from under me. I shake my head in disbelief, feeling nothing but rage course through my veins like poison.

I have to face the truth—a future with a woman is not meant for me. Never was, never will be. But I refuse to let her rob me of my career plans too. No chance in hell.

I pull into the underground car park with screeching tyres and take long, determined strides towards Buckman's office.

As I step in, I can barely contain the restless energy pumping through my body.

"Carter! Is it really true?" he greets me, sitting behind that ancient desk of his with concern etched into every line of his face.

I pace in front of him in a futile attempt to dispel the anger raging within me like a caged animal.

"Oh, it's true. She deceived all of us," I grate out. "The minute we walked into the golf club, we'd already lost the Windpower account. Her father was there, shaking hands with the Ravens, and then he walked out with that smug grin plastered on his face, like he just hit the jackpot."

My fists clench at the memory, at how easily my hopes were reduced to ashes in a matter of seconds. Yet Sophie stood there beside me, too calm, too composed for someone witnessing the chaos she'd caused. Buckman falls silent, his demeanour thoughtful as he assesses the situation.

"I get that her personal relationship with Andrew Rosen would naturally make her the prime suspect," he finally says, crossing his arms, "but do you have any solid proof? She's been here for four years, and as far as we know, she's never crossed that line before. So, why now?"

"She has," I spit the words out with both defiance and determination, pulling my phone from my suit pocket and slamming it onto his desk. The sound echoes in the space between us like a death knell to his doubts.

"The day Harman and the judge were caught scheming, she was there. She stood right next to them, probably hearing every word." I lean in, pointing at the picture of the woman beside Harman.

His expression darkens as he studies the damning evidence. "How do you know that's her? You can't even see her face."

"I know," I say, my voice steady with an undercurrent of fury that threatens to break through. "I've seen that mole before."

Buckman's brows shoot up, and I can practically see him pondering how I've made such an intimate observation. But instead of questioning me, instead of pressing for details I'm not willing to give, he absorbs the moment, processing my words.

"Fair enough," he concedes after a pause that feels too long. "So how do you want to handle this situation?"

I stride over to the window, needing distance, taking a moment to glimpse at the towering skyscrapers around us. They're glistening in the autumn sun like polished diamonds, beautiful and cold and indifferent to the chaos below.

"HR will conduct an investigation. This evidence should be enough to force her out without a massive severance package. God knows, she has cost us plenty already. Once she's out, I'll work on getting the Windpower account."

"Do you really think we still have a chance to get it back?" he says, joining me by the window.

I nod, certainty punctuating my response. "Absolutely. I have a plan to get her father to with-draw."

Buckman sighs, his gaze settling on the chaos below——the traffic, the people, the city moving on like nothing's changed. "I must admit, Carter, I don't like the sound of this. And regardless of whether Sophie was involved or not, I'm sure she wouldn't either."

In my peripheral vision, I see him turn to face me fully, concern written all over his wrinkled features.

"Is that something you could live with?" he asks quietly.

Because of her, I let my guard down. I allowed myself to explore feelings that had long been tucked away in the darkest corners of my heart, locked up and forgotten for good reason. All the while, she pretended to be the damsel in distress, refusing our undeniable connection to protect her vulnerable heart from the big bad wolf. It was a ploy. One, that worked so well that I lost sight of my mission to salvage the firm and, naturally, my own aspirations along with it.

"Sophie Rosen is, and has always been, nothing but a liability that needs to be dealt with." The words leave my lips like a verdict, cold and final, and I know without a doubt that I will see this through to the bitter end.

I pivot from Buckman, the weight of betrayal heavy in the air as I stride out of his office. Each sharp echo of my shoes against the marble flooring sends a jolt of resentment through me, hardening the pulse of my heart into a cold stone. I step into her vacant office, and the silence swallows me whole. My heart feels like nothing more than a lifeless slab resting in my chest, stripped of warmth and vitality, just the way it was before she came along and made me believe I could feel something again.

Liar

Sophie

There are thirty-two tiles in my bathroom. I know this because I've spent the last two days scrubbing each one of them at least nine times. I would have gone for a tenth round but I ran out of bleach. I haven't clawed at my thighs since last night—not that I don't want to, but they're so raw now that even the soft silk of my robe feels like sandpaper against the angry red marks.

So now I'm forced to turn to my other outlet for stress, even though the very idea of facing other people makes me want to curl up under my duvet and disappear into that safe cocoon of solitude where no one can see me fall apart.

I walk along the wall of the gym, keeping my head down, hoping to be noticed by as few people as possible. I'm really not up for idle chatter or forced smiles. I just want to go feral on the punching bag until I'm physically and mentally exhausted, until I can't think about him anymore.

I'm torn apart inside, split down the middle like I've been cleaved in two. Part of me wants to crumble in despair, wishing I had realised sooner that lying to Carter was a fool's errand, doomed right from the start. The other part of me simmers in rage, ready to scream at the top of my lungs over his icy dismissal, over how easily he threw me away. How can he be so cold? After everything we've shared, everything I let him do because he stirred a desire in me that no other man ever could—he can't even grant me the benefit of the doubt. Yet deep down, I knew this was the inevitable ending, the final spin of our dance in the grey shadows.

I've preached to myself about the dangers of mixing business with pleasure, and yet here I am, reaping the bitter harvest of my own defiance.

"Soph, over here!" Baron's voice slices through my thoughts, drawing my gaze as I set my water bottle down on a bench at the far end of the gym. I quickly zip up the high collar of my jacket and push my thumbs through the holes on my sleeves to hide all evidence of Carter's marks from him. The bruises have faded but are still prominent against my pale skin, and the last thing I need is Baron's interrogation about where they came from.

"I've called over to you like three times! Didn't you hear me?" His warm smile travels towards me, but today, it doesn't so much as graze my heart.

"Hey, sorry. I must have been lost in thought," I reply, forcing a smile that feels like a mask I'm barely holding in place.

"No sweat. Are you ready for a good session?"

"Sure," I respond, willing myself to focus on anything other than the ache in my chest. "I thought we could do a practice fight. What do you think?" I fasten my grappling gloves tightly, trying to ignore the cocktail of emotions gnawing at my insides and the dull pain of my bruises as the Velcro strap chokes my wrists.

"Yeah, let's do it," Baron agrees, his readiness evident as he prepares himself for the fight. His enthusiasm is infectious, but I can't shake this weight pressing down on my chest like a boulder. It's time to channel this chaos into something productive before I completely lose my mind.

I take a deep breath as I step onto the mat, my muscles taut with a mix of adrenaline and pent-up frustration. Baron stands opposite me, relaxed and easy, a hint of a smile tugging at his lips. He gestures for me to come at him, his posture open and inviting. But today, I'm not in the mood for an easy round or gentle sparring. I charge forward, feeling the heat of my anger coiling tightly in my chest. My first jab connects with Baron's midsection—a little too hard. He grunts, eyes widening in surprise.

"Contact, back off a little," he says, backing up slightly, but I'm already pressing the attack.

Another hit lands—this time on his shoulder, and the smile is replaced with confusion.

"Contact, Sophie!" His words pierce through my haze, but I'm too far gone, the memory of Carter's cold dismissal replaying in my mind like a relentless loop I can't shut off.

I throw an elbow towards his face and it grazes his cheek. I know exactly what I'm doing, and I don't care. Baron's eyes narrow, and he retaliates with a quick jab of his own, momentarily knocking the air out of my lungs as his fist connects with my ribs.

"Sophie, back the hell off!" he shouts, uncertainty creeping into his voice.

I whirl around, attempting a low kick, and connect again with a solid strike to his thigh. Baron staggers back, putting distance between us, raising his hands in a defensive stance.

"Sophie, stop! This isn't sparring anymore!"

I lunge forward, my fist aiming for Baron's shoulder, but he blocks the attack. I push through the haze of my heartache and charge again, throwing a series of jabs that land against his sides with satisfying thuds.

"Seriously, what's going on with you?" Baron urges, dodging my next punch but not entirely.

My knuckles graze his ribs, and I can see his expression shift from alarmed to genuinely angered.

"I said, back the fuck off!" he barks, his breath quickening, frustration bubbling over.

This isn't a game anymore; I'm not here to knock his ego down or prove a point. My heart is a pile of rubble, and I'm taking it out on him when all along I should have taken it out on Carter. I should have defended myself from the moment he laid a hand on me, but I was too stupid, too naive, too goddamn enthralled by his intoxicating demeanour.

I'm a pathetic bitch who deserves everything that's coming her way!

I swing wildly again, adrenaline clouding my judgement, each hit laced with the weight of my failures and self-loathing. I am not sparring; I'm fighting for my control. I don't even notice how my strikes are becoming increasingly frantic.

"Stop, just stop!" he commands, raising his arms, trying to block rather than hit. "This isn't you!"

But I can't hear him over the pounding in my chest. One last push—the swing of my arm is meant to daze him, but it hits harder than I mean it to. I feel the connection, his body jolting back, but instead of backing down, he whirls around, no longer holding back his own strength. He twists my arm behind my back before I can react.

I wince as he kicks into the back of my knee, folding me down to the mat. The thud echoes through the gym, and I'm left breathing hard, kneeling in defeat, my heart racing faster than my thoughts can keep up with. The fight drains out of me, and the tears flow freely, hot and humiliating.

Baron crouches beside me, his grip still firm but his voice

softening. "What's going on, Sophie? Talk to me."

I shake my head, unwilling to say the words that will make this nightmare a reality, but it's futile.

"Carter... he suspended me," I blurt out, the words tumbling from my lips with the weight of despair crushing down on them. "After everything... after that night together, after I gave him everything, he found out I was there with Harman on the golf course."

Baron's brow furrows deeper, and I can see the anger flashing in his eyes—not directed at me, but at the situation, at Carter.

"He can't do that," he says firmly, a protective fire igniting in his tone. "You didn't do anything wrong."

"Tell him that!" I cry, my body shaking with sobs. "He wouldn't even listen to me. He just... he looked at me like I was nothing."

"Hey," Baron says gently, turning me to face him, his hands steadying my shoulders. "Take a deep breath, and then you'll tell me what happened."

He waits patiently, his presence a soothing balm against the storm raging within me. Slowly, I draw in a shaky breath, wiping the remnants of tears from my cheeks with the back of my gloved hand. I begin to recount everything that unfolded—from the moment we stepped foot into the golf club and saw my father leaving, to the bitter end when Carter dropped me off at my flat.

As I finish my tale, Baron swipes a hand over his beard, exhaling sharply, as if he's trying to blow away the thick tension in the air.

"It sounds like you've had to deal with various shades of fucked-up shit." His voice is low, laced with an undercurrent of disbelief. "Any idea how your father could have found out about the client?"

I shake my head, mindlessly tracing circles on the mat with my fingertip. It's a question that has gnawed at me relentlessly for the past couple of days, eating away at my sanity. I know I didn't slip up when I spoke to him—I'm absolutely certain of that. And anyone else who knows about Windpower doesn't strike me as the traitorous type. The thought of confronting Father had crossed my mind, but the confidence to do so swiftly evaporated. He would never reveal who his source is, not even to me.

"To be honest," I admit, my voice tinged with resignation, "I'm not even surprised that my own father would pull this stunt on me. He'd say it's nothing personal, just business; and if I'm too sensitive to accept that, well, maybe I shouldn't be a corporate lawyer to begin with."

Baron growls at the truth in my words, but he holds back, refraining from launching into another tirade about my father—a man he clearly despises with every fibre of his being.

"What really hurts is that Carter wouldn't believe me," I continue, the pain in my voice sharpening with each sentence. "Yes, I lied about Harman, but only for good reason. But he lied to me, too. He promised if I'd accept him, he'd take care of me. But not even a day later, he throws me to the wolves without a second thought."

Baron remains silent for a moment, his piercing gaze fixed on me, brows knitted together in concentration as he processes everything I've told him.

"Then kick them in the snout," he finally says, his voice suddenly fierce with challenge. "Don't let him defeat you."

The unexpected defiance in his tone stirs a flicker of something within me—not quite hope, but close.

"But how? He won't even listen to me," I groan into my palms, feeling the hopelessness wash over me again.

"Then find a way to make him," Baron asserts, his voice fierce and unwavering. "You'll figure this out. You're stronger than you give yourself credit for."

But in this moment, as his words echo around me, I feel anything but strong. I'm engulfed by the sting of loss and the suffocating weight of mistrust and betrayal. The fight is gone now, but my heart still aches. And I don't know how to stop it.

Oxygen

Medard

"Mr Carter, I'm finished for the day," Mrs Ruthers announces as I shrug out of my suit jacket and pull the bottle of scotch from the cupboard. "I've put your dinner in the oven to keep it warm, and the grey suit arrived today. It's hanging in your wardrobe."

I know she's silently judging me for pouring myself a scotch the moment I arrive home, but I couldn't care less. Not now, not since I had to suspend Sophie a week ago.

I've been living in a dizzying haze of rage and feigned indifference, my heart fully detached from any hurt she inflicted. It's the fuel that keeps me on track to take her and her father down.

"Thank you, Mrs Ruthers. You may leave now."

She nods before slipping on her coat. Just as she opens the front door, a voice carries through my penthouse, setting my teeth on edge.

"Evening. Is he here?" Sophie storms past my baffled housekeeper.

"It's fine Mrs Ruthers," I assure her, "I'll see you tomorrow."

The old lady nods before closing the door.

"Sophie, didn't I make myself clear?" My voice cuts through the quiet. I turn towards her as she approaches the kitchen island. "You're not to contact any employee of Carter & Buckman."

She's infuriatingly stunning. The knee-length navy skirt clings to her curves, her white top tucked in neatly. It's off-shoulder—on purpose, I'm sure—to reveal the fading mark I left on her neck.

She truly is the prettiest picture of deceit.

"I didn't do it, Carter." Her voice is steady, but her eyes spark with fierce determination as she sets her handbag down, ignoring my warning.

I should tell her to leave. I removed myself from the investigation for a reason, but curiosity gnaws at me.

I down my scotch in one swallow and immediately refill the glass. The amber liquid trembles as I move towards the living room. It's a futile attempt at distance.

"What exactly?" The words spill out harshly. "Serving your

father the Windpower account? Or manipulated the case with Harman?"

"I told you, I don't know how my father found out about Windpower." She has the audacity to raise her voice as she follows me. "You have to believe me!"

"I don't have to do shit!" I spin around, the scotch sloshing violently in my tumbler as I point an accusing finger at her. "You fucking lied to me!"

She deceived me. And I was foolish enough to let my feelings blind me.

"I didn't lie about Harman. I just kept it from you, for that, I am sorry." She tries to reason, showing vulnerability I can't afford to care about. "But I thought you wouldn't understand. I didn't know the judge would be there. Harman and his wife invited me to lunch, and before I knew it, I was being introduced to him."

There's sincerity in her tone, and still, doubt lingers.

I back away as she tries to encroach my space, making a beeline for the kitchen island. I need to keep a level head.

"Why didn't you report it?" I ask, forcing her to meet my challenging gaze.

She throws her arms up, frustration spilling out. "How could I? If you won't even believe me, why would a bunch of strangers on the bar?"

She's got a point. If she'd reported it, she'd been dragged into an investigation that could have smudged her reputation.

Still, she was at the golf club, saw the judge, and didn't report it. The ethical breach justifies my decision to suspend her.

"I honestly believed you were one of the last people to overstep the ethical line," I say, hating the disappointment seeping through.

Her hands find their way to her thighs, her eyes searching mine with sorrow. I grab the scotch again, pouring myself a double with shaking hands. When I turn back, she's closer. Her fingers curl around my bicep, and her voice dips into that soft whisper designed to unravel me.

"Please, Medard. Reconsider the suspension. I swear I had no idea."

Medard—how often did I hope she would call me by my first name? But hearing it now feels like a manipulative tactic.

I pull away from her touch. I can't be near her, not without losing everything I'm clinging to. I sink down onto the sofa, my heart pounding. Every fibre of my being wants to believe her.

"So that's it?" she whispers, her voice splintering as she presses her tongue against her palate to fight tears.

Her eyes dart to the ceiling. The sight leaves a dull ache in my chest.

"I don't expect you to forgive me," she says at last, quieter now. "But please, don't make me lose my job."

"If you're as innocent as you claim to be—" My voice stays low, cool, though my insides burn. "Then you'll have nothing to worry about."

I swirl the scotch in my glass. God, I want to hold her, more than I've ever wanted anything. But if I touch her, I'd risk giving her whatever she wants.

"We both know with my personal connection to the opposition, I won't stand a chance at keeping my job," she says, voice breaking.

Her throat works as she swallows back tears. Her hands tremble. "Please, don't do this. I'll crawl on my knees if that's what you want."

"I don't want your false loyalty."

Fuck.

I want it. I want every shred of affection she's willing to give me, false or not. I've spent the entire week burying myself in work during the day, and drinking myself senseless in the nights while listening to soppy blues.

"Then spank me." Sophie's words barely break through the air, but it hits me like she's shouting them from the rooftops of this city.

"Sophie, I can't." I dare a glance at her, a single glance, and immediately regret it.

I down my scotch and set the empty glass on the coffee table, my fingers pinching the bridge of my nose. I can't look at her. Not like this.

She walks up and perches on the edge of the coffee table between my legs. There's an arm's length between us, yet it's close enough to make me struggle.

"Why not? You've done it before."

Her voice is desperate, and it pierces right through me.

"You can't have it both ways." My gaze drops to the floor. "You can't accuse me of abusing my position and then request that I do just that when it serves your interests."

I pull the tie from my neck and unbutton the top two buttons, because the lump in my throat feels like a stone pressing against the collar.

I've caused this. I've blurred the lines. I've left her believing that pain could be her penance.

"You did abuse your position! The cornering, the spanking, the choking, and that bloody CRA. You did all these things." Her voice raises.

"And you let them happen, just so I wouldn't find out about your little scheme!"

"I did not scheme against you! How could you even think that?"

"It's simple. You made sure to tell me how impossible and arrogant I am at every opportunity you got."

"Because you are, but that doesn't mean—"

"Enough. We're done here." I glare at her but she doesn't retreat.

"Medard—" Her voice dips into a quiet plea as she reaches for my shoulder.

I swat her arm away, and her gasp fills the quiet. I can't have her touch me, because I don't know what I'd do. She's hurt me, still hurts me. Yet I still want her.

I can't think straight. Don't know what to do, and I fucking hate it.

She gets to her feet, her heels clicking across the floor in symphony with her quiet sobs. She walks towards the front door, and it takes every ounce of willpower in me not to stop her.

Fuck, I'm pathetic.

This woman lied to me. Yet I'm still debating letting her come back to the firm, just so I'll have another shot at convincing her to be with me.

I pinch the bridge of my nose so hard, I'm sure the bone will crack. I undo a couple more collar buttons, and roll up my sleeves, but it's useless.

"No!" her voice suddenly rings out, prompting my head to snap up. "I can disobey you!"

She turns back and despite her eyes being glassy with mascara streaking down her cheeks, her look is fierce and angry.

She throws her coat and handbag onto the ground and takes

decisive steps towards me. "I can fight you," she continues.

"Sophie—" I drawl in warning.

She grabs the vase from the console and holds it aloft. "And I can throw the fucking china at you!" she bellows as the thing goes flying towards me. I duck, the vase shattering behind me.

"But you will never push me away again when I show you my affection!" I jump to my feet and meet her strides halfway as she bites out the words through tears.

Her fists hammer against my chest and it takes me a couple of attempts to get a hold of her wrists.

"This is all your fault!" she cries out, her knees buckling. I keep a firm grasp on her wrists to stop her from falling. "You did this to me! You forced yourself into my life and made me fall for you, and now you're just discarding me!"

Fall for me? Did she just admit that she wants me?

My brain short-circuits, rendering me speechless. I've been pleading with her for weeks to admit there's a connection between us. And now that she's finally said it, I can't compute.

She twists her hand outward and suddenly she's holding my wrist, pulling my hand towards her throat. My fingers loosely wrap around her throat—like muscle-memory—but she's trying to force my fingers to apply more pressure.

"Do it!" she demands, squeezing my hand. "Show me your worst, but don't push me away."

She squeezes my hand again, but all I can focus on is the single tear that drops off her chin and falls between her fingers onto my hand.

"Please, do it," she pleads, her fierceness depleting. "Be my oxygen, because I don't know how to breathe without you anymore."

My heart splits wide open. She needs me.

My lioness needs me the same as I need her.

I will my hand to tighten around her throat, but my fingers won't co-operate. I don't want to hurt her. Not like this, not now. I want to hold her and tell her how precious she is to me.

Her hand drops from mine, the fight draining out. Her shoulders drop in defeat as she turns away and heads for the door.

Panic surges through me. I can't let her go. This is all I ever wanted—Sophie Rosen to be whole-heartedly mine.

Fuck Harman.

Fuck Windpower.

I'll veto the suspension and threaten to pull my shares if anyone dares to fight me.

My body finally sets into motion, and I close the distance. I catch up as she kneels to pick up her coat. My hand reaches for her shoulder, but she shrugs it off. I grab her arm, but she yanks it back, losing her balance and falling onto her knees.

"Don't!" she bites out through sobs. "I get it. You don't want me."

"You don't get it," I say, squatting down and reaching for her shoulder to prompt her to turn around. "Now, come here."

"Screw you!" she cries out, shoving me hard.

The move comes unexpected, and I fall onto my arse.

That bloody stubborn woman.

Fuck, she makes me rock-hard.

"Lioness, stop fighting me!" I roar, reaching for her calf and pulling her back as she tries to stand.

She falls onto her belly and I drag her between my legs. But then she turns onto her back and kicks out wildly. I barely dodge her heel before I catch her ankles and pull the weapons masquerading as shoes from her feet.

"I hate you!" she yells, still kicking and lashing out.

Her fingers catch my shirt and the sound of fabric ripping tears through her sobs, the buttons scattering. I finally manage to catch her wrists and pin them down beside her head.

"I hate you!" she shouts again, still trying to thrash her legs before they too get pinned down by my thighs as I straddle her.

"You don't," I say, my voice calm as I drink in the intoxicating sight of her.

My fierce lioness, with a face of thunder and her blond mane wild, looks as stunning as ever.

"I want to hate you!" she shouts, but there's less heat in it now as another bout of tears spills free.

I shake my head. "I want you."

Three little words—that's as much as I can bring myself to say. As much as my heart allows me to admit, and I hope it'll be enough for her.

She finally calms and stops fighting, searching my eyes as the words register. Her breath stutters.

"Then kiss me already, you arrogant prick."

My mouth slams down onto hers, and she meets my kiss with hungry swipes of her tongue. I loosen my hold on her wrists, and her hands shoot forward to my belt. With impatient movements, she fumbles with the belt buckle before her hand dips inside and grips my cock in a firm grasp.

"Shit, lioness," I inhale sharply, my balls drawing up.

It's been too long. A whole fucking week of knowing how perfect she feels.

"Fuck me," she demands between kisses, her hand working my cock.

My hand finds her throat, and using my thumb, I tilt her chin up to kiss along her jawline, tasting the salt of her tears.

"My pleasure," I say, snaking my fingers around her neck to pull her up. She yanks my slacks and boxers further down before I kick them all the way off.

"Take off your top, lioness," I command, finding the zipper at the back of her skirt. "Show me those beautiful tits I've been dreaming about all week."

She pulls the top over her head, her hair falling in wild waves. Her hands reach behind to unhook her bra, and I watch transfixed as the lace falls away. I capture her lips in another searing kiss, my hands finally free to roam. My kisses wander down her neck, trailing heat before finding her breasts. I shower them with affection, my tongue circling one nipple while my hand kneads the other.

My kisses travel further down, across her ribs, over her stomach, while I work her skirt and panties down her hips. But as I pull the fabric down her legs, my fingers grazing the top of her thighs, she winces sharply.

I freeze.

"Sophie?" I pull back slightly, trying to get a look at her thighs, but she quickly pulls her legs against her chest, hiding them.

"It's nothing," she says quickly, too quickly.

"Lioness, show me." My voice is gentle but firm.

"Please, Medard, just—"

I grab her calves and pull her legs straight, needing to see what she's hiding.

The sight steals my breath.

Her thighs are red raw, covered in angry red scratches. Some are fresh, others scabbing over, creating a horrific pattern of self-inflicted damage.

I can't believe that she'd rather expose her most intimate parts to me than show me her thighs.

"Did you do this because of the suspension?" My voice comes out rough and thick with guilt. "Because I pushed you away?"

Her face flushes with embarrassment, and she won't look at me.

"Sophie, answer me."

But she remains silent, lips pressed together in stubborn refusal as she sits up and draws her legs back to her chest.

She's not willing to explain herself. The uncertainty twists in my gut like a knife.

I huff out a breath and get to my feet, stretching out my hand to help her up. She stares at my hand like it might bite her.

"Please don't send me home," she pleads, her voice small and broken.

"I'm not doing that, lioness." I take her hand and pull her to her feet. "I'm taking you to my bed."

Relief floods her features as I lead her through the penthouse, her hand trembling in mine. The tremor bothers me more than I want to admit—this woman who threw a vase at my head just minutes ago is now shaking like a leaf.

We walk to my bedroom, and I shed what's left of my torn shirt before moving to my side of the bed. She stands on the opposite side, insecure, arms crossed over her chest. She watches me with uncertain eyes.

She's more vulnerable than I initially thought. All this time, I saw her defiance and fire, mistook it for confidence when really it was just her way of keeping the world at arm's length.

As I settle against the headboard, I take off my watch and place it on the nightstand. "Come to bed, lioness."

"I'm not wearing any clothes," she says, stating the painfully obvious.

"I'm fully aware," I reply, my gaze sliding down her body while I run my hand deliberately up my hard length. "And you should get used to it. There will never be any clothes in our marital bed."

She giggles and rolls her eyes at my supposed 'delusion', but then she slides into bed beside me. I sit up, opening my arm wide in invitation. She accepts it immediately, snuggling into my side with a sigh that sounds like relief. Her warmth seeps into me, chasing away the cold that's been lodged in my bones all week.

I grab the remote from the nightstand, and a moment later the picture frame over the fireplace slides up to reveal the telly.

"Documentary or cooking?" I ask.

"Cooking," she decides.

I find a cooking competition show, and we settle in to watch. For a while, we exist in comfortable silence, occasionally commenting on what's happening on screen—a chef's knife technique, an ingredient neither of us have heard of, the ridiculous time constraints they're working under.

"I could never do that," Sophie murmurs as a chef frantically plates his dish with seconds to spare. "I'd be a disaster in a kitchen."

"You cook?" I ask, genuinely curious. I realise with a pang that there's so much I don't know about her, so many ordinary details I've never thought to ask.

"Not at all," she admits with a self-deprecating laugh. "I grew up with a housekeeper who did all the cooking. I never learnt."

I can't help but laugh. "You do remember teasing me about having Mrs Ruthers when we first met, right? Said I wasn't humble or something along those lines."

There's a pause. "Oh God, I did, didn't I?"

"You did," I confirm, still chuckling. "For the record, I didn't have a housekeeper growing up. My mum did all the cooking. Mrs Ruthers only came into the picture after I bought the penthouse."

She goes quiet. "I didn't have that luxury."

The words hit me like a punch. I immediately tighten my arms around her. She never got to have her mum cook for her. My heart aches for the little girl who never knew her mother's love. And the rage that follows is swift and fierce—rage at her father for driving her mother to such despair.

"I'm sorry, lioness," I murmur against her hair, meaning it.

She's quiet for a moment, then shifts the conversation. "What about you? Do you actually cook?"

I take a breath. "I cook a mean paella that even my best friend approves of, and he's Spanish, so that's saying something."

"Really?" She sounds genuinely surprised. "Paella? That's ambitious."

"Alex dragged me to Almeria a few years back," I explain. "We ate our way through the city, and I became obsessed with getting it right. Took me months of practice."

"I'd like to try it sometime," she says softly.

"I'll make it for you, and introduce you to Alex" I promise, pressing a kiss to the top of her head. "You'll like him."

The domesticity of the moment settles over us like a blanket. It feels natural, easy.

On screen, one of the chefs is having a meltdown, and Sophie makes a sympathetic noise. "Poor thing. I know that feeling."

"Do you?" I ask.

"Of course. When everything falls apart despite your best efforts, and you just want to curl up in a ball and give up." Her voice goes quieter. "I felt like that this week."

The confession makes my chest tighten with guilt. I did that to her.

"I'm sorry," I say, the words inadequate but necessary. "For pushing you away."

She doesn't respond immediately, just traces her fingers over my chest.

Out of the blue, she asks, "Will you ever believe me about Harman and Windpower?"

I consider it, turning it over in my mind before answering honestly. "I want to."

The words hang between us.

"But you don't," she says quietly.

"I don't know what I believe yet," I admit. "But I'm willing to try."

She relaxes slightly at that, and we fall into silence again.

"Would you be willing to take your father down? Destroy his law firm?"

I feel her stiffen against me. She's silent for a long moment.

Finally, she says, "I'm loyal to Carter & Buckman."

It's only half the answer I hoped for, and disappointment settles heavy in my chest.

"Is that answer enough for you?" she asks, and I can hear the uncertainty.

She turns around to face me properly, shifting in my arms. The vulnerability in her gaze makes my heart clench.

"It's enough to have you back at the firm," I tell her, and I mean it.

I kiss her, soft at first. But then her hand wanders down my chest, wrapping around my cock, and the kiss deepens into something hungry. I growl against her mouth.

I shift, positioning myself on top of her, caging her beneath me. She looks up at me with those beautiful blue eyes.

"Never lie to me again," I say, my voice rough.

"Never abandon me again," she counters.

"Deal." I kiss her like I'm sealing a pact.

Then I break away, trailing kisses down her body—over her jaw, down her throat, across her collarbone. I take my time worshipping her breasts again, her ribs, her stomach, moving lower until I'm sitting back between her legs.

"Now open your legs and show me what's mine."

She inhales sharply. Slowly, she opens her legs, revealing herself to me.

I place my hands on her knees and push her legs up to her chest, fully exposing her glistening pussy.

"Is this truly mine now?" I ask.

She moans a breathy "yes."

"What about the copper?"

She rolls her eyes, and I can't help but playfully smack her pussy. She jolts, gasping, but then I feel her get wetter.

Fuck, my lioness likes that.

"He doesn't matter any—," The words get cut off by her moans as I smack her once more.

Satisfaction courses through me. "So, you've ended things with him?" I slide a finger inside her tight heat, followed by a second.

"Yes," she tells me, nodding frantically as she holds her legs open while I pump her slowly, my thumb circling her clit with deliberate pressure.

I growl low in my throat, leaning down so I can press my tongue flat against her pussy and lick a long stripe up her centre. She moans loudly, her fingers threading through my hair and pushing my head harder against herself, grinding against my tongue.

I suck her clit into my mouth while continuing to pump my fingers into her, curling them to hit that spot inside. Her thighs start to tremble until she finally shatters, crying out my name—Medard, not Carter—as she comes undone on my tongue. My cock twitches violently at the sound, and my chest swells with satisfaction so intense it nearly chokes me.

Sophie's finally submitting to me—to Medard, the man outside of boardrooms and power plays—and it feels like I've hit the fucking jackpot.

Her legs are still shaking when I close my lips around her clit once more. She jolts like I've electrocuted her.

"Medard, don't," she yelps. "I'm too sensitive."

"Too bad, lioness." I plunge a third finger into her. "I'm taking what's owed, what's mine."

Her hands reach for my head, trying to push me off, but I pull out, grasp her wrists and pin them with one hand down on her stomach. Another swipe over her sensitive clit has her buck off the mattress with a cry that's half protest, half pleasure.

"You still owe me two orgasms," I declare, punctuating my words with deep thrusts while my thumb applies pressure with slow, torturous circles on her clit.

Her heels dig into the mattress, her arse lifting off the bed, pushing her pussy deeper onto my fingers, telling me her body wants this even if her mind is protesting.

"Medard, please," she cries out, shaking her head as tears spill down her temples. "No more, I can't—"

But I don't stop because I know she can take it. I suck on her clit while she screams loud enough to wake the entire building, and fuck if it isn't the most satisfying view of my lioness I've ever seen.

Her body starts trembling as she comes a second time. Her pussy flutters around my fingers, against my lips, and I have to push my cock harder into the mattress to keep myself from coming untouched.

"That was—" Sophie pants between heavy breaths.

"—act two," I say, easing my fingers out and pulling myself up to kneel between her legs.

"What?" she gasps. "No. Carter, no! I can't—"

I thrust in without warning, and instantly her pussy grips me like a vice.

"Still Medard to you," I bite out as my cock is finally back in heaven.

God, my lioness feels incredible.

I slide my hands under her knees and push her legs up further, opening her wider.

"No, no, no," she cries out, her eyes rolling back as I feel the tip of my cock touching her cervix.

Soon I'll have our child in there, and I'll get to watch her breasts swell with milk. The thought has me latching onto her nipples, licking and sucking them one after the other with reverence.

Her belly will swell too, round and full with our baby, and fuck—if it's even possible—she'll be even more beautiful than she already is.

"Medard," Sophie cries out. "Why, oh god—"

Her words falter as I plunge into her again. "You...angry. You look angry."

She glides her hands over my chest and snakes them around my neck, and I take it as an invitation to lean down and capture her lips.

"Not angry, lioness," I say between deep kisses. "Possessive. I imagined you pregnant with my child."

Her head rears back, and she looks at me like I've completely lost my mind. And maybe I have. When it comes to her, I'm wild, unhinged, morally black, but fucking complete in a way I've never been before.

"What? I'm not having your child," she says, shaking her head.

"Not yet, lioness. But if we keep fucking like this, it won't take long." I capture her lips and drive deep into her to make my intentions clear. There's a reason why I never thought about using a condom with her. The possibility that she could be pregnant with my child has not once frightened me, because Sophie belongs by my side with everything that life has to offer.

"I've been getting the shot since I was twenty, and I won't stop taking it."

Her admission stops me. I still inside her.

A sudden pang of disappointment hits my chest. It's unreasonable to already entertain the idea of building a family with her. It hasn't even been twenty-four hours since I thought she was only out to hurt me, and the jury is still out on how innocent she really is. Yet I want the white picket fence with her as soon as possible.

"One year, lioness. You have one year, and then you'll bear our child." I capture her lips in a searing kiss, and at the same time, I slowly drag my cock almost out, before slamming right back in.

She cries out against my lips.

"You're mine, lioness," I bite out between thrusts. "Mine."

It's unreasonable, downright controlling, and I should probably seek out professional help for the possessive thoughts running through my head. But fuck, it just feels right to stake my claim on her like this, to mark her as mine in every possible way.

She shakes her head frantically, panting heavily. Then suddenly her nails drag down my back, scratching hard.

I hiss at the sharp pain, and I thrust into her harder. "Say it! Say you'll have my child!"

"Screw you!" she cries out as I bottom out.

My defiant lioness.

I massage her breasts roughly, lowering my mouth to suck her nipple, teeth grazing the sensitive peak.

She tilts her head to the side, exposing the long column of her neck. I lean down and bite the spot where her neck meets her shoulder, sinking my teeth into the fading mark, claiming her all over again.

The bite sends her over the edge. She orgasms hard, her pussy squeezing me, and the sensation triggers my own release. I come with a roar, emptying myself deep inside her.

As we come down, our movements slow, and we kiss lazily. Her fingers trace gentle patterns on my back, soothing the scratches she left moments ago, and I can feel her smiling against my lips.

I roll to the side, pulling her with me so she's draped across my chest, both of us catching our breath. My hand finds her hair, threading through the tangled blond waves.

This is what I've been missing all week. This is what I nearly threw away, but I'm never making that mistake again.

I will fight with everything I have to make this woman my wife and the mother of my child, or die a lonely man.

"You're staying," I murmur against her hair.

"Is that a command?" she whispers back, and I can hear the smile in her voice.

"An observation," I say, pulling her leg over my groin until I feel fully engulfed by her warmth.

She cuddles into my side, her fingers drawing small circles over my heart.

"What about tomorrow?" she whispers with worry.

I kiss the top of her head while stroking her hair. "I'll take care of it."

And then, for the first time in my life, I fall asleep with a woman in my arms—a woman who makes me feel like I've finally come home.

Hypocrite

Sophie

I wake to gentle touches on my face, fingers tracing the curve of my cheek with tenderness that makes my heart flutter. My eyes slowly open to find Medard sitting on the edge of the bed, already dressed in one of his immaculate suits that makes him look infinitely sexy and powerful.

God, I'm the luckiest woman in the world.

"Good morning, lioness," he murmurs, his voice still carrying that rough edge.

I reach up and pull him down for a kiss, and he smiles against my lips in a way that makes warmth bloom in my chest. My hand wanders down his chest, heading toward his crotch with clear intention, but he catches my wrist.

Rude.

He brings my hand to his mouth instead, kissing my knuckles. "As much as I'd love to stay in bed with you and fuck you six ways to Sunday, I have a board meeting in an hour."

I pout, genuinely disappointed, and the sight makes him chuckle.

"That's only six positions," I point out. "I expected more expertise from you."

His eyes darken. "Don't tempt me to prove you wrong, or I'll be late and you'll be unable to walk."

Fair point.

He cups my face and gives me another kiss, slower this time, deeper, before pulling back and nodding towards the nightstand. "Eat your breakfast."

I turn to look and find a tray waiting—coffee in a proper mug and a plate of scrambled eggs with sourdough bread.

"I only have coffee for breakfast," I tell him, though my stomach betrays me with a small rumble.

He shakes his head, his expression taking on that stern quality. "You need to eat properly, Sophie."

"Yes, Father," I mutter, but I'm already reaching for the fork because it does smell delicious.

I take one bite just to appease him. But the moment the eggs hit my tongue I realise how delicious they are. I take another bite, then another, practically shovelling it in.

When I glance up, his face blooms with satisfaction.

"Good girl," he murmurs, and the praise shouldn't affect me the way it does, but heat pools in my belly anyway.

Suddenly, he pulls the duvet down, and mindful of being completely naked, I grab for the edge.

"Medard—"

"I've already memorised every single inch of your body, lioness," he says. "And you'll never be allowed to hide it from me again."

"You say that like you've got it catalogued in a spreadsheet somewhere," I mutter.

"Mental spreadsheet," he corrects with a smirk. "Filed between 'improving your diet' and our wedding plans."

I don't know if he's joking or not.

Before I can protest, he pulls a small tube of cream from his pocket. "I'm seeing to your thighs."

My cheeks flush with embarrassment as I look at the angry scratches. I wince at the contact, but then the cream feels soothing as he gently applies it to my damaged skin, his touch so careful it makes my throat tighten.

"Better?" he asks when he's done.

"Yes," I admit quietly. "Thank you."

I can't remember the last time someone took care of me like this—if ever.

He caps the tube and reaches for something else—my clothes from yesterday, neatly folded.

"We won't have time to stop by your flat, but your clothes are freshly washed," he says.

I blink in surprise. "Is your housekeeper already here?"

He shakes his head, and I watch as a faint hint of colour touches his cheeks.

Wait. "Did you... did you do my laundry?"

"I'm capable of operating a washing machine."

"The man who has a housekeeper did my laundry," I say, barely containing my grin. "At, what, six in the morning?"

"Five-thirty, actually," he says.

"Can you iron too? Please tell me you can iron."

He glares at me, but there's no heat in it. "There's a towel and a fresh toothbrush laid out. I'll wait for you in the living room."

"Running away from the laundry conversation, I see—"

He leans down and kisses me, effectively shutting me up, lingering just long enough to make me want to pull him back into bed despite his meeting. Then he's gone, closing the door behind him.

I finish my breakfast before heading into the bathroom. I tie my hair up and quickly shower, glad to find a generic almond-scented shower gel that doesn't smell like "Intimidating God of the Boardrooms" or whatever ridiculous names they give men's toiletries.

I brush my teeth with the new toothbrush, trying not to think too hard about how he thought of everything. Rummaging through my handbag, I'm glad to find the concealer I always keep on me for emergencies—spots, dark circles under my eyes, and now bite marks, too. It takes me forever to cover up Medard's stamp of possession, but when I step back from the mirror, it's only visible if you focus long enough on the spot.

When I step out of the bedroom, I find him sitting on the sofa in his signature pose—one ankle resting atop the opposite knee, finger brushing his lower lip as he scrolls through his phone. The image is so perfectly him, so devastatingly attractive, that I stop mid-walk.

I just drink him in, my heart fluttering wildly. I've won the lottery, basically. A slightly controlling, occasionally infuriating lottery, but still.

His eyes snap up to mine, and he openly assesses me from head to toe. The intensity of his gaze has me reaching for my thighs instinctively.

"Are you okay?" he asks, his brow furrowing with concern.

I nod, forcing my hands away from my thighs, and walk towards him. I take a seat on the edge of the coffee table.

"Do I make you nervous?" he asks, and there's something vulnerable in the question.

I hesitate. We agreed to no more lies, so with every ounce of confidence I can muster, I admit the truth. "Sometimes you do, because of the way you look at me all stern and intense."

"That's because I'm mentally undressing you," he says matter-of-factly.

"I'm already wearing yesterday's clothes. There's not much

mystery left."

"There's always mystery with you," he says, unhooking his leg and holding out his hand. "That's the beauty of us."

I take his hand and let him guide me onto his lap. I settle there with my legs draped over his thighs, and his hand strokes the side of my thigh.

"The only thought I have when I look at you," he says, his voice dropping to that sexy rough timbre, "is that I can't wait to spend a lifetime with you."

My heart blooms in my chest, expanding until I can barely breathe with the force of it.

I'm wholeheartedly in love with Medard Carter.

God help me.

He grips my chin and kisses me deeply, thoroughly. When he pulls away, I want to tell him—want to say the words—but before I can, he's already speaking.

"We should head out," he says, glancing at his watch. "I can't be late for this meeting."

The moment passes, and I swallow the confession.

We head out, and he takes my hand as we walk to the lift. He opens the car door for me, and soon we're driving through morning London traffic.

Aaron Frazer plays softly, his soulful voice filling the comfortable silence. Medard's hand rests on my knee, drawing lazy circles. I'm happy and content in a way I haven't felt in years, maybe ever.

But then the office building comes into view, and reality crashes back like I'm being dragged out of a dream I didn't want to end.

We haven't discussed how to handle our relationship at the office.

He parks in his reserved spot, and before I can think, his phone rings.

He glances at the screen and grimaces. "I have to take this. Walk ahead to the lifts, and I'll be right behind you."

I nod, relieved to have a moment to collect myself. I quickly pull my lipstick out and apply it, trying to look professional, like it's a morning like any other, like I didn't just spend the night being thoroughly debauched by the boss.

Then I head towards the lifts, push the button and wait, my

mind racing.

What am I doing? What are we doing?

Surely, it's best to keep our relationship quiet for now.

Right?

The lift arrives with a soft ding, and I step inside. As I turn around, I see him walking towards me, phone still pressed to his ear.

My eyes land on the lift panel and the two buttons—one to open, one to close.

I know I should press the button to keep the doors open. It's the polite thing to do, the expected thing, the thing a normal person who isn't having a minor panic attack would do.

But my finger moves to the close button instead.

What am I doing?

The doors begin to slide shut, and I watch as Medard's eyes widen. He increases his speed and grabs the edge of the door before it can shut. The doors bounce back open, and he steps inside next to me, ending his call with a curt "I'll call you back."

The lift doors close, sealing us in together.

Nervously, I dig my nails into my palms. "So, funny story about the doors—"

But then he reaches for my hand, and instinctively I pull away as panic floods my mind.

"What are you doing?" I ask, my voice barely steady.

"What am I doing?" His eyes narrow dangerously. "What are you doing? Did you really just try to close the lift doors on me?"

"I just... I thought we should talk first," I say, hating how weak I sound. "Before we get upstairs and everyone sees us and—"

"About what?" He steps closer, and I instinctively press back against the wall. "About how you want to pretend last night didn't happen the moment we step into the office?"

"No! That's not—" I take a breath. "I just think we need to discuss how we're going to handle this at work. People will talk, and I—"

"And you what?" His voice drops to that commanding tone. "You want to hide what we are?"

"I just think we should be discreet," I say. "At least for now, until—"

"No." The word is flat, final.

Well, that was easy. For him.

"Medard—"

"I said no." He steps closer, caging me against the wall. "We're not going down that path. It's either all or nothing, and nothing has never been an option."

"But—"

"You made me a promise," he continues. "You promised me your loyalty. I expect you to show me that loyalty as my employee and as my girlfriend."

The way he says 'girlfriend' makes my heart race.

"I am loyal to you," I insist, my hands coming up to rest on his chest. "But this is different. People will judge—"

"Let them judge," he says, his jaw clenching in that way that means he's about to be incredibly stubborn. "I don't care what they think, and neither should you. You're mine, Sophie, and I'm not going to pretend otherwise."

"You don't understand," I say, frustration bleeding into my voice. "It's easy for you to say that. You're the managing director. Your position is secure. But I—"

"You what?" he challenges. "You think your position isn't secure? I lifted your suspension this morning before I even got out of bed. You're back at the firm. Fully reinstated."

"You... what?"

Why didn't he tell me that this morning?

"I told you I'd take care of it," he says, his expression softening slightly. "Did you think I wouldn't?"

"I just... I didn't know you'd already done it," I admit. "When did you even have time? You were doing my laundry at five-thirty!"

"I'm an excellent multitasker."

"Apparently," I mutter.

His lips twitch. "Are you finished?"

"No, actually. I have notes. Starting with the fact that you just decided—"

"I take care of what's mine," he says simply. "And you are mine. Which means we're not hiding. We're not being 'discreet.' We're being exactly what we are—together."

"Medard—"

"No," he cuts me off, "been there, done that. This is official, and that's the end of the discussion."

He pushes off the wall as the lift dings, announcing our arrival.

Oh God. This is happening.

The doors slide open. Buckman is standing there, coffee in hand. I nearly die on the spot. His eyes move from Medard to me, but his expression doesn't change.

"Morning," Buckman says, turning to Medard, "board meeting in ten minutes, Carter."

"I'm aware," Medard says, stepping back to let me out.

I seize the opportunity and leap out, my feet carrying me as fast as they discreetly can.

"Sophie! How are you feeling?" Ben's voice calls out. "Mr Carter said you had the flu."

I blink, confusion washing over me before I realise—that's what Medard told everyone. The flu. That's why I wasn't here yesterday, and last week. Before I can respond, Medard steps up beside me and wraps his arm around my waist. This is it—this is him making our relationship public.

I'm going to kill him.

"She's feeling much better. Thank you for your concern, Reynolds," he responds smoothly.

Ben looks at me, clearly puzzled.

"Yeah, much better," I manage to squeak out. "Modern medicine. It's just...fab."

Ben nods, still looking slightly confused, but then walks off.

"The flu?" I hiss under my breath. "That's what you went with?"

"Would you have preferred I told them the truth?" he murmurs back.

I try to create some distance as we continue walking, but Medard's grip around my waist is unyielding.

And everyone is looking now. I can feel their eyes on us, see heads turn, hear whispers starting to build.

As we reach Millie's desk, he turns to me. "Have a great day, and don't forget to sign the CRA," he says, the twinkle in his eyes catching me off guard.

The CRA. Right. Because apparently, we're doing this, and there's paperwork.

I huff, trying to step away, but he's quicker, catching my wrist and spinning me around until I collide with his chest.

Oh no.

The world narrows, his lips finding mine with searing passion. He's kissing me. In front of Millie. In front of half the office.

Before I can fully comprehend the moment, Millie's shocked

gasp drags me back to reality.

Someone drops something that clatters. There might be actual gasping.

I wrench myself away and dash into my office.

As I shut the door, I hear Medard greet Millie with a bright "Good morning!" as if he didn't just snog me senseless.

The audacity of this man.

I rest my forehead against the cool door. My hands are shaking. My whole body is shaking.

He just kissed me. In front of half the office.

There's no taking that back. No pretending it was anything other than what it was.

I'm in a relationship with Medard Carter, and now everyone knows it.

I've been hiding in my office for hours, pretending to work while actually just staring at my computer screen and reliving that kiss.

Millie knocks and pokes her head in, her expression a mixture of concern and barely suppressed curiosity that makes me want to crawl under my desk.

"Miss Rosen? Are you alright?" she asks. "It's just... you haven't taken a single break all morning."

"I'm fine, Millie. Really."

"It's been five hours, Miss Rosen," she says softly. "I got you a salad when I went to lunch."

Five hours? I hadn't realised.

"Thank you for your concern," I say, offering a smile. "I'll grab my lunch now."

As I step out and head to the staff kitchen, I scan my surroundings, half-hoping, half-fearing to catch a glimpse of Medard. It's only been a few hours, but I already miss him, which is absolutely ridiculous. But he was so sweet this morning—doing my laundry, making breakfast, applying cream to my thighs—that I can't wait to spend more nights with him.

I quickly cover my mouth as giggles burst out. I feel giddy and happy, and...queasy as Amina walks past and throws me an indignant glare that could freeze hell.

Right. Because he was also completely unreasonable when we got to the office, literally forcing the outing of our relationship without trying to understand my side.

I shake my head and retrieve my salad from the fridge. There's no point spiralling. Medard and I will just have to sit down and come up with a plan.

"Spill the beans, you sexy little minx!"

I nearly jump out of my skin as Ben appears with a broad grin.

"I don't know what you're talking about," I brush him off.

He leans down onto the counter and pulls my salad towards him. "Come on, Soph! It's me. What's he like? Hung like a horse, or more like the little sting of a bee?"

"Ben!" I whisper-shout while frantically looking over my shoulder.

"Never mind, I already know the answer," he says. "A man like him? Hung like a horse. I'm sure of it."

"Sooo...?" he starts again, when I don't respond.

"So, what?"

"So, is he hung like a horse or not?"

I steal a glance at him, catching him wagging his eyebrows.

My mind wanders unbidden to last night. I try to suppress the grin, but my burning cheeks give me away.

"Oh, yes! I knew it! You lucky bitch!" Ben exclaims with a clap. "You and me, lunch, this week. I want all the dirty little details."

Before I can respond, he pivots and heads out, leaving me in a fit of giggles.

But then footsteps echo in the corridor, and my heart does this stupid fluttering thing.

I glance over my shoulder just as Medard steps into the kitchen, and all the air leaves my lungs.

"Lioness," he says, crossing the space between us.

Before I can react, he's there, his hands on my waist, pulling me close. His lips find mine, and oh God—

"Medard, stop," I hiss, pushing at his chest and stepping back. "This is completely unprofessional!"

He pauses, his eyebrows rising. "Unprofessional?"

"Yes! You can't just... maul me in the staff kitchen where literally anyone could walk in! People could see us—"

"I'm not mauling you," he says with infuriating calmness. "I was giving my girlfriend a kiss."

I stare at him, shaking my head. "Same thing when we're at work!"

His eyes narrow dangerously.

"People are already talking," I continue. "That kiss this morning was bad enough, but if they see us groping each other in the kitchen—"

"Let them talk."

"No. You don't get it!" I snap, setting my salad down with force. "You don't have to deal with the whispers and the looks. You're Medard Carter, untouchable managing director. But I'm just the woman sleeping with her boss!"

His jaw clenches. "That's not—"

But I'm already moving, heading for the door because if I stay, I'm going to either kiss him or kill him.

"Sophie." His voice carries a warning tone.

I don't stop. I hear his footsteps behind me, and I increase my speed. He matches my pace effortlessly, and suddenly this has turned into the world's most ridiculous chase scene.

People are definitely staring now.

As I reach Millie's desk, I turn to her. "Millie, I'm not to be disturbed for the rest of the afternoon—"

But Medard is right behind me. "We'll be a while, so you're welcome to take another lunch."

Great!

Perfect!

Now she'll definitely think we're planning on shagging in my office.

"No," I insist, stopping abruptly. "We won't be anything. I'll have my lunch and then get back to work. On. My. Own."

The satisfaction lasts approximately two seconds before he snaps his fingers at Millie and barks "Out!"

The poor girl practically runs off.

"Was that necess—"

"Big mistake, lioness," he bites out, grabbing my arm and pulling me into my office. The door slams behind us.

"You will never say that again, understood?"

I pull my arm out of his hold with a defiant raise of my chin. "You're a complete hypocrite! Last time I stood up to you in front of others, you told me I'd have the right when I'm your girlfriend. Now I am, and you're still pissed off?"

He actually huffs and pinches the bridge of his nose like I'm an ignorant child throwing a tantrum instead of a grown woman with legitimate concerns. I hope he breaks his perfectly shaped nose in the process.

"Lioness—" He huffs again before dropping his hand, and I can see him physically restraining himself. "You can defy me any day—here at work or at home. It gets me off every goddamn time."

He cups his crotch to make a point, his gaze dragging over me in a slow, deliberate way that makes my skin prickle and my core clench traitorously.

"But I won't allow you to say that 'we won't be anything' when we're fucking everything to each other."

"What? I didn't mean it like that—" I start, backing up as he advances.

But he doesn't let me finish. He closes the gap in two strides, and his mouth crashes onto mine with bruising intensity. My knees buckle instantly, and my salad—my poor, forgotten salad that I never even got to eat—drops to the floor with a sad little splat.

His hand finds my throat, not squeezing but holding, possessive.

"No more excuses, lioness," he growls against my lips. "The suspension is gone. The staff already knows about us. All that's left for you is to accept your place by my side."

I should be angry. I am angry. But I'm also breathless and dizzy.

"Now be a good girl," he continues, his voice dropping, "and get down on your knees and suck my cock."

The words should offend me. Should make me slap him and storm out in righteous indignation and feminist fury.

Instead, heat floods through me.

But I manage to find my voice. "And what if I don't? Will you spank me?"

He smiles suddenly, and it looks almost menacing. "Always playing the defiant damsel in distress," he says softly, his thumb stroking my throat in a way that makes me want to purr like a cat. "When really, that's exactly what you want. Isn't it, lioness?"

Before I can respond, his hand slides up my skirt, dipping underneath my knickers. Two fingers push inside me without warning, and I gasp at the intrusion, at how easily he slides in.

He snickers as he pulls his fingers out and holds them up, glistening.

"Look how slick you are for me," he murmurs. "How wet. You want me to put you over my knee and spank that defiant little bottom."

My cheeks burn.

"Get on your knees, lioness."

I should refuse. Should tell him to get out, that he can't just barge into my office and demand sexual favours like some kind of—

But I'm already sinking to my knees, my hands reaching for his belt with trembling fingers that betray how much I want this.

What is wrong with me? When did I become this person who drops to her knees in her office?

I undo his belt, his zipper, and free him. He's hard and thick, and my mouth waters.

"That's it," he murmurs as I wrap my lips around him. "Good girl."

I take him deeper, and his hand threads through my hair, loosening the pins. My hair tumbles down as he gathers it in his fist, guiding my movements.

"Such a good, obedient lioness," he coos. "You're staying at my place tonight, and if you behave for the rest of the day, I might give you that firm hand you so clearly need."

I hate how his words affect me, how they make me even wetter, how I want to be good for him despite his complete trampling of every professional boundary I've ever had. How I can't wait to go home with him tonight and let him do whatever he wants to me.

His grip tightens in my hair as I work him with my tongue, my hands, learning what makes his breath catch, what makes his hips flex, cataloguing every response like I'm studying for the most important exam of my life.

Just when I think he's going to finish, he pulls me up roughly, spins us around so I'm leaning against the door. His hands are on my hips, pushing my skirt up, and he yanks my knickers to the side hard enough that the fabric tears.

He lifts me into his arms, aligning himself. But he doesn't push in. Not yet.

"Now tell me, lioness, do you want me to fuck you?" he asks. "Right here, against your door, where someone might hear us?"

My breath stutters. I should say no.

"Yes," I breathe. "Yes, I want it."

He thrusts into me in one hard stroke that makes me see stars, and I cry out. The door rattles with the force of it, and oh God, if someone just walked by, they definitely heard that.

"Medard—" I gasp.

He sets a punishing pace, each thrust making the door shake, making the hinges protest, making my whole world narrow down to the feeling of him inside me and the mortifying knowledge that everyone outside must know exactly what we're doing. There's no way they don't. The door is literally rattling like it's trying to escape its frame.

"This is what you needed," he grates out. "To be claimed. To be owned."

"You're insufferable," I gasp, but it's a lie and we both know it, and I can't even put any heat into the words because they come out too breathy.

"Yet you want me," he counters, his fingers circling my clit. "Say it."

The door rattles again, louder.

"Say it," he demands, his thrusts becoming harder, deeper, more desperate, and I can feel his control fraying at the edges.

"I want you," I sob out as my orgasm builds. "God help me, I want you—"

"That's my good girl," he growls, and then his fingers press down hard on my clit and I shatter.

I come with a cry I can't suppress, and he follows moments later with a groan that's definitely loud enough for everyone to hear.

We stay like that for a moment, both breathing hard, my head pressed against the door that probably has a dent in it now.

Then reality crashes back in.

"Oh my God," I whisper. "Everyone probably heard—"

"Good," Medard says, pressing a kiss to my shoulder. "Then they know you're mine."

As he helps me straighten my clothes, his touch gentle now, I realise something that should probably terrify me but doesn't.

I don't actually want to fight him on this anymore.

I'm in love with him, and that's worth more than any scrutiny I'll face. It's worth the whispers because at the end of the day, I get to go home with him.

"I'll be out of the office for a couple of hours," he says, tugging at my chin. "But come by my office at five. We can stop by your flat to stock up on some clothes, and get a takeaway."

"Stock up?" I ask, raising a suspicious brow even though I think I know exactly where this is going.

His mouth splits into that dimpled smile. "I'm not planning on returning you home any time soon."

"Medard—" I try to scold him, but he cuts me off with a kiss.

"I'll see you later, lioness."

Leech

Medard

Rosen looks up from his over-sized chair, his lopsided grin exuding an air of mock unconcern.

"Mr Carter, to what do I owe this pleasure? Have you come over to personally congratulate me on my latest client acquisition?"

He leans forward. His polished bravado is meant to disarm, but it only fans the embers of my anger into something that shines. I take his hand, revelling in the connection, knowing that barely an hour ago my fingers were knuckle-deep inside his daughter. The intoxicating surge of power courses through me, tightening my grip on his fingers.

"You don't strike me as a man who needs praise," I say, my voice low and deliberate.

I ease into the chair opposite him, unbuttoning my jacket with the kind of slow, confident movement reserved for people who know they're about to win. The tension in the room crackles with anticipation, and the smile that tugs at my mouth is sharp as a knife. This is the opening move of a very exquisite game.

"True, for a man with my track record, praise can swiftly become repetitive. But you should know that. After all, you have made quite a name for yourself." He says it like he's offering me a compliment and a consolation prize rolled into one.

I laugh—not soft, not kind. It's a dark, low sound that flattens his attempt at civility. "I must admit, your scheme did take me by surprise. For a moment, I was naive enough to believe Sophie would side with you."

His smug grin falters, replaced by a look of disdain as I toss his failures back in his face.

"Sadly, my daughter's choices are steered by feelings and not professional gain."

I can't help the grin that splits my face; it's broad and a little predatory. I point a finger like a judge delivering a sentence. "That's true. I don't have the impression she's trying to gain anything from me other than my affection."

"Don't take it personal. I suspect she did the same with

Harman." Rosen's laughter is as dark as it is sinister.

I lean back, quiet for a moment, utterly gob-smacked by his ignorance. How can he be so blind? Sophie isn't seeking out lovers. She's looking for something he never gave her—warmth, guidance, the kind of steady hand she never had beneath his iron rule.

She sleeps with me because we click in ways that are electric and inevitable, the way death is inevitable. She sleeps with me because we're meant to shape this city together. Being her boss has, if anything, kept her from exploring those feelings for me sooner.

"Contrary to you, I know where I stand in my relationship with Sophie." The words are soft but absolute.

He snorts, feigning superiority. "No offence, but you know nothing about my family. Now, say what you came here for or get the hell out of my office." The calm in his voice is a brittle thing as fury is curling at its edges.

It's satisfying to witness the little cracks forming in his composed facade. I watch him like a man studying a map, and then I say what I came for.

"I want the Windpower account, and you will give it to me."

Rosen laughs in a cavernous, dismissive boom that bounces off the tasteless art and the out-dated wall panelling. "And why would I ever do that?"

"Because if you don't, this will hit the news." I drop a folder on his desk with a deliberate thud.

The sound is theatrical and precise. We stare at one another; the air inside the room thickens, viscous with the unspoken. He flips through the pages. The expression that creeps over his face is a slow unravelling. It's all there, wrapped up neatly in a tapestry of his failings: his late wife's medical records, court transcripts, police reports.

"You son of a bitch! Those records were sealed!" His voice is ragged, higher than he intends.

I shrug, feigning indifference as the corners of my mouth curl into a grin once again.

"You have 48 hours to withdraw from the account, or the tabloids will learn exactly what kind of a man you are– a bastard of a husband and father."

"You are gravely mistaken if you think you can blackmail me.

I will not stand for it." He rises, all theatrical indignation, like a toddler who's been called out and is trying desperately to be taken seriously.

"Accept it or not, throw a tantrum or shag your frustrations out with the next best hooker who's desperate enough to touch your shrivelled little dick. The facts remain: you are being blackmailed and you will give me the account."

His face drains of colour, only to be doused with a furious crimson as his nostrils flare. The sight is grotesque, a reminder of just how poorly Sophie's bloodline is represented in this room. Her fierceness and beauty did not come from him. No, that was her mother's gift. She got the grit, the hunger, the fire from somewhere kinder.

"This discussion is over, and my daughter will under no circumstances work for you anymore! And note this, you piece of shit, no Rosen will ever bow to your demands!" He slams his fist into the desk.

A glass of scotch tips, an amber wave soaking into papers that once mapped his empire. But his fury is like sugar to my soul – it sustains me and urges me on. His family loyalties mean nothing when he's willing to have sacrificed the one thing that should have mattered to her.

"Well, it's a good thing then that Sophie won't be a Rosen for long." I rise, buttoning my jacket with deliberate care as I revel in the chaos I've sown within him.

"How did you put it?" I snap my fingers, pretending to mull it over. "Oh, that's it! Her choices are driven by her feelings. And her feelings for me will soon have her renouncing the Rosen name to become a Carter."

His hands ball into fists, crushing paper like it's made of his dignity. "You disgusting leech!"

I tut at him, shaking my head like a disappointed father. "Let's play nice, Daddy dearest. After all, we'll soon be family."

He stammers, rage choking his words, and I turn, taking my leave while throwing one last parting shot over my shoulder: "48 hours, Rosen. Tick tock tick tock!"

Backstabber

Sophie

Reality slams into me like a freight train the moment the door closes behind him.

Oh God.

What have I done?

I need to clean up. I need to fix my hair. I need to get to the bathroom before anyone sees me like this, before the evidence of my complete and utter lack of professional judgement becomes even more obvious than it already is.

I grab some tissues from my desk and do a quick cleanup of the salad carnage on the floor, shoving the container into my bin. My hands are shaking as I try to smooth down my skirt, but I can feel him—feel the evidence of what we just did trickling down my thighs—and my cheeks burn with hot mortification.

This isn't me. I don't do shit like this.

Deep breath. You can do this.

Just walk to the bathroom like a normal person who didn't just get thoroughly shagged against her office door by her boss while half the floor listened.

I crack open the door and peek out like I'm checking for snipers in some kind of corporate warfare.

Millie's back at her desk, and she won't meet my eyes. She's staring at her computer screen with the intensity of someone pretending very hard not to have heard anything, which means she definitely heard something.

Kill me now.

I step out into the corridor, trying to project an aura of professionalism and composure I absolutely do not feel. My legs are still slightly wobbly, which isn't helping matters, and I'm acutely aware of every single person I pass, every eye that might be tracking my walk of shame.

Sarah from accounts looks up as I walk by, and her eyes do this thing—this quick scan from my face to my body and back up again—and I watch her expression shift from neutral to knowing to judgemental in the space of about two seconds. She says nothing, just turns back to her conversation with Martin, but I hear them start whispering the moment I'm past.

My cheeks are on fire. This is a nightmare. This is an actual waking nightmare.

I turn the corner and nearly collide with Mrs Henderson—who knows exactly what that CRA form is for, who probably took my moans as some twisted form of consent and just processed the bloody thing. She gives me this look. It's not quite pity, not quite disapproval, but something in between that makes me want to sink through the floor.

"Miss Rosen," she says, her tone carefully neutral in that way that's somehow worse than outright judgement. "Any news on the CRA?"

"No. Still under review," I squeak out, which is absolutely not convincing and we both know it. "If you'll excuse me, I just... need the loo." I speed-walk past her before she can say anything else, before she can give me another one of those looks.

More heads turn as I pass. More whispers start up in my wake like I'm leaving a trail of scandal behind me, breadcrumbs of gossip for people to follow.

Finally—finally—I reach the bathrooms and practically throw myself through the door.

The door swings shut behind me, silencing the chaotic hum of the office outside. I rush to the nearest cubicle, my heart still racing from what just happened with Medard in my office—and from the gauntlet of judgement I just ran through. I close the stall with an unsteady hand, locking it firmly, and lean against the cool metal, trying to catch my breath.

This is fine. Everything is fine. I just need a minute to pull myself together and then I can go back out there and pretend I'm a functioning professional adult who makes sensible decisions.

I grab a handful of toilet paper, my movements frantic, mechanical, trying not to think too hard about what I'm doing. When I pull down my torn knickers and dab away what's left of my recklessness, I almost laugh—a hollow, joyless sound that sticks in my throat.

Futile.

The goo clings like a second skin, an echo of everything I shouldn't have done, every boundary I shouldn't have crossed.

Professionalism: shredded. Boundaries: incinerated. Sophie: complete and utter idiot.

Flushing the paper feels symbolic, but the shame doesn't go down with it. I step out of the cubicle and catch my reflection in the mirror above the sinks. It shows someone unravelling. My hair is slightly dishevelled, a few strands sticking to my damp forehead, and just beneath my skin, the warmth of his touch lingers with a mix of pleasure and guilt that I'm suddenly desperate to wash away.

As I reach for the tap, the bathroom door swings open again, and instinct has me leap back into the cubicle like a frightened rabbit.

Amina's voice cuts through the silence, sharp and unforgiving.

"Honestly, Farid, she's nothing but cheap for sleeping with the boss."

My breath hitches. I bite down on my lip to stifle my breathing, and dig my nails into my thighs without thinking. My skin screams in protest—sharp, hot and unbelievably painful—but it keeps me still.

"I should have known Sophie was just waiting for her chance to climb the ladder, to lure Carter under her skirt. He practically groomed her for the position. It's just sad that he doesn't see she's using him."

Every word cuts deeper than I could've imagined, slicing through what's left of my composure.

The bathroom door opens and closes again, leaving me wrapped in silence. I take a shuddering breath and swipe at the tears that finally spill over, hot and angry on my cheeks. Alone in this small, suffocating space, I feel the weight of her words settle in my chest, heavy and unforgiving.

Against all my efforts, despite all my careful planning and protests and attempts to keep this professional, I yet again find myself under the scrutiny of my peers.

And this time, I have absolutely no one to blame but myself.

I sit down on the toilet seat and wipe at my tears with shaking hands. The pulsing pain in my thighs flares to an unbearable level, and I slowly peel my skirt up to inspect the damage I've inflicted. My thighs are bleeding. The wounds that were scabbed over are ripped open again, trickling dark red. The skin burns so hot it feels like someone took a sanding block to them and didn't stop. This is the worst it's ever been. This is the worst I've ever done to them.

Another bout of tears bursts free.

I should be happy, shouldn't I? Full of joy and butterflies and all those things people feel when they're in love. I'm finally with Medard—a man who wants me, who claims me, who cares about me. Even if it's in a slightly twisted and controlling way that probably requires therapy. Still, I should be happy.

But I'm not. I'm not okay.

I'm not okay, at all.

I'm scared, and lonely.

Where's Medard?

I pull my legs to my chest, and another bout of tears ripples through my body as the raw skin stretches by the movement.

I want my mum.

I take what feels like an eternity to compose myself—drying the tears off my cheeks with rough toilet paper that scratches my skin—before I feel brave enough to face the world outside this tiny cubicle.

I hurry back to my office, my head bowed, purposely ignoring anyone who crosses my path.

"Sophie, I've come to apologise," Buckman greets me as I step back into my office.

"For?" I hesitantly ask as I step further into the room, closing the door behind me.

"The suspension. We never should have doubted your loyalty. Jason Miller from IT accessed your email account, presumably to get his girlfriend a job at your father's firm."

"Julia Michaels," I gasp, the name hitting me like a slap in the face as the pieces slot into place.

"Indeed. She didn't take Carter firing her lightly. So, you see, we owe you an apology."

Anger should be pulsing through me right now. But instead, all I feel is the raw ache of betrayal. All day, Medard has known about my innocence? And yet, he let me walk into this office, tethered to the belief that his "saving grace" was my only chance at redemption.

"Thank you for your apology," I manage, my voice steady despite the lump wedged in my throat, and the tears that threaten to spill again.

He nods, just as my phone erupts into the silence.

"I'll let you take this. It's good to have you back, Sophie."

As the door closes behind him, I pick up my phone and glance at the screen.

Father.

I haven't spoken to him since the golf club, since everything went to hell with the Windpower account. And now that Medard finally knows that I'm innocent, he doesn't have the courtesy to tell me himself.

I press the button to answer, hopeful that speaking to Father might soothe some of the ache in my chest.

"Sophie!" his voice booms through the receiver, sharp and unforgiving, as if he's standing right in front of me with that scowl he reserves for his greatest disappointments. "How dare you pull this stunt on me!"

"Father, what do you—" I stammer, taken aback by his unexpected outburst.

"Your boss, or should I say fiancé, just came by my office," he interrupts, each syllable dripping with disdain that makes my blood run cold.

I can't believe it. Medard went to my father and told him about his "proposal". My heart sinks, dropping into my stomach. I grip the phone tighter, trying to steady the tremor in my hand that's spreading through my entire body.

"That's not true, we've just—" I protest weakly, but it sounds pathetic even to my own ears.

"It is not?" he barks, laughter laced with contempt. "You think I am so naive? He told me how happy you were to spread your legs for him."

His hurtful words slam into my chest, yet they hold no surprise. This is my father, after all.

"Father, please, just listen!" My voice falters, breaking on the last word.

"Listen? Is that what you want me to do while some greasy bastard plays puppet master with my life, with your life?"

"Your life? Who I'm with has no bearing on you. I want to be with him, and he wants—"

"You stupid girl!" he cuts me off with a chuckle void of any joy, any warmth. "He used you, and yet you are still so naive to think that he wants you. I know you had a hand in getting him the file on your mother. Fuck knows how you managed to get your nosey little paws on it."

What?

How can Medard do this to me, using my tragic past as leverage? Using my mother—my dead mother—as some kind of bargaining chip?

I swallow hard, the bitterness coating my throat.

"You better think long and hard about what you are doing, Sophie. You think I am going to let you or some jerk jeopardise my career? My reputation?"

"I didn't do—" I fumble for words, feeling more cornered with each breath. "I can explain. It's not—"

"I do not want to hear your excuses," he cuts me off again, his irritation bubbling over. "What are you even thinking? Is this how you have been making your way up at the firm? First Harman, now Carter? Close your fucking legs, for Christ's sake, before the whole city knows I have a promiscuous slut for a daughter!"

Anger flares inside me, a defiant fire against his insults, but it's immediately doused by shame because part of me—a horrible, traitorous part of me—wonders if he's right.

"You've got it all wrong!" I bite out, the words tasting like venom on my tongue. "I've worked hard for my position so I can prove myself to—"

"Prove yourself? You think rolling in the sheets with your boss makes you a professional?"

The derision is unmistakable, cutting, and I feel the heat of humiliation wash over me in waves. He's right in a way, isn't he? Although I didn't sleep with Harman, I did—I still am—sleeping with Carter. I did blur those lines I swore I'd never cross.

"And do not even think about sending me a wedding invitation. Save the seventy-five pence for a stamp, Sophie, because I will not attend that joke of a wedding."

The finality of his words lands like a blunt force trauma, knocking the air from my lungs. I want to scream back, to declare that this isn't how it ends. That I won't let him control me like this. That I'm more than his disappointment. But instead, the air leaves my lungs, the free-fall devastating.

"Father, please," I whisper, but the line clicks dead before I can say anything else.

I'm left clutching the phone, the cold plastic pressing into my palm, silent disbelief swirling in my head.

I stare at the wall, the reality crashing down around me in pieces I can't put back together.

Medard never cared for me. He only wanted to get close so he could use me for his personal gain, to get information about my father, to stab me in the back when it suited him.

And I let him. I let him in. I gave him everything.

God, I'm such an idiot.

Bad Catch

Medard

I stride through the glass doors of Carter & Buckman with the kind of satisfaction that comes from a day well executed. The afternoon meetings went exactly as planned—contracts signed, the board appeased, and one particularly satisfying conversation with Andrew Rosen that will bear fruit in the very near future.

Everything is falling into place.

"Mr Carter," Janet greets me with her usual efficiency as I pass her desk, already sorting through what I assume is tomorrow's agenda.

"I'll be leaving in about an hour," I tell her, checking my watch. Four o'clock. Perfect timing. "Clear my calendar for the rest of the evening."

"Of course, sir." She makes a note, her fingers flying across her keyboard. "And the—"

"Tomorrow," I say, already moving towards my office. "It can wait."

Because tonight is about Sophie, and Christ, I can barely contain the anticipation thrumming through my veins.

I close my office door behind me and settle into my chair, pulling up the spreadsheets I need to review before I leave. Numbers swim across the screen—projections, forecasts, revenue streams—but my mind keeps wandering to far more pleasant territory.

The Windpower account will be ours within the week. Andrew Rosen will hand it over on a silver platter, gift-wrapped with his desperation to keep certain files from seeing the light of day.

It's not my finest moment, playing hardball with Sophie's father, but business is business, and the firm will flourish because of it. We'll be swimming in the black by Q2, and every partner in this building will have me to thank for it.

And Sophie, my lioness, finally stopped fighting me on going public. It took some convincing—some rather spectacular convincing against her office door this afternoon, if I'm being honest—but she's accepted it. No more hiding, no more pretending we're just colleagues. Everyone knows she's mine now, and that's exactly how it should be.

Never again will I be the fool who hides his relationship like it's something shameful. Lisa taught me that lesson the hard way, insisting we keep things quiet while she played me like a fiddle, making me believe she wanted me when all she wanted was my brother.

But Sophie's different. She has to be.

Tonight, I'm going to show her exactly how different things can be when she stops fighting what we both want. Dinner first—something simple but good, maybe Chinese or Indian. Then home, where I'll have her strip down and bend over my knee for the spanking, she's been earning all day with her defiance and attitude. I'll make her count each strike, make her sob and beg and promise to be good before I finally give her what she's desperate for.

And then I'll fuck her until my cock is red and raw and she can't remember her own name, let alone how to walk. I'll fuck her until she understands that this—us—is everything.

After that, a bath. I'll wash her hair, tend to those thighs she keeps damaging, hold her while the water cools around us. Then we'll curl up naked in my sheets and watch whatever film she wants, her head on my chest, my fingers tracing patterns on her skin until she falls asleep.

Perfect. Absolutely fucking perfect.

I'm grinning at my spreadsheet like an idiot when I hear it—raised voices outside my office, one of them distinctly Sophie's.

What the fuck?

I push back from my desk and stride to the door, yanking it open to find my lioness squaring off with Janet, who looks somewhere between professional concern and genuine alarm.

"—don't need an appointment," Sophie is saying, her voice sharp with an edge I don't recognise. "I've put up with enough of his bullshit to warrant barging in unannounced."

"Miss Rosen, Mr Carter has protocols—" Janet tries, her hands balled into fists that do absolutely nothing to calm the situation.

"Protocols?" Sophie huffs, waving her off dismissively like Janet's concerns are beneath her consideration. "Right. Because heaven forbid the great Medard Carter be interrupted without a formal written request."

The casual disrespect in her tone—towards Janet, towards

me—makes something cold settle in my chest.

"Sophie." My voice cuts through their argument. "That's enough."

She spins to face me, and there's pure anger in her eyes. But also, something deeper. Something that makes my earlier fantasies feel suddenly, dangerously naive.

"Oh, wonderful," she says, her voice dripping with sarcasm that would be amusing in different circumstances. "His Highness has finally decided to grace us with his presence."

Janet's eyes widen at Sophie's tone, clearly shocked that anyone would speak to me like that.

"You will not speak to my assistant that way," I say evenly, keeping my voice controlled despite the irritation building behind my ribs. "And you will certainly watch your tone with me."

"Or what, exactly?" Sophie challenges, stepping closer with her chin raised in defiance.

Janet makes a strangled sound, her professional composure cracking at the edges.

"My office. Now." I don't wait for her response, just grab her wrist and pull her past Janet, who's doing an admirable job of pretending she's suddenly very interested in something on her laptop screen.

I slam the door and turn to face Sophie, who's standing in the middle of my office like she's ready for a fight. The afternoon light streaming through the windows catches her hair, and even now, even angry, she's the most beautiful woman I've ever seen.

"You know," I say, crossing my arms and leaning against my desk, trying to regain control of the situation, "I had plans to spank you tonight in the comfort of my home. But the way you're behaving, I'm seriously considering doing it right here, right now, so you remember how to show some goddamn respect."

It's meant to defuse the tension, to shift this into familiar territory where I'm in control and she's bratty but ultimately pliant. Where this ends with her bent over my desk or pressed against the window, both of us getting exactly what we need.

But she doesn't blush. Doesn't graze her thighs. Doesn't show even a flicker of the arousal I was expecting.

Instead, her eyes narrow, her jaw clenches, and when she speaks, her voice is pure venom.

"Is that what this is to you?" she asks, her voice shaking with barely contained rage. "Everything's just another opportunity to bend me over and fuck me into submission? Is that what gets you off—having the Rosen-Girl kneel at your feet?"

The words hit me like a slap. This isn't play. This isn't her being defiant because she wants me to dominate her into submission. This is real anger, real hurt, and I've completely misread the situation.

"You can shove your patronising bile up your arse, Medard."

She turns to walk out, and panic flares in my chest, hot and fast.

"Sophie, wait—" I push off the desk, closing the distance between us and catching her arm before she can reach the door.

She whirls on me, and the look in her eyes stops me cold. It isn't just anger. It's an inferno. A fire that sears straight through me, scorching my composure to ash.

This isn't going to end well.

"What's going on? Don't run away, just speak to me," I implore, my voice laced with a panic I can't disguise.

"Run away?" Her voice trembles, but it's not weakness. It's a symphony of indignation and betrayal, every note perfectly tuned to shred me. "I ran towards you! I stepped into the lion's den because you promised you'd take care of me. But you lied—again. Thank you for letting me keep the job that shouldn't have been threatened in the first place."

Fuck!

Buckman. He must have told her about Julia Michaels, about how I knew she was innocent before we even stepped foot into the office.

"Sophie, let me explain," I plead, feeling the tension crackle between us.

"Don't!" She warns with a raised hand, like a fortress I can't breach. "All day, you've known I'm innocent, yet you didn't say a word. Did you ever plan on telling me the truth?"

Her words are pointed daggers, aimed straight at my heart.

"No," I bite out, frustration tearing through my calm façade. "But what if I had? You would have regretted coming to my home last night. You wouldn't have opened up to me. So, I kept my mouth shut and instead showed you how fucking perfect we are together."

This, us, I won't let her destroy it over a situation that's already been handled. Not after everything we've been through, not after

I've finally gotten her to accept what we are.

A laugh escapes her, but it's not light. It's dark, brittle. It cracks in the air like splintering glass.

"We're nothing. You've done your best to prove it to me at every turn. Especially today. You are my boss and nothing more."

"Sophie—" I try to catch her with her name, but she's already retreating, already pulling away from me.

"All you care about is your own agenda. It doesn't matter who you hurt or compromise in the process. I hope it was worth blackmailing my father behind my back."

"Is this why you're really hurt?" My words come sharper than I mean them to, the edge of my own anger bleeding through despite my best efforts. "You told me you'd side with me when push comes to shove!"

"I gave you my loyalty," she shouts, her head shaking violently, "not permission to weaponise my tragic past, my own feelings! I'm done being tossed around and used without a shred of regard."

"Without regard?" I bark, my voice cracking in disbelief. "I've given you everything!"

She looks at me then, and her eyes are devastating in their calm, in their absolute certainty. "You've given me nothing. You've lied, you've manipulated, controlled and bloody abused me. You've done every bad thing imaginable to me, and I still chose you. But now I'm done, Medard. I'm done with this fucked-up game of yours."

"No, you're not!" I protest, stepping forward, aching to bridge the chasm between us like a wound.

But she steps back again, a perfect choreography of rejection. Every move she makes is a wall slamming down between us.

I've bared my soul to her, my fears, my darkest corners, and still, she recoils like I'm poison.

"I mean it, Medard." Her voice softens just enough to be lethal, to cut deeper than if she'd screamed it. "I don't want to be under you—neither in work nor in bed. This is over."

The finality in her words feel like a kick in the balls.

"Sophie." Her name is a plea now, a breathless sound caught between desperation and command.

I step forward and place my hands on her shoulders, as if grounding her to this moment, to us, to everything we've built.

But with fierce, graceful precision, she knocks my hands away. Before I can recover, before I can even process what's happening, her palm strikes my throat in a deliberate hit. The shock steals my breath, a white-hot ripple of pain stunning me as I stumble back, my lungs pleading for air.

The distance between us stretches into an abyss, widening with every step she takes away from me. My hands reach out, but I'm left grasping at shadows.

My footing slips. A cascade of folders spills to the floor around me as I struggle to regain my balance, papers scattering like the pieces of my control. Chaos erupts in my head, spilling out into my limbs. Fury swells my heart, feral and consuming, before it enters into a dizzying dance with devastating grief. I hurl a glass against the wall. It explodes into a hundred sharp echoes, each one taunting me, mocking me. A reckless sweep of my arm sends a flurry of papers spiralling into the air, like a physical manifestation of the tempest inside me.

The door bursts open. Janet rushes in, her eyes bulging at the destruction before her. "Mr Carter, are you alright?"

"Get out!" I bark, the rawness of my torment leaking through the cracks of the cold mask I usually wear so perfectly.

Her eyes widen even further, wet with tears she doesn't want me to see. She flees, her sobs trailing behind her like a haunting melody.

"Fuck!" I roar.

The word ricochets off the walls, back at me, mocking, relentless. Control slips through my fingers like sand, every grain a reminder of what's gone. Sophie. She's gone.

My legs give way under the weight of everything I've just destroyed—her, me, us. I slide down the cold glass wall until my backside hits the floor, the sound a dull thud in the echoing quiet of my office. Around me lies the wreckage of my perfectly curated life: shattered glass, crumpled papers, and the stale air of regret.

Tears break free before I even realise what's happening. I swipe at them roughly with trembling fingers, furious at the weakness staining my face, at this loss of control I never allow myself. I can't even remember the last time I cried. Maybe it was when my nan died, maybe never. But now, they won't stop.

The realisation hits with violent clarity: she's my lifeline. The only one who's ever managed to pierce the armour I wear like it's welded to my skin.

And she's gone.

The sobs rip out of me, raw and uncontrolled. My chest tightens, refusing air. My hands claw at my tie, yanking it loose, buttons flying as I tear at my shirt like a man desperate for oxygen or salvation. My throat constricts, vision blurring, panic slicing through the edges of my thoughts.

The door bursts open again. Buckman strides in, his presence impossibly distant in the midst of the chaos consuming me.

"What's going on?" He halts mid-step, eyes sweeping the scene: the unravelling mess that is me. His expression sharpens, the concern in his gaze far too genuine for my liking.

"I can't breathe," I choke out, clutching my chest like I can physically force air into my lungs. "What's happening to me? I can't—"

The words splinter as I gasp, my lungs refusing to cooperate. Buckman moves with deliberate control, lowering himself beside me on the floor, his voice firm, grounding.

"Calm down. Deep breath in. Then out. Slowly."

I try, inhaling like it's an Olympic sport, each breath scraping the inside of my lungs.

"You're having a panic attack, son," he says quietly, matter-of-fact.

The diagnosis lands heavy. I nod, but the motion is jerky, unfocused, like my head's not entirely attached to my body. The minutes stretch, my breathing easing slowly, the sharp edges of panic dulling into a steady ache. When I finally lift my gaze, Buckman is looking at me like he's assessing structural damage after a hurricane.

"Now get up," he orders, his tone shifting from fatherly to commanding, "and tell me why your assistant is crying out there, saying you've lost your shit."

"I'm fine," I mutter the lie through gritted teeth. "Tell her I didn't mean to shout."

"You're going to tell me what's going on," he says, his voice calm but unyielding, "and then you'll apologise to her yourself."

He extends a hand, pulling me from the wreckage of my emotions. My knees protest, my lungs still tight, but I let him haul me upright. I collapse onto the sofa, the cushions swallowing me whole as the weight of what I've done drags me down like an anchor.

Buckman pours two scotches, his movements practised, his expression a blend of weary understanding and exasperation.

"I'm glad you didn't smash all the glasses," he mutters dryly, handing me one.

I down it in one go, the liquor scorching a path down my throat. It's fire and punishment in liquid form. Without missing a beat, he refills the glass, his brow lifting just enough to make the silence between us scream.

"Now talk," he says simply. "I've been watching you spiral for weeks."

The words hang in the air like smoke. I stare at the glass in my hand, watching the amber liquid tremble with my pulse.

"I've screwed up," I admit finally.

It comes out hoarse, stripped of the bravado I wear like armour.

"With Sophie?" His tone is clipped, too casual, and that's what makes it sting. "Yeah, I figured that would happen."

I blink, turning to him. "You know?"

Buckman exhales a long-suffering sigh, settling into the opposite sofa. "Everyone knows. You practically paraded her around the firm like she was your new favourite acquisition. But I've known for weeks. Over thirty years in this business, Carter. You start seeing patterns."

My brows knit together, confusion seeping through the exhaustion. "What patterns?"

He ticks them off on his fingers. "An unexpected promotion without added responsibilities. A corner office. Swapping assistants for no reason. Late nights at the office. And a mole that's usually covered by a bra."

Despite everything, a startled laugh escapes me, half-choke, half-incredulity. "Christ, Buckman."

He lifts an unimpressed brow. "Don't 'Christ, Buckman' me. I've seen colder men than you melt faster than ice in July once they mix business with pleasure. It's textbook."

I stare down at the floor, the laughter dying as quickly as it came, leaving nothing but hollow emptiness.

"And HR gave me a copy of her CRA," he continues, his voice cooling, "which she never signed."

"Ugh," I grunt, dragging a hand down my face, frustration thick in my voice. "And she never will."

"Why would she?" he retorts, his eyes narrowing. "I certainly wouldn't have signed it."

"Am I that bad of a catch?" I scoff, a humourless smirk twisting my lips as I take another sip.

"That depends." He leans forward, elbows on his knees, eyes pinning me in place. "Can you, for once, get off your damn high horse and think about what she wants? What she needs?"

The question lands like a blow I didn't see coming. I exhale, sinking deeper into the cushions, staring into the distance where her face lingers in my mind—fierce, wounded, heartbreakingly real.

"I don't know what she wants," I admit quietly. "Her body says one thing, her voice says another. I've given her everything, and it's never enough."

Buckman shakes his head slowly, disappointment threading through his gaze. "That's because you've been giving her the wrong things. She doesn't need your power, Carter. She needs your presence. There's a difference."

I stare out the window, the reflection staring back at me looking nothing like the man I thought I was.

"You're not that dumb," he says finally, standing and straightening his suit. "Take a step back. Forget yourself for five damn minutes, and look at her. Really look."

He moves towards the door, pausing with one hand on the frame. "And apologise to your assistant. These women are the backbone of this firm. You treat them with respect or you'll find yourself answering to me."

The silence he leaves behind is deafening. I glance around at the scattered papers, the splintered glass, the bottle of scotch warming my veins, and realise the truth I've been avoiding:

I love Sophie. I love her with everything I have, everything I am.

Man Of Steel

Sophie

I'm on a war path.

One man down, one to go.

I storm into Father's office, the door slamming against the wall with a violent thud that reverberates through the opulent space. The air is thick with the scent of polished wood and expensive leather, but all I can smell is betrayal.

He glances up from his laptop, slightly annoyed, his meticulously styled hair untouched by my outburst.

"Really, Sophie?" he drawls, sarcasm dripping from his words. "Is this how you choose to make an entrance?"

"Screw you!" My voice is a shaky mix of indignation and hurt. "How dare you paint me as the villain after you've schemed your way into getting the Windpower account? This could have cost me my job!"

"I am doing what is best for my firm," he replies, his tone chillingly calm, and it only infuriates me more, "and it seems you have found a way to secure your position. So much for keeping things professional. Sleeping with your boss? Really classy, Sophie."

"You know nothing!" I inch nearer, fists clenched at my sides, anger sparking in my chest. "I've worked so hard to prove myself to you, and all you—"

"All I have done is provide for you!" he cuts me off, his voice rising. "You should be grateful. Look at everything I have sacrificed! And now you want to shame me with your sordid affairs? You are just as weak as your mother was."

The words hit me as painfully as his cane always did on my fingers when I was little.

"What did you just say?" I breathe, the betrayal slicing deeper. "You know nothing about strength. You've lied to me about her life. You've painted her as a junkie, when she—"

"She took her own life because she couldn't handle it!" His voice is thunderous now, a storm unleashed. "Your mother was a weak woman, Sophie. Postpartum depression or not, she made choices that led to her failure. I did what I had to do to ensure our future was secure. I would not risk her dragging us down."

"Dragging?" I snap, stepping closer. "You're the one who dragged me down! You took me from her. You made me believe she didn't care about me, that she chose drugs over her own daughter, when really—" I choke on the words, anger morphing into sorrow. "When really, you stole me from her like I was just some trophy. You took everything from her and then crucified her memory!"

His sharp intake of breath fills the silence before his composed facade slips back into place.

"Yes, I did, so you could have a comfortable upbringing; and what do you do to repay me? You disgrace this family by scheming against me, by spreading your legs for your boss. You are as weak as she was. No ambition, no respect for what I have given you. Instead, you are following in her footsteps. Congratulations, you are a disappointment."

"Don't you dare talk about her like that!" Tears of rage prick at my eyes, but I refuse to let them fall. "You ruined her, you—"

"And you are ruining yourself!" He snaps, his voice cracking like a whip through the air. "I expected more from you. I thought you were stronger than this pathetic spectacle."

"Stronger?" I scoff, resentment lacing my words. "Is that what you think strength is? Being a cold-hearted, self-absorbed monster?" My voice rises, but it's steady, deadly. Years of silenced screams condensed into one moment.

My eyes scan his face, searching for something, anything. A flicker of the man who once held my tiny hand, of the father I begged to impress. Kindness. Love. But there's nothing. Just the sneering mask of a man drunk on his own power, eyes flashing with disdain, lips curled into the kind of snarl that belongs on predators, not parents.

And in that moment, like a veil lifting, I see it clearly. The years of clawing for his approval. The bending, breaking, reshaping of myself to fit into a mould he carved out of his own emptiness. The cold reality slams into me: nothing I say, nothing I do, will ever be enough for him. It never was. It never will be.

I take a small step back, then another, my body moving before my mind catches up. My heart thunders but my voice drops, calm and quiet, sharp as a blade.

"You've twisted my reality for too long."

Another step back, the distance between us finally feeling like freedom.

"I'm done, Father. I want nothing to do with you anymore."

For the first time, his face flickers with confusion, maybe fear; but I don't give him the satisfaction of seeing me hesitate. My hands don't tremble. My back doesn't bend. With one final glare of defiance, I turn sharply on my heel and storm out. The door slams behind me with a finality that echoes my resolve.

No more lies, no more deceit. I'm ready to reclaim my truth, even if it means leaving him and Medard behind.

Stepping out into the road feels like stepping out of a lifetime.

The city air rushes around me, cool and unapologetic, and for the first time in forever, the weight I've carried—Father's expectations, his criticism disguised as guidance, his love dangled like a prize I could never quite earn slides from my shoulders.

Fighting for his recognition has always been my life raft, or so I told myself. In truth, he was the damn anchor tied around my ankle, dragging me to the ocean floor while I called it devotion. But now... now I'm finally free.

The chaotic symphony of London embraces me. Taxi horns blare. Conversations overlap in a dozen accents. My heels click in a steady rhythm against the concrete, a soundtrack of independence, sharp and satisfying.

I have every intention of catching the tube home, being sensible, responsible even. But when the train screeches into the station, that metallic scream splitting the air, something inside me rebels. The doors open. People rush in. I... don't move.

"It's time to break out of the mould," I whisper to myself, and for once, I mean it.

The words feel dangerous on my tongue, a tiny rebellion that sparks something feral in my chest. With a deep breath, I shrug off twenty-eight years of obedience and expectation. My fingers find my hair, tugging it loose from its sleek restraint until it tumbles free. The wind catches it instantly, tossing it around my face. It feels wild. Alive. Mine.

I keep walking, letting the city swallow me whole. The scent of coffee, grease, and questionable street food fills the air, wrapping around me in a heady mix. My feet ache inside my heels, each step a stabbing reminder that perfection comes with discomfort. But I'm too stubborn to stop. Until I see it.

A fluorescent-lit souvenir shop, glowing like sin and bad decisions. Rows of neon key chains, plastic snow globes, and oversized "I *heart* LONDON" T-shirts practically scream for attention. It's tacky, it's ridiculous, and I love it instantly.

I push open the door, greeted by a wall of colour and a cashier who looks like she took a bath in a rainbow —pink hair, green eyeliner, and a smirk that says 'I've seen worse'.

"Hey there! Can I help you with something?" she chirps, leaning on the counter.

"I need a pair of those." I kick off my heels and point to a pair of neon-orange flip-flops hanging from a rack. They're offensive to the eyes, their gaudiness almost mocking my sense of decorum.

She blinks, half amused, half scandalised. "Seriously? Aren't you a little overdressed for flip-flops?"

I grin, placing my shoes on the counter. "Let's just say I'm having an adventure tonight."

Her smirk grows into a laugh, shaking her head as she takes my heels like I've just handed her the crown jewels. "Alright, adventure girl. Enjoy your evening."

"Oh, I plan to," I reply, wiggling my toes under the plastic straps. They're ugly, absurdly bright, and feel like heaven.

Back outside, I'm grinning like an idiot. The pavement under my feet feels different—softer, freer, almost intimate. It's ridiculous how something so small can feel like a revolution.

With renewed energy, I wander further until the smell of greasy fried food hits my nose. My stomach growls, loud enough to turn heads. It's been almost twelve hours since I had Medard's scrambled eggs, and I never got to eat the pathetic little salad at the office. I'm so done eating like a rabbit!

I walk up to a fast-food joint, its sign promising salvation in the form of cholesterol. I stride inside, order a cheeseburger and walk out with my paper-wrapped trophy in hand. The first bite is hot, messy, glorious and... awful. Grease, salt, disappointment. I chew once, twice, grimace.

"Never again," I mutter, wiping my mouth with the back of my hand like the 'commoner' Father always told me not to become. I toss the sad excuse for rebellion into the nearest bin and keep moving.

Then I see it.

A quaint chocolatier standing proudly between two corner shops. In its window golden pralines shimmer like tiny treasures. I don't even think; my feet are already carrying me in. The air inside is thick with cocoa and temptation. Heaven. Pure, sinful heaven.

"I'll take one of each, please," I tell the woman behind the counter, flashing her a smile.

She packs two dozen truffles with delicate care, and I tap my phone to pay the small fortune it costs to soothe a broken spirit.

Outside again, I unwrap one and pop it into my mouth. The chocolate melts instantly, rich and velvety, the sweetness coating my tongue like a promise. This—this is what freedom should taste like.

I stroll through the streets, box in hand, praline after praline dissolving on my tongue. The city hums around me, alive with movement. I've walked these streets a thousand times before, always on autopilot—rushing, performing, surviving. Gareth's words spring to my mind. I truly was a foreigner in my own hometown. But tonight, I see it.

I see the vibrant life of this city as people rush to their destinations, tourists snap photos of iconic landmarks, and street performers showcase their talents. I see the double-decker buses gliding along the busy roads, weaving in and out of the constant movement. I smell the scent in the air—a concoction of curry, perfume and exhaust fumes. I hear Big Ben chiming faintly in the distance, marking time I no longer care about. The energy is palpable, a vivid reflection of this city's diverse spirit.

The life of London. It's messy, relentless, beautifully imperfect; and for the first time, I soak it all in.

I plop another truffle into my mouth, when the tightness of my skirt digs into my hips, a sharp reminder of the woman I usually am—polished, controlled, always composed to the point of suffocation. The kind of woman who crosses her legs properly and eats salad when she's starving for cake.

But not tonight. Tonight, I'm a rebel in flip-flops and bad decisions.

I let out a soft, defiant sigh and tug at the zipper of my skirt until it gives with a satisfying hiss. The relief is instant, scandalously good. My blouse pulls free as I drag it out, shirttails brushing my skin, my fingers still slick and sticky with chocolate. I don't even care that I'm leaving little smudges of indulgence against the crisp white fabric, like fingerprints of freedom.

Somewhere deep inside, the version of me who always has her lipstick perfect and her emotions caged gasps in horror. But I ignore her. She's boring. She's predictable.

Right now, I'm a mess and it feels delicious.

I meander past the antiques shop, and there it is—the ugly goose lamp, glowing like it's proud to be the ugliest thing ever created by human hands. Its ceramic feathers glint beneath the dim light, its beady eyes practically daring me to judge it.

And I do. Oh, I absolutely do.

But there's something about it that pulls at me. That lamp, hideous as it is, saw the first cracks in me. It stood proudly in Mrs Saunders office when I began to realise, that my father's affection came with a rulebook. That lamp had watched every moment of it. Every confession, every time I swallowed tears and smiled like the good little daughter he raised me to be.

And now it's here, my ugly little witness to the very beginning of my rebellion.

The bell above the shop door jingles as I step inside, and the musty scent of dust and time curls around me. The shopkeeper glances up from a newspaper, eyes narrowing as they track my path straight to the glowing monstrosity in the window. I crouch beside the lamp, running a fingertip over its ridiculous golden beak.

"You've seen me at my worst," I whisper under my breath. "Might as well come home with me."

"I'll take the goose," I declare aloud, straightening with a strange sort of pride. I hoist it from its perch like I'm reclaiming a part of myself—the quiet girl who once sat under its light and dared to question the man who taught her to be silent.

The shopkeeper blinks, clearly not used to this level of emotional commitment to poultry-themed decor. But I don't care.

I stride to the counter and tap my phone against the reader, not even glancing at the price. The machine beeps like it's stamping approval on my impulsive little act of rebellion.

Outside, dusk is rolling in. The pulse of nightlife begins to thrum around me. Bars hum with afternoon survivors—people knocking back what's left of the day's dignity. I sling the lamp under my arm and keep walking.

A shriek of glitter and laughter pulls me towards a glowing doorway.

"Bunny!" a voice calls, warm and theatrical.

A drag queen, radiant with sequins and charisma, beckons me over. She sizes me up—my clothes in disarray, my hair a tangled mess, and that grotesque goose cradled in my arms like some badly behaved pet.

"Rough day?"

"You could say that," I reply, trying for humour and missing by a mile.

"Come on in," she insists, waving me over with an exuberance that's hard to resist, "I'll get you a cocktail on the house."

I hesitate for just a moment, thoughts of my life, my responsibilities, creeping back in. But tonight is about breaking free, about shaking off the weight of expectation; and I am ready to embrace whatever this luminous city has to offer.

"Alright, I'm in!"

As I step into the dimly lit bar, the vibrant energy wraps around me like a warm embrace, its charm a stark contrast to my rough day.

"Brenda, baby!" the drag queen shouts, her eyes glinting with mischief. "Give this lovely girl a Blowjob, will you?"

My eyes widen in horror at her outrageous request.

"Oh bunny, relax! It's a cocktail." She snickers with a reassuring squeeze of my shoulder. "I can spot real titties from a mile away. Now, fly off little birdy."

She motions for me to go to the bar like I'm some fledgling about to be set free. I approach Brenda, the bartender in a sparkling green dress and a voluptuous ginger wig, who spins around with a wide grin.

"Sophie!" she exclaims, her brows furrowing with recognition.

"Ben? You—" My surprise is palpable as I take him in, plastered in make-up and fake eyelashes, but looking effortlessly gorgeous.

He bites his bottom lip, his eyes nervously darting around the bar so not to look at me.

"You look amazing!" I offer, hoping to ease the tension building between us.

He lets out a sharp exhale, "thank you, Soph."

We stare at each other, silence wrapping around us like a curious cocoon as my brain is trying to comprehend what my eyes are seeing.

"Come on, let's hear it," he finally breaks, cocking a brow.

"What?" My defences go up reflexively. I'm not sure which of me I'm protecting tonight—the professional, the wounded child, or the woman in flip-flops clutching a ceramic bird.

He laughs, that delighted, mischievous sound. "I know you've got questions. So, ask."

"How long have you been doing this? Does anyone else at the office know? Why didn't you tell me?" I fire the questions out as curiosity and embarrassment flush my cheeks.

"Since I was eighteen," Ben replies, with a hint of pride masking his vulnerability. "No one else knows; and you, little Missy, didn't tell me you're shagging our sinfully hot boss!"

His grin knocks the wind out of me.

I splutter, eyes big. "I knew it was more than professional admiration! So much for him being a *turner*."

My attempt at ridicule is feeble as he shrugs like it's obvious.

"Please, look at that fine specimen of a man," Ben says, eyes twinkling. "Who could resist those eyes of steel? Mh, those abs of steel."

That heart of steel.

I laugh, taking a sip of the cocktail he slides over to me. "Wait! What about your ex, Olivia? Or do you like both? You know what, never mind. I shouldn't have asked."

Ben waves a dismissive hand. "Relax, Soph. I'm gay. Olivia is actually Oliver."

We share a laugh, the air around us softening as he catches sight of my atrocious lamp resting on the barstool next to me.

"What on earth is that?"

"Honestly? I don't know. Something compelled me to buy that ugly thing. Maybe it was an act of rebellion or liberation. I don't know yet."

I gaze at the lamp, wondering if they made more of these or if this particular abomination was once Mrs Saunders', when I spot someone familiar.

"Ben, Brenda... if you'll excuse me for a moment," I say, feeling the excitement surging through me.

I stride towards a man who is very, very wrong for this bar, and yet somehow so entirely right for tonight's performance.

"Mr Ravens, what an absolute delight to find you here!" I call out, feigning enthusiasm to mask my surprise.

In an instant, he yanks his arm away from a drag queen who's wearing the same dress I wore the first time we met. It all clicks into place—he wasn't eyeing me up, he was ogling the frock.

"Miss Rosen, what are you—" he stammers, colour draining from his face.

"Say, is the Mrs close by? I'd love to say hello," I ask innocently, my inner mischief bubbling to the surface.

He grabs my arm, urgent and flustered. "Miss Rosen, I implore you to forget that you've seen me here tonight. I have a reputation to uphold."

The classic excuse, just like Father always said. I stifle an eye roll with a practised smile.

"Absolutely, Mr Ravens, Gerald, if you don't mind," I tease, a smile creeping onto my face.

Relief washes over him, but I press on. "And in return, you will let me represent your company."

"I can't." He snorts a laugh that's more sorrow than humour. "My wife won't allow it."

"Your wife said it's your company," I cut in, hand on his shoulder, my teasing grin softening to something almost kind. "You call the shots. If you can hide this, you can persuade her."

He steels himself. "Alright. I'll call Carter in the morning."

The diplomatic fallback. Predictable. Dull.

I wag a finger theatrically, tutting at him as though he's a misbehaving little boy. "You're going to call Buckman, not Carter."

"Why?" He's baffled but curious.

"Let's have a drink and chat. You've got to try the Blowjob. It's delicious!" I say, delivering the line with a theatrical wink that would make the drag queen proud.

With my hand guiding him towards the bar, I feel the delightful excitement of planning my small revolution.

Soon enough, I'll have them all by their balls.

But unlike Father and Medard, I won't squeeze unless I have to. Professional leverage, not personal destruction. I'm better than both of them.

Beggar

Medard

I spend the night tossing and turning in bed, like a man at war with himself and losing on every front. Sleep doesn't come—it's just me, my demons, and the ghost of her haunting every inch of my mind, every corner of my penthouse that suddenly feels too empty, too cold.

Sophie.

Every moment with her replays in torturous clarity, each memory a fresh wound. I see her walking into my office that first day, eyes blazing with fire and determination, daring to challenge me in a way no one ever had. I was a stone-faced, career-driven bastard then, every inch of me hardened into armour, sharpened by years of calculated moves and untouchable power. I built my life on control—my suit, my schedule, my heart. I was the most feared man in this building, and I wore that reputation like a crown.

And yet she slipped under my skin with a single look.

One glance from those eyes, and my fortress cracked. I wasn't the cut-throat lawyer I'd crafted myself to be; I was a fool. A complete and utter fool, jerked around by the pull of a woman whose allure I couldn't resist, whose depths I couldn't fathom no matter how hard I tried.

I knew I should have stayed away. I should have remained the arrogant prick whose reputation kept even the boldest at bay. That mask had protected me for years, a shield against the confusion and chaos she poured into my carefully controlled world. Yet every attempt to ignore her, every night I spent with other women trying to forget her, landed me back at square one. She was my forbidden fruit, and I was too weak to resist the taste.

She captivated me in a way no one ever had. Just thinking of her was like striking a match inside my chest, igniting a possessiveness I didn't recognise in myself.

I thought I was being her saviour, her protector, when really, I was just a control freak, a tyrant who demanded she feel the same electric connection tearing me apart. And when she finally did, when she reached for me and gave me everything, I did the unthinkable.

I shackled her with my control. Demolished her agency. Became the backstabber, the liar, the hypocrite she accused me of being.

And still, my beautiful lioness broke free.

The realisation hits me somewhere around three in the morning as I stare at the ceiling of my bedroom where she should be sleeping beside me: I've been giving her all the wrong things. Power. Position. Protection. When all she ever wanted was my presence. My honesty. My trust. My respect.

I've been an arrogant bastard, a tosser who thought he knew what was best for her.

I've been the executioner of her trust, the devil in a suit who used her tragic past as leverage. I've been everything she called me and worse—a narcissist, a lunatic, a psychopath who couldn't see past his own agenda.

But I can change. I have to change.

Because she's not just part of my life. She's my oxygen. And without her, I'm suffocating.

By the time dawn breaks over London, painting the sky in shades of pink and gold, I have a plan. It's not much—Christ knows I'm operating on desperation and caffeine at this point—but it's something.

I shower, dress in my best suit like I'm preparing for the most important case of my career, and head to the office with a single piece of paper tucked into my jacket pocket.

My letter of resignation.

If being her boss is the issue, then I'll remove that barrier. I'll step down, hand the firm over to Buckman, do whatever it takes.

I don't want the power or the prestige if I can't have her.

The stone-faced, career-driven bastard I used to be would never have considered this, but that man is dead. She killed him the moment she walked into my life.

The lift doors open on my floor, and my heart is hammering like I'm about to walk into battle. Each stride towards her office feels heavier, my breath dragging like a man at the gallows. I'm teetering on the edge of hope when Buckman's voice cuts through my thoughts.

"She just left," he says flatly, not even looking up from his coffee.

The words slice through me, sharp and final.

"Where to?" My voice strains, desperation seeping through as my hand tightens around the envelope in my pocket like it's salvation itself.

"Home, possibly," he shrugs with infuriating nonchalance, and a knot tightens in my stomach, panic clawing its way up my throat. "If you hurry, you might catch—"

I don't let him finish. I turn on my heel and dart around him, my feet already propelling me towards her, towards my last chance. Buckman's chuckle echoes through the corridor behind me, but I'm already pushing through the door into the stairwell, taking the stairs two at a time because waiting for the lift would cost me precious seconds I don't have.

I fly into the lobby just in time to see her slip through the glass doors, her silhouette framed by the morning sunlight like she's some ethereal angel escaping my grasp. My angel. My salvation.

"Wait!" I shout, the word tearing from my throat.

The moment freezes in time. She turns, surprise flickering in those deep-set eyes I've memorised in excruciating detail, caution mixing with something that feels like a stray bullet to my chest.

"Sophie, wait!" The words tear from me as I close the distance between us. "I've been up all night trying to find the right words, and I'm still not sure I have them, but I need you to hear this."

She stops on the pavement and the fact that she's even listening feels like a small miracle I don't deserve.

"I'm sorry," I say, and my voice cracks on the words. "So fucking sorry. I shouldn't have blackmailed your father or suspended you without giving you a chance to explain. I should have trusted you from the start. I should have told you the second Buckman told me you were innocent. I've fucked up in so many ways I've lost count."

Her gaze sharpens, dissecting me with that mixture of vulnerability and guardedness that makes my heart ache.

"You said you no longer want to work under me," I continue, pulling the envelope from my pocket with shaking hands. "So, I'm removing that obstacle."

I thrust the letter towards her like it's a peace offering, like it has the power to fix what's splintering between us.

"This is my letter of resignation," I say, my voice steady despite the chaos in my head, despite the fact that I'm offering to destroy everything I've built. "If me being your boss is the issue, then I'm not your boss anymore. I'll step down today. Right now. All that matters is having you in my life, Sophie. However you'll have me."

She stares at the envelope in my hand, not taking it, and confusion clouds her beautiful face.

"Medard—"

"I know I've been an idiot," I interrupt, because if I stop talking, I might lose my nerve. "A complete and utter moron who thought he could control everything, including you. I've been a sadistic bastard who used your pain as leverage. But I'm trying to be better. I'm trying to be the man you deserve."

The words hang in the air between us, raw and exposed, and I watch her eyes widen slightly at the confession.

"Marry me or don't marry me. Have one child with me, or two, or five... or none. Be a career woman and travel the world, or stay home. Hell, do both if you want. The choice is yours—and I'll be whatever you need. All I'm asking is to be by your side in whatever capacity you'll allow."

She looks down at the letter, then back up at me, and something shifts in her expression—something that looks almost like pity, which is somehow worse than anger.

"I can't," she says softly, pain surfacing in her voice like a wound reopening.

"Sophie, please—"

"I've already taken care of it," she says, and there's a strange calmness in her voice now that makes my stomach drop. "Turn around."

I do, slowly, confused, and that's when I see it.

The sign above the building entrance, gleaming in the morning sun.

Carter & Rosen.

"What have you done?" I gasp, my heart stuttering in my chest.

"Buckman signed over his shares to me in exchange for the Windpower account," she says, her voice steady now, resolute. "My father is off the hook, and my past is where it belongs: in the past. We're partners now, Medard. Equal partners. You're not my boss anymore."

Her words floor me, and despite everything, despite the panic clawing at my chest, I can't help but laugh. She's fiercer, stronger, more savvy than I ever gave her credit for. She's taken my power play and turned it on its head, restructured the entire firm while I was busy having a breakdown. I should be furious. I should be threatened by this coup.

Instead, pride rises inside me. She's incredible.

"Did you just hear what I said?" she asks, searching my face.

"Oh, I did. Loud and clear," I reply, my heart racing as I step closer. "But it doesn't change a thing. If anything, it makes me want you more. You're brilliant, Sophie. Absolutely fucking brilliant, and I'm so goddamn proud of you."

I reach for her, my hands finding her face, cradling her cheeks like she's something precious I'm terrified of losing.

"Please," I whisper, all my pride stripped away, leaving only raw desperation. "Please, just have me. I know I've been an arrogant prick who thought he knew better. But I lo—"

"Don't!" she interrupts sharply while stepping back, breaking my grasp.

"I'm sorry, Medard," she says, and her voice is sad but resolute, final in a way that makes my blood run cold. "I can't do this. After everything you and my father put me through, I need time to find myself. I'm taking a sabbatical."

The words land like a bomb, destroying what's left of my composure.

"Sophie, please don't go," I beg, and I don't care that I sound pathetic. "I'll give you space, I'll give you time, I'll give you whatever you need—just don't leave. Not like this."

"I'm sorry," she repeats, and there are tears in her eyes now that mirror my own. "This is over."

She turns and walks away from me, from us, and each step echoes painfully in my heart like a death knell.

My legs give out, and I sink to my knees right there on the pavement, not caring who sees me falling apart. My heart explodes into a million pieces, and all I can do is watch her retreating form blur through my tears.

I've lost her.

I've lost the only thing that ever mattered.

My phone buzzes in my pocket, but I can barely feel it through the numbness spreading through my body. With shaking hands, I pull it out and somehow manage to dial Alex's number.

"Oh man, I'm glad you're calling," he says after a couple of rings, his voice bright and oblivious. "I think I've just made a huge mistake. I wasn't even thinking when—"

"Alex." My voice cracks, the sobs breaking through despite my best efforts to hold them back.

"Qué pasó? What happened? Talk to me!" His concern is immediate, cutting through whatever he was about to say.

My heart feels shredded, its shrapnel cutting me from the inside. I clutch the phone tight, my free hand tangled in my hair, pulling hard as if pain might dull the agony tearing me apart.

"I can't do this anymore," I cry, not caring who hears, not caring that I'm on my knees on a public street. "It hurts too much. I've lost her, Alex. I've lost her and I don't know how to get her back."

"Tell me where you are," Alex's voice is sharp now, commanding. "I'm heading over right now. Don't move, hermano. Just stay where you are."

Roadblock

Sophie

One month later.

Panic grips me. I hastily clasp my clothes, flee from his penthouse and race down the corridor to the lift. I watch the indicator slowly move up. Level six, nine more levels to go. My foot taps nervously as I glance over my shoulder to his open door. He emerges clad in nothing but boxers and strides towards me with a slow, deliberate pace; his gaze fixed on mine. Desperately, I press the lift button again, hoping for a faster arrival. But he reaches me before the doors open, leaning casually against the frame as he studies my face in silence. I clutch my belongings tightly, the tension between us palpable. Finally, the doors slide open with a sharp ping, but I'm rooted to the spot, unsure of what to do next.

"You want to run, so run." He gestures towards the lift.

I hesitantly take a step forward, his words echoing in my mind.

"But you and I both know," he murmurs, his eyes locking with mine, "whichever direction you take, you will always end up in the exact same place."

Is he right? Have I been trying to escape something that is already a part of me? Despite countless chances to resist him, I have allowed him to consume me, to take control. I let him dig his claws into me. I let him feast on me and I loved every moment of it.

I glance towards his front door before meeting his intense gaze once more.

"The lion's den," I whisper.

His expression darkens, a deep growl rumbles in his chest.

"Run!" he commands, his eyes burning with passion.

Without hesitation, I drop my clothes and race towards his penthouse, the thrill of his pursuit igniting a fire within me. He slams into my back, his arms circling my waist. His hand dips into my knickers, cupping my pussy, teasing my clit in the most delicious way. His mouth finds my neck and his teeth sink into my tender flesh. My body arches into him, relishing his burning touch. He frantically rips my knickers down, scratching my thighs in the process, and then without warning, he thrusts into me.

I cry out, his forceful intrusion the relief I've been silently craving for far too long. He slams into me with such vigour my hands slide across the worktop of the kitchen island, unable to find purchase. But then his thrusts, erratic and toe-curling, suddenly stop. Pulling out of me, he grabs my arm and spins me around. I crash into his solid chest but he holds me steady.
His hand flies up to my throat, squeezing it hard enough to stop my breath. But I'm not scared anymore. I lean into his hold, daring him to do his worst.
"I'm done running," I gasp, before everything goes black.

"Sophie!" A voice pierces through the fading remnants of my dream, shattering the delicate illusion of him.

I thrash, limbs tangled like a chaotic mess in a sea of sheets.

"Wake up!" The voice cuts through the air again, firm and insistent, shaking me by the shoulders.

In an instant, I blink awake, the vivid images of the dream swallowed by the blinding light streaming into the room.

"Are you okay? You had a bad dream again," he says, his tone warm and kind, wrapping around me in comfort.

I roll onto my side, aligning myself with him on the enormous bed. His smile is a balm, and with a gentle touch, he brushes a stray strand of hair behind my ear.

"You're a true friend, Gareth." The words slip out, and I watch amusement dance in his eyes.

His chuckle resonates through the room, soothing the jagged edges of my heart.

"I know! Not only did I let you crash my Gibraltar-trip, I even accompanied you on countless shopping trips," he quips, a teasing glint in his eyes.

"Forgive me if I needed a break from looking at rocks," I laugh, hurling a pillow his way.

His expression shifts from disbelief to a broad grin before he launches into a round of tickles. Laughter echoes around us, dispelling the last remnants of sorrow.

"Stop!" I gasp between giggles, hands flailing in mock protest. "I take it back! I love rocks!"

"Good girl!" His mocking praise pierces the air as he finally retreats, plopping back onto his hunches.

For four weeks now, we've been performing this tightrope

act. By day, we're exploring the landscapes and attractions of Gibraltar, soaking in its calming allure. By night, he pulls me away from the clutches of my troubling dreams. He never pries. He doesn't have to, as I often call out his name when he infiltrates my subconsciousness again.

It feels like a never-ending game of push and pull.

Spending time away from London, and everyone in it, has given me a chance to discover who I am, what I like and what I've clearly forced on myself all these years, just to please others. Yet, my feelings for Medard linger relentlessly, unwilling to accept that I had to put myself first.

"What if I shag you?" Gareth's unexpected question jolts me from my thoughts, making my jaw drop.

"Pardon? Where did that come from?"

He shrugs off my surprise and hops out of bed, slipping into a pair of shorts.

"You know how the saying goes: the best way to get over someone is to get under someone else. It's been weeks and you're clearly still pining for him. Maybe my magic cock could finally break the spell he has on you," he teases, a cheeky wink accompanying his words.

I can't suppress the laughter erupting from deep within me as I swing my legs over the side of the bed, adjusting my pyjama bottoms and collecting my clothes for the day.

"You would do that for me? Sacrificing your involuntary celibacy for the greater course of mending my broken heart?" I swoon dramatically, placing my hand over my chest in mock disbelief.

He shakes his head, chuckling as he pulls on a t-shirt.

"First off, it's not involuntary; I choose to spend my time with you. Secondly, I absolutely would. You've become a really good friend, and I want you to be happy—whether that means dusting your little cooch or shoving you on the next flight to London."

He steps closer, his presence disarming in that quiet, steady way only Gareth can manage. His hands find mine, warm, grounding, and he brings them to his lips, pressing a soft kiss to my knuckles. The gesture is gentle, almost reverent, and it makes something fragile stir in my chest.

"I think this trip has been really good for you," he says, his voice low and sincere. "You've finally let go of your restraints.

You're not performing anymore, Soph. You're just... you. Unapologetically you. But now," his eyes flicker with something almost apologetic, "it's time to face the truth."

My throat tightens. "And what truth is that?" I ask, though dread already curls in my stomach, heavy and molten.

"Life can be steered," he starts, in that annoyingly philosophical tone he gets when he's about to sound like a fortune cookie. "But sometimes you hit a roadblock."

I blink at him. "Gareth, I'm glad you're moving to the Drug Unit. You've clearly spent too long in Roads Policing." My brow furrows. "Roadblock, what does that even mean?"

He exhales a long-suffering sigh, dragging a hand along his neck before his arms reach for me again, catching my hands like I might try to make a run for it.

"Billy... Medard, is your roadblock," he says finally, with all the gravitas of a man dropping the world's most inconvenient truth. "He's standing right in the middle of your heart, Soph. Until you face him, you're stuck. Spinning your wheels on the same stretch of emotional tarmac."

I scoff, because it's either that or scream.

"What if I just... take another route?" I ask, doing my best impression of casual indifference, even though we both know I'm one wrong word away from spiralling.

He smirks, that knowing look in his eyes.

"There is no other route, Soph. One life, one road. And as smug, arrogant, and emotionally constipated as that man might be," he pauses, giving me a pointed look, "he's part of it. He's part of you."

I want to argue, to tell him he's wrong, that Medard is nothing more than a detour I took in a moment of weakness. But the truth sits between us, undeniable and heavy. Because deep down, I know Gareth's right.

But Medard isn't just a roadblock.

He's the bloody road itself.

The one, I can't stop driving down, no matter how many warning signs I pass.

Gentle Heart

Medard

"Right in that corner over there would be the perfect place for it," Dad points at the empty space at the end of the patio with his cigar, the smoke curling into the cold morning air. "13ft x 5ft is all they need, and with the right filtration system it'll be easy to maintain."

He puffs contentedly before letting the ash fall into Mum's prized roses.

The morning sun no longer holds any warmth, hinting that autumn has finally surrendered to winter's approach. I pull up the lapel of my coat to shield my neck from the cold wind and watch the coloured leaves on the grass take flight.

"Didn't Mum say she wanted to plant another rose bush in that corner?" I ask with a quirked brow, knowing full well that Mum would never agree to have a pond in their garden.

There's something about fish that she doesn't like the look of—she says they have dead eyes, which is ironic considering that's exactly how I feel these days.

"She did," he points his cigar at me like he's making a closing argument, "but that corner is too dark. So now I can build my pond."

"Not this again!" I hear Mum holler behind me before she steps out onto the patio with a tray in hand, her expression somewhere between exasperation and fond amusement.

The day Sophie left—the day she walked away from me on that pavement and took my heart with her—Alex brought me up here to my parents' house in the countryside. I ended up staying the entire week, working from my old childhood bedroom during the day like some kind of pathetic teenager nursing his first heartbreak, and catching up with my parents in the evenings. That was four weeks ago, and since then I've spent every weekend here, sitting out in the garden with Dad when he has his cigar, trying to figure out how the successful lawyer became such a spectacular failure at the one thing that actually mattered.

At first, I thought I was seeking out the comfort of my parents' love after I had realised and lost my love for Sophie in the same breath. But after a while it felt therapeutic to come back to my roots, to remember who I was before I became the bastard who thought control was the same as caring.

When I spoke to Alex that night—the night I called him from my knees on the pavement—he told me that I had changed over the years, hardened into something he didn't recognise. So maybe coming here has been a way of helping me find some of that old version of me. The one, who wasn't the accused in his own relationship trial.

I am the accused, and I've been found guilty. *The executioner has become the executed*—that's how my therapist phrased it. And there's a poetic justice in that which would be almost funny if it didn't hurt so fucking much.

Still, the pain I feel, the grief, it pales in comparison to the hurt I inflicted on Sophie.

Christ, some of the things I told the therapist were so bad, he immediately decided to see me twice a week.

Now, that's an achievement I'll never be proud of.

"I've told your dad that it's not that simple to build a pond for koi fish," Mum explains while placing a pot of tea on the table before taking a seat next to me, her movements practised and soothing. "The pond needs to be at least 6ft deep, and we can't dig that deep because of the concrete foundation underneath."

"We'll just get rid of the concrete," Dad waves off her concerns with typical male bravado, holding his cup out as Mum refills our drinks with a long-suffering sigh.

I smile behind the collar of my coat at his typical approach. There are no hurdles for him—if something gets in his way, he simply bulldozes over it.

A trait, I've come to realise with painful clarity, I inherited from him. The same trait that made me think I could force Sophie into accepting my vision of our future without considering what she actually wanted.

Mum pinches the bridge of her nose as she, no doubt, has already had this conversation with him plenty of times before.

"Don't be daft, Alfred! I've told you we would have to dig up the patio slabs which will disturb the roots of the rose bushes. So, we're not having this pond."

He nods in acceptance, but then I see him worrying his lip as his eyes try to anchor on a different spot in the garden, already planning his next angle of attack.

"So, when's the digger coming?" I ask, trying to suppress a smile because at least someone's romantic dreams aren't completely dead.

His eyes snap to me with the look of a man caught red-handed. Mum gasps as she too sees the guilt written all over his face.

"Couple of weeks," he admits with forced nonchalance that fools absolutely no one.

"Alfred!"

I burst into laughter at their customary dynamic, the sound surprising even me because I hadn't realised how much I'd been missing this—this normal, ordinary display of love and negotiation and compromise. The things I never learnt to do with Sophie.

"Can't blame me for trying, Eleanor," Dad laughs, completely unrepentant. "But I will cancel it tomorrow morning."

Mum doesn't look convinced, but she still nods, and I watch them with a pang of envy because they've figured out what I couldn't.

We all fall silent, enjoying the scenery before us. Despite the cold temperatures and the trees being bare of any leaves now, their garden still looks like a peaceful sanctuary amidst the calm countryside. They've truly built a home for themselves and their kids to find comfort in. A place where even the biggest asshole can come to lick his wounds. It's a place I now realise I always wanted to build for myself and my family.

But that ship has sailed, hasn't it? I scared Sophie off with my controlling ways, trying to force something on her that she only could have given to me willingly. I was the groom at a wedding that will never happen, the husband she'll never have, the stalker she's running from.

I'm just a loser. A madman. A hypocrite who preached trust while lying to her face.

"She'll come back," Mum's voice pierces through the quiet and my spiralling thoughts.

"I know she will," I deadpan, blowing into the steaming hot cup of tea that burns my tongue. "She has a firm to run now... with me."

I try to swallow the lump in my throat that's become a permanent fixture over the past four weeks. Inevitably, I'll have to face her again when her sabbatical ends, and with it my broken heart that hasn't learnt how to function in her absence.

"I meant she'll come back to you," Mum says with a warmth in her voice that briefly soothes the raw wound in my chest.

I look over at her, searching her face for the tiniest shred of hope that Sophie would forgive and take me back, that I haven't completely destroyed the best thing that ever happened to me.

"What makes you think that? I was horrible to her," I almost whisper, remembering the day I dropped her off after Theo's and Lisa's wedding rehearsal.

"I'm sure you were," she deadpans to my surprise, no sugar-coating, no maternal blind spots.

Although I really was horrible—a complete tosser, actually—I didn't expect my Mum to agree to it so easily.

"Whose side are you on?"

"Yours darling, always yours," she squeezes my knee in a reassuring gesture that makes my throat tighten. "But as your mother I will never shy away from telling you the truth, and the truth is, you have controlled your heart for far too long."

I let her words sink in, settle into the hollowed-out space where my confidence used to live. She's right, of course. I have controlled my heart over the years, but I did so to protect it from the heartbreak I kept experiencing. It was a mechanism to protect myself after watching what vulnerability did to people. But in protecting myself, I became the very thing I feared—someone who inflicted that pain on someone else. On Sophie.

I hurt her so much that even when I gave up everything to win her back, it wasn't enough. Nothing I have is enough. Because what she needs isn't my resignation or my shares or my power. What she needs is time to heal from the damage I've inflicted, time to become whole again without me controlling every aspect of her life.

"You're a lot like your father, you know?" Mum continues, her voice gentle but unflinching.

Dad grunts in agreement, though I'm not sure if he's happy about it or not, and honestly neither am I at this point.

"You both have a very tough shell. So tough, most people think you're lacking any warmth or empathy. But underneath that hard shell, you're very vulnerable. I'd say more so than most."

I silently agree with her, still feeling the raw pain of Sophie's breakup as though it happened yesterday instead of four weeks ago. Every morning, I wake up and for a split second I forget she's gone, and then reality crashes over me like I've been kicked in the balls.

"Then isn't it understandable that I chose to control my heart?" I whisper more to myself than to her, trying to justify the unjustifiable.

Mum leans over and gently cups my cheek in her warm hand. It's a gesture I thought for a long time I didn't need anymore, that I'd outgrown, but now I embrace it like the lifeline it is.

"That's the problem, darling. The heart cannot be controlled. Your head kept telling you that you had to mould Sophie into someone she simply isn't, while your heart kept yearning for her exactly as she is."

The truth of it hits me square in the chest, and I have to look away.

"All I ever wanted was to have a relationship like you both have," I admit in this moment of truths, my voice rough with emotion I can't quite contain. "A partnership built on love and trust that could weather anything. But I fucked it up spectacularly, didn't I?"

"Son, we're not perfect, by a long stretch," Dad speaks up, setting down his cigar with uncharacteristic seriousness. "But what we have works for us because we learnt to compromise."

"What your father is trying to say," Mum translates with the patience of decades, "is that the kind of relationship you're describing doesn't exist without work. Sometimes, you do get hurt because people make mistakes—and when it's someone you love, it can hurt particularly bad. But their job isn't to shelter you from that pain, but to mend it together."

I nod while trying to wrap my mind around her advice, trying to understand how I got it so catastrophically wrong. Sophie is the first woman I've wholeheartedly fallen in love with—truly, completely, devastatingly in love with. Despite all my efforts to convince myself that she would hurt me like Lisa and all my previous ex-girlfriends did, I still wanted her. I still knew she could mend my fragile heart, so I forced her into my embrace and ignored her worries clawing at my skin, dismissed her needs as obstacles to overcome rather than truths to honour.

"Have you heard from Theo?" Dad's question pulls me from my

thoughts, probably intentionally.

I nod, rolling my shoulders to throw off the heavy weight of sadness that's threatening to pull me under again. "They're still enjoying their honeymoon. They left Paris yesterday for Verona."

"How lovely," Mum says with a warm smile that reaches her eyes. "I'm so happy to see you boys finally getting along again."

I think back to my first weekend back home after Sophie left, when Theo stopped by on his way to play squash. His mouth dropped in disbelief—first at seeing me at our parents' house without the necessity of a family event, and secondly when I asked if I could join him.

We played again the following weekend, and I realised that I actually like the man he's become. Last weekend was his and Lisa's wedding, and to my own surprise, I found myself standing by his side as his best man after the original choice fell through. Mum was overjoyed and kept telling me how proud she is of my personal growth, though it felt hollow because none of it has filled the void that Sophie left behind.

Alex was the only one who wasn't impressed at seeing me take on best man duties at the last minute. He saw his claim on being best man at my wedding threatened by Theo's sudden reappearance in my life. I told him with Sophie gone, there won't be a wedding in my cards. She's the only woman I ever wanted to spend the rest of my life with.

There won't be another woman like her. I know it deep down in my bones with a certainty that's almost frightening, but Alex is adamant that I'll end up in front of the altar eventually.

I want to fool myself into believing that my romance-stricken friend has some magic power that sees me ending up with Sophie,

that this is all just a temporary setback in our epic love story. The reality of it though is that Alex is simply high on oxytocin and grateful for my help in getting his girl back, projecting his happiness onto my misery.

But I'm happy for him. I'm happy for Theo and Lisa.

I'm happy, I'm happy, I'm happy.

I repeat the words like a mantra until I can almost believe them, until the lie tastes less bitter on my tongue.

Partner

Sophie

Carter & Rosen.

I look up at the sleek black sign mounted to the skyscraper, the letters gleaming in the morning light. My name, right there on the door. And I put it there.

My mouth splits into a wide grin, matching the pride swelling in my chest like a champagne bottle about to pop. It took me a few unconventional methods to achieve this goal, and perhaps a minor emotional breakdown followed by a sabbatical in Gibraltar, but at the end of the day I like to tell myself I only played as dirty as the men in my life always have.

The corporate world is cut-throat, ruthless, and painfully unforgiving—but if you've got enough bite, you don't have to be a pawn in this game. You can become the player. And then it's a thrilling, adrenaline-soaked rush that makes every sacrifice worth it.

Yesterday afternoon, Gareth really did shove me on a flight back to London despite my protests. I told him that I had so much more to figure out about myself, my life, my questionable decision-making skills. But he was adamant that anything left undiscovered, I'd only find once I cleared things up with Medard.

He wasn't wrong there.

By the time I arrived home, jet-lagged and emotionally wrung out, I was battling with myself not to head straight over to his place. But this could be a new beginning for both of us. Especially now that we're equals—partners in every sense of the word. So, I thought it best to first meet on neutral ground, on professional territory where I can maintain some semblance of control.

I push through the towering glass double doors and halt for a moment as the memory of seeing Medard standing on that landing on his first day flits through my mind, vivid and sharp. So much has happened in such a short amount of time that I still struggle to wrap my head around it. The woman who walked through these doors that day barely resembles the one standing here now.

I cross the lobby with purpose. Some colleagues do a double-take as they clock me, recognition dawning followed by something that might be respect. Others nod in silent greeting. I suppose putting your name on the door changes the perception of your peers. Funny how a sign can do what years of excellent work sometimes can't.

The lift doors ping open, and Mrs Henderson steps out looking exactly as impassive as always.

"Miss Rosen, you're back," she notes, greeting me with her trademark neutral expression. "Any chance I could get feedback on that CRA? I'd really like to get it off my desk before I retire."

"No, sorry," I say with a smile as we switch places, me stepping into the lift as she exits. "Still under review."

The lift doors begin to close, but before Mrs Henderson vanishes behind the metal barrier, she nods with a smile flickering across her usually stern face. Progress.

I walk down the corridor, noticing a few colleagues glancing up from their work to offer courteous nods before resuming whatever they're doing. I make my way towards my office, briefly befuddled that Millie's desk looks different—rearranged somehow—but when I step into what I think is my office and Ben straightens in his chair, I realise my error.

Right. I requested to be moved into Buckman's old office.

"Soph!" Ben cheers while trying to discreetly wipe what looks like foundation off the back of his hand. "Or should I say bombshell? You look amazing!"

He openly assesses me as he practically bounces over, taking in my casual outfit with appreciation. I can't believe how much I've missed this dramatic little gossip. I pull him into a hug, and he briefly squeals like an excited teenager.

How I never clocked his feminine side before is beyond me. Now that I know he likes to dress in drag, the signs are so blatantly obvious it's almost comical.

"Thanks, Ben. I missed you too. How are things?" I squeeze his arm for emphasis before he takes his seat behind the desk again, suddenly clearing his throat and schooling his features into something more professional.

"Good. No accounts lost. Windpower's happy," he mumbles while his eyes aimlessly dart around the room.

"Alright," I drawl, moving closer and perching on the edge of his desk. "Are we good? Because you're being weird."

"Yes," he stammers, too quickly, too nervously, propping his chin on his palm like he's posing for a portrait. "Of course we're good."

Great.

Of course he's nervous.

I'm basically his boss now. I didn't even think about how my promotion would affect our relationship, our friendship. I'm starting to understand how Medard must have felt all this time, that impossible balance between authority and connection.

I suppose I'll have to figure out what kind of boss I want to be. I certainly don't want to be like Father—distant, demanding, impossible to please.

"Stop this nonsense," I say to Ben, my tone flat but determined. "Don't be a stranger now just because there's a new sign on the wall. I'm still me."

He eyes me warily for a beat, suspicion and hope warring on his features, but then he lets out a massive huff.

"Thank fuck! Because I'm bursting to tell you everything that went down while you were gone, like Amina resigning after she had a mental breakdown at the office."

"And I can't wait to hear it," I say, standing and heading towards the door. "But first, there are a few people I need to talk to."

"You mean Carter?" he asks cautiously, his voice dropping.

Just hearing his name makes my stomach flutter with anticipation and dread. I don't know how he'll react to seeing me, but whatever reaction it may be, it'll be better than the unknown. Better than spending another night wondering.

"For one," I respond, closing the door behind me and heading towards my actual office.

"Miss Rosen, you're back!" Millie jumps from her chair, her excitement palpable as she darts around her desk to greet me like I'm some sort of celebrity.

"And you look different too! You've got your hair down and—are those jeans and loafers?"

I can't help but chuckle at her infectious enthusiasm, the kind that lights up a room and makes you feel like maybe the world isn't such a terrible place.

Who knew an over-sized dress shirt paired with cropped jeans and loafers could be so effortlessly chic? Gibraltar taught me that comfort and professionalism aren't mutually exclusive.

"Well, at least we know now that your glasses prescription is accurate," I muse while pulling her in for a hug, feeling her surprised gasp against my shoulder.

But then she embraces me back, her squeeze warm and genuine, like a promise of brighter days ahead.

"Has everything been all right while I was gone?"

She follows me into my office, and relief washes over me at seeing my instructions have been followed. Buckman's heavy, oppressive furniture has been replaced with my own—lighter, more modern, actually reflective of who I am.

"Yes, all good," she confirms with a nervous nudge to her glasses. "Mr Reynolds has been working tirelessly on the Windpower account. I checked in with him just yesterday, and he says they're very happy. Your father called about three hundred and eighty-two times—" she pauses for emphasis, "—but it's been quiet for the past four days. So, I believe he's finally given up."

"Good," I say, then notice something on my desk that doesn't belong. "What's this?"

A vase sits there holding a sad bunch of wilted gladioli, droopy and forlorn, like they've given up on life.

"They were delivered the week after you left. I didn't want to throw them out without you knowing about them."

I pluck the small card nestled among the wilting stems and flick it open, my heart doing something complicated in my chest.

> I always knew your name belongs on the door.
> Congratulations, Sophie!
> I'm proud of you.
> C.H.

Harman.

A smile creeps onto my face as I take in the brown-speckled petals. Gladiolus—a symbol of loyalty. Of course he'd know that. Of course he'd choose these.

"He's asked about you," Millie says, catching my attention. I look at her over my shoulder, my brow knitting in confusion. "Mr Carter, I mean. A few times, he's asked if I knew how you were doing. He pulls really long shifts at the office now. Always seems to be the first one in and the last one out."

Something in my chest tightens. "Does he still intimidate you?"

She shakes her head, a small frown crossing her features. "No, not at all. He's actually been quite nice to all of us. Patient, even."

"That's good," I smile, a glimmer of hope igniting within me as I turn towards the corridor. "I should probably say hi to him."

As I step down the short corridor, my palms suddenly grow clammy. I wipe them on my thighs, trying to dispel the tension as I release a slow, deliberate exhale that does absolutely nothing to calm my racing heart.

I haven't seen him since I walked away outside this building. That was over a month ago. The memory of the hurt in his eyes still haunts me, plays on repeat during quiet moments.

Though my voice was steady that day and my posture resolute, I too was consumed with pain. But time has passed since then, and the ache has morphed into an acceptance of mistakes—each one a lesson I can't erase, can't undo, can only learn from.

All that remains is the desperate need for my heart to spark to life again.

I just hope he feels the same.

"Good morning, partner!" I stride into his office with what I hope is a casual air, but beneath the surface I'm so anxious I want to scratch my thighs bloody.

He looks up from his paperwork, surprise evident on his handsome features—those sharp angles, those grey eyes that see too much.

"Sophie. I didn't expect you." His voice carries a fragility I've never heard before, tinged with something electric that sends a thrill up my spine.

I take a few steps closer, noting how he rounds the desk, his tall frame commanding yet somehow inviting. There's a rawness to him I haven't seen before. A neatly trimmed full beard now frames his face with rugged appeal, making him look older, more seasoned, like he's been through something and survived it.

His hair is untamed, curling slightly at the tips, as if he's just rolled out of bed. I can't help but drink in the sight of him, cataloguing every change, every detail.

"You look healthy. Happy." His throat works as he speaks, his hands slipping into the pockets of his suit—his typical shield against whatever this moment might unleash.

He studies me with that intense focus I remember so well, eyes flicking over my face—free from the usual armour of lipstick—to my hair cascading loose around my shoulders. Then they slide lower in an undeniable assessment of the fifteen pounds I've gained under the sun of Gibraltar.

"Healthy and happy," he repeats, and the words drape over me like soft ripples at the edge of the shore.

"You look more mature. It suits you," I say with a smile, relishing this unexpected moment of vulnerability from him.

He chuckles, though the smile doesn't quite reach those captivating silver eyes. He brushes his fingers over his beard thoughtfully, then looks past me as if the room's décor has suddenly become fascinating.

The atmosphere around him feels different somehow. Every interaction between us has always been charged with sexual tension, anger, or intimidation—that crackling electricity that made the air feel alive. But now there's just a serenity that envelops the space, calm and settled.

I kept wondering how I would feel once I was in the same room with him again. I expected a riot of emotions—hurt and anger, joy and longing, maybe even indifference.

But all I feel is comfort. The kind that feels like finally coming home.

"Are you happy?" His gaze snaps back to mine, sincere and probing, like my answer actually matters to him.

"Actually, yes. I really am." The conviction in my voice surprises even me, but the smile is genuine. I am happy, in ways I never thought possible.

He studies me, those intense eyes trying to decipher the truths hidden behind my words, to read what I'm not saying.

"Have you met someone?" The way he phrases it is low, hesitant, like he's afraid of the answer but needs to know anyway.

It prompts a laugh from deep inside me, taking me straight back to our very first encounter when he asked me the exact same thing.

"I have," I admit, a warm rush of excitement fluttering in my belly like a thousand butterflies taking flight. "It's still early days, but he's very handsome and caring in his own twisted and complicated way. A bit too cocky for his own good, though."

The disappointment flickers across his face—quick but palpable, like a shadow passing over the sun.

"I'm happy for you," he says, though the heaviness in his voice betrays him.

The statement compels me to close the distance between us, but I keep myself at arm's length—far enough away to think clearly, to maintain perspective.

If I've learnt anything from the mess, we found ourselves in over a month ago, it's that we need to take things slow. Build a foundation instead of just diving right back in where we left things in tatters.

"Thank you. I hope everything was all right while I was gone?"

"Yes, all good," he forces a smile, but the fist clenched at his side gives him away completely.

He walks back to his desk with measured steps and shuffles through a pile of paperwork until he eventually exhales sharply and takes a seat. He crosses his legs in that way he always does—right ankle propped on left knee, index finger brushing along his lower lip in that gesture I've seen a hundred times.

"We should discuss how we're going to co-lead from now on," he says, his voice thick. "I have a few meetings booked already for today, but I can free up a couple of hours in the afternoon."

His gaze snaps up to mine for just a fraction of a second before returning to the papers in front of him.

"That would be good," I say, taking slow steps backward towards the door. "But it'll have to wait until next week. I thought with it being Thursday, I'd use the rest of the week to settle back in at home. Unpack. Breathe."

He nods briefly before resigning himself to the documents in front of him, like they're suddenly the most important thing in the world.

"Oh, and Carter?" I say as I reach the door, drawing his attention back to me.

His head lifts, those grey eyes finding mine.

"If you'd like, I thought you could take me on our first date tomorrow evening."

His mouth splits into a wide grin, showcasing those beautiful dimples I've missed more than I care to admit.

"I would love nothing more."

"Good," I nod with a smile of my own, feeling warmth spread

through my chest. "Just tell me where and when."

"Eight o'clock, my place," he fires back before I've even pushed the door handle down, his response immediate and certain.

I turn back, pointing a warning finger at him. "No sex!"

My warning bounces off him as he grins with a mischievous glint in his eyes that makes my stomach flip.

"We'll see about that," he says, smugness dripping off his handsome features like honey.

I bite my lower lip to stop myself from grinning like an idiot, step out of his office, lean back against the closed door, and let myself grin like the Cheshire Cat anyway.

"Yes!"

I hear him cheer without restraint from inside, his voice carrying through the door, pulling a bout of giggles from me that I can't suppress.

I can't believe how much I've missed his impossible smugness.

How much I've missed him.

Lion

Sophie

"I can't believe it took you this long to invite me over," Brenda says over her shoulder while she's walking through my flat and is taking in everything from the furniture to the decor.

"I used to think it's best to keep my work and personal life separate," I call out from the kitchen, filling us both a glass of white wine.

"Well, obviously not anymore," she shouts down the hallway. "You're literally my boss now! I still can't believe how you pulled that off!"

I shrug as I find her sitting comfortably on my bed. Her bright rainbow-coloured sequin dress and voluminous ginger wig makes her look like a bird of paradise against my white linens.

"It doesn't change a thing. I believe in flat hierarchies these days. And anyway, you could have invited me over to your place."

"No, I couldn't," Brenda laughs, "the minute, you would have stepped foot into my flat, you would have known I'm gay and a drag!"

"That much glitter, huh?"

"Oh, yeah! Expect your bed to be covered in it by the time I leave. Can't wait to see the sparkles on Carter."

"I'm not planning on letting him into my bed any time soon."

"Oh, please! I give it a week tops. You won't be able to resist that smouldering package, no one could."

"First, I need to find something to wear for tonight, or we won't make it past our first date."

"You're right. Let's get to work," Brenda exclaims with a clap of her hands.

She gets up and shuffles through my dresses, pulling out a tight-fitted emerald number.

"How about this one?"

"The zipper pinches in the back," I decline with a scrunch of my nose.

"This one?" she asks, holding up a pale pink dress with ruffles at the bust.

"It's lovely, as long as you're standing."

"What about this one?"

"It doesn't fit me anymore, and neither do these five," I admit with a shrug, pointing at the dresses I once thought I was wearing like an armour. Now I know they were a mask, hiding my true self. So, I'm not in the least disappointed that I no longer fit into them.

"How about the dark red one?" she shoots back, holding up the dress I wore to our first meeting with Windpower. The same dress, I saw Ravens' affair in.

"No, thank you. I don't need to give Medard a reminder of the day I flirted with Ravens like a fool," I mumble, feeling a shudder run up my spine.

"Oh, can I have it? With a couple of panels sown into the sides, it'll fit like a glove, and I love to shove it in Ivana's face—you know, Ravens' mistress—how I look a thousand times more gorgeous in it than her. Stupid cow, calls herself Ivana, and she isn't even Russian."

"Be my guest," I say with a shrug, "but aren't you worried Ravens might find out about you if you quarrel with his misses like that?"

"He knows," she deadpans with a gentle sweep over the dress.

My jaw drops to the floor, but Brenda simply shrugs unperturbed.

"We share the same secret, so it kinda built trust. Plus, I'm fucking brilliant at my job. You should tell my boss next time you see her," she says, bumping her hip against mine.

I laugh as Brenda wags her brows playfully. It's these moments when I still catch my friend Ben shining through the layers of make-up and glitter.

"Believe me, she knows," I say, wiping the mirth from the corners of my eyes, "she knows, she wouldn't be where she is now, if it wasn't for your support."

"Aw, I love you too, my sexy blond bombshell," she coos, pulling me in for a hug. "Now, stop crying or you'll mess up your make-up!"

"I'm not wearing any," I mumble into her fake-boobs, prompting her to pull back and study my face.

"You bitch! How is your skin so flawless? What moisturiser are you using?"

Another bout of laughter erupts in my chest and I turn away from her to rummage through my wardrobe again.

"I'll tell you after we've found an outfit for me."

She huffs with a theatrical sweep over her pompous ginger wig.

"I don't know, Soph. At this rate, we'll have to grab you a potato sack and cut three holes in it."

"That might work with a little brown belt," I suggest as I watch her eyes widen in horror.

"Absolutely not! Carter has class, so you can't show up there in bloody burlap!"

She dismisses me with a wave of her hand, frantically pulls more and more dresses from their hangers and mumbles, "although, he's so infatuated with you, you could wear just about anything, or better yet, nothing at all."

"How do you know? How do you know he's 'so infatuated' with me?"

The questions spill from my lips with curiosity. I know he tried to declare his love for me, the day I dumped him outside the firm. So, when I came back, it wasn't a question of whether he loved me or not; but whether he still loved me after I'd been gone for so long.

Brenda stills for a moment, her gaze slowly moving down to my thighs and settling on my nervous swipes. She drops the dresses in her hands and leads me to the bed. As we sit down, she takes both my hands and rests them in her lap.

"For a start, he made sure your new office was all prepped and ready for your return. He also covered all of your clients. He wouldn't let anyone else come near them, claimed it was your decision who would handle them in the future now that you're his partner. In fact, he almost ripped my head off when I suggested to take them over. "

"That sounds like something he would do," I say with a smile, imagining his authoritative tone of voice that always makes my tummy tingle.

"And the one day, he came in with this pretty little thing. He kept telling everyone who passed them, that she was just his mate's girlfriend. He wanted to make sure no one gets the wrong idea that he'd moved on from you."

"And is it true?" I ask with bated breath.

I know Medard still wants me but insecurities are not so easy to dispel.

"Oh, yes! I asked Millie to spy on him. The poor thing was bored with you gone," she reassures me with a warm smile, before releasing my hands with a clap of her own. "Right, let's get you dressed for your date!"

She jumps off the bed and flicks through the clothes on the rail once more.

"What are we looking for? What's important to you?"

"Comfy," I shoot out, "and sexy, but definitely comfy!"

Brenda nods and then pulls a dark blue wrap dress out.

"That's the one, Soph! It's comfy, it's sexy and it's very easy to take off," she says with a mischievous wink.

The fabric is a soft ribbed cotton that clings to my curves but it can easily expand around a belly full of food—and with a single strap holding it in place, it merely takes a little tug for the fabric to fall away from my body—not that I have any intention to sleep with Medard tonight. I'm determined to take things slow this time.

"That's the one!"

An hour later, the taxi driver drops me off at Medard's new address, and I spend a moment staring up at the building like some sort of awestruck tourist. Turns out, while I was on my mission of self-discovery—eating my weight in tapas and pretending I wasn't thinking about him every five seconds—he decided to make some rather significant changes to his life too.

I walk through the grand foyer, all marble and understated wealth, and give the concierge a polite nod. He nods back before his attention immediately shifts to whatever film he's watching on his computer.

I step into the lift and press the button, taking deep, steadying breaths with each floor the lift passes. When the lift finally arrives at the top floor and the doors ding open, I smooth down my hair one more time and tug my wrap dress into place, suddenly hyper-aware that the neckline might be too low, the hem might be too high, and I'm about three seconds from a full-blown panic attack.

It's ridiculous how nervous I am. Sure, it's technically our first proper date, but it's not like Medard is a complete stranger.

Hell, we've been through so much together—the arguments, the proposals, the mind-blowing orgasms—that if anything, he feels more like my husband than someone I'm just getting to know.

And still, I feel as nervous and giddy as a teenager who's never been kissed, let alone thoroughly shagged by her boss.

I cross the short hallway to his front door and gently rap my knuckles against the wood, my heart hammering so hard I'm certain he'll hear it before he even opens the door. It takes him a couple of moments, but then the door swings open and my heart doesn't just leap into my throat—it does a full gymnastics routine.

He's wearing an off-white linen shirt that's unbuttoned at the top, sleeves rolled up to showcase golden hair on his chest and forearms that makes my fingers itch to touch. His trousers are loose-fitted linen in beige, making him look like he's ready to enjoy a good aged scotch on the French Riviera while seducing unsuspecting women with nothing but a smouldering look.

He looks so utterly delectable that I'm certain my mouth is watering from the sight of him alone, and not from the delicious aromas wafting over from the kitchen.

"Hey," I manage to press the small word out with what I hope is a casual smile, suddenly feeling ridiculously shy in his presence.

"Hey, yourself," he says, and that effortless charm in his voice nearly makes me whimper. "Come on in."

I step inside and take in his new place, my eyes widening despite my best efforts to appear unimpressed. It looks similar to his old flat—the large window fronts, the open-plan concept, those dramatic pillars and soaring ceilings that scream "successful alpha male with excellent taste."

Yet, somehow it feels warmer. More inviting. The cold white marble tiles have been replaced with mid-tone wooden flooring that looks like it's been nicked from a chalet in the Alps. The walls are off-white or cream, same as the pillars, instead of that stark concrete he had before. It's the perfect canvas for a cosy family home, and I absolutely refuse to think about what that might mean.

Turning my attention back to him, I notice he's been watching me with an expectant gaze, like my opinion actually matters to him.

"Your place looks lovely," I say, and immediately want to kick myself for such an underwhelming compliment. Lovely. Like I'm commenting on someone's garden gnome collection.

"I was hoping you'd like it," he says, stepping behind me to help me out of my coat with practised ease.

As the thick material glides down my arms, his fingers slightly graze my shoulders, and a little spark runs up my spine like an electric current I have absolutely no defence against.

Trying desperately to ignore the effect he still has on me—so easily, so effortlessly—I turn my attention back to my surroundings. I'm glad I didn't put on tights but opted for thick knitted socks that peek out of my brown ankle boots, because his home is heated to a comfortable level. Though I'm not sure it's quite warm enough to be barefoot like he is.

"Aren't you going to get cold feet?" The question slips out before I can stop it.

His brow furrows at my unexpected question, confusion flickering across his handsome face before understanding dawns. "With you, never."

The words land like a promise, heavy and loaded, and I have to remind myself to breathe like a normal human being.

I point at his bare feet with a giggle. "I meant, you're barefoot."

He chuckles, shaking his head in that way that makes me feel adorably foolish rather than just foolish. "There's underfloor heating. Take off your shoes and try it."

I do as he says, slipping out of my boots with far less grace than I'd like. Instantly, I feel the warmth seeping through my socks, and I can't help but wiggle my toes in pure delight.

"Toasty! I love it!"

"Good," he grins, and then he's offering me his hand like we're about to embark on some grand adventure rather than just walking to his kitchen.

On instinct—or perhaps because I've completely lost my mind—I lace my fingers with his. His hand engulfs mine, warm and solid and somehow exactly right. He walks me to the kitchen area where I'm greeted by the largest rose bouquet I've ever seen in my entire life.

The roses are enormous and vibrant in various shades of pink, red, and white, arranged with the kind of artistry that probably cost more than my monthly salary.

"These are gorgeous!" I swoon, unable to stop myself as I lean in to inhale their fragrant scent, which is somehow only half as intoxicating than the man standing beside me.

"They're yours," Medard says, stepping up next to me, his hand coming to rest at my lower back in a gesture that feels both possessive and protective. "Courtesy of my mother."

"They're your mother's? From her garden?" My voice pitches higher with surprise.

He nods, and the warmth of his hand at my lower back sparks that fuzzy feeling in my chest to life—the one I've been trying very hard to ignore for the past month.

"I don't know what to say. These are truly beautiful, and not what I expected," I admit truthfully, gently touching one of the perfectly shaped petals. "Thank you."

"I'll tell my mum you love them."

The casual mention of his mother, the ease with which he says it, makes something warm and terrifying bloom in my chest. Lost for any other words that won't reveal how completely undone I am by this gesture, I whisper another "thank you."

"Right," he suddenly clears his throat and walks around the kitchen island with purpose, and I can't help but notice the way his linen shirt moves across his broad shoulders. "Let's start on dinner."

He pulls out a plain navy apron from a cabinet and ties it around his waist, and God help me, does this man ever not look devastatingly sexy? He could probably make a hazmat suit look like haute couture.

"You're cooking for me tonight?" I ask, trying not to sound as surprised as I feel.

He shakes his head with that mischievous look I've come to associate with trouble, and pulls another apron from the cabinet. "We both will. I even got you your own apron."

He holds up a half-folded cream apron, and I catch a glimpse of what appears to be geese—geese of all animals—printed across the fabric. My mind immediately wanders to the ugly goose lamp that's currently residing on my side table in the living room, the one I bought in a moment of rebellion and have grown inexplicably fond of.

"How do you know—" I start to ask, but then he unfolds the apron completely and I see the word "HONKERS" written in bold yellow letters across the top.

I burst into laughter, the sound bubbling up from somewhere deep in my chest, and he joins in, that deep, rich laugh that I've missed more than I care to admit.

"You like it?" he asks, eyes crinkling at the corners in genuine pleasure.

"I love it!" I say, taking the ridiculous apron from him and tying it around my waist with more enthusiasm than any grown woman should have for poultry-themed kitchen wear. "So, what are we cooking?"

"Penne Arrabbiata," he says with a smile that promises this is going to be far more interesting than just making pasta.

We start cooking, and it's surprisingly... normal. Comfortable, even. He shows me how to properly chop garlic—apparently, I've been doing it wrong my entire life—while I tease him about his unnecessarily extensive knife collection. We work side by side, our movements synchronised in a way that feels practised despite this being the first time we've cooked together. Every time our hands brush, every accidental touch, sends little sparks through my nervous system that I'm trying very hard to ignore.

"A little something to tie us over until dinner is ready," he says, sliding a small bowl of olives across the counter towards me.

"Green olives," I muse, remembering our conversation at the shop what feels like a lifetime ago. "I usually prefer black."

"I know," he smirks, that insufferably confident expression that irritates... No. It just arouses me now. "But I'm sure you'll like these."

I quirk a brow skeptically and tentatively pop one olive into my mouth, fully prepared to prove him wrong. The flavours explode across my tongue—briny, rich, with hints of herbs I can't quite place. "They're delicious! Like the ones I had in Italy."

Medard chuckles in that deep, sexy way I've missed hearing every single day I was gone, and quirks his own brow in response. Realisation dawns on me.

"You didn't?"

"Let's just say I've exhausted my quota of CO_2 emissions for the year," he says with a nonchalant shrug that's completely undermined by the pleased gleam in his eyes.

I can't believe it. He got the actual olives from that little restaurant in Rome. The one I mentioned exactly once, weeks ago, in passing.

"How did you—" I stammer, utterly gob-smacked by the sheer sweetness of this gesture. "Did you fly to Rome this morning?"

"I didn't. My brother did. And to be fair, he was already in

Verona, so the journey wasn't that long."

Oh my God.

He's roped his entire family into creating this perfect date. I want to melt into a puddle on his expensive wooden floors.

"You're setting the bar quite high for me, you know?" I jest, popping another olive into my mouth as I watch him stir the pasta in the pot with practised ease. "If I ever meet your family again, I'll have to repay them for their kindness."

I watch him with bated breath, expecting him to correct me for saying "if" instead of "when"—expecting that trademark arrogance to surface, that possessive certainty that used to infuriate yet somehow really excite me. But he simply shrugs with a smile that's almost... humble?

"I think you'd already repay them just by being with me."

His words are sweet. Humble. Genuine.

And I don't like them.

Where's his smugness gone? Where's the man who declared I'd be his wife with absolute certainty? This gentler version of Medard is throwing me completely off balance.

We continue cooking, falling into easy conversation as the pasta sauce simmers and fills his flat with mouthwatering aromas. Eventually, we plate up the food and move to his dining table, and I'm impressed by how good it actually looks—we might have actually created something edible.

"How was your sabbatical?" he asks once we're seated, and there's genuine interest in his voice rather than polite small talk.

"It was good. Gibraltar is a beautiful place, and the landscapes are simply stunning." I twirl pasta around my fork, trying to find the right words. "It gave me time to think. To figure out what I actually want."

"How come you decided on going there?"

I take a bite of pasta to buy myself time, then admit, "I sort of hijacked Gareth's trip—as a friend. Nothing happened between us."

I watch his face carefully for any sign of jealousy or possessiveness, but he just nods. "If you say so, I believe you."

"But you don't believe him," I observe, catching the subtle clench of his jaw.

"He's a man, Sophie, and any man who wouldn't want you is a moron." He says it so matter-of-factly, like it's an undeniable truth rather than a compliment.

Heat creeps up my neck. "What about you? What have you been up to while I was gone?"

"Not much. I've been spending a lot of time with my parents. And I'm rebuilding my relationship with my brother."

There's something vulnerable in his admission, a softness I'm not used to seeing.

"That's good," I say sincerely, reaching across the table to squeeze his hand. "Really good."

"What about you? Have you heard from your father?" He pauses, concern flickering across his face. "I'm sorry. If you don't want to talk about him—"

"It's okay," I interrupt, surprising myself with how much I mean it. "He's tried calling me a few times, but I'm done with him. Since he's been out of my life, I've never felt better. So as sad as that may sound, it's for the best."

He nods, sadness softening his features. We're quiet for a moment, the soft sound of Aaron Frazer crooning in the background filling the comfortable silence, when a question slips from my lips before I can stop it.

"So, a little birdy told me you brought a visitor to the office while I was gone."

He chuckles, and I catch the hint of amusement in his eyes. "Reynolds, the little gossip. Yes, her name is Laura—I like her. She reminds me of a younger version of you."

"Ouch!" I press a hand to my chest in mock offence.

"I don't mean it like that." He leans forward, his gaze intense and sincere. "You're the most beautiful woman I've ever laid eyes on. Laura reminds me of you because she's still very much trying to find her own voice. I can see you having been just like her when you were twenty."

The compliment lands somewhere deep in my chest, warm and unexpected.

We talk some more about nothing in particular—his plans for the firm, my thoughts on potentially switching practice areas, whether Christmas is best celebrated in the heat or the snow. Just comfortable, interesting conversation where he tells me so much about his life that I never knew before, filling in gaps I didn't even know existed.

We've long finished our dinner, plates pushed aside and wine glasses refilled, when he stands and holds out his hand to me.

"Will you dance with me?" he asks, and there's something almost shy in the question that makes my heart squeeze.

I nod, unable to form words past the lump in my throat, and let him lead me into the living area. He pulls me close, one hand settling at the small of my back while the other captures mine, and our bodies begin swaying to the music. I lean my head against his chest, breathing in that fresh ocean scent I've missed every single day while I was gone—the one that invaded my dreams and made me ache with longing I refused to acknowledge.

"You've been different tonight," I murmur against his shirt.

"Because I don't want to step a foot wrong." His admission is quiet, vulnerable in a way that's entirely unlike him.

"I don't like it. I want you to be yourself," I admit, pulling back slightly to look up at him.

"I can't." His jaw tightens. "If I'd be myself, we'd be rolling naked in the sheets by now. But you told me no sex tonight, remember?"

I pull back further, a daring grin spreading across my lips. "Well, look at that. The almighty Mr Carter, all tamed."

He grins back, showing me those captivating dimples. "Careful. My self-restraint has a limit."

"I'm not so sure." I shake my head slowly, my fingers grazing down his chest with deliberate provocation. "I think the lion has lost his bite."

I give him a gentle shove, expecting him to let me go, but his arms fly up lightning-fast, seizing my wrists and pulling me back against his chest with enough force to make me gasp.

His lips slam onto mine, and my senses immediately hum to life at the sweet invasion of his tongue. But then he pulls back, searching my face for consent, for permission to continue, and something in me rebels at his restraint.

Oh, this lion needs to find his claws again.

I slowly walk backwards, maintaining eye contact as I dare him with a crooked finger. "Come here, little kitty."

His brow lifts at my audacious command, and I watch as something shifts in his expression—something darker, more primal, distinctly him. It sets him into motion. Before I can tease him further, he moves to close the gap between us, but I spin on my heel and sprint towards the hallway, laughter bubbling from my lips.

He's right on my heels as I pass multiple closed doors, his footsteps heavy and determined behind me. I fly through the last door at the far end—his bedroom, I realise belatedly—when he catches me. I trip, lose my footing, and brace myself for the inevitable impact with the floor.

But his arm shoots out and clamps around my waist, and then he's spinning us both during the fall in what must be some sort of protective instinct he can't control.

Medard's back hits the ground with a solid thud while I land safely on his chest.

"Oh, fuck!" he groans, and the pained sound immediately sobers my playful mood.

I scramble to turn around, straddling him as I frantically examine him for damage. "Are you okay? I'm so sorry! It looked a lot hotter in my head."

"I'm fine," he chuckles despite the wince, his hands finding my hips and gripping them possessively. "More than fine."

He grins as I feel his cock harden beneath me, pressing insistently against my core through too many layers of fabric.

Heat creeps onto my cheeks as he tries to pull himself up, but he stops with a pained expression that makes my stomach drop.

"Shit," he winces, his hand reaching for his shoulder. "My shoulder hurts."

"Let me get you some ice." I move to stand, but his hand on my hip tightens.

"I'll be fine, lioness."

The pet name slips out so naturally, and my heart bursts at hearing it after four long weeks of silence.

He grasps for my hips, clearly intending to keep me exactly where I am, but with his shoulder hurting, he's too weak to stop me. I'm already on my feet and sprinting to the kitchen, determined to help even if he's too stubborn to admit he needs it.

I return moments later with a bag of frozen peas and a kitchen towel, finding him sitting up and leaning against the foot of his bed. I kneel down next to him, gently positioning the makeshift ice pack and securing it to his shoulder with the towel tied in a careful knot.

I can feel him watching me in my peripheral vision, his gaze heavy and intense, and when I'm done nursing his injury, he holds my waist and nudges me back onto his lap.

"Come here, lioness."

I comply, even though I know it'll be infinitely harder to resist temptation with his cock pressing insistently against my core. But I've missed being close to him, missed feeling the solid warmth of him.

His eyes drink me in slowly, deliberately—perusing over my face, my neck, travelling down to my breasts before they snap back up to mine. He swallows visibly, and a pang of sadness overshadows his handsome features.

"I'm sorry I hurt—"

I cup his face and press my lips to his, cutting off his apology with a kiss that's meant to be gentle but quickly deepens into something more desperate. A moan escapes my throat as his tongue sweeps through my mouth, caressing mine with gentle reverence that makes my toes curl.

"Fuck, lioness," he murmurs, his breath hot against my lips. "You're making it really hard for me to behave."

"I'm sorry," I say with a sheepish smile as I lean back, though I'm not sorry at all. My hands glide down his firm chest, feeling the rapid beat of his heart beneath my palms.

He quips a brow, then reaches for the little belt of my wrap dress with deliberate slowness. The knot unravels easily, and my dress falls open to reveal my dark blue lace bra and matching knickers. Even though I prefer comfort these days, nothing makes me feel more sensual than beautiful lacy underwear. And still, my hands fly to my dress instinctively as I try to wrap it back around myself, suddenly painfully aware of the weight I've gained since he last saw me naked.

Medard shakes his head, drawing a shaky breath as he gently but firmly pulls my arms away, opening my dress again. He drinks me in with undisguised hunger, and I feel him harden further between my legs.

"You're even more beautiful than the day you left," he gasps, swallowing hard. "Soft, and warm, and incredibly sexy."

His hand glides up my hip with aching slowness, over my waist, cupping my breast before travelling higher to wrap gently around my throat.

My breath stutters at the familiar gesture, and I can't help but gyrate my hips against his hardness.

We kiss for what feels like hours, lost in the taste and feel of each other, until he pulls back just enough to murmur against my mouth, "How am I performing so far?"

"Hmm?" I'm too dazed to process actual words.

"Do I have a chance at a second date?" There's vulnerability threading through the question that makes my chest ache.

I pretend to mull it over, tilting my head thoughtfully while trying not to smile at the way his jaw tightens with impatience. "I'm not sure. I'll have to think about it."

He leans forward, gently sweeping my hair aside with reverent fingers before pressing his lips to the sensitive skin of my neck.

"You're torturing me, lioness," he whispers against my pulse point, and I feel the words as much as hear them.

"You're doing alright so far," I gasp.

"Just alright?" He pulls back with mock offence, but there's a wicked gleam in his eyes. "Well, I think I can help you along with making a decision." He shifts slightly beneath me, nodding toward his nightstand. "Get the piece of paper from the top drawer for me."

My lower belly hums at his words. That's the Medard Carter I've missed—command, instead of humble request. "What paper?"

"You'll see. Top drawer."

Curiosity wins over suspicion. I climb off his lap—ignoring his disappointed groan—and pad over to the nightstand. The drawer slides open to reveal a surprisingly organised collection of items, and right on top is a folded piece of paper that looks distinctly official.

I grab it and return to my perch on his lap, straddling him once more as I hand over the mysterious document. "What is this?"

He unfolds it carefully, turning it so the typed writing faces me, and says with complete seriousness, "By the way, your bin collection day changes from January."

My eyes widen. "My what?"

I grab the corner of the page, straightening it to read properly, and sure enough—there's my address printed at the top of what is unmistakably a letter from my local council advising of changes to rubbish collection schedules.

"Why—how do you have this?" I sputter, completely baffled.

He shrugs with studied casualness. "I found it when I tidied up your flat. You know, after you'd completely wrecked the place and passed out in bed."

Oh God.

The memory—or rather, the fragments of memory—come flooding back, and I cover my face with both hands, mortification burning through me like wildfire. "Don't remind me. To this day, I only remember snippets. Tearing books from the shelves. Flinging that vase from the side table in the hallway like some sort of drunken maniac." I peek at him through my fingers. "But I still can't figure out why the hell I was wearing my graduation gown."

His mouth splits into the widest grin I've ever seen, dimples on full display, eyes absolutely dancing with mischief. "You were playing judge."

"I was what?"

"Playing judge," he repeats, clearly delighted by this revelation. "I found this paper alongside a hammer, which I'm assuming you were using as a gavel, on your living room floor."

I frown, trying to piece together my vodka-soaked rampage, but then a giggle escapes despite my embarrassment. "What case was I presiding over?"

Medard clears his throat theatrically, shaking out the paper with exaggerated formality and—oh no.

He reads in his best courtroom voice: "Submit to Carter: Pros and Cons."

Oh no no no. God no.

My eyes widen in absolute horror, and I lunge for the paper. "Give me that!"

He laughs—that deep, rich sound that does things to my insides—and holds it out of reach. But then he hisses in pain, his injured shoulder protesting the movement, and I immediately stop my assault.

"Oh God, I'm sorry! Are you okay?" My hands flutter uselessly, wanting to help but afraid to hurt him more.

"I've never been better," he assures me, that smile returning as he pulls me closer with his good arm. "With you sitting on me like this."

I narrow my eyes at him. "You're using your injury to manipulate me."

"Is it working?"

"Unfortunately."

He grins, then holds up the paper between us like evidence in an actual trial. "Let's start with the cons, shall we?"

My head drops into my hands immediately, and I shake it in utter mortification. But curiosity is a terrible, terrible thing. "Go on, then. Let's hear how terrible you are."

"Boss," he reads, and I can hear the amusement in his voice. "Fair enough. But I did offer to give up my position for you."

I roll my eyes and giggle despite myself. "That doesn't count."

"Arrogant prick." He pauses, shrugging with complete nonchalance. "Is it really arrogance when you just happen to be right all the time?"

"Oh my God," I laugh, shoving at his chest half-heartedly.

"Intimidating glare," he continues, and there's something darker in his tone now. "I'd call it possessive."

"That doesn't make it better!" I protest, but I'm still laughing.

"Boundary-stomping." His expression sobers slightly. "Guilty as charged. And I do feel shitty about it."

The sincerity in his voice makes my chest tighten. "Medard—"

"Controlling," he reads, cutting off my protest. "Half-guilty, because you do like it when I bend you to my will."

His hand grabs my hip and drags me deliberately over his hardening length, and the friction makes us both groan.

"That's—that's different," I manage breathlessly.

"Is it?" He's smirking now, knowing exactly what he's doing to me.

"Next one," I demand, trying to regain some composure.

"Stalker." He actually has the grace to look sheepish. "Yeah, Alex told me from the start that was a stupid idea."

"You think?"

"Stubborn," he reads, and quips a brow. "Debatable."

"Not even remotely debatable."

"Chauvinistic." He frowns, looking genuinely confused. "When was I ever chauvinistic?"

"Our first meeting," I remind him, crossing my arms. "When you told me my clock was ticking to have children."

His eyes widen with recognition, and he winces. "Right. Forgot about that one. That was spectacularly out of line."

"Yes, it was."

"Drives a fancy car," he continues, and now he just sounds offended. "What's wrong with my car?"

"Nothing. Drunk me was clearly grasping at straws."

"And finally—" He twists his hand to examine it closely. "Has a mole on left hand." He looks up at me with mock indignation. "Now you were just making shit up to have more cons than pros."

I bite my lip, trying not to laugh. "It's a very noticeable mole."

"It's barely visible!" He shakes his head, but he's smiling. "You know, this list isn't too bad. Considering everything I've done." His expression grows serious again, vulnerable. "I'm sorry, Sophie. For all of it."

I cup his face, feeling the slight stubble under my palms, and nod. "I know." I try to lighten the mood, needing to break the heaviness settling over us. "What about the pros? How bad can they be? They're compliments, right?"

He raises a brow, a warning if I've ever seen one. "Are you sure you want to hear them?"

"How bad can it be?" I shrug with false bravado.

"Alright then." He clears his throat again. "Hot as hell—well, that's just factual."

"Modest too," I mutter.

"Magic tongue." He grins wickedly. "No comment necessary."

My cheeks flame. "Moving on."

"Eyes to lose yourself in," he reads, and his voice has gone softer. "I rather like that one, although I don't quite get how you'd like to lose yourself in them while they also intimidate you."

"Welcome to my world!" I huff, throwing my arms up with theatrical flair.

He laughs, pinching my chin between his fingers and pressing a kiss to my lips.

"Knows me—sometimes better than I know myself." He looks up from the paper to meet my gaze. "That works both ways, lioness."

My throat tightens with emotion I wasn't prepared for.

"Smug as hell," he continues, grinning with that cocky glint in his eyes. "I just know how good I am."

"You're impossible."

"Makes me feel special and wanted." His voice has dropped even lower, almost reverent. "You have no idea how much I needed to read that."

"Medard—"

"Smells divine." He pauses, and I watch as he reads the last item silently. His entire expression shifts—softens and intensifies all at once—and he slowly lowers the paper to give me his complete attention.

"I love him," he says, and the words hang in the air between us like a confession.

I smile shyly, suddenly unable to meet his eyes, my hands automatically moving to rub my thighs in that nervous gesture I can never quite control. "It's true," I whisper.

"I love you too, lioness." The words are firm, certain, leaving no room for doubt. "So fucking much."

And then he's kissing me, the paper fluttering to the floor beside us, forgotten as his hands roam over my body with renewed purpose. This kiss is different from the others—deeper, more meaningful, weighted with everything we've just confessed.

It's slow and sensual, our hands caressing and exploring like we have all the time in the world. Like we're learning each other all over again. It feels like an eternity but somehow not nearly enough time at all when I finally lean back, my lips swollen and my mind fuzzy with want.

I almost hate myself for the words that form on my tongue.

But I say them anyway, because I know it's for the best.

"I should head home. It's late."

The words taste like lies even as they leave my lips, but I force myself to stand anyway, my legs slightly unsteady as I tie my dress back into place with fingers that tremble just enough to be annoying. Medard rises too, taking off the towel that kept the bag of peas in place, and we start the long journey towards the front door.

Except it's not long at all—distance-wise, it's maybe twenty feet. Time-wise, it takes approximately forever.

We make it about three steps before he catches my hand, spinning me back around and pressing me against the bedroom door frame. His mouth finds mine, and I melt into him like I have no backbone whatsoever, which at this point might actually be accurate.

"I should really go," I mumble against his lips, though my hands are fisting in his shirt in a way that completely contradicts my words.

"Mmh," he agrees, but doesn't stop kissing me.

We manage another few feet down the hallway before I'm the

one pulling him back this time, pressing him against the wall and rising on my toes to reach his mouth. He groans into the kiss, his hands spanning my waist, and for someone with an injured shoulder, he's remarkably good at holding me exactly where he wants me.

"Seriously, I need to leave," I say between kisses, more trying to convince myself than him at this point.

"Absolutely," he murmurs, but his mouth is trailing down my neck in a way that suggests he has no intention of letting me go anywhere.

Another few steps. Another stop. This time it's mutual—we meet somewhere in the middle of the hallway, mouths crashing together like we're oxygen-starved and the only air available is in each other's lungs.

"Stay," he whispers against my lips, and the single word reverberates through my entire body.

"I can't," I protest weakly, even as my fingers thread through his hair.

"We could just keep doing this," he suggests, pulling back just enough to look at me with those devastating silver eyes. "Just kissing. Nothing more. I'll be good."

I let out a slightly hysterical giggle at that blatant lie. "Could you actually behave yourself?"

He shakes his head slowly, that mischievous smile playing at his lips. "Not even remotely."

"That's what I thought," I say, but I'm smiling too as we somehow make it a few more steps.

We finally reach the front door, and I think I might actually escape with my plan intact, but then he's crowding me against it, one hand planted above my head, his body a wall of heat and temptation in front of me.

"Stay," he tries again, and I can hear the smile in his voice. "We could carpool to work tomorrow. Very environmentally friendly. Help me level the scales on my CO_2 consumption."

"Tomorrow's Saturday," I point out, trying desperately to ignore how good he smells this close.

He doesn't miss a beat. "Breakfast in bed, then. There's a very good French bakery around the corner. Best croissants in London, I'm told. Buttery, flaky, still warm from the oven—" He trails off meaningfully, watching me like he knows exactly what he's doing.

"You drive a hard bargain," I admit, biting my lip. "But I still have to be the sensible one who goes home."

I'm leaning against the front door now, feeling the cool wood at my back.

He steels himself, drawing in a deep breath, then sighs dramatically. "You're leaving me no choice but to get the big guns out."

"The big guns?"

He pulls his phone from his pocket with the kind of deliberate movement that suggests I should be very worried about what's coming next. A few taps on the screen, and suddenly smooth blues music fills the room—the rough, gravelly timbre of a singer crooning about heartbreak and longing.

"Won't you stay with me? 'Cause since you've gone, it's pain and misery..."

And then—oh God—he starts swaying his hips to the music, moving with a sensuality that should be absurd but is instead devastatingly effective. His hands move to the buttons of his shirt, and he slowly, so slowly, begins unfastening them one by one, revealing more of that golden chest hair and tanned skin with each button that comes undone.

I bite my lower lip hard, trying and failing to suppress the giggle that bubbles up from my chest. My head shakes slowly from side to side, even as my eyes stay glued to the strip tease happening in front of me.

"You're impossible," I manage to get out, though my voice has gone breathy and weak.

"Is that a yes?" He grins, still swaying, still unbuttoning, still looking at me like I'm the only thing in the world that matters.

I nod, because apparently, I've completely lost my mind and all ability to make rational decisions. "Yes."

His grin turns absolutely wicked as his arm moves past my hip, and I hear the distinctive click of the lock engaging.

"But no sex," I blurt out, suddenly very aware that I've just agreed to spend the night with a man who looks like he wants to devour me whole.

He smiles—that mischievous, trouble-making smile that tells me I'm in serious trouble—and I know instantly that he's going to be a very, very naughty boy.

"We'll see about that, lioness," he murmurs, and the promise in those words makes me shiver as his lips find mine again.

I'm definitely going to regret this.

Or maybe not.

Probably not.

Oh, who am I kidding? I'm absolutely not going to regret this.

Epilogue

Medard

One year later.

Another day done in court, another step closer to bringing Andrew Rosen to his knees. Sophie will be absolutely delighted when I tell her we've finally gotten ahead again. My balls tingle at the mere thought of wrestling with my lioness in the sheets tonight. Anticipation coils through my body like a live wire.

Since we entered into this legal battle with her father, we've established a little ceremony between us. When he gets ahead—which frustratingly happens far too often—I let my anger out boxing with Baron. Afterwards, I cook something nice for Sophie and make sweet love to her while she tends to my wounded ego. She reminds me that there are more important things in life than beating Andrew Rosen. Her.

But when I get ahead? Oh, then the claws come out. I get to wrestle my lioness into submission.

Total control. Total victory. Total ego-boosting thrill that makes me feel like I could conquer the fucking world.

I slide into my car and start the engine when my phone pings with Sophie's reply.

Me: Sushi or Latvian?

Lioness: Sushi. That's my lion. x

My mouth splits into a wide grin. Asking her what takeaway she wants tonight—that's all it takes for her to know I've gotten ahead again against her father.

Simple. Elegant. Perfectly us.

I truly am the luckiest motherfucker on this planet.

I step on the gas and make a quick pit-stop at Nobu before heading straight home, the anticipation swirling through me to see my woman.

It's been almost a whole year since she gave me another chance, and I'm still as madly in love with her as though she only stepped foot into my office yesterday. Maybe more so, if that's even possible.

I finally arrive at the penthouse, the plastic bags filled with her favourite dishes dangling from my hand as I step through the front door.

"Honey, I'm home," I call out playfully, but quiet myself when I spot her standing by the kitchen island. Her phone is pressed to her ear and she signals that she's on a call.

I drop the keys into the little dish on the side console, and give the beak of the ugly goose lamp a gentle rub.

A snicker escapes me as I think about the day I brought it home. Six months of Sophie leaving more and more of her things at my place. Six months of her taking longer periods of sleeping at hers. When I realised, she was basically moving herself into my home, I helped her along by discreetly bringing her things over—books, kitchen utensils, bathroom towels. The usual stuff that women seem to accumulate.

Until the day I walked through the front door with that ugly goose lamp clutched to my side. We both burst out laughing, and she never went back to her flat afterwards, because we terminated her rental agreement the same day. Best fucking move I ever made—bringing that hideous lamp.

As I approach her by the kitchen island, she greets me with a swift kiss before we fall into our usual routine. She boils the kettle for my tea. I check the mail. It's domestic bliss, and I'm not ashamed to admit I love every second of it.

"I still can't believe how you've met her," she says into the receiver. The phone is wedged between her ear and shoulder as she dumps a tea bag into my mug. "But yes, I could do the 20th, if that suits you?"

"Who is it?" I whisper when she turns back to me.

"Gareth," she mouths.

I can't help but roll my eyes. She giggles at my reaction, then giggles again when I realise, I've copied her mannerism. It annoys me. Eye-rolls are adorable on a defiant lioness. When I do them, I look like a petulant fourteen-year-old who's just been told he can't have the car keys.

I turn my attention back to the mail, though my focus remains on Sophie's conversation. It's Gareth, after all. Apparently, he's just a friend. I try to be civil with him. But I don't trust him. I trust her, but not him. That's something that'll never change. The man looks at her like she's the last glass of water in the Sahara, and I'm not blind.

Still, I've come to accept him as her friend. She's accepted that we'll never be best buddies. It's a delicate truce that works for us.

My attention snags on the latest bill from Sophie's therapist, and I instantly feel the impulse to crumple it into a ball and fling it into the bin. I've spent thousands on her therapy now, and she's still rubbing her thighs from time to time. It's a lot better, sure, but it's still there. I could swear the fucker is prolonging her recovery to bank more fees.

Maybe I should have a word with him. Make him understand that I'd willingly give him my last penny if, in return, he'll just.Do.His.Bloody.Job. I want Sophie to finally overcome this trauma.

And my therapist can go fuck himself if he wants to tell me again that healing takes time. I don't have the patience for it. Nor the heart to watch her have another episode.

The good thing is though, I can tell these days when one's on the horizon. When she feels particularly anxious. She'll graze her thighs more often. She'll tuck her hair more behind her ear to keep her hands occupied. Her eyes will dart more. Like she's doing now.

Shit.

I drop the letters onto the tabletop, and watch as she says goodbye to Gareth and scribbles something into her planner.

"How was your day?"

"Good," she smiles, then leans in to give me a proper hello-kiss.

For a moment, I forget about my concerns and let myself soak into her warmth—her hand resting atop my heart, her finger grazing the spot below my ear, her soft tongue caressing mine. This woman could make me forget my own name with a kiss like that.

"We got the account," she beams and leans back slightly to look at me. "Four accounts down, two to go."

That's our strategy. Operation take-over. While I'm distracting her father in a public legal battle to destroy his biggest client, she's been sneaking in through the back door to pick up his smaller clients. So, by the time I'm done with him, he'll have nothing left to fall back on, and his firm will have to shut its doors.

It's the perfect tactic. His overblown ego keeps him focused on me while his typical underestimation of his daughter makes him blind to the carnage she wreaks at his firm. The old bastard never saw her coming. Never thought his 'little girl' would have the balls to take him on.

He was wrong.

"That's my lioness," I say, giving her another kiss. "I wouldn't expect anything less."

She rewards me with a grin that I feel right through my shirt and into my heart.

"Oh, before I forget," she says, turning away from me to hand me my tea. "Lucy had to cancel our brunch for Sunday, which works perfectly for me. I can go to the farmer's market with your mum and Lisa again while you play squash with Theo."

"That's good," I note, taking a sip of the perfectly brewed tea. "I've had lunch with Alex today, and he confirmed the ceremony on Friday ends at four. So, the table's booked for four-thirty."

My gaze tracks her every movement. That's four. I glance over to the clock on the microwave. Four times in five minutes that she's resisted reaching for her thighs and instead played with her hair. Something's definitely wrong.

"Alright, I'll let Millie know to adjust my schedule," she says, trying for casual but missing by a mile.

She's pumping her fists. Her eyes keep snapping back to her planner like it holds the secrets of the universe.

"How's Alex? Is he nervous?"

"Shaking like a leaf," I confirm, watching as her hand finds her thigh again.

Enough of this dance.

"Lioness," I start, watching her as she hesitantly locks her gaze on mine.

She tempts to graze her thigh again but balls her hand into a fist at the last second. She knows I've clocked something's off.

I take a step towards her. She swallows visibly. Another step. Her eyes dart away from me.

"Lioness," I demand her attention once more, my voice dropping lower.

Her eyes flick back to me, but then she suddenly smiles and plays at nonchalance. "Yes, my lion?"

Her voice is sugar-sweet. Her performance though? Nowhere near good enough to fool me. Not even close, and she knows it.

I close the distance between us and reach for the hem of her dress. I already know what sight awaits me when she takes a deep breath and closes her eyes the moment my hands slowly move up the fabric.

Red skin. Thin lines. Not too bad, but worse than her latest episodes. My chest tightens. The lump forms in my throat at the sight of her thighs and the shame written all over her face.

"Are you okay?" The question comes out calm and controlled, but it takes every ounce of composure in me to keep it that way. To just be present for her instead of marching down to that therapist's office and demanding answers. "Do you want me to schedule you an extra session this week?"

Her hands find mine, and she brings them behind her back to put herself into my arms. The fabric of her floaty dress falls back over her knees, hiding the evidence of her struggle.

"I'm okay," she whispers, her bright blue eyes finding mine.

Fuck, I'll never get tired of drowning myself in them. I could stare into those eyes for the rest of my life and die a happy man.

"Are you sure? This doesn't look like 'okay'," I say, swiping a lock of hair behind her ear.

She nods before nuzzling into my chest, and taking a deep breath. "I just had to work through something for a moment, but I'm fine now. Actually, I'm more than fine. I'm happy—well, almost. I really want to eat that sushi."

Still holding her, my gaze drifts over to the bags on the counter. The aromas have long since infused the air, making my stomach growl in anticipation. I'm hungry too. Starving, actually.

"Then let's eat—"

My words falter as Sophie pulls a plastic stick from her dress pocket, and lays it on the counter in front of us.

"I'm pregnant," she mumbles into my chest, her hands caressing my back with slow, calming strokes.

Two lines.

Two pink fucking lines.

"You're pregnant," I repeat, my brain working overtime to compute the news.

My lioness is pregnant.

I'll be a dad.

Fuck, she had a couple of glasses of wine last night. Is that bad? I need to google that.

Fuck. Focus, Medard.

"I'm happy," she says, looking up at me again with those bright blue eyes. "Are you happy?"

Her question floors me in the sweetest way possible.

"Am I happy?" My mouth splits into a wide grin that probably makes me look like a complete idiot, but I don't care. "I'm fucking mad with joy!"

I spin her in my arms and let the happiness break free. We laugh without restraint, the sound filling the penthouse with pure, unfiltered joy. My heart beats so fast I think it'll break free from my chest any moment and do a victory lap around the kitchen.

I hoist her onto the counter before pulling her mouth down onto mine, kissing her with everything I have.

My lioness is pregnant.

She's carrying my child. Our child.

Fuck, we're having a baby.

I never dared to believe this would be possible. We discussed having children. She was sure she didn't want to be a mother. She kept getting the injections—

My thoughts grind to a halt like a train hitting the brakes.

Wait a minute.

"Lioness," I drawl, my eyes flicking from her stomach to her face. "I'm sure my sperm has supreme qualities, but—"

She bites her lip as though to hide a grin, and I know I'm about to discover something entertaining.

"How exactly did I manage to knock you up while you're on the injections?"

She doesn't answer immediately. Instead, she just slides her planner towards us, showing me a week from three months ago. I pick up the book and scan her appointments until I land on the one for her injection. Next to the time is a big fat red arrow—Sophie's code for 'reschedule'.

I flip to the next pages. And the pages after. All the way to today's date.

There's nothing. She never re-booked the appointment.

"You didn't for—"

She wouldn't forget. Sophie's structured. Organised. Overly-prepared. The woman colour-codes that bloody planner, and has twenty different symbols for every possible scenario. She has a system for her systems, for fuck's sake.

She nods slowly, the corners of her mouth twitching with barely suppressed amusement. "I did."

Now I'm biting my own lip, trying hard to suppress the urge to laugh at her mistake. But it's too good. Too delicious. Too perfectly Sophie to mess up the one thing that would change both our lives forever.

"Come on, laugh it up," she teases, reading me like a book.

And I do. I howl with laughter as the book slips from my hands and hits the counter. Sophie rolls her eyes, but then she can't help herself and starts laughing too, her shoulders shaking as the giggles take over.

She made one wrong decision by wanting to reschedule the appointment. And it had to be a life-changing one. Only Sophie Rosen, my lioness, could get herself in a situation like this. The irony is fucking beautiful. Poetic, even.

"I'm sorry, lioness," I gasp, wiping mirth from my eyes. "I shouldn't laugh, but I never thought I'd be so happy about you making a wrong call."

Her hands fly to her face in embarrassment, but her shoulders are still shaking from the giggles. "I know, but I blame Ben!" She drops her hands to point an accusing finger at me, her eyes sparkling with mischief. "Since we made him Head of Acquisitions, he's been triple-checking everything with me. The man's determined to prove himself, keeps asking for feedback, wants to make sure he's meeting your expectations." She pauses for dramatic effect, and I can already see where this is going. "So come to think of it—I blame you too!"

She's always so utterly adorable when she plays the little damsel. I can't help but laugh, clasping her hand to bring it to my lips.

"If that's the case," I say between kisses to each of her knuckles, "then I'll give Ben a big fat bonus tomorrow." I close the small gap between us and snake my arm around her waist while my hand finds her stomach, spreading it wide over where our child is growing. "And I—I already have mine."

Soon my lioness will be big and round. I'll get to watch in awe as she grows this little life inside her. Watch her body change. Watch her glow with that pregnancy radiance everyone talks about.

Christ, I'm going to be insufferable.

"You're impossible." She giggles, her hands threading through my hair and tugging it gently.

"And yet, you love me."

"More than anything." She tugs harder in a plea for me to kiss her.

And I do with gentle brushes to her lips, and languid swipes of my tongue that speak of the deep love I feel for her.

I thought I'd be her saviour. Turns out, she was mine. Saved me from a life of cold, empty perfection and gave me this—messy, beautiful, real love.

"Now I want to play with the lion," she hums against my mouth, her voice dropping to that sultry tone that always makes my cock stand to attention.

I lift her off the counter and carry her towards our bedroom, pausing only to grab the bags from Nobu and dump them into the bin.

"What are you doing? There was nothing wrong with it," Sophie leans back in my hold and protests, looking at me like I've lost my mind.

The movement presses her arse harder against my crotch, eliciting a growl to rumble through my chest.

"You can't eat it while you're pregnant. Raw fish. So, neither can I."

Because I'm not about to sit there enjoying sushi while my pregnant girlfriend watches. I'm a possessive bastard, not a monster.

Her eyes widen at my reason, and then her mouth breaks into the most beautiful smile. Her hands fly to my cheeks and she presses a kiss to my lips that I only break when we're standing in front of the bed.

I drop her to her feet, and take a deliberate step back. The anticipation to have my way with her is already thrumming through me like an overly excited dog ready to run through fields.

Down, boy.

"Take off your clothes and kneel on the bed. Arse towards me, cheek to the mattress," I command, my hands already moving to the buttons on my shirt.

She gasps. Her pupils dilate instantly, and I'd bet my life that she's already soaking through her panties. I know my lioness.

She pulls the dress over her head and unclasps her bra.

The lace falls off her beautiful breasts, and my mouth waters at the sight of her. I pull off my shirt and watch as she slides down her panties, revealing what I already knew—she's drenched.

Satisfaction courses through my chest and leaves my body on a devilish grin.

Fucking perfect.

I work on my belt and slacks as Sophie takes her position on the bed, leaning down to give me a nice full view of her glistening pussy. I fist my cock, feeling the hard muscle pulse against my palm as I drink her in.

"Medard—" she mewls impatiently.

"So needy, my lioness." I tut her, enjoying this little moment of her desperation for me. It's a power trip, and I'm not ashamed to admit I love every second of it.

My hands move to her arse, and grab her cheeks with enough pressure to make her understand that I won't be gentle tonight. That the lion is here to play. I slide my cock through her pussy, revelling in the feeling of her wetness coating every inch of it.

Fuck, I love this woman with everything I have. Everything I am. She's my entire world, and now our child is too. A child I never thought I'd have. That Sophie never wanted because of her tragic past.

Fuck. Of course.

I'm a bloody idiot.

"Turn around," I tell her as I pull my cock away from her. "Lay on your back and spread your legs for me."

Sophie blushes at my words, but looks clearly confused that I'm changing course mid-game. Still, she obeys my orders like the good girl she is. Seconds later, I settle between her thighs and slide right into her, groaning at the feeling of her tight heat wrapping around me. Her moans swirl through the room as she stretches around me while I keep a leisurely pace.

"Medard—" she whines, digging her heels into my lower back. "—go faster, harder."

I shake my head between kisses to the column of her neck, my slow rhythm never wavering.

"Where's my lion? I thought you got ahead today in court." There's confusion in her voice, mixed with arousal and frustration.

She digs her nails into my back to spur me on, but I resist the desire to slam into her.

God knows, I want to fuck her hard and fast right now. Have her cry for mercy while I pull the orgasms from her trembling body. The victory in court earlier is still coursing through my veins like liquid fire. But right now, that's not what she needs.

"Not today, lioness," I whisper close to her ear. "Now, tell me."

Her breath stutters as I tilt my hips to drive into her deeper, my groin dragging over her clit in the way that always makes her lose her mind. "Tell me."

"I...I don't know what you mean," she moans, but I can hear the frustration shining through, the fear creeping in at the edges.

I gently clasp her throat, and tilt her chin up to look at me. "Don't lie to me, lioness. Be a good girl and tell me."

Her eyes flicker between mine for a beat, a silent war raging behind those blue depths. But then she exhales sharply, surrendering. "I'm scared."

"I know," I say, my thumb caressing her cheek as I continue to slowly rock into her. Of course she is. How could she not be?

"What if I get post-partum like my mother did?" The words tumble out now, the dam breaking.

Her eyes start to fill with tears. Her bottom lip wobbles as I pull her confession out with each slow thrust, making her feel safe enough to voice her deepest fears.

"Then we get you the help you need," I reassure her, meaning every word. "The best doctors. The best therapists. Whatever it takes."

"What if I can't handle it all—motherhood, work, my own problems?" Her voice cracks on the last word.

"Then we make arrangements. You can take time off work to see to yourself and the baby. I can take time off too. We'll have Ben step up some more. My mum can help with the baby as well." I kiss away the tear that escapes down her cheek. "Hell, we'll hire a whole team of nannies if we need to. Whatever you need, lioness."

She nods as the tears run down her temples. I kiss them away, tasting the salt on my lips. "You're not alone, Sophie. I've got you. Always."

She nods again, and a small smile rushes past her lips before she pulls me down to bury her head in the nook of my neck.

"Marry me," she whispers against my skin.

My movements still. My brain has passed out. My heart has declared itself king of my entire body and is currently doing a fucking conga line through my chest.

"You're serious?" I hesitantly press the words out, afraid that if I move or breathe too loudly, this moment will turn to smoke.

She nods, pulling back. The small smile breaks into a big grin that lights up her entire face.

"Marry me," she says again, louder this time. More confident.

Before I can even try to form a coherent word, I pull out of her, scramble off the bed and stumble over to the chest of drawers like a drunk man.

"Medard!" she whines, thrashing her arms and head against the mattress in frustration. "What are you doing?"

I grab the box and rush back to her. I settle between her legs again and position myself at her entrance. Sophie watches me with curious eyes as I take out the ring. I grab her wrist, and slide the ring onto her finger while I thrust back into her.

"Finally, my lioness," I say with a kiss to her ring, my voice rough with emotion, before continuing the slow, sensual thrusts that make her gasp. "I was starting to think you'd never say yes."

"You never asked," she says with a shrug.

What the—?

I stop mid-thrust. "I did, seven times over the past year!"

Sophie rolls her eyes on a resounding huff. She digs her heels into my lower back to get me to move again, but I'm too stunned by her words to comply.

I've asked her at her flat. At Cian's club. On Valentine's Day. On her birthday. The day I brought the goose lamp home. On my birthday. On some random fucking Friday.

Seven times.

And every time she said no.

I've already been planning the eighth for our one-year anniversary. I even hired a bloody string quartet. Spent two weeks coordinating the perfect moment.

Through the fog of my thoughts, I hear Sophie groan in frustration. Feel her pushing against my chest with determination. Before I can compute what she's doing, I'm falling back onto my arse, the mattress bouncing beneath me. She straddles me and lets herself sink down onto my cock in one smooth motion.

"Fuck, lion—" I hiss as she starts to ride me like a wildcat. Her tits bounce as she plummets down on me relentlessly, taking what she wants.

"Oh God, I need this," she moans, cradling my face and kissing me with an eagerness that strips me of my restraints.

I grab her arse with both hands and push her down onto my cock, meeting her movements with upward thrusts. My mouth latches onto her nipples where I let my teeth graze over them, hard enough to make her gasp.

"You kept telling me 'Marry me.' That's not a question," Sophie pants between ragged breaths, looking down at me with that knowing smirk.

Semantics? That's why she hasn't said yes yet? Because I didn't phrase it properly?

Jesus Christ, this woman will be the death of me. The absolute death of me.

My hand slides up her back to gather her wild blond mane in my fist. I tug until her back arches, her breasts pushing towards my face.

"Lioness." Her pet name comes out strangled, desperate.

She smirks, knowing exactly what she's doing to me. She rides me faster, harder, chasing her release.

I grab the base of her neck and her thigh with bruising force and throw her back onto the mattress before slamming into her with enough force it knocks the breath out of her lungs.

Instinct has me grip her throat, muscle memory taking over. But then I remember it's no longer just her and me.

And although I know how to safely choke her—always have, thanks to one particular woman called Gianna—there's a baby growing in her belly now. Our baby. Everything's different now.

Fuck, I can't wait to be a dad. To hold our child. To watch Sophie become a mother.

I move my hand to her cheek instead, caressing it gently with my thumb.

"No more of that while you're pregnant," I say softly, though my hips keep driving into her relentlessly.

"Yes," she pants, understanding immediately.

Then my thrusts come hard and fast, the way she's been begging for. Her orgasm inches closer with each hit, each drag of my cock against her walls. The moans spill from her lips like a symphony. The climax ripples through her as her whole body tenses up, clenching around me.

And I say what I should have asked months ago if I wasn't such a smug control freak who thought he knew better.

"Sophie Rosen, lioness, will you marry me?"

Her beautiful laughter rings out, mixing with her moans as the orgasm continues to roll through her.

My fucking heart beats a million miles per hour for the love of my life.

My lioness.

"Yes, yes, yes! I'll marry you!"

Of course, she will.

Teaser

Now that you've survived One Man's Control, let's talk:
Was Medard the villain? The hero? Both? Neither?
Did you want to shake Sophie? Shake Medard? Shake them both until they made better life choices?
And most importantly—did you howl with laughter at the sheer audacity of these two messy disasters, or did you just scream into your pillow?

Because here's the thing about complicated characters making catastrophically messy choices: they're exhausting. They're infuriating. They're also impossible to stop reading about.

Which brings me to Alex.

You remember Alex, right?
Medard's best friend.
The one who was always there—picking up the pieces, offering terrible advice, believing in love like some kind of optimistic lunatic.
The funny one. The loyal one. The one who made you laugh while Medard made you want to stage an intervention.

Here's what you didn't know:
While Medard's weakness was **control**, Alex's weakness is **obsession**.

And remember that tutoring job he mentioned? The one for his boss's daughter?

Yeah. About that...

"This is it. My last chance to escape this madness. I should run as fast as my feet will carry me. To snuff out this morbid intrigue before I end up dead in these bushes.
But my gut is telling me that I'm still safe, even as a stranger in a

skull mask is following me through a dark park and is literally telling me that he's going to grab me.

I should run.

"You understand, girl?" He bites the words out as though he's fighting the urge to restrain himself.

I should definitely run."

Stay tuned to find out how Alex gets his girl.

Book Two of the **Men Of London Series - One Man's Obsession**
will be released <u>1st May, 2026</u>.

About The Author

R.K. Everleigh believes the best romance novels make you feel everything—the butterflies, the rage, the "oh no he didn't," and the "finally, thank god" in equal measure.

She writes dark romance that doesn't apologise for being messy, complicated, or uncomfortable. Her heroes are the kind of alpha males who make terrible decisions before they make better ones. Her heroines are strong enough to bend without breaking—and fierce enough to break back when they're ready.

She lives in rural Wales, UK with her husband, their child, and a cat who wishes she'd get a normal hobby. When she's not writing about men who desperately need to learn what boundaries are or managing chaos at work and home, she's plotting the downfall of her next morally grey protagonist (and the woman who'll bring him to his knees).

Trigger Warning

This book tackles themes of

Dub-Con (workplace relationships that blur consent)

Possessive behaviour

Mental health struggles including self-harm (scratching)

Minor blood

Parental abuse

Blackmail

Explicit sexual content
(including but not limited to spanking, breath- & primal play)

Printed in Dunstable, United Kingdom

78542035R00270